"A smart thriller. Readers will find themselves educated about the history of cryptology, from grille texts to Vigenère solvers. . . . Gruber's themes may be lofty, but his people are fully fleshed. An engaging adventure."
—*Boston Globe*

"If you love books, make room on the shelf for a new guilty pleasure. Smart, packed with excitement. . . . Gruber mixes in fascinating details about rare manuscripts, intellectual property, and ancient and modern cryptography."
—*Washington Post*

"An intricately crafted and literate work [that] should give the [thriller] genre a good shake. A rich cast of characters who are difficult to leave when the final pages are turned. Gruber is a master of his material. He sidesteps the obvious risks with disparate plot lines, and his remain unmuddied and ultimately join together naturally."
—*Denver Post*

"Fearless, intricate, and intelligent. Stylish and confident prose. Realistic characters. Dialogue that respects a reader's intelligence. A smart and original plot. A smooth sense of timing, a healthy dose of skepticism, and by no means least, a sense of humor."
—*Seattle Times*

"A fire in a rare bookstore leads to the discovery of some letters from [Shakespeare's] cousin . . . one of the many tantalizing threads in [this] narrative. At the end of this tantalizing run, you hope to hear from Gruber again soon."
—*Daily News*

"A dead genius, a sleuthing couple with romantic chemistry, and some bad guys . . . it's a fun party."
—*Entertainment Weekly*

"A gripping literary thriller. A taut novel that offers ingenious puzzles plus murderous threats along the way."
—*Seattle Post-Intelligencer*

"Michael Gruber pulls out all the stops [in] an elaborate game of cat and mouse."
—*Newsday*

"[An] intelligent thrill ride."
—*Tampa Tribune*

"Ingenious. . . . Engaging. . . . The mysterious murder of a Shakespeare scholar, shootouts in the streets of Queens, and an unlikely romance all combine to make for a gripping, satisfying read."
—*Publishers Weekly* (starred review)

"[With] intelligence and engaging style . . . Gruber raises the thriller stakes and accelerates the plot, while still creating convincing personal journeys for his characters. All that and a tantalizing imagining of Shakespeare's personality too."
—*Booklist* (starred review)

"Not since A. S. Byatt's *Possession* has an author so successfully combined literary puzzle, tempestuous duplicity, human adventure, and good storytelling. In a thriller written with remarkable flair, Gruber serves up an elaborately layered and devilishly detailed masterpiece."
—*BookPage*

D0249779

"Bold, provocative, and frightening. . . . An extraordinary debut."
—*USA Today*

"Gripping. . . . Gruber has written an undeniably strong book."
—*Seattle Times*

"Michael Gruber has written a book with such intelligence, confidence, dazzling bits of arcane knowledge, and downright page-turning scariness that other novelists are going to want to just smack him. Absolutely mesmerizing. . . . Equal parts literary novel and thriller. . . . Gruber has an astonishing way of pulling in the reader."
—*Cleveland Plain Dealer*

"Reminiscent of Peter Hoeg's *Smilla's Sense of Snow*. . . . Original, unconventional, and intricately plotted. . . . A gritty, edge-of-the-seat crime novel."
—*Fort Lauderdale Sun-Sentinel*

PRAISE FOR
# NIGHT OF THE JAGUAR

"Almost no one matches [Gruber's] talent for blending the supernatural with gritty street grunge. His latest is no exception."
—*Entertainment Weekly*

"A worthy addition to this heretofore terrific series. . . . The novel fires on all cylinders, once again displaying Gruber's skill at blending genres."
—*San Francisco Chronicle*

"[A] highly entertaining thriller . . . hotly spiced with hit men and guns, demon gods and piranhas."
—*Publishers Weekly*

"Superior entertainment that raises sincere, provocative questions of intellect and faith."
—*Seattle Times*

"Compellingly original. Gruber gives more to ponder than intriguing clues to the identity and motive of the killer—both of which, when they arrive, are as satisfying as they are unthinkable—and he does it with prose that is efficient yet rich and hip. His characters have lives; they care about issues in ways that compel them to wax enthusiastic as they are sucked into the labyrinth of the case."
—*Sunday Oregonian*

"His novels are elevated to the level of literature . . . enjoyed by the masses and admired by academics for years to come."
—*Denver Post*

PRAISE FOR
# THE BOOK OF AIR AND SHADOWS

"Breathlessly engaging. . . . Brilliant. . . . Few [thrillers] will surpass *The Book of Air and Shadows* when it comes to energetic writing, compellingly flawed characters, literary scholarship, and mathematical conundrums. *Air and Shadows* is also incredibly smart. . . . Unpredictable. . . . We never had this much fun reading *The Da Vinci Code*. Gruber has raised the stakes in the thriller genre."
—*USA Today*

Nina Subin

## About the Author

MICHAEL GRUBER began freelance writing while working in Washington, D.C., for the Carter White House's Office of Science and Technology Policy. He later worked as a policy analyst and speechwriter for the Environmental Protection Agency, and he has been a full-time writer since 1988. His novels include *The Book of Air and Shadows*, *Night of the Jaguar*, *Tropic of Night*, and *Valley of Bones*. Married with three grown children and an extremely large dog, he currently lives in Seattle.

www.michaelgruberbooks.com

Books by Michael Gruber

THE FORGERY OF VENUS
THE BOOK OF AIR AND SHADOWS
NIGHT OF THE JAGUAR
VALLEY OF BONES
TROPIC OF NIGHT

# MICHAEL GRUBER

# VALLEY OF BONES

HARPER

NEW YORK • LONDON • TORONTO • SYDNEY

## HARPER

Grateful acknowledgment is made for permission to reprint the following:

From *The Collected Poems of Wallace Stevens* by Wallace Stevens, copyright ©
1954 by Wallace Stevens. Copyright renewed © 1982 by Holly Stevens. Used by
permission of Alfred A. Knopf, a division of Random House, Inc.

From *Given Sugar, Given Salt* by Jane Hirshfield, copyright © 2001 by Jane
Hirshfield. Used by permission of HarperCollins Publishers, Inc.

From *Gravity and Grace* by Simone Weil, translated by Arthur Wills, copyright
© 1952. Copyright renewed © 1980 by G. P. Putnam's Sons. Original French
copyright: © 1947 by Librarie Plon. Used by permission of G. P. Putnam's Sons,
a division of Penguin Group (USA), Inc.

A hardcover edition of this book was published in 2005 by William Morrow, an
imprint of HarperCollins Publishers.

HarperCollins books may be purchased for educational, business, or sales
promotional use. For information please write: Special Markets Department,
HarperCollins Publishers, 10 East 53rd Street, New York, NY 10022.

FIRST HARPERTORCH EDITION PUBLISHED 2006.
FIRST HARPER PAPERBACK PUBLISHED 2009.

Library of Congress Cataloging-in-Publication Data is available upon request.

ISBN 978-0-06-165074-1

09  10  11  12  13    RRD    10  9  8  7  6  5  4  3  2  1

For
E.W.N.

There are four evidences of divine mercy here below. The favors of God to beings capable of contemplation (these states exist and form part of their experience as creatures). The radiance of these beings, and their compassion, which is the divine compassion in them. The beauty of the world. The fourth evidence is the complete absence of mercy here below.

—SIMONE WEIL, *GRAVITY AND GRACE*

The hand of the Lord was upon me, and carried me out in the Spirit of the Lord, and set me down in the midst of the valley, which was full of bones.

—EZEKIEL, 37:1

# BLOOD OF CHRIST, SOCIETY OF
## NURSING SISTERS
### OF THE (SBC)

Founded by Bd. Marie-Ange de Berville in 1895, the Nursing Sisters of the Blood of Christ are dedicated to giving succor and providing healing to the innocent victims of war and oppression. The order, which was one of the few to retain the habit after the reforms of the Second Vatican Council, is noted for its almost military discipline and its custom of recruiting very young girls from the ranks of abandoned and disabled children throughout the world, although this aspect of its work has been widely criticized. Sisters of the order have distinguished themselves by their bravery and self-sacrifice during both world wars and thereafter in many fields of strife. Although counting no more than three thousand professed sisters and oblates at the present time, it has lost to death over 120 of its number, more than any other order in modern times. Traditionally, its members categorically refuse to leave patients and communities for which they have taken responsibility, in keeping with the order's motto "Where we go, we remain." *See also* Bd. Marie-Ange de Berville; Pope Pius XI; Cardinal Matteo Ratti.

—*ENCYCLOPEDIA CATHOLICA,* 2D ED., 1997

# One

The cop happened to look up at just the right instant or he would have missed it, not the actual impalement, but the fall itself. It took him a disorienting second to realize what he was seeing, the swelling black mass against the white stone and glass of the hotel facade, and then it was finished, with a sound that he knew he would carry to his grave.

After that, he took a minute or so to sit on the bumper of his car with his head down low, so as not to pollute the crime scene with his own vomit, and then reported the event on his radio. He called it in as a 31, which was the Miami PD code for a homicide, although it could have been an accident or a jumper. But it *felt* like a homicide, for reasons the cop could not then explain. While he waited for the sirens, he looked up at the row of balconies that made up the face of the Trianon Hotel. The thought briefly crossed his mind that he ought to go and check the guy out to make sure that he was actually dead, that perhaps the wrought iron fleur-de-lis spearheads protruding from the man's neck, chest, and groin had missed all the vital organs in their paths.

He was a dutiful officer, but this was his first fresh corpse, and he decided not to investigate more closely than a couple of yards, telling himself that it was better not to contaminate the crime scene. The corpse had been a good-looking guy, he thought, leather-dark skin but aquiline features: hooked nose, thin lips, a little spade beard. There was something foreign about the face, although the officer could not have said what it was.

Turning away from it with some relief, he inspected the facade of the hotel, noting that there were three vertical columns of balconies adorning the twelve floors of the building, which was capped by a copper roof styled after a French château. That was the theme of the Trianon Hotel, as much French as would fit: besides the roof, there were gilt cornices, coats of arms, New Orleans–style wrought iron on the balconies, and, of course, fleurs-de-lis on the iron fence that surrounded the south face of the property. People were coming out of the hotel now, frightened men in the hotel's white livery, a few guests from the lobby. A woman's shriek recalled the cop to his duty, and he herded them all back into the cool interior.

A broad man in a double-breasted cream suit accosted him at this point and announced himself as the manager. He knew who it was, a guest, 10 D, and gave a name. The cop wrote it down in his notebook. The manager departed, dabbing at his mouth with a handkerchief, and the cop resumed his study of the facade, although his eye kept drifting over to the victim. The flies arrived and got to their buzzing tasks, and shortly after that an ambulance pulled up. The paramedics emerged, took in the scene, declared the man officially dead, made wiseass paramedic remarks, and went back to their bus to wait in the cool of the AC. The crime scene van arrived, and the CSUs started to assemble their various implements of investigation and their cameras, while making some of the same cracks (that's what I call piercings; sorry, he can't come to the phone right now) that the paramedics had made, and after a little while an unmarked white Chevy pulled up, and out of it came a neatly built, caramel-colored man, in a beautifully cut gray-green silk and linen suit. The cop sighed. Of course it had to be him.

"Morales?" asked the man. The cop nodded, and the man held out his hand to be shaken, saying, "Paz."

"Uh-huh," said Morales. He knew who Jimmy Paz was, as did everyone on the Miami PD, as did everyone in Metropolitan Dade County who owned a television. Morales had not, however, met him professionally until now. Both men were first-generation Cuban immigrant stock, but the patrolman considered himself white, like 98 percent of the Cuban migration to America, and Paz was not white, yet also undeniably Cuban. It was disconcerting, even without the tug of racism, which Morales was conscious of trying to resist.

"You're the first response on this?" Paz was not looking at the corpse. He was looking at Morales, with a pleasant smile on his face and little lights glinting in his hazel eyes. He was looking at a man in his early twenties, with a fine-featured beardless face, in the complexion usually called olive, but which is more like parchment, a face that might be choirboy open when relaxed but was now guarded, tense, the intelligent dark eyes focused on the detective so hard they almost squinted.

"No, I was here already. Somebody called in a disturbance at the hotel. It was a hoax call. I was just about to pull out when he came down."

"You saw him drop?"

"Yeah."

Paz looked up at the face of the hotel and saw what Morales had seen. It was perfectly clear from which balcony the victim had begun his fatal descent. All the balconies but one had their glass doors closed against the afternoon heat. In the single exception the door was open and the white curtains were flapping like flags. Paz counted silently.

"It looks like the tenth floor," he said. Now for the first time he inspected the corpse. "Nice shoes," he said. "Lorenzo Banfi's. Nice suit too. A dresser. Tell me, why did you call it in as a homicide?"

"He didn't yell on the way down," said Morales, surprising himself with this statement. Paz grinned at him, a catlike grin, and Morales felt his own face breaking into a smile. "Very good. Good police work. Guy slips off a terrace, you have to figure he's going to make some kind of noise on the way down. And now that we know that, this little line of blood dripping under the back of the skull here is more interesting, huh?"

"He could have hit his head on the way down."

"Against what? You saw it: it's a straight shot from that balcony to the fence, and he made a perfect three-prong landing. No, he went over with that wound already on his head. He was probably out cold when he landed. Probably a good thing too, considering." They both looked for a moment at the fly-crawling corpse.

Then Paz said, "I tell you what, Morales. This guy isn't going anywhere. Why don't you and me go on up to that room and try to find out what he was doing before he came down?"

"His name's Jabir Akran al-Muwalid. I got it off the manager. He's a guest, 10 D."

Another big grin from Paz.

"Very good, Morales. Great! Terrific! Thank you. I wasn't looking forward to going through that guy's pockets for ID."

Morales was thinking that maybe the book on Paz was wrong, that he wasn't an arrogant pain in the ass after all. Morales had been on the force for nine months, and this was the first time a detective had treated him like anything but a useless doughnut-dunker who had probably messed up the crime scene and helped the perp on with his coat. The other funny thing was that the guy didn't have a partner. All the homicide guys worked in pairs, but apparently not Jimmy Paz.

They picked up a key card from the desk and went up in the elevator, which was, like the lobby, decorated in cream and gold. It even had a little Louis Quinze chair in it, with a brocade seat. As it turned out, they did not need the key card. A rolled towel had been placed on the floor to thwart the automatic-closing feature of the room door. They stepped over it and into the room.

It was a suite, furnished in the same Louis Quinze style as the lobby and the elevator; and they were now in the spacious sitting room thereof. One whole wall was lined with gilt-framed mirrors, and on the opposite side they had a view of the balcony and the French windows that led onto it; the heavy drapes, printed with heraldic ancien régime designs were pulled back, and the filmy white sheers fluttered in the breeze from Biscayne Bay.

Paz started to walk toward this balcony but caught a glimpse of something in the mirror and stopped. There was a woman in the room. She was kneeling on the faux Aubusson, her hands clasped to her breast, eyes wide open, staring. Paz moved into her field of vision, but she didn't appear to notice him. He observed that she was speaking in a low voice. Praying? He moved closer, at the same time gesturing for Morales to check out the bedroom.

It didn't sound like prayer, not that Paz was particularly familiar with the sound. She seemed to be talking to someone conversationally, although he could not make out the words. It was much like the one-sided conversations one heard lately on the streets from the people with cell phones. Paz looked carefully: no cell phone. The woman was tall and thin and had the bony good looks of a country-and-western star, a little faded. A C & W singer who'd never really made it, or one that *had* made it and then got ruined by drink and/or shiftless men, living small in a Hialeah motel. A hard face, he might have said, the kind you saw in the tank when the cops had rounded up a bunch of whores, except that there was something transcendent in the expression on her face that didn't go with the picture. She was dressed in a faded blue T-shirt, very loose and a little soiled, a calf-length brown cotton skirt, and tire-tread sandals. Dusty feet. Her hair was crow black and cut into a boy's cap from which small lobeless ears emerged, close to the head. No earrings. Her eyes, set deeply within a hedge of thick dark lashes, were (surprisingly, given her hair and complexion) the color of washed blue jeans, against which the pupils looked unusually small, like BBs. Drugged, maybe? That might explain that expression too. She wore neither makeup nor nail polish, and her skin was sallow in the way that indicates a deep tan faded. Against her neck, just above the fabric of her shirt, he could make out a thin leather cord, perhaps attached to some ornament she wore under the T-shirt.

"Excuse me," said Paz. To his surprise, the woman rolled her eyes back into her head so that only the whites showed and toppled gently over onto her side. Paz immediately knelt beside her and put his hand to her neck. Her skin was moist and felt unusually hot, but the pulse beating beneath it was strong and regular. A scent came off her, sweat and something gas-station-ish, like oil or gas, and a faint floral note. Paz had handled many floral arrangements in his time and recognized the odor: lilies.

The woman's eyelids fluttered, her eyes opened, she jerked and looked surprised when she saw Paz staring down at her.

"What happened?" she asked. "Who're you?" A rural-sounding voice. *Hur yew.*

"You were kneeling and then you kind of keeled over," Paz said. "I'm Detective Paz, Miami PD. Who are you?"

"Emmylou Dideroff. Is he here?" She sat up and looked around the room.

"He would be Mr. al-Muwalid, yes?"

"Uh-huh." She rose somewhat shakily to her feet, and Paz saw that she was tall indeed, somewhat taller than his own five ten.

"You ought to sit down," he said, "you look a little shaky." She did, on one of the silly uncomfortable-looking French chairs. "You're from the police?" she asked, and when Paz nodded, she said, "Are you here to arrest him?"

"Why would we want to do that, Ms. Dideroff?"

"Oh, he's a murderer," she said. "A criminal. That's why I followed him. I couldn't believe it, walking down the street in Miami, like nothing. He drove into the parking garage and I parked my truck on the drive—where you check in? And I waited in the lobby for him to come by. I wanted to go up to him and look him in the face, I mean to make sure it was really him. And he didn't show up and I thought, Oh darn, he probably came up right from the parking garage."

She met Paz's eyes and said, "Oh my gosh, I fainted again, didn't I?"

"Yes, ma'am. What exactly were you doing before you went out?" In the mirror Paz saw Morales in the doorway of the bedroom. Their eyes met, Morales shrugged and gestured with his thumb at the room behind him, meaning, no one there. With a slight motion of his head, Paz indicated the balcony. Morales slipped along the wall, silently for a cop, and went through the open French windows.

"Oh, talking to Catherine," the woman said. "Anyway, I just took the elevator up to the top floor and found the chambermaid and asked her which was his room, but he wasn't on that floor, and then I just went down floor by floor, talking to the ladies there, until I got to ten and that one knew him right off. So I went to the room and I saw that the door was propped open and . . . I went in. I guess I shouldn't have, right?"

"Not really. Who's Catherine?"

"Catherine of Siena."

"As in Saint?"

"Uh-huh. She's extremely wise in the ways of the world."

"Was. I thought she was dead."

The woman gave him a smile. He saw that she was missing two teeth on the right side, but besides that it was a lovely open smile. "Well, yes. But the dead are all around us. It's the communion of saints. Are you a Catholic?"

"Raised. I'm not much of a churchgoer." The woman had nothing to say to that.

Throat clearing behind Paz: he turned, and there was Morales with the curtain flapping around him and an excited look on his smooth face. "Ah, Detective, I think you need to see this out here."

Paz waved him in and walked across the room. They conversed in low voices.

"What've you got?" Paz asked.

"I think the murder weapon's lying out there. Looks like an engine part with . . . ah, like blood and hair on it. I didn't touch it or anything."

"Good. Anything interesting in the bedroom?"

"The vic's ID. A Sudan passport with a bunch of business cards stuck in it. A wallet with a couple of grand in fresh hundreds. I looked in the top drawer of the dresser. Was that okay?"

"Not really, but we'll let it slide. The dead have no rights, but we like to wait for crime scene before we touch stuff. Now, why don't you keep Ms. Dideroff there company while I take a look at your clue."

"What's her story?"

"Damned if I know," said Paz and walked through to the little balcony terrace. He squatted low and peered at the thing. When he was sixteen and poor as dirt, Paz had rebuilt the blown engine on his first car, a '56 Mercury, and so he knew just what he was looking at. It was a rod, the short, strong, steel forging that connects the piston of an internal combustion engine to the crankshaft, larger than the Merc's was, maybe from a big diesel. It consisted of a ring designed to grip the crankshaft and a smaller ring that went around a fat pin inside the piston. There was a smear of blood along the side of the large ring and a few curly dark hairs that looked like they could have come off the head of the victim. He leaned closer, balancing like a chimp on the knuckles of one hand. The rod was brand-new, it seemed, and covered with a sheen of oil. Low on the shaft were several almost perfect fingerprints, where someone had gripped it. Well, well.

He stood and looked over the wrought iron railing. He could see the impaled victim, ten stories below, with the CSU swarming around him, photographing and taking samples. Paz wished them well but thought that most of the relevant evidence would be found right up here in 10 D. He pulled out his cell phone, called the CSU team leader on her cell phone, and was amused that he could actually see the person he was cell-calling to. He waved and she waved back and he told her to get up to 10 D with all speed.

He went back inside and pulled up a chair so that he was facing Emmylou Dideroff.

"So, Ms. Dideroff—can I call you Emmylou?" She nodded. "Emmylou—what's your connection to Jabir al-Muwalid? You a friend of his?"

"Oh, no. He was our enemy."

"'Our' being . . . ?"

"My tribe. The Peng Dinka. The Monyjang."

"Uh-huh. And this was because . . . ?"

"Oh, he was responsible for the deaths of hundreds, maybe thousands of people. I don't mean just in the war. He was the leader of a kind of special death squad."

"I see. And this was where? Here in Miami?"

Her face underwent a change, as if she had suddenly realized where she was and what was happening. Paz got a stare that could have come from any Overtown chippie. "Excuse me, but what's going on? Where is he, and why're you here in his room?"

"He's dead," said Paz bluntly. "He went out that window there about twenty minutes ago and impaled himself on a spiked fence."

A swift intake of breath, a slight widening of the eyes. "Well," she said, sighing. "God have mercy on his soul," and then something in a clanging language Paz did not know. He studied the woman's face. The surprise looked genuine, but then again if she was half the nut she seemed at present there was no telling what sort of unconscious states she could drop into. Paz had somewhat more experience with exotic mental phenomena than the average police detective. An annoying little prickle had begun a couple of inches in from his belt buckle.

"And so, Emmylou . . . ah, do you know anything about how he came to go out the window?"

"No. I never saw him. I told you, I came here, I found the door open, I came in and waited."

"And prayed."

"I saw the apparition. I hadn't seen her for quite some time and I guess I drifted, you know, a little ways off." He saw a little color appear on the bar of her high cheekbones. Embarrassment? Or guilt?

"Right. Tell me, do you know what a connecting rod is?"

"Sure. It's part of an engine. Why?"

"Do you have one? I mean not as part of a car, a separate one. Like a spare part."

"Not on me. Look, I don't understand why you're asking this about conn——"

"But you do own one."

She shook her head. "There's one in the foot well of my truck. I mean Jack Wilson's truck. Wilson Brothers Marine on South River Drive. I work there. I do their office, and I'm a parts runner when there's a rush. That's how I came across the colonel. I was at Shattuck Machine on Southwest First, picking up a remanufactured C rod for a Mermaid Meteor they're working on. And he was there, waiting by a pay phone outside the 7-Eleven across the street. So I followed him back here."

"Uh-huh. And basically you came up here and waited for him and you had the rod handy and you slugged him with it, hard, and after he went down you dragged him over to that balcony and tossed him over. Is that how it went down, Emmylou?"

Her mouth became a little pink O. She was good, he had to admit, if this was an act. "You think I *killed* him?"

"Well, there's a connecting rod out there with blood and hair on it. It looks like someone whacked Jabir across the head and then tossed him over. And you're sitting here praying. And you said he was your enemy. And you followed him all the way back from the river. What am I supposed to think?"

She stared at him. He looked into her eyes and felt a little shock: it was like looking into the eyes of two completely different people, one set being the icicles of a stone killer, and the other the sorrowful soft sky blues of the Blessed Virgin in a chapel.

It was only for an instant, and Paz briefly thought that he had imagined it, but he'd felt the sweat pop out on his lip and in the small of his back. Weird shit, he said to himself, with an inward sigh. Weird shit *again*. This, however, passed; routine took over. Paz read Emmylou Dideroff her rights and Morales cuffed her.

The woman seemed to be back in her trance. "She said there would be more afflictions." She spoke in a soft wondering voice.

"Who was that, Emmylou? Who said?"

"Catherine. This is so strange. You never can tell what He has in store for you. Life is so *interesting* that way. But you know, really, I didn't kill him. I wanted to, at one time, and it might even have been appropriate then, but not now."

"Then why did you follow him back here?"

She said, "I wanted to forgive him."

Paz couldn't think of anything to say to that. He made a little motion of his head, and Morales led her away.

The booking took some hours, as it always did. While they hung around the complaint room at the state's attorney, Paz chatted with Morales, who turned out to be Tito. Tito and Iago: they shared a Cuban moment about their names. A little Spanish thrown in too, although Morales understood a good deal more than he could speak. He was a second-generation immigrant, or *exile,* depending on who in the community you were talking to. In his easy detective manner, Paz was able to find out nearly everything there was to know about Tito Morales, without revealing anything of himself, except for the stuff that was public knowledge. Morales was twenty-three, unmarried, living at home, had tried Miami-Dade for a couple of semesters, liked it all right, but wanted something more physical, more adventurous, had thought about the marines, but didn't want to leave his mother, who was ailing. The cops seemed like a good deal. Paz asked him where he wanted to go in the cops, and Morales said that he liked the idea of being a detective. A little conversation about how one got into the detectives. Paz told the story of how he had got in, which was catching a guy from Overtown who'd killed a Japanese tourist, a story that Morales seemed already to know.

It took a while, but two observations finally struck Jimmy Paz with some force: one was that although he was only about ten years older than Morales, the young cop was far more of an American than he himself was. Paz did not ordinarily think of himself as Cuban foremost, but he realized now that this was because he had been unconsciously comparing himself with his own mother and because he spent a good deal of time immersed in the *cubanismo* of her restaurant and milieu. But compared with Morales, he might as well have been wearing a straw hat and leading a donkey and a cart full of sugarcane. The other observation was that he was receiving hero worship, not obnoxiously, but it was clear that the kid was enormously pleased to be having a private conversation with Jimmy Paz, and that he was going to tell all his pals about it, and his mom, and that they in turn would be impressed. And the kid was white. Paz had been on the TV and had been on podiums, having his hand shaken by the mayor and a congressman and the state's attorney for Dade County, but that was all connected with a particular event, or rather with a particular version of the event—the capture of the infamous Voodoo Killer, so called—which version Paz knew to be a fabrication. Paz was the only person in Dade County who knew what the truth was, and he was practiced in not thinking about it at all. Getting this flash of admiration from a patrolman was different somehow, more real. It really seemed to transcend race, which transcendence in Paz's experience was so uncommon as to be hardly a blip on the radar screen of his life. He realized, not entirely with pleasure, that he was moving, in a tiny parochial way, into the realm occupied by the single-named chosen people of his race: Oprah, Tiger, Shaq.

The booking completed, he bid Morales good-bye and went back to homicide, where he ran the name Emmylou Dideroff through the National Crime Information Center. It came up with a blank, which meant the woman had never been convicted of a crime as an adult. How many crimes she'd committed without being convicted the computer did not say. Although Social Security numbers are not supposed to be used for purposes of identification, this rule is now something of a joke, so Paz ran her name through a commercial agency to get a credit file for her and was somewhat surprised to draw a blank again. Same with driver's license records. The woman did not exist on paper, which was impossible, so the name had to be a fake. He had an address, though, of a sort, and he quickly obtained a search warrant.

Before executing it, Paz attended the autopsy of the late Colonel Jabir Akran al-Muwalid, and learned that the victim had indeed been bashed on his occiput by a blunt instrument, which instrument could very well have been a connecting rod. The theory was clinched later that same day by the crime lab report, which found that the hair and blood on the connecting rod matched that of the victim. Cherry on top? The prints on the rod matched those taken from Emmylou Dideroff.

Whistling a happy tune, Paz took this material down to the interview room at the Miami PD's Fifth Street headquarters, where they had parked the woman. He found her in the company of a female detective. The detective was reading a worn copy of *People*. Emmylou was reading a Bible. Paz was heartened to observe that there was no counsel present. He pulled up a chair across from her and watched her for a moment. She was reading intently, moving her lips. Paz wondered whether she was a poor reader or if this was something to do with prayer.

"Emmylou," he said at last, when it had become clear that she was not going to respond to his presence. She closed the book and regarded him benignly.

"What does *I.X.* stand for?" she asked, pointing to the picture ID that, like everyone in the building, he wore on a chain around his neck.

"Iago Xavier," he replied.

"That's a lovely name. Which saint do you consider your patron?"

"Let's talk about you first, Emmylou," he said. "You're in a lot of trouble." And now he laid out the evidence against her—the blunt instrument, the forensics on it, the autopsy, her presence at the murder scene, the absence of any evidence that anyone else had the opportunity to whack Mr. al-Muwalid across the skull and toss him to his death.

"The thing of it is, we sort of got you on this. I don't know what this guy did to you to get you mad enough to kill him, but you did it, and the only thing you got going for you now is your story. The only story we have now is that you were lying in wait and killed him in cold blood. No signs of a struggle, if you get what I'm driving at. That's a special circumstance."

"I don't understand."

"It's like multiple murder, or murder with extreme cruelty, or murder for hire. It allows them to go for the death penalty. I got to say, when the state's attorney shows what happened to the victim here, what he looked like on that fence, I think the jury will go for it. I mean, it's something to think about. Whereas, if you tell your story, write out your confession, save the state the expense of a trial, that's a whole different situation."

"You mean confess to murdering him?"

"That's what I mean."

"But that would be a lie. I couldn't lie. And it would be under oath, wouldn't it?"

"Yes."

She smiled, and he thought, Why am I feeling bad? She's the killer. She seemed to pick up his discomfort. "I'm really sorry. I just couldn't. I mean, lie like that. Also, it would mean you'd stop looking for the killer, and that wouldn't be right. He might kill someone else—"

"Oh, cut it out!" Paz cried, rising and slamming the thick case folder he was holding down on the table, hard, and was glad to see her jump. He stood over her and yelled in her face. "For crying out loud, Emmylou! We're not talking *lying* here! You killed him, you know you killed him, and I am giving you your one damn chance to keep out of that little room up in Raiford. The needle? Do you want to die?"

She seemed to consider this for longer than, in his experience, anybody had ever considered the question. "Do you really think that there's a possibility that I'll be executed?" she asked quietly.

"Damn right!" said Paz, trying to get more conviction in his voice than the facts warranted. Florida had only killed one woman in recent years. "They executed Aileen Wuornos, and they'll do the same to you. You want to kill someone and you don't feature getting the needle, don't do it in the state of Florida."

The woman seemed to consider this proposition. She cleared her throat and said, "I guess I should consider it an honor."

"What?"

"To be executed unjustly, like Jesus himself. What more could I ask?"

A little jolt of rage flashed through Paz, and then a wave of regret. He really needed his old partner Barlow on this one, Barlow would know how to handle the woman, they'd have a nice chat about the Holy Spirit and the end times or whatever, and then she'd sign a confession. Paz had his doubts about the death penalty, given what he knew about how the cops collected evidence, but he liked that you could wave the flag of death in a murder interrogation. He found it concentrated the minds of the suspects. Unless they were nuts, as in the present case.

"Provided it's unjust," said Paz. "And that's interesting, Emmylou. Most people are afraid of death." A nod and a murmur. "But you're not?"

"I've been there. It's not much."

"So what *are* you afraid of, Emmylou? Help me out here. I can't threaten you if I don't know what scares you the most?"

He saw a small smile bend her mouth. "Oh, you know I talk a good game, but I'm not really that brave. I'm a runner and hider. Sneaky. And what I'm afraid of you can't threaten me with, I don't think."

"Try me. What is it?"

"Do you believe in the soul?" This almost in a whisper, her head down. Paz could hear the female detective turn a page in her magazine.

Paz was actually not sure what he believed in this regard, but he thought that the right answer now was yes.

"Then you could say I fear for my soul, I fear being dragged down to hell."

"The devil's chasing you, hmm?"

She raised her head slowly and looked at him. "Not *chasing,* no."

Their eyes locked. Paz saw the small pupils expand, covering the blue wash of the iris, then expand impossibly to consume the whites the whole face the whole room, he saw the deadly beauty of hell revealed, he felt its pull, the events of his life spun in his head, changing meaning, yes, he was meant for this, the lovely power of it, the moral compass spun like a pinwheel. . . .

Paz stood up violently, knocking the chair backward. At the noise, the other detective glanced up from her magazine, a puzzled look on her round face. He felt nauseated, he was going to puke on the table, lose control of his functions, blackness closed in, red rimmed, he was looking at the suspect down a tunnel, at a face now entirely ordinary.

Post-traumatic stress, he'd read about it, some flashback from all that voodoo stuff, it went with the nightmares, oh yes indeed, triggered by this lunatic woman and the talk of devils, and the whiff of African weirdness he'd experienced earlier.

"Are you all right, Detective?" the woman asked.

"I'm fine," said Paz. He took out a pocket handkerchief and wiped his face. He made himself look at her. She was back in Blessed Virgin mode. "So you're worried about your soul— well, I always heard that confession was good for the soul."

"Yes, that's true." She emitted a deep sigh. "All right."

"All right what?"

"I'll confess."

"Good. You make a full confession and the state's attorney is a lot more flexible on leniency, on—"

"I'm not interested in that," she said. "I've been told to do it."

"By . . . ?"

"The saint, I told you. I had to forgive and confess."

"To the murder."

She shook her head impatiently. "No, I didn't murder al-Muwalid, I told you that. I mean to my other sins and crimes."

Paz pushed a legal pad and a ballpoint across to her. She didn't touch them.

"No, I need a bound notebook, not a spiral, nothing I can tear pages out of."

"Because . . . ?"

"I'll lie. I'll write down the truth and then I'll tear it out. It has to be bound so you can tell if any pages are missing."

"Uh-huh. Okay, bound notebooks. Like in grade school? Black with those little white dots?"

A blazing smile that made her look eight. "Yes, perfect. I think I'll need . . . say, four."

"You got 'em. You wouldn't want to give me a little teaser now about some of these crimes?"

"No. I have to write it. In that kind of notebook."

A sinking sensation in his gut. A nut, it was clear, and she'd probably work an insanity plea behind it, and all the beautiful evidence he'd collected would be moot. Was she in fact crazy? Paz knew he'd seen something for a second there in the hotel room that wasn't crazy at all, that icicle woman, but that meant zero in a court of law. Paz didn't think at all about what had seemed to happen a few moments ago, and except for the drying sweat on his back, he would have believed that it hadn't happened at all. Some kind of attack, low blood sugar or stress or something, nothing to worry about, nothing compared with this loony getting away with it. In any case, not his business anymore. Paz felt like he'd wasted his whole day.

The little town of Pony-aux-Bois lies in the Forest of Vaux, on the shores of the river Mance, which flows a few miles south into the Moselle at Metz. The town is of great antiquity. The church, Saint-Martin-de-Tours, dates from the ninth century, and in late summer when the water is low, the people will point out to you the piling of a Roman bridge, pale angular shadows under the golden water. It is a peaceful and lovely place, much favored by the wealthy men of Metz for the construction of summer cottages and shooting lodges. One such was Georges Hippolyte de Berville, a merchant of that city and a trader in coal and oil. In 1851 he had built for himself and his family a comfortable cottage of local stone, overlooking the river. The family consisted of three sons, Alphonse, Jean-Pierre, and Gerard, and his wife, Sophie Catherine. They were all loving and healthy, for which they all gave thanks to God, for they were very devout, especially Sophie Catherine. After the cottage at Pony was finished, they used to spend the whole summer on the river, where they occupied themselves with such country pastimes as angling for tench and bream and shooting pigeons and woodcock. In this gentle place upon a summer's morning in the year 1856, Sophie gave birth to a child, whom they would name Marie-Ange Bernardine, for Sophie was much devoted to the Queen of the Angels, and it was August 20, the feast day of Bernard of Clairvaux.

—FROM *FAITHFUL UNTO DEATH:*
*THE STORY OF THE NURSING SISTERS*
*OF THE BLOOD OF CHRIST,*
BY SR. BENEDICTA COOLEY, SBC,
ROSARIAN PRESS, BOSTON, 1947.

# Two

## The
## CONFESSIONS
### of
### Emmylou Dideroff

### Book I

*Just plunge in. Just plunge in, in my daddy's voice, just plunge in, sugar pie, ain't nothin in that river meaner'n you. I must have been four, the river was the Coelee in Caluga County, Florida, tea dark, with the Spanish moss and the live oak and palmetto overhanging. He was teaching me how to swim. So I plunge in and really I have no idea, I am a reader not a writer, I should have started with praise as Augustine did but of course I forgot and what vainglory comparing myself but perhaps God sees us all the same, He loves us though we are all beneath contempt the greatest saints and me. Augustine begins with I recall only the famous line You stir man to take pleasure in praising you, because you have made us for yourself, and our heart is restless until it rests in you. Of course, we don't really know that, do we St. A? We think we want other stuff, more easily available and so when we remember to pray at all we pray as you did for so long—God make me good but not yet.*

*If I had not been so wicked, the possession of devout and God-fearing parents, together with the favor of God's grace, would have been enough to make me good.* I laughed out loud the first time I read that, in a priory library where laughter was not encouraged, and then I was sad because I would have liked so much to have had parents like that or to have been as little wicked as Teresa of Avila, and I could have started my confessions with that line as she did her Life. And I find it interesting how I am not in fact plunging in but filling the page with buzz to avoid it, my genuine and not chastely imagined wickedness. Now, for real.

I was born to Joseph R. and Ellen May (Billie) Boone Garigeau in Wayland, Florida. Billie was seventeen at the time, and my father, called Ti Joe by everyone, was twenty-two and a Cajun from Plaquemines Parish in Louisiana. I think neither of them feared God very much, and their devotion, though strong, was not to Him. Momma was devoted to Ti Joe, at about the same level as Teresa was devoted to Jesus (or so I later imagined), and Daddy was devoted to two propositions, first that owning and driving a Kenworth truck was the only life for a man worth having, and two, that being a good husband and daddy did not in any way preclude him from getting as much pussy as he possibly could. Oh, now it seems I can write what I decline to say. Bastard. Prick. Cunt. Fuck. An exhibition of hypocrisy now I must be prissy mouthed although I have known nuns who could strip the paint off a Buick. Or maybe this is a dispensation, in the service of absolute honesty.

We lived in a double-wide at the Karefree Trailer Park close by the Coelee River, about eight miles out of Wayland on Route 217 in Caluga County. It was a nice place as those kinds of places go, four neat lines of mobile homes, a playground, a ball field, some red picnic tables by a muddy beach on the river, a wobbly dock, and a small convenience store. While he saved for that Kenworth, Daddy drove a rig for an outfit in Panama City, and he'd be gone different lengths of time during which life entered a kind of limbo, us sitting around waiting for the second coming like the early apostles although without the Holy Spirit to keep us company. He was a handsome devil though, my daddy, and Momma thought she was lucky to get him, although she was no kind of dog herself, a tow-headed skinny girl with long pale legs. She was a local person, a Caluga County belle, he was maybe a hair shorter than she was in his stocking feet, which you practically never got to see because he always had the cowboy boots on with the two-and-a-half-inch heels raising him as close to heaven as he was ever likely to get. That's my Granny Boone talking, not me, I have to believe in the infinite mercy of God. After death, not now.

I say Granny Boone, that's got to conjure up a picture of a bent crone in a faded flowered dress, maybe with a corncob pipe clenched in her toothless jaws, but Maureen Boone was about thirty-eight or so when I was born and not bent or faded at all. I guess Granny Boone was about the only what you could call a citizen among the whole Boone clan, being a bookkeeper for the Coelee River Lumber Company and a high school graduate, with two years of college, where all the other ones were what I guess they used to call white trash. Or trailer trash too, and as a matter of fact I guess Granny was the only Boone in the county who lived in a regular house, an old Florida frame house with deep verandas, painted white, with the gray pine boards showing through where the sun had faded it off.

What I got from Gran was the written word. That's what <u>she</u> was devoted to. She taught me how to read, one of my earliest memories. Sitting on her lap on my daddy's lounger chair, with the TV for once silent, we're in our trailer and Momma is off with her high school friends, the prom queens a little bleached, the football stars just starting to go soft around the gut, and Daddy's on the road with a load, and her quiet voice in my ear reading I can't remember what it was Goodnight Moon or Are You My Mother? Poky Little Puppy. One of those. I must have been three or four. And watching her bookkeeper's finger moving across the familiar black shapes that meant BOX,

*or whatever the word was, I suddenly realized I could
make its sound in my head without Gran having to say it,
and that meant that I could turn on the story in my head,
just like when you turned on the TV. And that meant, I
soon came to realize, that I could read anything, any book
in Granny's house, any book in the tiny town library in
Wayland.*

*Probably it is a fabrication that this happened, I am
backfilling to make a story, as perhaps St. Augustine
made up the famous story of his conversion in the courtyard, the child's voice calling take up and read and he
took up and read the verse that allowed the Holy Spirit to
enter his heart, but so it is with memory. Who knows what
really happened and really, who cares? It's what we make
of it now that counts, and the truth is by the power of the
Holy Spirit burnt into our bodies, so even now I can re-
capture the elation, the quivering joy I felt when I discovered what reading was, the second most important
spiritual event of my life.*

*I kept it secret from Momma and Daddy, because I was
I am trying to think honestly here. Because I was either a
controlling monster even then, like kids you hear about
who hide their poo, or because I figured out even as a little thing that neither of them would be happy to learn
that I was going to be smarter than them. Both of them
could read somewhat, but there was not a book in the
house, so that keeping the secret was no strain, even for a
four-year-old.*

*(You don't believe this denial of accomplishment? You
think kids want to be praised, why would I hide my gift?
Why is there the perversion of gifts at all? Or their salvation? St. Ignatius Loyola wanted to be a conquistador,
Hitler wanted to be an artist. Let's call it satanic while we
wait for the final revelation of psychology.)*

*Gran had a lot of books, of course, and for the longest
time I thought that this was what was meant when she
called herself a bookkeeper. Momma did not like me staying over at her mother's place, or maybe she was just be-*

ing mean to Gran because Gran always wanted me to, or to me because I did too. She was a jealous person, Momma, although not particularly interested in me when she had me to herself. Mean jealous, may God forgive her as I have.

By the time I was five and starting in school I was reading Black Beauty and Misty of Chincoteague and could use a dictionary to look up words I didn't know. I thought I had invented looking up in the dictionary, as a matter of fact, that I had discovered that all the words in this fat book were arranged in the same order as the alphabet! I recall being annoyed when I saw Gran look something up and asked her what she was doing and discovered that it was an open secret. Or maybe that is another fabrication.

In the first grade at the Sidney Lanier Elementary School they were doing the alphabet and I said I knew all of that and I could read but the teacher didn't believe me and that was when I first heard the voice in my head. Pay attention, Emmylou, she was saying, because I was looking out the window wishing I was reading something, she was saying what comes after H and I said I know all this already, this is stupid. She got red across the cheeks, Mrs. Barrett her name was, and I could feel the kids get excited, a murmur like wind in the grass, and she said don't be rude if you know so much say the rest of the alphabet and the voice told me no, you don't have to, you're smarter than all of them put together. I even looked around it was so clear, like one of the other kids was talking, but it wasn't, just a nice soft voice, you couldn't tell if it was a man or a woman. If this never happened to you you don't know what I'm talking about, and if it has you may tremble at the memory of it.

Anyway, that was my first crime that the devil made me do, I had to sit in a corner for half an hour and miss recess but when they all left and I could hear the screaming of play outside I got off the chair I was in and went to the shelf where Mrs. Barrett kept the storytime books and took down a copy of Alice in Wonderland and started to read it. How I explained it to myself was that keeping the secret kept me in control of things, it seemed to me, and even at six I knew that my poor parents were not all that good at controlling stuff. Momma came to school a time or two and let Mrs. B. lecture at her and then she stopped coming entirely and I was on my own, a problem child, slow. And bad. Momma said, honey child, you better turn out pretty because it don't look like you're gonna be no big brain.

After first grade I was in the dumb kid class. On most fine days I would run away at recess and go to Gran's and read. Gran would take books out of the library for her to read to me, and I read through whatever was on the hall table, mostly animal stories and Nancy Drews, and Judy Blume stuff, and Madeleine L'Engle. The hardest part of all this was keeping it from Gran. She did want me to be bright like her, and it was sad her trying to teach me how to read and me not learning. I believe that was the worst thing I did before I got in with boys later. But the devil is all will and hardness of heart and the pleasure I got from being in his favor and the power of fooling the whole world was to me better than pleasing someone who loved me, and the way he did it was to say imagine the pleasure on her face when you finally show her who you really are, and that comforted me in my evil. And he also made me understand that if I showed, they would put me in the gifted and talented where the rich kids were and they would despise me for my clothes and my cracker ways. So many excuses for doing bad!

Besides those books I read her World Book Encyclopedia. In the second grade I got from Aardvark, a large nocturnal burrowing mammal of Africa, to Dysprosium, a rare earth metallic element found in certain minerals. It wasn't until the third grade that I got to Eidetic Memory and found out what I was and that not many people were like me. And the devil said it was his gift, making me so that I wouldn't forget, so that all the treasures of the world's knowledge that he would show me would stay in

my mind always, and poor fool that I was then I thought
that not forgetting was a good thing instead of what it is,
poison acid and gall, but I am a true witness with God's
help.

So of course I remember it perfectly, a day in fourth
grade after lunch sloppy joes carrots fries white cake with
banana frosting, a rainy day so I'm in the classroom
lounging with the dummies and there is Gran at the door
of the room wearing her long yellow slicker and a plastic
kerchief on her head pressing her dark curls like grapes in
shrink wrap at the Winn-Dixie. She spoke to the teacher,
who gave me a sympathetic look that sent a chill down
into my belly, and then we got my little plastic raincoat
with the hood and went out to the Dodge and drove off.
The car smelled of cigarettes and the cologne she used lily
of the valley and we drove in silence for a while and then
she said there's no easy way to tell this sugar but your
Daddy drove his rig off a bridge in Alabama and he's
dead. I took it pretty calm considering, a lot calmer than
Momma anyway who was screeching and banging her
head on the arm of our sofa when we got home. I just
watched her, feeling blank as the back wall of a garage. A
good thing about being in thrall to Satan is you don't feel
much of the pain of human existence. He doesn't care so
why should you?

Daddy's people came in from Louisiana to bury him, a
bunch of dark-skinned, black-haired people I never met
before, the Garigeaus. They were Cajuns but they are not
part of this story, since I never did them any harm, nor
were they much interested in me. Along with the
Garigeaus came a heavyset girl who turned out to be the
first, and I guess only, Mrs. Garigeau. That was a cruel
blow to Momma, to find out that way she wasn't a true
wife, and I was a bastard. They let us all come to the
church though, St. Margaret's, the first time I had ever
been in a Catholic church and the last for many years until I was whipped into it kicking and screaming by God,
like the dumb dog I was and am. I remember liking the in-

cense and trying to get up and follow the rest of them to communion and Momma pinching my arm and making me sit still. They had the mass and cremated him and took him in a little box back to Plaquemines Parish, where they all came from. They have their graves in stone boxes above ground there, because of the floods, this fact told to me by a little cousin I never saw again.

The other wife meant there was no survivors' money for us, and the insurance company wouldn't pay the insurance the shippers made Daddy carry because they claimed negligence in the accident, which was what they called getting a blow job off a fifteen-year-old whore he'd picked up in Decatur and in the midst going off the Tennessee River bridge on 20 east.

Well, we were stony broke after that. Momma went back to work at the Tasty-Freeze, and we all moved back with Gran. When I think of the torments of hell, I often think of it like that, two women and a girl in a small little house, all the time fighting both ways, hot and cold. I guess I hated the cold kind the worst, the banging of doors, nobody talking, food slammed down on the table, silent meals. Gran was a good woman, I guess, or started out good, but she had put all her hopes on her daughter and then on me, that one of us would get out of this what she called the stinky armpit of Florida and amount to something, and it was pretty certain by then that one of us was a man-crazy slut without a lick of sense and the other was a retard, me. Retard was Momma talking, not Gran, and for days at a time when I'd done something she didn't like she would call me that, or Ree, or Emmytard.

But a few weeks into the summer after fourth grade, Momma started taking better care of herself and cleaning and cooking, because of Raymond Robert Dideroff, who came one warm summer Sunday night to supper. Ray Bob, as he was known, was the chief of police of Wayland. He had been married to Louellen Pritchard for a long time, and had two boys—Jon Dideroff was in my class at school and Ray Jr. was a year ahead of me—but a couple of years *back she had run off, no one could figure out why, because Ray Bob it was agreed in Wayland was quite the man. Which he was, a big, broad-shouldered, square-jawed fellow with slick-back sandy hair and crinkly blue eyes. The Dideroffs had been in Wayland since the year zip, had plenty of money, what they call prominent citizens, which the Boone family was definitely not. Ray Bob was also a deacon in the Amity Street Assembly of God Church. I believe that when we sat down that night it was the first time anyone had said grace over food in our house, and I got a wicked kick under the table from Momma just as I was about to grab a drumstick beforehand.*

*Well, it was pretty clear to me what was going on, and as I sat there eating chicken I began to think about what I could do to mess things up for Momma without getting caught out and killed. Toward the end of pie and coffee I had thought up a few good ones, but then something strange happened. Ray Bob leaned back in his chair after his second hunk of key lime pie and looked around the room, as if he was planning on buying the place and remarked to Gran about how many books there were in the room and asked if we were all readers. Gran said she had always like to read and she talked about writers she liked for a little while and Ray Bob and her agreed on how they liked some of them, and Momma said she loved to read too but never got the chance because she was working double shifts to keep the money coming in, which was a lie, but Gran knew better than to call her on it just then, and then . . . it is hard to explain but something came into the room with that lie, like a smoke, like Satan himself was there and we were his little dolls he was playing with and having just the best old time.*

*Ray Bob turned to me and locked those blue eyes into mine and the hair stood up on the backs of my arms and on my neck because I saw that he could see right into me right through to my deepest secrets, that he could see the evil working deep in me and that he thought that it was kind of cute. And I saw that what was looking into me was* something that not even Ray Bob knew about in his own heart, which was the scariest thing about it, like you're playing in the river and all of a sudden you realize you're not where you thought you were, not on a safe sandbar but out in the main current and there was no bottom under your feet and the river had hold of you. I had thought I was the wickedest thing going but right then I knew I was just paddling in the shallows of it.

He had a deep, pleasant voice like a TV announcer, and he said how about you, honey, you a reader too? Momma broke in and said oh she wants to so bad but she's <u>dyslexic</u>, we tried everything, and where she dug up that word I don't know, maybe retained against need from one of Mrs. Barrett's lectures, but he paid her no mind, just kept boring inward and stripping me with those eyes, and he said, oh, I think Emmylou can read pretty good when she wants to. Gran spoke up and started to say no, really Ray Bob, she can't read a lick but I cut her off and said I <u>can</u> read, my own voice seeming to come from some other little girl. He said go read us something honey.

Now as part of her act Momma had gone up into the attic and brought down her grandfather's family Bible and dusted it off and sat it on a doily on the sideboard next to the table, like we had Bible reading every day, and so I just had to reach out and grab it and I opened it at random with the blood pounding so hard in my head that I saw red spots. It was I Kings 14 that the book opened to and I read At that time Abijah the son of Jeroboam fell sick And Jeroboam said to his wife, Arise, I pray thee, and disguise thyself that thou be not known as the wife of Jeroboam and get thee to Shiloh: behold there is Ahijah the prophet, which told me I should be king over this people.

I read the next verse too about the cracknels and the cruse of honey and then Momma yelled real loud and said that it was a miracle that she had prayed for so long and came over and dragged me off the chair and gave me a hard furious hug. Over her shoulder I could see the look on Gran's face, the shock of betrayal. I guess she had really wanted to make me into a little her, someone who would enjoy the things she did, books and good music, and might attend the limited cultural events available to the Caluga County bourgeoisie, maybe a girl to take on trips to Atlanta or Miami, who'd go on to a four-year college like she did, only not get pregnant in junior year and have to drop out, and here I was, all what she wanted but keeping it hidden, and then trotting it out for the likes of Ray Bob Dideroff. She aged about ten years while I was looking at her. After a while, me showing off my reading prowess to Momma and Ray Bob, she kind of busied herself with clearing the supper things away. Of course, she never read to me anymore, or called me on how come I did that to her. She kind of faded out of our lives after that, nothing violent, but Ray Bob didn't much care for her, stuck-up was the word mostly used and also she wasn't church and she was a member of the ACLU, which was more than enough to put her in his bad books. Actually, now that I think of it, nearly everyone Momma knew from before was in Ray Bob's bad books, an imposing set of volumes, and I guess that should've told us something, but did not, Momma being so happy to finally be on easy street.

Gulf Avenue was the actual name of the street we were on, a big two-story brick on a five-acre plot that me and Momma moved into after the wedding. Momma was in her glory those first couple of months, I have to say, Ray Bob could not do enough for her, and the rest of us might as well have been invisible. She got rid of her old Ford truck and drove around in a yellow Mustang convertible that had belonged to the first Mrs. Dideroff and that Ray Bob had kept nice and clean in his garage. I had my own room and on the other side of the wall was their bedroom, from which nightly I could hear them going at it, which even at nine I knew what it was. I guess he had not got much nooky since Louellen had left, him being a pillar of the church and all and Wayland being a small place, so he was making up for lost time and Momma was certainly *willing enough. However, around six months into the marriage, when I guess Ray Bob's tank had been pretty much drained to normal, I noticed a change around the place. There was a night when the sounds from the other side of the wall were not what they had been, Momma yelling real loud and high not the kind of words you would expect from a saved church lady and the low rumble of Ray Bob's voice. (I never heard the man raise it once, he was the kind who you do what he says without him ever having to.) Then her voice went up real high and cut off and I heard some thumps, not the thump of the bed but other kinds of thumps. Momma stayed in bed the whole next day, and the day after that she walked kind of stiff and didn't say much. Ti Joe had whapped Momma once in a while when they were both drunk, but this wasn't like that. There was not a mark on her I could see and I peeked at her in the bathroom. So I was mystified, but they did not have the answer in the World Book that I could see.*

*I started fifth grade with a new name, Emmylou Dideroff, since Ray Bob said that we were all one family and should have the same name. Two weeks after school started, on a Friday, I came home in the afternoon and Momma was not there, and the yellow convertible was missing from the garage. She was still gone when Ray Bob got home. He was real calm about it and gave me one of his looks that you better not lie to me and asked me if I knew where she was and I said no sir I do not. Then he made some phone calls. Later that night I heard sirens.*

*They found Momma down in Dixie County, she was speeding and a local cop pulled her over and called Ray Bob because of the registration and he went down and brought her back. I didn't see her then or for a while after, because Ray Bob said she had a nervous breakdown and it was sad but we all had to pray real hard for her to get better. Ray Bob's uncle Doc Herm Dideroff ran a kind of rest home in Wayland Beach, they called it a rest home, but what it was was a place where rich people could kick the habit while not running into anyone they knew, one ad-*

*vantage of it being in a no-account place like Caluga County, Fla. So Momma was put in there for her nervous breakdown and got the electric shock treatments to straighten her out, or so I overheard, and I imagined Doc Herm making her stick her finger in a light socket with her feet wet, a picture I kind of cherished because I was pretty mad at her for running off and not taking me and didn't think even for a minute about what might have been the reason for her to do a stunt like that. What I was thinking about then, may God forgive me, was how I could turn this event to my profit, and at first I was worried that because Momma was no longer around I would lose my position in the family.*

*But the next day, Ray Bob took me aside, actually he came into my room and sat on the frilly rocker Momma had bought, and said that God sometimes sends travails into our lives to test us to see if we be worthy for the kingdom, and that he wanted me to know that whatever happened he would be there for me just like I was his own natural child. Then he asked me what I was reading and it was Kidnapped by R. L. Stevenson and he said that had been a favorite of his when he was a boy, and he asked me if I liked people reading to me. The answer to that was no, but I sensed that the answer that he wanted was yes, and he picked up Kidnapped from where it was on my bed and said come sit on my lap and I'll read to you and that's how it started.*

*I never did figure out whether Ray Bob could see and hear the shiny man like I could, or whether he had his own route to the power of Satan. I write shiny man now because that is what he seems to me in retrospect, although I don't recall calling him that as a child, no more than you would call your conscience or your bodily needs by names. He was just there in my head or sometimes something bright would cross my field of vision, bright as sunlight on dark waters, beautiful as a tiger, and I knew it was him. And he is here too, now, attached to me, by cords of steel, you are supposed to be exorcised when you enter the church but maybe it doesn't work the way it did once, maybe even the priests don't believe in him. You saw him I know and then you decided to forget like most people do, he's learned how to slide off the memory. Can he break me even now, while I am in God's hands? Only if I let him and God help me God help me I still want to, my intention to resist is rotten it always has been I want to slide down into it again away from the crushing light. He doesn't want me to*

*No stick to the story, little Emmylou.*

*Anyway Ray Bob had the devil in him of some kind. Momma sure knew it, and after she got back from her six weeks in the rest home she never gave him a lick of trouble until the very last. They sent her home with a big white plastic bottle of Librium caps so she would not cause any more problems, and with that one exception, she did not. She seemed pretty happy, all told, not that I cared at the time.*

*The sounds on the other side of my wall resumed, although not with the frequency of before and also with a few new ones, one a long grunting wail that it was hard to recognize came out of Momma, kind of a surprised sound like she had not expected whatever it was to hurt so much. Ray Bob told me at the time that he couldn't believe something as sweet as me come out of a wicked woman like Billie Boone, and if he had known about her beforehand he never would've given her his sacred word and married her in the Amity Street Assembly of God Church.*

*How boring now the rape of children is and I'll try not to take up too much time with it. There was nothing crude about Ray Bob's seduction of a nine-year-old child. I was entirely in his power, but he moved very slowly and I have to say gently, and at no point did I ever think or say to myself this is bad or wrong. Of course, there is hardly anything I would have called that, except something that frustrated me in any of my many desires. I had not had any moral instruction from my poor parents, and although Gran surely tried to lead me right, I think I did not have enough exposure to her thin liberal teachings or maybe her one clear principle, do what you please as long as you're not hurting anyone, is not armor strong enough to ward off the Prince of this World, if he takes an interest.*

*Did I enjoy his tickles? I have to say that I did, although I understand that we are not supposed to acknowledge that debauched children feel anything but horror and fear. I had much to do with raped children later on, and this is the story they tell—they hated it and the men who did it to them, and ran away from home because of it. But I never heard of anyone who was as good at it as Ray Bob. I think it is worse if the child enjoys it, actually, because then it's a rape of the heart and not just the body. In my case, the shiny man told me it was all right and that I had power over Ray Bob because I let him and wasn't it pleasant to have and just for letting him touch me there and give me that funny warm shivery feeling. I have heard that men who do this often make dire threats so that the girls (or boys) won't tell, but Ray Bob never did that, being way too smart, since if you make dire threats and all, the victim will know it's a bad thing and get all guilty and tell anyhow, or else wait and then call the cops years later. He said he loved me the best of anyone alive, and I pretended to believe him, as I knew that I was beyond the love of anyone, least of all a piece of shit like Ray Bob Dideroff. And anyway, why would I tell? I didn't think it was anything special.*

*On my tenth birthday, he bought me Solera, my darling mare, and taught me how to ride and also how to work his penis with my hand and mouth so that it squirted, which I privately thought was pretty amusing but didn't say. Little Ray was its name, and it made him cry out to the Lord and take his name in vain, also amusing considering he was a deacon and often slapped his sons on the head when they would do likewise. Did I mind? Maybe a little, but for that horse I would have let him fuck me on the steps of the Assembly of God. I was a perfect whore at ten.*

*Sometimes I would catch Ray Bob looking at me, and there was something in his eyes, not fear exactly, but a kind of worry, like maybe he wasn't all that much in control as he thought. I believe that was the best part of my ruin, seeing that look.*

*Meanwhile, Ray Bob's shaking the bed a couple of times a week finally produced a result. Momma got pregnant and bore a little girl, which Ray Bob named Bobbie Ann. Well, I believe something popped in Momma when that child got born, some dammed-up slough of love from which never a trickle came my way finally broke open, because she truly loved that child. Of course, she only got to love it when she came off the pills, which was rarely. We had a girl from the migrant camp, Esmeralda, to take care of the little thing. I could go on, but this is not a novel, so you don't need to know anything about what life was like for us. Aside from Momma's unfortunate breakdown, we must have appeared like a normal family to Wayland society. We went to church and participated in community events. Every summer Ray Bob took us Gulf fishing and every fall we went out and shot doves. He bought me a 16-gauge just like Ray Jr. had and taught me to shoot it.*

*About two years after Bobbie Ann was born I got my period and Ray Bob made me understand that now that I was a woman I would have to take Little Ray inside me, which I did one April night in my narrow bed, lowering myself down upon it, with not much discomfort I must admit, which owed a lot to Ray Bob's fingering over the years plus all the horse riding I had been doing. This could have been part of the reason he got me the horse, I don't know. He was pretty smart that way, although not smart enough, as it turned out. He got me a heart locket with a real diamond in it for my twelfth birthday, with a little picture of him in it in his police chief uniform.*

*Shortly after I became a real woman, Ray Jr. started to hang around the stable when I was grooming Solera, he must have been fourteen then, a real ox, red-faced and dull. I asked him why, and he said he thought he'd like* some of what I was giving his daddy, and he grabbed me and threw me down in the straw, ripping at my clothes and I said for shit's sake you creep you'll scare the horse and rip my clothes and then what will Ray Bob say? And he came to his senses when I said I would yank him off if he helped me muck out, and I did. Mucking out was one thing I definitely did not like about having a horse, and I figured better to do one messy thing that lasted eight seconds than another that took an hour.

Do you think this could be the source of my pathology? Sexual abuse in childhood leading to religious fanaticism later in life? It's a theory. Only it's hard to explain, but kids accept as normal whatever is going down in their families. Momma burns you with a red-hot poker, you don't like it much, but that's life, and you figure every kid gets the poker too, and you never ask or tell because why would you? It'd be like saying Momma pours milk on her cereal or goes to the bathroom. My error was my god, as Augustine says, although I hadn't read Augustine then. I read nearly everything else in that town though. The library was only open three days a week, and I got through the skimpy shelves pretty quick, except that Mrs. Oster the librarian wouldn't let me take out any really adult books. There was a place in town though, Jake's Junk, which bought up dead people's houses, and he had a whole back room full of books. He'd strip out the good stuff and sell the rest for small change. There I bought Nabokov's Lolita because of the girl on the paperback cover sucking a lollipop with those heart sunglasses on. A key book that told me finally what I was and then I fell in love with his language. I read the rest of Nabokov, nearly, Pnin and Pale Fire and the stories and essays, although there was a lot I couldn't understand, and from there I did all the big Russians, or all that ended up in paperbacks in Caluga County. War and Peace, Brothers K., Crime and P., Dead Souls, and strangely enough Babel's Red Cavalry in a ratty hardbound edition from what seemed like a lefty book club. Strong stuff for a twelve-year-old you will say, *but the chewiness of those fat books and their exotic people*

(I am avoiding again. I mention my literary intoxications to avoid writing about the denouement of our family drama. Although the word denouement doesn't go very well with this cracker voice I am using, and how about a long digression on voice in fiction, in memoir, which voice is the real Emmylou. How the voices in fiction inhabit us, those of us who read and for those of us who don't there are the movies and TV. That's who we are. Yes, our parents form us, we who are so fortunate, or unfortunate as the case may be, to have any, but they were formed mainly by what they read or saw all the way back to stained glass windows and Bible stories and tales of saints and heroes and monsters. Stories teach us how to live, says Anatole France. And he also says, The law, in its majestic equality, forbids the rich as well as the poor to sleep under bridges, to beg in the streets, and to steal bread. Never read the man, have no idea who he was, that and much more is from the Collier's Book of Quotations, Jake's Junk, seventy-five cents.)

Now I was in middle school, in the gifted and talented, since I was now rich. God in His great mercy gave us middle school so that we could see what hell would be like and learn to avoid it in later life, although like so many of His good ideas it has not worked out all that well. I of course was one of the demons of that hell. Having money and looks and things and not giving a shit what anyone thought of me and being smart enough so that I could both ditch school whenever I wanted and keep my grades up enough not to disgrace Ray Bob, all that put me in the fastest clique. I was a cheerleader too, naturally, and naturally was able to make life hell for those girls who desperately wanted to be and never would, and I had a mouth on me too, what with all the reading I was doing, so my cruelty was more refined than the usual your-momma's-so-fat-she-got-her-own-zip-code middle-school insults.

And there I met Randolf Hunter Foy. Hunter was in Ray

Jr.'s class, and my, he was all totally gorgeous in that Elvis–Jimmy Dean–Brad Pitt way and the biggest dope dealer in the school and I decided I would have him. He was trash like me, there was always a Foy or two in county jail, and Raiford was full of them by report.

In seventh grade I produced a burst of smarts so that I would qualify for advanced placement, and as a result I got to Wayland High a year early, a fourteen-year-old freshman just a year behind Hunter, who I guess was seventeen at the time. In any case he was old enough to drive and he had a vehicle, a late-model Ford-250 pickup with a camper back, and funny enough nobody wondered how a kid with a mother on welfare and a father in state prison could afford a rig like that. I lost no time in seducing Hunter. Jake's Junk had a substantial number of cheap porn books, the kind where they use lots of capitalization to indicate the money shot (I'm COOOOOOOMMMMMMING!), and these were my instructors along with Ray Bob, who truth be told was a meat-and-potatoes kind of pedophile, nothing exotic. I was sort of scared of being in the bed-pounding position, having heard all that stuff through my wall, but it turned out the pounding aspects were only for Momma. With me he was really almost delicate and concerned about what I was feeling. (Answer: not much. I always sort of drifted away while he was doing his thing, although not so far away that I couldn't answer his questions or fake the required responses. Do you love it, baby? Ooh, yes, daddy, jam your big love pole in my cunt! For Ray Bob had read his share of the same books, life following art down into the dank cellar.) I really think he wanted to turn me into the love slave of his toxic fantasy world, but I was never that. Now that I think on it, he was more like mine, although we did not actually discuss the subject.

Truth to tell, Hunter Foy didn't take much seducing. One day he pulled up in his truck and said hey and I said hey and got in and we went to Sand Creek County Park close by the sluggish flow of the tea-colored water and we smoked a couple of numbers in the camper back. After the second joint we started in chewing face and I tore my T-shirt and bra and panties off like they was on fire and then I leaped upon him and like they say in the bodice-ripper paperbacks I slaked my lust, although it wasn't until the second time we did it that afternoon that I felt more or less what you're supposed to feel on such occasions, and it surprised me so much that I yelped like a puppy.

I walked into the house knock-kneed on account of my soggy underwear, but with my head in a spin, thinking oh this is love all right like in the songs and movies and I am the star. It was just like me then to go from a pedophile abuser who at least liked me to a boyfriend who put me a little lower than his dog. The devil likes to break his tools, it's the most fun thing for him, but did I know that? It all made such sense to me, the shiny man whispering in my ear every time I thought Whoa, girl, what _are_ you doing? By that time he wasn't a shiny man anymore like when I was small, but more like my own self talking to me with my own voice.

This has happened to you too, hasn't it?

Well, we carried on like that for a couple of months, every afternoon practically, but sadly our idyll could not last, like they say in the romance books, or used to back when I read them, and one Saturday night when I walked in around ten or so, Ray Bob was waiting there with a look on his face that I hadn't ever seen directed at me, and he asked me where I had been, and when I repeated the lie I had told about being out with a couple of my friends studying, he whapped me across the face so hard I flew halfway across the room. Then he told me all what I'd been doing with that Hunter Foy, in some detail. I don't know, maybe Ray Jr. tipped him off and he had been spying on us with his police night-vision scope, and then he dragged me into my room, knocked me facedown on my bed, yanked my shorts and panties off, put his knee on my back, and beat me to ribbons with my own riding crop. I made a lot of noise.

When he got tired of whipping me he started in cursing me for a slut and how could I go with that trash after all he did for me, bringing me up like I was his own flesh-and-blood daughter and buying me anything I wanted, and things were going to change around here he'd been Mr. Softy but no longer, missy. And he said how he was going to arrest Hunter and send him to state prison. I said if he did that I would tell about what he'd been doing to me all these years from the time I was nine and it would be him who went to state prison and he said no one would believe a little white trash slut like me and if I said anything at all he would say I had lost my marbles and get Doc Herb Dideroff to lock me up in his rest home forever and give me the electric shock treatment. And I said we'll see about that, and I pulled on my pants again.

He tried to grab me then, but despite all my pain and suffering I dodged past him and ran out in the living room, and there was the whole family, because of all the noise, Momma holding Bobbie Ann, and Ray Jr. looking so pale his zits stood out like stars, and Jon, who was always half a step slow, but looking real interested. And I screamed out he's whipping me because I wouldn't fuck him anymore, he's been fucking me for years. And he tried to grab me but I ran around and hid behind my momma and Bobbie Ann, me now yelling out all the intimate details of our sex life together so she would know it was true. But he said, she's lying, Billie, you know that. She's lying, she always was no good just like you said. I saw him give her that look and while I couldn't see her face I could feel the spine shrivel right out of her. Bobbie Ann just got the side blast of it, but still it was bad enough to make her start in wailing. Momma said I got to go lie down now, and she took the girl up in her arms and walked away from me, and Ray Bob yelled at his boys to go to their room and snatched me by my hair and dragged me out to the yard, and locked me in the big red toolshed from Sears. That was Saturday night. He kept me in there two whole days with no food or water but plenty of palmetto bugs and spiders. No one came out to comfort me or bring me anything to drink, not one human creature, and it was like an oven in there stinking of chemicals and manure, and it was like an oven in my soul too, cooking away with thoughts of revenge and violence and how I could get back at them all and get away with Hunter Foy.

On the third evening I was in there, and starting in to wonder if he was going to keep me there until I died, I heard Ray Bob's voice say, you gonna be good now, Emmylou, and I said, I will if you promise not to arrest Hunter, and he waited a long time, I thought he'd gone away and then he said well I do believe in giving people another chance, but you better keep your dirty lies to yourself from now on and I said fine, okay. He let me out then, blinking into the end of the day. I thought to myself that it was a good deal if that was going to be all my punishment, plus I wouldn't have to fuck Ray Bob anymore, but it wasn't. While I was in the shed, Ray Bob had gone and sold my horse and he wouldn't tell me where. Ray Jr. said he sold it to the dog food place up by Preston. I cried for a week on and off far longer than I had when my real daddy died partly from the loss and partly because I couldn't get them all and grind them under my foot like cockroaches. But then I found that he'd moved the rocking chair out of my room and into Bobbie Ann's, and I started my plan.

# Three

TRANSCRIPT
COMPETENCY INTERVIEW

Prisoner: Dideroff, Emmylou (NMI) MPD CASE # 7716
Dade County Criminal Court Docket # 331902
Interviewed by: Lorna C. Wise, Ph.D.
Tape #: 2
Recording Started: 11:02 a.m.

Lorna Wise: Now about this voice you mentioned to the police officers. Are you still hearing it?

Emmylou Dideroff: No.

W: Did you at one time?

D: Yes.

W: And this voice identified itself as a saint?

D: Yes. St. Catherine of Siena.

W: I see. Any besides that?

D: No.

W: No other hallucinations at all?

D: They're not hallucinations.

W: Yes, well, do you still hear voices or sounds that no one else can hear? See people or things that no one else can see?

D: Not since the day of the murder. But sometimes before I drop off to sleep I hear the sound of my gun. And sometimes during the day too. Is that what you mean, stuff like that?

W: Tell me more about it, please.

D: Well, it's not exactly hearing it, like I can hear you, like I hear the noises in the jail, or people talking and like that, but like an extra-sharp memory. Like I *just* heard it, so I get startled out of whatever I'm doing.

W: What kind of gun? Like a pistol?

D: A pistol is a pistol. A gun is an artillery piece.

W: You thought you had an artillery piece? You mean like a cannon?

D: Yes. It was a L-70 Bofors gun. A forty-mm automatic cannon.

W: Mm-hm. Can you describe this sound?

D: It was very, very loud. [laughs]

W: Well . . . yes, cannons are very loud.

D: Uh-huh. And it's hard to describe, if you've never been near gunfire, um, how loud it is. It's louder than thunder, louder than a jetliner flying low. It's louder than one of those pneumatic drills. The only thing louder is bombs. A lot of noise. Of course, we all stuffed rags in our ears, but you can hear a sound like that through your nose. Through your elbows and feet. [laughs] After you've been firing on auto for a while, the sound takes you over, like God, in a way. I mean you're completely deaf, but it seems you can still hear things *inside* the noise, like the clang of the breech closing, a kind of hammer-on-anvil sound, and the rattle of the pawls and rammer in the autoloader, like a train on railroad tracks? And the brass falling, tinkle tankle, like bells. You shouldn't be able to hear any of that, but you do. Or seem to. And then there's the sound of the shells, the roar in the air and the bang of the explosion, but you're not so aware of that so much, except when you're firing single rounds. Are you bored yet? [laughs]

W: Not at all. You make it sound very interesting. Where did you learn all this about . . . what did you say it was? An automatic cannon?

D: Yes, a Bofors gun. From the manual. Foy always said read the f . . . read the dah-dah, manual, RTFM. And I did. Plus I had some help from a friend.

W: Who is Foy?

D: Percival Orne Foy. The late. A teacher I had.

W: In school.

D: This was more extracurricular. He taught me a lot of stuff, and I just sucked it in, never mind if I thought it was worth anything. I just gave myself over, I was so tired of thinking for myself. That was before I joined the Bloods and God found me. I was real surprised when so much of it came in useful. His providence is sometimes extremely strange in its working out.

W:  By Bloods—do you mean the street gang?

D:  [laughs] No, I meant the Society of Nursing Sisters of the Blood of Christ. The Bloods. Which we're not supposed to call ourselves, but we all do. Did. I did.

W:  Excuse me, are you saying that you're a nun?

D:  Oh, no. I was only a postulant. I never took vows. And they threw me out, needless to say.

W:  Why was that?

D:  Because we're a medical order. We . . . I mean they take the Hippocratic Oath on top of their vows of poverty, chastity, and obedience. To do no harm. And I did a lot of harm, may God forgive me.

W:  What sort of harm did you do?

D:  It's in my confession.

W:  Yes, but Emmylou, this, what we're doing here, is not part of the criminal case. We're dealing here on a basis of confidentiality. What you tell me won't be part of the court record and can't be used against you.

D:  You're supposed to find out if I'm crazy or not.

W:  Well, really, if you're fit to stand trial, to aid in your own defense.

D:  You wouldn't understand.

W:  Try me.

D:  Do you believe in the devil?

W:  The important thing here is do you believe in him?

D:  Oh, I'm so tired! I am so tired of this. I thought it was over, that he didn't have a use for me anymore, that I'd be let alone to live in peace, and now it's all starting again, and people are going to get hurt.

W:  Who's using you?

       [Silence, thirty-two seconds]

W:  Who's going to be hurt?

D:  Anyone. Anyone around me. Maybe you.

W:  And . . . the devil is going to make this happen, to hurt people?

D: Or God. It's a crossfire. You can't understand this. It won't fit in your kind of head.

W: Then help me to understand.

D: It's right in front of your eyes, but you can't see it. I'm sorry. That detective did, though . . . Oh, Christ, oh Christ have mercy!

W: Emmylou? It's very important that you talk to me. I just want to help you.

[Silence, one minute, twenty-two seconds]

W: Emmylou, what is it? Did you see something?

D: Could I go back to the jail now? I don't feel like talking anymore.

INTERVIEW TERMINATED AT 11:38 A.M.

Lorna Wise listens to the tape a third time, checking it against the transcript, occasionally stopping the flow of words with the foot pedal and writing in her notebook. After that, she reads through her notes, feeling dissatisfied with the familiar jargon. Inappropriate affect. Hallucinations. Fabulation. Resistance. Religious mania. Particularly disturbing, this last. Is Emmylou Dideroff a religious maniac? How is that different from being merely religious, if mere religion means ascribing reality to what cannot be verified by others? And what happened there at the end? An actual hallucination? She leans back in her squeaking swivel chair, kicks off her shoes, puts her stockinged feet up on the table, and rubs her eyes.

She is in a room reserved for such interviews in a nondescript county building on NW Thirteenth Street, convenient to both the Dade County Women's Detention Center and the main jail. It is a small room, the size of a rich man's bathroom, in two shades of brown, like a mutt. There is a wooden table with an artificial wood-grain surface, a swivel chair for the interviewer, a straight chair for the interviewee, one dirty window with a heavy grille on it, a four-tube fluorescent fixture with one tube dimmed out. And a wall clock, which she now consults. No time for this mooning, she thinks; she has another interview in twelve minutes. The county likes her to keep things churning.

Religious mania. Lorna picks up her copy of *DSM-IV*, the *Diagnostic and Statistical Manual*, a thick maroon-colored paperback that exists to classify all the ills that mind is heir to, and thumbs through it. She does not recall such a classification, and if she does not, there is most probably none, for she has the whole volume practically by heart. Yes, here it is: a one-liner noting that some schizophrenic hallucinations took religious forms. And, helpfully, *"Hallucinations may also be a normal part of religious experience in certain cultural contexts."* But not ours, typically. One can apparently no longer officially be a religious maniac. In the materialist religiosity of America we don't see saints or demons anymore. Other than that, there was no way that Dideroff is schizo. She had a job, no history of hospitalization, was clearly alert, well spoken, in control, or at least in as much control as any number of mental health professionals Lorna knew. So: initial diagnosis is: 297.1 delusional disorder, grandiose type. The "grandiose" type is because of the religion stuff. If you think God is talking to you, that's grandiose per se, according to the *DSM*.

Lorna writes this diagnosis down on the appropriate line on the court form. There is a larger space for describing the subject defendant, and here she inscribes a précis of her impressions, or as much of it as she thinks is to the point, and copies in the results of the tests—Rorschach, MMPI, Wechsler IQ—she has had administered to Emmylou Dideroff over the past week. Now her ballpoint hesitates, because here is where she must write down the magic formula, attesting that in her professional opinion the subject knows the nature of the charges against her, and the consequences if she is convicted, and that she is capable of assisting in her own defense. She finds that she is reluctant to write this statement.

She puts her pen down and again leans back in her chair. Five minutes, the clock tells her. She is thinking about something her forensic psych professor once did in class. Professor Benicke, one of her favorites, may be the reason she's chosen this peculiar and not very prestigious and certainly unremunerative branch of psychology. A winter's afternoon at Cornell, the sun slipping behind the bluffs at a quarter to four, scant leaden light through the windows, the room darkened, the clicking sound of a film projector. He'd shown them nearly the whole of Carl Dreyer's 1928 film, *The Passion of Joan of Arc*. They had all watched the silent movie in silence, and then as the lights came up on the blinking class, he'd demanded: Well? Is she competent? Forget she's a saint, forget the trial was rigged, forget the politics. From what you see, is this woman competent to stand trial on a capital charge?

It had been an interesting debate. What had she said? She knows where she is, she knows the gravity of the charge, she puts up a spirited, logical defense, and it doesn't matter if she's hearing voices. If we declared everyone who heard voices incompetent, there wouldn't be *any* trials, because we all hear voices, in a manner of speaking. We hear the voice of our conscience, don't we? And if some people project the voice of their conscience outward onto the figures of saints, what does that have to do with competence? What indeed? After ten years of practice, however, the distinction seems less clear in the tangled life of the crazy poor than it was in the classroom or the law books.

She finds herself checking the box for Further Consultation Required and is somewhat surprised at herself. She is one of three experts charged by the criminal court of Dade County to determine competency in this case, and very, very occasionally the three experts do not agree, in which case the judge has the option of calling in another panel, or going with the majority. But it is considered bad form in the shrink world not to present a united front on competency, which is one reason for the consult request box. Lorna is signaling to her peers that this is a hard case and that the three of them should get together and try to get their ducks in a row. Into the out basket with Emmylou, then, and push the button to tell the guard to bring in the next one. She examines the top sheet on the file. Oh, good, a grounder!

A knock on the door and a big guard brings in the familiar shambolic figure of Rigoberto Munoz. This is his eighth run through the system. Munoz is a stocky man with tangled lank hair, skin the color of an old grocery bag, and a lot of tattooing on his thick arms. His face twists into bizarre expressions from time to time, for he suffers from tardive dyskinesia, the result of all the Thorazine and other major tranquilizers the helpful state has pumped into him over the decades, in order to, among other things, render him competent to stand trial. Munoz has no money and nowhere to live and has a venereal disease and, of course, the tardive dyskinesia, but his main problem, Lorna now learns from him, is that space aliens have implanted a robot in his belly, which robot is gradually pulling his penis into his body cavity. The robot is activated by alien agents, who use remote control devices disguised as cell phones. But Rigoberto is not fooled. That's why he's here, he explains to the interested lady, he stabbed one of the aliens on Flagler Street with the nail-equipped pole he uses to pick up the bits of trash that often contain secret messages from the good kind of space aliens.

It does not take Lorna long to classify Mr. Munoz as: 295.30, schizophrenia, paranoid type. The guard takes him away. Lorna knows that they will conduct him to a locked ward at Jackson, shoot him full of Haldol, drag him zomboid and tractable before the court, register his plea of guilty, sentence him to time served, and dump him back on the street with a prescription for antipsychotics and a pat on the back. Sooner or later he will kill someone, and after a good deal of passing forms similar to the one Lorna now slips into her out box, Florida will kill him by lethal injection. This evil was not in her department, however, and she had learned to confine her thoughts to zones affecting personal action. She declares him unfit to stand trial, signs the form, and now it is time for lunch.

The ladies' room in the facility is tiny, as befits an institution (the Jail) run and populated almost entirely by men. After using the toilet (and wasn't a capacious bladder essential to doing psychological work in the public sector!), she checks herself out in the spotted mirror. Fawn cotton suit, pale gray knit underneath, unobtrusive. The mad do not like screaming colors, or so she justifies her taste, but she has dressed in such shades since long before she became a demi-shrink. Girl, why you want to look like some dead leaf? Her pal Sheryl. She is going to have lunch with Sheryl today, in fact, and she knows Sheryl will make a comment of that type. Look like a damn tree. To please Sheryl, she carefully applies rather more makeup than is her usual wont. Eye shadow barely blue, mascara on her pale lashes, blusher, darkish lipstick, matte. She does not really need the blusher because she has flawless skin. Her best feature, she thinks, although "she has beautiful skin" is what they always say of fat, unattractive girls.

As she was. As she sometimes still thinks she is. She is tall, and has to stoop a little to get her face in the mirror. She will retain part of this stoop when she leaves the ladies' room, for it is her habitual posture. Stand up straight, her father was always telling her, but here as in so many other aspects of life she had not been a dutiful daughter. She walks with her broad shoulders rolled slightly forward and her neck drooping slightly from the vertical. This is to hide her breasts, which are large and round. Jutting, as the pulp writers like to say. She has also a defined waist, and broad hips, which she conceals with her suit jacket. This she removes briefly to dab her underarms with industrial strength antiperspirant. Lorna was not made for the tropics, and once again a vagrant query registers in her mind: why does she stay here? Again, no answer, for the answer is inertia. Although she is courageous in defense of self and her prerogatives, she fears change.

Her other good feature is her hair, which is long, silky, honey-colored. She knows she should cut it into a sensible shape, but she resists this and wears it instead pulled back in a troublesome French knot. She adjusts this now and tucks back the various pennants that have come loose. Jacket back on, a final frowning inspection. A century ago, Lorna Wise would have stopped traffic in any large city of the western world, teams of horses would have run wild through shop windows, and even fifty years before she would have been considered Marilyn-esque, but now she is 180 degrees out of fashion, and women are required to resemble seventeen-year-old male basketball players. Lorna has what she thinks of as good feminist credentials, but her conviction stops at her skin. So she dresses sub-fusc and stoops.

Stooping then, she leaves the bathroom and the building, waving to Ernesto in his security window on her way out. Ernesto sighs with desire as he watches the sway of her fine ass, but Lorna does not hear this, and would not have appreciated it if she had, not because of any class or ethnic bias (from which she is remarkably free) but because she has only ever been attracted to men who want her to lose weight. All her psychological training has not hipped her to this catastrophic twist of taste.

Outside it is, of course, hot and humid, although not as hot and humid as it will be in a few hours. It is late September, still summer in Miami, and the city yearns for the relief of tourist season. She crosses to the shady side of NW Thirteenth and pauses on the curb, in the shadow of the huge redbrick jail. Even in the shade she begins to sweat, and she hopes that she can avoid armpit stains on her suit. Before long, a silver Chrysler sedan pulls up to the curb and she enters it, grateful for the air-conditioning within. Sheryl Waits, her best friend, is wearing a linen suit too, but hers is fuchsia. Under it she wears a white polyester shirt gushing ruffles at the throat. Her lipstick is fuchsia too, and glossy, startling in its effect against her skin, which is the color of a large drip coffee into which one of those little plastic cups of half-and-half has been poured. Sheryl is nearly as tall as Lorna and twenty pounds heavier, but she has absolutely no body image problem. She thinks she looks terrific. She goes dancing with her husband all the time, and from what Lorna can observe, he thinks she looks terrific too. Lorna often wonders if this difference is basic to their friendship, and she is occasionally subject to shaming thoughts, yet another exploitation of black womanhood, fat white girl gets fat black friend so she doesn't look bad? But she genuinely loves the woman and feels loved in return. Is that an illusion too? Who can tell nowadays?

The two have been friends since the first day of classes at Barry College, where they both took their MSW degrees. Except for the years when she went north to do her psych Ph.D. at Cornell, she has had lunch with Sheryl Waits on average once a week and is thoroughly integrated, so to speak, into the Waits family circle. Sheryl is a psychiatric social worker and runs a unit in a community mental health center in Liberty City, an impoverished black district of Miami, where she is considered both a saint and a tough-ass bitch, often by the same people on different days.

They go to a moderately expensive restaurant in a waterfront hotel, with a nice view of Biscayne Bay. It is rather overpriced, they both agree, but they are worth it. They are scrupulous about taking turns picking up the tab; what they never do is to minutely divide up the bill, arguing about who had what and how much to tip. While they wait for their meal, they exchange news, which given their lives means that 80 percent of the news will be Sheryl's, always announced with the phrase "dysfunction in the intact black family," a torrent of amusing folderol about the husband, Leon, a patrol lieutenant in the Miami PD, the most useless husband ever invented, and the three children, defective, insubordinate, no 'count, doomed to failure and the streets. None of this is true. Sheryl is creating a mythos, propitiating the gods to continue what Lorna knows she believes is the most colossal good fortune. In return, Lorna tells some anecdotes about her patient load, including the Dideroff woman and her saints—no names, of course. Sheryl seems particularly interested in this one, but Sheryl is a church lady, a Catholic, strangely enough, and thus pretty much in the same bin, in Lorna's mind, as Dideroff. The remainder of their conversation is devoted, as it usually is, to Lorna and men.

"Anybody on the horizon?" Sheryl asks.

"Not as such."

"Ticktock."

"Oh, stop! I'm only thirty-four."

"Uh-huh. And as far as I know, you ain't never yet been out with anybody really gave a damn about you. All of them're these skinny little white-boy intellectuals want you to be they momma, while they play around on you. You need to get your life sorted out, girl."

"I'm *fine,* Sheryl. Being between men is not a felony in this state. And, you know, I'm wondering why every lunch we have ends up with an elaborate critique of my sex life. I mean it's getting a little old, don't you think?"

"I'll tell you what else is getting *old,* darlin. You ringing on my phone at two A.M. in the morning, oh, wah, Sheryl, he done it *again,* boo hoo hoo!"

"All right, I'll never call you except during business hours," snaps Lorna.

"Oh, for God's sake! That's what friends are for, you nut! All I mean is it just breaks my heart. I want you to be *happy*! Regular. Walking in green fields full of flowers with a nice guy."

"Like in a toilet paper commercial."

"Exactly. And every fourth commercial the couple is black, except you can tell the dude is, like, a little queer? Seriously, hon, you got to change your way of living."

"And if that ain't enough, I'm gonna change the way I strut my stuff."

"Oh, right, be a smart-ass about it. But the songs don't lie, honey. Uh-uh. They don't lie."

"You're bound and determined to reshape my life into domestic bliss, aren't you? Guided by the eternal wisdom of old popular song lyrics?"

"And my highly honed social worker skills. Let me ask you something: you ever thought about a cop?"

"When I got my stereo ripped off, sure."

"Moron. I mean to date one."

"You're still confusing me with you, dear," Lorna says uncomfortably. "It's not my kind of thing."

"Because . . . ?"

"Because. Let me think. Look, you know I love Leon, but I need . . . how can I say this without sounding like an arrogant shithead . . . ?"

"Oh, go on, go on! If I was going to dump you for being an arrogant shithead, I would've done it years ago."

"Thank you. I want someone I can talk to. I don't respond well to 'how about those Marlins' as a conversational gambit. I want someone who reads books."

"Leon reads books."

"I mean *books*. Come on, Sher, I don't want to get into a fight. You're happy, God bless you, but I need something different. Let it go."

"Got to be an intellectual, huh?"

"I think so."

"Just like Daddy."

Lorna mimes looking around, as if searching for a public notice. "Excuse me, I thought this was a psychotherapy-free area. Waiter!"

Sheryl ignores this and studies her friend appraisingly. "Mm, I just had an interesting thought."

"What? And I don't like that look on your face."

"My thought was you ought to meet Jimmy Paz."

"And why is that? He's an intellectual?"

"He reads books is what I hear. Leon says most people in the department think he's the smartest guy who ever worked there."

"And he's probably got three semesters at Miami-Dade Junior College too."

"Now you *are* being an arrogant shithead."

Sheryl is now giving her the stare she usually reserves for one of her children gone seriously over the line or a junkie trying to hustle her. Lorna feels herself blushing again. "All right. That was low."

"I forgive you, or I will forgive you if you show up at our place the Saturday from next. We're throwing a retirement party for Amos Greely. You've met him."

"The mentor."

"Uh-huh. Anyway, Paz will be there. We'll have white folks too. We ain't prejudice or nothin."

"He's a Cuban, right?" There is some eye-rolling action here.

"An Afro-Cuban."

"So *not* another male chauvinist piggie?"

Sheryl laughs long and loud, drawing looks from some of the neighboring tables.

"Darlin, they're *all* male chauvinist piggies, and your skinny whiteboy intellectuals are the worst kind because they'll never admit it. And Paz cooks too."

"He cooks?"

"Yeah, he's a chef in his off hours. His mom owns Guantanamera."

"Very impressive," says Lorna, who is actually impressed. She has eaten at that restaurant, widely considered to be the finest Cuban place in Miami, the best of a tough league. "Let's see, reads books, cooks for his mother, unmarried at what . . . ? Thirty-five?"

"About there."

"Gay."

Another laugh from Sheryl, even louder than before. She has to dab at her eyes with her napkin. "Oh, no, sugar. You don't have to worry about that. Not Jimmy Paz. The book on him is he likes smart girls. Smart white girls. I am going to get cast out of the sisterhood for setting this up, but I'll have to learn to live with it."

"Lucky me," say Lorna sourly.

"No, this is right," says Sheryl. She looks up, cups her hand to her ear. "What's that you say? No lie? Made in *heaven*? Well, lawsy me!"

"I'm calling 911," says Lorna.

"You may laugh, but I got a good feeling about this. And let me slip a little professional note into your file, honeybunch. Us Catholics talk to the saints all the time. And sometimes they talk back. You need to find out some more about Emmylou's religious background before you toss her among the lunatics."

Lorna finesses this uncomfortable moment by signaling for the waiter, and then she makes much out of checking the time and fretting about an appointment she has at one-thirty. That Sheryl is sincerely religious she regards as an amusing flaw, like the fat. On the other hand, Sheryl's point is a good one and supported by the *DSM*. She will find out about that the next time she sees Emmylou. As they leave the restaurant, she is already planning her questions. She will have to get through the consult first, but that should not pose a problem. Mickey Lopez thinks *everyone* is crazy, which means she will only have to roll Howie Kasdan, which she knows she can do and will take grim pleasure in doing.

# Four

Paz was at last having sex again. It had been a long time between and he should have been more excited, for although he rammed away valiantly, and although the woman sighed and moaned beneath him, he seemed to have become somewhat detached from his sexual apparatus and also disturbed because he could not recall the woman's name. They finished, leaving him drained but not satisfied. What the *fuck* was her name? He rolled off her. She chuckled. "That was great, Jimmy," she said. So she knew who he was, why couldn't he . . . ?

"Could we turn on the lights?" he asked.

"You sure you want to?" she asked. She had a throaty, pleasant voice.

"Yeah, turn it on."

He felt her moving, reaching for the switch, and then the light went on, a little pink bedside lamp. Paz was out of bed in an instant going for the door, scrabbling, kicking at it, although it was clear now that the door was just painted on the wall, crudely at that, a child's drawing of a door. There was no way out of the room. The woman was still chuckling, although it was hard to know how she managed it, since her face was as smooth and featureless and white as an egg.

It was the pain that woke him up, the pain from his toes. He cursed vividly in the two languages he commanded when he realized he was standing in the little hallway leading to the rear door of his apartment. He'd kicked his right toe bloody against its base. Paz staggered to the kitchen sink and leaned into it, running cold water over his head. He turned the water off, dried himself with a dish towel, and listened. Mrs. Ruiz, his upstairs neighbor, was moving around. The old lady was a light sleeper and his screams and the kicks had awakened her, as they had before. Maybe the rest of the neighborhood too. He prayed no one had called the cops.

He had a tendency to be paranoid about his status in the department. At present he was untouchable because he had almost singlehandedly cracked the biggest mass murder case in the history of the city, but that was fading in memory, or rather the false story of the so-called Voodoo Murders was fading. The memories of what had really happened were still pretty fresh in Paz's mind.

He limped to a kitchen chair and examined his foot. The big toe on the right foot was nearly half again as large as its mate on the other foot and turning plum. The nail looked loose and was rimmed with drops of blood black as India ink in the crime-light glow coming in through the kitchen jalousies. He wiped the blood away with a paper napkin and used it also to wipe the sweat from his forehead and neck. Paz had been having nightmares every night for the past week, and walking in his sleep, and he took this as touching on his mental stability, a real concern after what had gone down last year. A flashback, a delayed thing from those events? Maybe, but there was also that . . . *whatever* in the interview room with Emmylou Dideroff. Was madness contagious? Or something even scarier? As this thought emerged, Paz used all his considerable intellectual and emotional energy to shove it back in its box.

The main thing was that it not happen again. The next time he'd be out the door and walking through the staid Cubano neighborhood, a black guy dressed in a T-shirt and nothing else, howling. Some householder would shoot him, or the cops would grab him up, and that would be it. They'd give him a rubber gun and sit him behind a property room grille for the rest of his career. Which was also why he couldn't go to the department headshrinker. What he ought to do, had he any real balls, was talk to his mother . . . Uh-uh, no; he dismissed the thought.

He checked the clock on the stove: four-ten, too late to go back to bed. He put on a bathrobe and grabbed the *Herald* off the tiny front lawn, noting that he was going to have to cut it this weekend, or else Mrs. Ruiz was going to complain to his mother. His mother owned the duplex, and Paz lived in it rent free, which was where he got the money to buy the kind of clothes he wore. It was not exactly a free deal, because besides the routine maintenance around the place, Margarita Paz expected her son to help out at her restaurant. Paz did not mind helping his mother, but Mrs. Paz often failed to understand the exigencies of police work and gave Paz considerable grief when he chose to catch murderers rather than chop up snappers in her kitchen. She did not consider police work a real job.

Paz fired up a big hourglass metal espresso pot and made half a pint of Cuban coffee. He was getting hungry. Ordinarily, he took breakfast out, but he didn't want to drive to an all-night joint. He opened his refrigerator. Paz did not dine at home, but sometimes he used his place to store the restaurant's overstock of perishables. In the refrigerator were ten-pound bags of flour, a box of butter pats, a bag of powdered sugar, a box of salted cod, six dozen eggs. Stacked near the refrigerator were three five-gallon cans of peanut oil and a crate of mangoes.

Paz took flour, butter, salt, and water and made a dough, to which he added a healthy shot from a bottle of Anis del Mono that happened to be keeping company with the bottle of Ketel vodka in his freezer. He heated up oil in his only big pot and hand rolled the churros because he didn't have a star press. As he dropped the pastries into the fat, he recalled, as he always did at such moments, how his mother had taught him at the age of seven to test the temperature of the hot fat by flicking drops of water at it, listening for just the right sort of crackle. He made a dozen, eating two and a half fresh from the fat after sprinkling them with powdered sugar. The others he put into a paper bag. He ate a mango over the sink, dripping juice, and washed his face again.

This apartment had two bedrooms, in one of which lived a rowing machine and a set of weights. Paz put on headphones and listened to Susana Baca sing Afro-Peruvian songs for thirty minutes of rowing. Then he did a routine with twenty-pound barbells and a set of crunches and push-ups. He exercised every other morning, and ordinarily he used the tedium to think through his day. A methodical man, Paz, despite his reputation on the cops as something of a cowboy.

Slow steps sounded above him. Mrs. Ruiz would wait until

he was out of the house before calling his mother to report in. Mrs. Ruiz was a pretty good spy, and Paz often wondered if his mother gave her a deal on the rent in return for this information. Or maybe it was just a normal service of the Cuban Mothers' Mutual Aid Society. Mrs. Ruiz's boy was a graduate of Florida Atlantic University, a certified public accountant, married with two, and he was a year younger than Jimmy Paz. He also resembled a Bartlett pear, but this fact cut very little ice with the mom when Paz pointed it out, as he did whenever she started on the why-can't-you-be's. Paz thought once again of discussing the dream and the other weird stuff with his mother but again dismissed the idea. He had spent most of his conscious life defending his privacy from her, and this habit was now too strong to break. Although his mother, as it happened, knew a great deal about dreams and other states of consciousness that differed from plain vanilla awake-and-aware.

Dressed, he poured another cup of coffee, added hot milk, grabbed a dish towel and the remains of his third churro, went out to the small backyard. There he wiped the dew from a seat of a redwood picnic set and sat down. The eastern sky was rosy with dawn and the air was as cool as it was going to get, scented with jasmine, citrus, the hot dough and coffee of his breakfast. So by dawn's early light, Paz drank, ate, and read the *Miami Herald*. He skimmed the national news, checked the local news for crime and scandal, then the obituaries: here was a guy dropped dead in an office lobby, a developer, clipped at forty-seven. Paz was still a relatively young fellow, but being the sort of young fellow he was, he had discovered unusually early that he was not immortal, and so he had started this past year to read the obits with interest. Then he read the sports pages to have something to talk about to the men at work, and then he turned with somewhat more attention to the arts page. Paz was not a regular close reader of this section, which counted (if column inches of space meant anything) the movies and TV as the primary arts of mankind, but recently he had studied it with some care, especially the continuing coverage of the Miami Book Fair. There was a half-page announcement of the day's event at Miami Dade's downtown campus, and he found the name he was looking for and noted the time at which this particular author would appear. For the first time since his cruel awakening he felt a smile blossom in his heart.

That morning, Paz was the first one in the homicide unit, a suite on the fifth floor of the Miami PD headquarters building. Unlike the versions presented by the cop shows on TV, police work is largely desk work, using phone, typewriter, ballpoint, and, latterly, the computer. Despite the drop in the murder rate, the homicide unit remained busy, because it was also responsible for assault and domestic violence, which had not declined at all.

The unit was commanded by a lieutenant named Posada and was part of the Criminal Investigation Section, under a major named Oliphant. Paz thought Posada was a useless excrescence but had not made up his mind about the major. Major Oliphant was a newcomer. The city fathers had finally concluded that after two generations of almost continuous scandal and corruption they would try an outsider. This was fine with Paz; he didn't have many friends among the old guard. Oliphant was ex-FBI, which did not endear him to the Miami cops. There were rumors, too, about why he had left the Bureau, some obscure Bureauesque imbroglio.

Paz was making phone calls, looking for a gold Lady Rolex watch bearing the inscription "To Estelle from Eddie, Love Always" because the love hadn't lasted quite that long. Eddie had just put Estelle into a coma and proved to be a cad in the bargain, making off with all his gifts. On the eighth call, he found the right pawnshop. He put the phone down, smiling, and spun around on his swivel chair like a small boy but stopped when he saw that Major Oliphant was standing in the doorway of the detail bay, looking at him curiously. Paz stood up.

Douglas Oliphant was an offensive-tackle-size man, a shade or two darker than Paz. He smiled and asked, "Good news?"

Paz told him about the case. Oliphant nodded and gestured in the direction of his own office. "Come on, I'll buy you a cup of coffee."

"Want a churro with it?"

A little hesitation at the sight of the greasy bag Paz held up and then, shrugging, "Sure, whatever."

Oliphant's office had a big window looking north, but the

blinds were already drawn against the glare of early morning. He poured Paz a cup and one for himself and sat behind his desk. Paz noticed that his cup was a souvenir item from the 1998 National Association of Chiefs of Police convention, and that Oliphant's had "FBI" on it, with a golden seal. Oliphant examined the churro with interest and took a bite.

"Mm, my, that's good! Where do you get these?"

"I made them."

"You *made* them?"

"Yes, sir. I'm really a girl, but they make me cross-dress because otherwise I would have too much affirmative action. They'd have to make me the chief."

This was delivered deadpan, and it took Oliphant a few seconds to get it, but he managed a laugh.

"Yeah, I heard you were a pisser . . . is it Jimmy?"

"Yes, sir."

"Yeah. Why don't you have a partner?"

The unexpected pertinent question of a skilled interrogator. Paz was impressed but not discomfited. "I prefer to work alone, sir. They fired my partner last year and none of the new guys seem to have worked out."

"No, and what I hear is you ran them off. I also hear you got an attitude." Paz did not comment on this. Oliphant regarded him over the rim of his coffee cup for a while. "And a perfect disciplinary record, an unusual combo in my experience. Well. The fact of the matter is, your preferences aside, you have to have a partner and you know why. This department, I can't have detectives wandering around the town all by their lonesome. You make a case, I got to have two people saying what went down. And if the shit happens to hit the fan . . ." He made an indeterminate gesture with his hand, and Paz filled in, "You want to be able to get each of them in a room with a bunch of snakes and get one of them to rat the other one out."

"You got it."

"You could hire Barlow back."

"Uh-huh, I could, just before I handed in my resignation and packed my bags. Your guy held the former chief of this department hostage at gunpoint while spouting all kinds of racist crap."

"He was emotionally disturbed. The perp slipped him some kind of drug."

"That's the story, although I have to note that the docs found no drugs whatever in his system after you arranged for his capture." He paused and waited, but Paz was not forthcoming. "I always thought there was something really fishy about that whole Voodoo Killer thing. Care to comment?"

"I wrote a report. Eighty-seven pages without appendices. And there was a book out."

"I read both of them," said Oliphant and pinched his nostrils together meaningfully. Paz kept mum. The major went on: "Okay, you need a partner and I'll tell you what I'll do. Since I think we can call this a special case, I'll let *you* pick your guy. Anyone in the department who's got the right grade and time in service. I want a name by close of business tomorrow. And this arrangement stays between you and me. Are we clear on that?"

"Yes, sir," said Paz and stood up.

"Sit down," said Oliphant. "That wasn't what I wanted to talk to you about." He took another churro out of the bag, then smiled, patted his belly, and placed it on his desk blotter.

"Later, I think. Okay, this homicide at the Trianon you put away the other week. That was fast work."

"A grounder. The perp was sitting there, the murder weapon was at the scene."

"Still. There's no doubt the doer was this woman Dideroff?"

"Not in *my* mind," said Paz, and then had an uncomfortable feeling. "Why do you ask?"

"Oh, no reason. Know anything about the victim?"

"A guest in the hotel. Flew in from Mexico City three days before he died. Some kind of Arab businessman is what I gathered from his stuff. A Sudanese passport."

"Uh-huh. I got a call about the case."

"Oh?"

"You know I used to be with the Bureau."

"Yes, sir, I heard that."

"The call was from a guy who works for the people who watch certain individuals from that part of the world. At the Bureau, I mean. This Jabir Akran al-Muwalid was on a watch list."

"That's interesting. Did he say why they were watching him?"

"Not really," said Oliphant brusquely, discouraging curiosity. "He was mainly interested in knowing if it was really him, Muwalid. I had the file faxed up to D.C. He also wanted to know if the woman, the suspect, was going down for it. Is she?"

"That's not up to me, sir, but you read the file: I can't see how we could deliver a more unbreakable case. What'll happen at trial . . ." Here Paz shrugged elaborately. "She's a wack job was my take on her. Talking about mystic voices. She might try an insanity defense, I don't know."

"That would be a long shot, in my opinion," said Major Oliphant. "But it might strengthen the case if we had a good sense of what the connection was between them. She say anything about that?"

"Only that the vic was her enemy and that he'd done some bad things back home in Africa. I gathered she was talking about massacres and stuff, war crimes."

"Uh-huh. She elaborate any on that? What went down in Africa?"

"No, sir, not to me. But she's writing out what she calls a confession."

"Really. What does it say?"

"Well, actually I haven't seen it yet. She says she has to write it in a special kind of notebook." Paz had a certain expression on his face when he said this, and Oliphant's eyebrows rose.

"Oh, *that* kind of confession."

"It's a good bet. She's a total loon."

"Mm. Be that as it may I'd feel more comfortable with a fatter file. More of the background. So follow up, her movements, her background, the vic's movements. It'd be nice to paint a picture she had a major hard-on for this character and was lying in wait. That would speak against the insanity plea."

"Okay, sir, I'll get on it. Was that all?"

Oliphant nodded. Paz rose, and the major said, "And thanks for the . . ." He gestured to the bag.

"Churros, sir," said Paz helpfully, and left.

Back at his desk, Paz found the bay had filled with its usual complement of detectives and cops and clericals, and that the usual noise of telephones and talk and clacking machines had replaced the quiet of a few minutes before. Paz's mind was also considerably less quiet than it had been. All right, the partner business, put that to one side, he'd deal with that in some way. What bothered him was Oliphant's interest in a firmly closed case. Bosses were normally interested only in open cases, and in these mainly when there was some political pressure to catch some particularly egregious villain, someone, for example, who had made the grave error of killing a white person in the state of Florida. They were interested in closed cases only when there was some suspicion that a cop had screwed up, had, for example, dropped a gun to cover a bad shooting, or strong-armed a witness into perjury. But Paz knew the Dideroff collar was Tide clean, so that couldn't be it.

So it was the FBI connection, someone in D.C. was interested in his little grounder. And interested in seeing Emmylou Dideroff go to prison, maybe to a berth on death row. Okay, let's take another look at Ms. D. He pulled a file from the vertical rack on his desk. He read through the A form, the arrest affidavit in the case, the initial summary of why the cops thought the arrestee had in fact committed the crime. Then he read the transcript of the interview tapes he'd made with the woman, and as he read them there arrived in his mind the memory of what had happened in that interview, what he had seen. Or thought he had seen. And then came the intense desire never to look her in the face again. Suppress that. Divert to something else: ah, here was a search warrant. With relief he fled the office to do some police work.

The address on the warrant led him to a houseboat moored on the Miami River, in an undesirable location shadowed by the East-West Expressway overpass. The houseboat was an undistinguished mass-produced unit, flat-bottomed, flat-roofed, made from peeling beige fiberglass. He stepped down onto its deck and broke open the jalousied aluminum cabin door. Inside, a plain Formica table with a philodendron in a clay pot in its center, some aluminum and nylon mesh deck chairs, a stove, a sink, a small refrigerator. A long padded seat ran over storage cabinets on the opposite bulkhead. Yellow plaid curtains, much faded, covered the windows, mellowing the sunlight that passed through them. Paz checked the storage and the pantry and the refrigerator and found only the usual kitchen equipment and linens and food: no drugs, no guns. The one berth was forward, a tiny place with barely room for a double bed. The storage here was built into its base. Paz tossed it quickly, finding only a simple selection of clothes—straight cotton skirts, T-shirts, one cotton sweater, cotton socks, cotton underwear, all with low-end labels from Penney's and Kmart. In a plastic bag was what looked like a cook's apron, a gray wool dress, a white scarf, and a pair of high lace-up black boots. A cheap slicker hung from a peg.

Was he missing something? No, the occupant seemed to be the only woman in South Florida with no bathing suit, no shorts. No suntan oil or makeup either, on the shelves in the tiny toilet–shower room. Hairspray, though, which seemed a little out of place for a woman with two inches of hair. He checked the can, shaking it, and did not hear the little ball rattle. Uh-oh. A hard twist and the top came off, revealing a wad of currency. But it was only two hundred and some dollars, what you would expect a working stiff without a bank account to have squirreled away.

Back in the bedroom, Paz stood for a moment in thought, as he always did in such situations—home of victim, home of suspect—and tried to feel the character of the occupant. The place was first of all spotless. Paz had done a hitch in the marines, and he believed that the boat would have passed an inspection by any gunnery sergeant in that organization. And he had also been in any number of women's dwelling places and he had never seen one so sparse. The woman owned next to nothing. He knelt on the bed and examined the contents of the box shelf behind it. Books first: a New American Bible in the paperback study edition, much thumbed and containing numerous bookmarks. If the distribution of these were any indication, then Job and the Gospel of John were her favorites. A book written in Arabic script, also heavily thumbed, with gilt edging, that Paz supposed was the Quran. A life of Catherine of Siena, and the *Discourses* by that saint, and a Penguin edition of the autobiography of Teresa of Avila. A thin book with crumbly yellowed pages called *Faithful Unto Death: The Story of the Nursing Sisters of the Blood of Christ,* by Sr. Benedicta Cooley, SBC, and a paperback of Simone Weil's *Gravity and Grace,* quite worn. Paz leafed quickly through each book. In the Weil he found a Polaroid photo. It showed a white woman in the center of a group of a dozen or so very tall, very black soldiers, with a background of thin tree trunks and dark foliage. The white woman was deeply tanned and wore a blue mechanic's overall and a white scarf covering her hair, like the headdresses worn formerly by nurses or currently by some nuns. The woman and the soldiers were all grinning at the camera, the teeth and eyes of the latter startling against skin that was almost purple. The soldiers were dressed in ragged khaki tunics, shorts, and sandals. They had bandoliers crossed on their chests, and they were brandishing AKs and big dark rifles of an older design. Paz took a folding hand lens from his pocket and brought it to the photo. As he had expected, the woman was Emmylou Dideroff. The surprise was that all the soldiers were young women. He slipped the photo into his pocket and resumed his search.

The books were held in place by half a brick on one side and a big pink conch shell on the other. There was a large-beaded rosary sitting in the opening of the conch, as if it had been spawned there, a disconcerting sight. Behind the books was a cheaply framed photo of a statue of a woman in three-quarter view. Her head was swathed in a nun's veil, the face strongly featured and beautiful, with remarkable long, narrow eyes that seemed to be squinting against the sun or focused on some inner reality. Paz thought he'd seen those eyes somewhere, but he couldn't quite connect them to a person. Stuck between the glass and the frame was a color photo of a handsome freckle-faced woman wearing a white apron, white headdress, and gray dress, standing in front of an elaborately carved doorway. A nun of some kind, and Paz had the cruel thought, What a waste! The woman was hotter-looking than nuns were supposed to be.

Next to the big seashell was a small, free-standing crucifix. Paz picked it up and examined it closely. It was finely carved from some dark, hard, and heavy wood. The corpus was not shown peacefully expired, as in most such items, but writhing in agony, the body twisted nearly into an S, each individually carved finger curled to indicate pain. The crucifying nails were actual metal nails, driven through the wrists rather than into the conventional palms. He was excruciatingly thin, ribs and joints staring, and he had a Negro face, with the cheeks marked with parallel scars. Paz felt the skin prickle on his neck when he saw this. First that weirdness in the interview room, now Africa, again. And he thought also that, although the figure was not strictly realistic, the artist was not just using his imagination. It looked almost as if the artist had sculpted from life, as if he had actually seen a crucifixion. He found a canvas suitcase and loaded it with the personal items and books, including the money. It was none of his business whether the woman lost all this through theft, as was almost inevitable on the river, but for some reason he could not bear for someone who had so little to lose the little she had.

A motion of the boat snapped Paz out of this unpleasant reverie. Someone had come aboard, and now a voice called out, "Can I help you?"

Paz emerged from the sleeping cabin to confront a soft-looking man of about forty with a buzz cut over an undistin-guished set of white-bread American features. His eyes were uncertain and nervous behind horn-rimmed glasses, and he held his right hand out of sight.

Paz slowly withdrew his badge wallet from his breast pocket and showed his ID.

"Paz, Miami PD. Who're you?"

The man leaned forward and examined the credentials for longer than most people did when so confronted. Seemingly satisfied, he straightened and brought his other hand into sight.

The man said, "I'm David Packer. This is my boat."

"You're renting it to Emmylou Dideroff?"

"Yeah," he said, and then his brow knotted with concern. "Hey, did anything . . . I mean, is she okay?"

"She was fine the last time I saw her. How is she as a tenant?"

"Perfect. Doesn't smoke, doesn't drink, doesn't have skanky men come by all the time, or dope parties, like the last one I had in here. No broken glass. So if she's okay, how come you're here?"

"She's involved in a crime and we're checking her out. Look, could we go up on deck, it's getting warm in here."

"Yeah, it'll do that. Boat's got an AC, but she don't use it much."

The man turned and walked out. He was overweight, and his T-shirt was too tight to conceal the butt of the pistol he had shoved into the waistband of his faded cutoff jeans.

On deck, Packer said, "We could go to my place, get out of the sun if you want to talk." He gestured to the next moorage where loomed a large structure covered with redwood shingles. Technically a houseboat, it was more like a house *on* a boat, flat-roofed, wooden-shingled, with big picture windows, a balcony, and a deck full of redwood lawn furniture and well-grown potted plants.

"Lead the way," said Paz, and they both walked off Dideroff's houseboat, along the bulkhead and up a ramp onto the larger craft. They had to squeeze past a huge motorcycle on their way to the deck facing the river.

Packer directed Paz to a padded mahogany chaise lounge, but he chose a canvas chair instead. Packer dropped down into another lounge, winced, pulled the pistol out from behind him, and placed it carefully on a side table. He said, "Sorry about my attitude. We've had break-ins, theft, vandalism."

"Uh-huh," said Paz. See a black guy, naturally you reach for your gun. He looked at the pistol. It was a Walther PPK/S. The man saw his look and said, "Don't worry, Officer, I have a license."

"Detective, and I'm not worried, sir," said Paz. "So . . . Mr. Packer. You know Emmylou for long?"

"Just since she's been here. A year or so. I could check my records."

"She just showed up one day?"

"No, she was . . . I mean I was recommended to her by mutual friends. She was looking to settle here in town, I had a boat to rent . . . like I said, she's been a tenant from heaven."

"And you're here most of the time?"

"Oh, I'm out and about. Got a motorcycle over there on the stern deck, you probably saw."

"Yeah, the Harley. And you're what? Independently wealthy?"

Packer laughed. "I wish. No, I'm just a retired civil servant with some lucky investments. And a pension."

"Mm. What agency were you with when you were working, if I may ask?"

"Excuse me, but I thought we were going to talk about my tenant," said Packer. "You said she was involved in some crime?"

"Yes, sir. A homicide."

"Emmylou *killed* someone?"

"That's what we're trying to determine, sir. Now, did you ever see her with anyone who might have been African or Arab?"

"No, we didn't socialize, and I never saw anyone visit at the boat."

"Did you ever know or hear her talk about a man named Jabir Akran al-Muwalid?"

"No. Is that who she's supposed to have killed?"

Paz ignored this and took a steno book and a pen from his breast pocket. "We're trying to find out something about Emmylou, her background, where she's from. Can you fill in any of that?"

"No, I'm afraid I can't. Like I said, we weren't pals. We exchanged small talk if we happened to pass and once a month when she brought the rent. Paid in cash, by the way, and always on the day."

"Well, then, those mutual friends . . ."

"Hilda and Stewart Jameson. I have a P.O. box number for them at Methodist World Missions you could have, but I have no idea how you'd get in touch with them. They're on the road a lot."

"In Africa."

"Yes, as a matter of fact. How did you know?"

"Oh, just a lucky guess." Paz did not appreciate being snowed, which he was pretty sure was what Packer was doing to him, but he had no leverage on the man at present, so he took his leave (noting the license plate number on the bike as he did so) and drove to the Wilson Brothers Marine engine shop to check out Dideroff's employment. It was a big shed by the river, smelling of dank water and engine exhaust. He located the proprietor in his office, a small cubicle lined with cheap luan paneling. This was decorated with a whiteboard listing active jobs, framed photos of boats, a calendar supplied by Volvo Marine and another showing a naked woman, which was heavily marked with circlings and phone numbers. Jack Wilson was a big heavily tanned guy with a long back-sweep of golden hair down to the neck in back and not too clean, dressed in the usual grease-stained khaki cutoffs and sleeveless T-shirt of the Miami water rat. He had massive biceps on which were tattooed LIVE FREE OR DIE (left) and a marijuana leaf (right). A shark's tooth on a thong decorated his neck.

"I've been expecting you guys," he said after Paz introduced himself. "When Emmylou didn't come back with my truck I figured something was up. I called and they told me she was arrested."

"We're questioning her. She may have witnessed a crime. So tell me a little about her. A good worker? Reliable?"

"Yeah. She was great. Is great. I mean everybody around here really liked her."

"She ever mention any Arabs? Guy named Jabir al-Muwalid?"

"Not that I ever heard," said Wilson. "What kind of crime?"

"Why don't you let me ask the questions, sir? I'll be out of your way a lot quicker. How did you come to hire her?"

"A guy we did some work for steered her here when my old girl quit."

"So you hired her on a boater's recommendation. A friend of yours?"

"No, just a customer. Dave Packer. She rents a houseboat from him."

"I know. I met Mr. Packer a while ago. And so . . . she ran your office? Handled the petty cash. Looks like you got a lot of expensive stuff for sale. She cut your checks too?"

"Yeah, what about it?"

"Just that it seems an important job to give a stranger on the recommendation of some guy you hardly knew. Did she have references?"

Paz kept up the cop stare, buoyed by the cop instinct that he was in the presence of someone with something to hide, a violation of the criminal code type of something. This was the kind of leverage he did not have on Packer, and he was going to make the most of it. After a little pause, Wilson said, "Look, I'll level with you. This is the Miami waterfront, huh? People come and go. I mean decent office help's hard to find, and most people'd rather work in a bank, nice office, air-conditioning, quiet . . . I mean this place, a crummy little room, fumes from the shop . . . so I was paying her off the books—cash, no withholding. She wanted it like that anyway."

"And why was that, do you think?"

"Hey, she was a good worker. And I'm not nosy."

Paz waited, staring.

The big man shrugged. "It's the black economy." A little grin, here. "There's thousands of people not in the system. They don't pay taxes. They're into cash, barter. A lot of them pass through Miami, and a lot of them end up on the water. You gonna turn me in to the feds for this?"

Paz didn't bother to answer this. With a few more questions he determined that the woman had in fact been sent out after a connecting rod an hour or so before the murder.

Paz thanked Wilson and made to leave.

"What about my truck?" Wilson asked.

"You can pick it up at the police pound. I don't think we're going to need it."

"And my C rod?"

"I believe you ought to think about getting another one of those," said Paz with a smile, and left.

Paz sat in his car with the engine and the AC running and gave himself over to discontent. If this was a grounder, and the woman had done it in the way the evidence suggested she had, then these interviews should have been simple formalities. But both men were clearly lying. Now his view of the case began to shift; he tried to fight it, but the little nagging details kept adding to the mystery. Why the lies? Why was a cop right there when the victim went out the window? Someone had called the cops to report a disturbance was why, but the only disturbance had been the murder itself. Someone had wanted the police at the scene. And the strangeness of the woman herself . . . he didn't really want to think about that. Instead he thought about his need for a new partner, and the face of the policeman from the hotel, Morales, was right there at the surface of his mind. Well, why the hell not?

For a long time after Sophie died Georges de Berville sat disconsolate in the darkened bedroom in the house on Rue d'Orléans in Sedan. He neglected his business, leaving the burden of his affairs to fall on his eldest, Alphonse, then barely sixteen. He rarely emerged and spoke to no one, not even the servants, for very long. Marie-Ange's nanny, Mlle. Rosière, was instructed to keep the child away from her father, for the sight of her little face, so similar to that of her mother, reduced him to such sobs and cries of grief that they feared for his sanity.

Yet, Marie-Ange, even at the tender age of seven years, had a powerful will and a mighty desire to bring comfort to the afflicted, and she loved her father very much. One evening, while Mlle. Rosière nodded by the nursery fire, the child slipped out and trotted down the corridor to her father's bedroom. She found him tossing in fitful slumber, often waking with a cry and then falling back into his uneasy dreams. She sat on the edge of the bed and held his hand, and prayed to the Blessed Virgin and to St. Catherine to give her dear father peace. Now her father opened his eyes and, as he later confided to his eldest son, he saw around his daughter's head a halo of light, and heard a voice saying, "Be at peace, Georges de Berville, for your wife is with us in Paradise!" After that he fell into a deep and refreshing sleep, and when he awoke he was himself again. This occurrence was in later times regarded as a true miracle in the de Berville family, and was the first notable instance of the special favors the Bd. Marie-Ange was to receive from Our Lady during the course of her life.

—FROM *FAITHFUL UNTO DEATH:*
*THE STORY OF THE NURSING SISTERS*
*OF THE BLOOD OF CHRIST,*
BY SR. BENEDICTA COOLEY, SBC,
ROSARIAN PRESS, BOSTON, 1947.

# Five

---

The
## CONFESSIONS
of
## Emmylou Dideroff

### Book I

*I took up with Hunter Foy again, but it wasn't exactly the same as it was before, because the little tiny part of me that was still able to love had got totally squashed by what all had happened at the house and there was nothing in my heart but gravel and old oyster shells. I started to help him in his dope business at that time and I was amazed to learn how big it was. Hunter used to make regular trips into Gainesville and Panama City to sell to his customers there, bulk sales, bricks of compressed seedless marijuana, shiny with brown resin. He had a very superior product, Hunter, and it made me curious. I watched TV like everyone else, and I wondered how he was able to do like that, without other drug gangs coming in and how he got it all organized and who his supplier was. I wondered pretty hard because it wasn't long before I knew that Hunter Foy did not figure all of that out for himself, him being smart enough for a Foy but not by any means the sharpest knife in the drawer.*

*It was February 3, 1985, a Monday, when I found out the secret. I biked over to Hunter's trailer, and there was an old rusted Dodge pickup with Virginia plates sitting in the yard with a couple of big feist dogs in it that growled at me when I went by. I wasn't supposed to be there that night but I had forgotten a book and I wanted it. The book was Atlas Shrugged by Ayn Rand, and like every ill-educated fourteen-year-old in the world I thought it was hot stuff. I went barging into the trailer like always, saying Hey whose truck . . . and then I stopped because I was looking into the barrel of a big revolver. On the other side of the pistol was my first sight of Percival Orne Foy. Hunter said real quick and nervous oh that's just my girlfriend, unc, and the older man slowly dropped the pistol off of me and said we got business, girl, you'd best be on your way, and I said sorry, I just forgot my book, and I went and got it.*

*When he saw the book he gave me another look. He was fair and rangy with the white-gold hair and the blue eyes that all the Foy clan have and around thirty-five at the time. He favored Hunter a little, or I guess you could say Hunter favored him, on account of him being the son of Orne's brother, but where Hunter was soft around the jaw and mouth and a little empty in the eye department, Orne Foy was steel hard in both places, and not like any other man I'd met until then, and the first thought that raced through my mind as he held that pistol was this man could kill Ray Bob Dideroff for me, if I could get him to want to. He looked at me for what seemed like a half hour but couldn't've been more than a couple of seconds, and I felt a little like I had when I first got that look from Ray Bob, like he could see me not the mask I showed to the world, but there wasn't any of that evil in it, no lust at all, only an interested regard from a being higher than me, one of those winged lions from mythology, or like a man sizing up a dog he was thinking about buying. He said you reading that book and I said yes and he asked me how did I like it, and I said I thought it was great. He said I guess you think you're one of the people who hold up the* world and I didn't say anything and he said, what you got there is a shadow of a shadow of a shadow. Would you like to see the real thing, the source of the light? And I said, yes, sir, and he got up and took my arm and took me out to his truck. I guess there might be another major drug trafficker somewhere who travels with a copy of The Viking Portable Nietzsche never more than a reach away, but if so I never met him. He handed me it, and I looked at it and said Nitscha? And he said it right, and I said, I teach you the superman. Man is something to be surpassed. He looked at me funny like I might want to bite him and said you've read Nietzsche? And I admitted it was just Collier's Book of Quotations, although it was on my lips to say oh, sure all the time, I wanted him to respect me so much, and that was the first time I had that particular and useful feeling. He told me to get out and he'd be back in a month and we might talk about it. Later I found out he bought them by the case and gave them out like Gideon does Bibles, a missionary in his way was Percival Orne Foy.

Well, started reading that night and I'll admit that there was a lot that left me confused in it, mostly references to things I never read and philosophical terms. I had to look up Wagner and all the Greeks he mentions in the encyclopedia, which wasn't a bad thing. But the core of it set me on fire, seemed pretty much designed to set on fire any bright heartbroken fourteen-year-old with a lust for revenge. The will to power! The tyranny of the weak! And fuck Christianity while you're at it, all those hypocrites at Amity Street. Mediocrities! Slaves! I did the usual blasphemies, including dragging poor Hunter out and busting into Amity Street and making him fuck me on the table up front while I howled and laughed like a goblin.

When Orne Foy came back next month I was there and sat at his feet and drank in wisdom. Nietzsche had been right, Western society was hopelessly decadent, was moving inexorably toward chaos, Atlas shrugging away, fundamentalists and Jews running the country trying to turn us into a nation of repressed slaves. But it couldn't go on. The environment would collapse, poisons would flood the air and the water, new diseases brought by filthy immigrants that we didn't have the sense or guts to keep out would ravage us all. The economy would collapse because all the weak couldn't stand for the strong to flourish and chained them with all their rules and regulations, so a real man couldn't breathe . . . but after the collapse the faithful remnant would emerge, heavily armed, from their hidden fortresses and reclaim the world for glory and honor and savage beauty.

And a lot more in that vein. I had never really thought much about the world, except to despise it, so Orne's teaching fell on rich virgin soil and flourished. He had a place in the wilds of Virginia where he grew dope in defiance of the slave government, and where, after the final collapse, he would establish the nucleus of the new civilization. I wanted in on all that, needless to say, a perfect fascist disciple, me, maybe all teenagers are fascists of one kind or another. And also he said he was paying off Ray Bob to let Hunter operate in the county, which I should have figured out, given Hunter's soft brains. He was bored by all our talking and he usually lay stoned in his headphones while we philosophized and his uncle raped my mind the way Ray Bob Dideroff did my body. It was terrific, better than dope, really, the only funny thing being that he seemed not to be interested in my actual body, which I shoved under his nose as often as I could manage. In those days only actual professional whores had access to the kind of clothes they sell for little girls at every mall nowadays, but I wore my thinnest T-shirts and tightest jeans, and once I even brought along one of those cold packs you use in coolers and ran it over my nipples so they would poke out when I went into the trailer. But nothing. I had to make do by imagining it was him when I fucked Hunter.

Meanwhile, the year advanced, the weather got hot again, and I waited patiently as I could for events to transpire, and as it happened I had to wait for Memorial Day weekend. The police always threw a big barbecue, and of course we all had to go because of Ray Bob being the chief. I was happy to see that Momma was losing it ever more frequently, fits of screaming in public. Ray Bob kept getting her to take more pills, but it didn't seem to do any good. I saw him talking to Doc Herm at the party, looking over at where Momma was downing beer after beer and popping large numbers of those green-and-black caps in an effort to resume her equilibrium.

After the picnic I sneaked off with Hunter and we went to the beach and listened to some people play music in a house there and we sold some dope, and then we fucked a couple of times on the beach and then I said I wanted to go home and take a shower. He dropped me off at the end of our street. We had this long driveway leading to the house and I could hear the crying from halfway down the drive. When I walked in the front door I could hear that it was Esmeralda and Bobbie Ann doing it. They were in the kitchen. Esmeralda looked at me and said something in Spanish that I didn't understand and I walked off to see what was what.

Ray Bob was lying in Bobbie Ann's room at the foot of the famous rocker, with his fly open and his skull in a couple of big pieces hanging on to the end of his neck. She had used more bullets than were strictly necessary. She herself was in the yellow Mustang in the garage, looking like she was about to drive off, had she not been dead. They say that women never shoot themselves in the head out of vanity and Momma was true to type, having placed the muzzle of the Colt Python against her breastbone and blown most of her tiny cold heart into the rear seat. The place stunk of gunpowder, blood, shit, and Jim Beam, so I did not tarry long.

I honestly had not really expected Momma to kill herself, I figured she would make a run for it, but I was not unduly dismayed either. I was sadder, to tell the truth, when I found she had also killed Jon Dideroff, who had *never as far as I known done anything to hurt her. Collateral damage, I guess, he just got in the way, or maybe she just didn't like the way he looked just like a little Ray Bob. Esmeralda and the girl had been out on a shopping trip when it happened, or she might've taken them out too. She also missed Ray Jr., who'd been off at the beach with his friends, and I remember thinking oh, well, you can't have everything. I was the blond beast then and that is how we think.*

*The Colt Python was Ray Bob's, of course, one of a dozen firearms he owned. He was the county NRA president and a great believer in gun safety, so there was a big gun safe in his den, with a key and a five-button combo lock. The manufacturer had provided two sets of keys, and one of them had lived in a tackle box on a high shelf in the Sears shed until I pocketed it when Ray Bob locked me in there. Conveniently, it was still in the manufacturer's little plastic envelope, along with a printed card that had the combination on it. Ray Bob kept his pedophile pictures in the gun safe too, as I learned when I tested the key. I grabbed a few, stunned-looking little girls holding big hairy erect penises or lying on beds with their pudenda exposed and that bruised look around their eyes. I had left some of these and the key packet in an envelope on Momma's vanity table a couple of weeks ago, as a hint, and had been happy to observe that she had grabbed them up shortly afterward. Who did she imagine had supplied them? I wonder. She never said a word to me, and I guess by then she was not thinking too clearly.*

*Supplying the key and the combination was actually the easy part. Much harder, really, was taking apart every single Librium cap in the house, pouring out the sleepy powder, and refilling each one with cornstarch. It took hours and hours. Momma must've felt sort of strange when real life came back after so many years, she couldn't sleep as well through those long afternoons, when the rocker went squeak, squawk and Ray Bob's gentle voice reading Wind in the Willows filtered out of her precious little girl's* room. She tried booze, but you know booze doesn't give you that guaranteed sleep like Librium does, and besides it doesn't suppress the violent urges. Kind of stimulates them as a matter of fact. Momma always went crazy when she drank, everybody in the Boones knew it, and that's why she had always previously been careful to remain a pill head.

I paused only to stop by the kitchen and scream at Bobbie Ann, this is all your fault! And then I picked up the little bag I had packed against this day and as the police sirens wailed I rode off on my bike to Hunter's place to tell him what we had to do.

# Six

The consulting room is large and bright, the walls covered with dun rice paper, relieved by several marine-themed paintings and prints, ships under sail, tropic shores with boats, the framed diplomas and accolades. A model of a yacht in a glass case. Dominating the room a mahogany desk, also the canonical leather couch, leather side chairs, a long credenza in rosewood, on which sit examples of Haitian and Cuban folk art, statues of saints and demons.

Mickey Lopez, with a genuine smile, comes from around his desk and hugs Lorna, plants kisses on both cheeks. She has to bend slightly to receive the kisses and a pong of his Acqua di Parma, for he is short and blocky. He beams at her, and she smiles back. He tells her she looks marvelous. Hardly any accent, just enough to be distinguished, although it is, of course, a Spanish one rather than the prized mittel-European model. But good enough for Miami. She tells him he hasn't changed a bit, and he hasn't, the same beautifully cut gray sharkskin suit, white silk shirt, maroon tie, very Manhattan. Mickey Lopez resembles to a startling degree the late Israeli prime minister David Ben-Gurion—the blunt-featured determined face, the famous untamed aureole of white hair around the high shiny pate. He says it's because all psychoanalysts summon forth their inner Jew, and this is his. She was in analysis with him for twenty months, terminated at her request last year.

Howard Kasdan is standing too, and now he leans into her with a handshake and a kiss on the cheek, an all-friends-together kind of kiss that lasts a sadistic forty milliseconds too long. The pheromones hit her like a blow to the base of the skull. No suit for Howard; Howard, M.D., is not that kind of shrink. He has on the silk/linen Hugo Boss cream jacket he always wears, and today it is worn over a black silk turtleneck, black slacks, shiny Italian woven loafers. A scientist exploring the mind is Dr. Kasdan. She doesn't have to bend for him, no, he's six two and buffed, dark eyes under thick brows and lashes, deep eyes, she always called them penetrating to herself, and they were, so much that she has to look away at the palm tops waving outside the silvered glass of the window.

After they have all taken seats, Mickey begins chatting about sailing, the expense, he is going to sell the damn boat, and Howard, whose boat is five feet longer than Mickey's, tells him that's bullshit, that everyone in town knows Mickey Lopez is rich as God. Lorna does not care for sailing very much. That is, she rather likes the thing itself, but not the endless talk about it, the mystique. I mean, it's a *vehicle,* for God's sake, not a person, she has told Sheryl, also no sailor. The talk runs down after a few minutes and Lopez says, "Speaking of money, unlike you public sector parasites, I have to see a patient in twenty minutes, so could we get this going, please? I think this is your party, Lorna."

She opens her briefcase and pulls out three photocopied packets and a notebook, and hands each of the men a packet. Clears her throat, breathes in, out, in, and begins, the professional screen falls, the emotions still roil in the pit of her belly, but nothing shows. In psych testing she is The Man, and everyone knows it.

"The subject here is a native-born white female, age thirty-three, in good general health. No sign of recent trauma, but we observe old scars on the backs of the thighs, and somewhat more recent scarring on the ventral surfaces. Heavy keratinized scarring on the soles of the feet. X-ray shows cartilage damage in the region of the proximal humerus and the glenoid process, both sides, suggesting recent dislocations, with treatment. She has trouble with arm elevation—"

"Excuse me, Lorna," says Lopez. "Does she give a history for these injuries?"

"She says she was tortured. By the man she killed. Allegedly." There is a meaningful pause here, but no one comments, and so Lorna continues. "Subject presents a somewhat flattened affect, or maybe an unnatural calm would be a better way of putting it. I mean unnatural in someone accused of committing a capital crime. We expect a little anxiety, but nothing shows. She understands her situation rationally, but there doesn't seem to be any emotional component. I think that's indicative, considering her test results. To which we now turn. Page one of your handouts. We administered the Wechsler, and she's not intellectually impaired; on the contrary, she scored above normal on almost all the segments, but especially high on the nonverbals. Her picture completion score is off the scale, actually the highest I've ever seen."

Kasdan says, "Remind me, please . . . ?"

"Picture completion measures visual perception, long-term visual memory, and the ability to differentiate essential from nonessential details."

"Thank you. Please go on."

She does, taking them through the psychometrics, comforted and calmed by the precise figures. Emmylou Dideroff was not lying or trying to manipulate, was unusually self-critical, was not easily influenced by social standards or customs but socially extroverted, not a psychopath, a rejector of normal female roles.

Kasdan asked, "A lesbian?"

"Not in that range of scores, typically," Lorna replied. "You know those stories about people who have lifelong successful careers as coal miners or cavalry officers, and then when they die it turns out they've really been women? That's this."

"So was she a cavalry officer?" Lopez, smiling.

"Not that we know of, but it could tie in with the gun fantasy, which I'll get to in a minute. She's a perfectionist, and scores unusually high on scale eight, the schizophrenia scale."

"You must have messed up, dear," said Kasdan confidently. "This woman is not a schizophrenic, or not one like any I've ever seen."

"Actually, Doctor," says Lorna, exercising considerable self-control as she recalls yet another of the reasons she is no longer with this man, "scores over ninety-one are associated with subjects under acute, severe situational stress. People in combat, for example, or in the grip of an identity crisis. It's not diagnostic for schizophrenia. The subscale is Sc3, which is associated with lack of ego mastery. We would expect to see strange thought processes, feelings of unreality, defects in memory, false memory. As we in fact do observe in interview. So: did either of you get the gun fantasy?"

Lopez looks at Kasdan. "Gun fantasy?"

"Not with me either," says Kasdan. "What's the gun fantasy?"

"An elaborate . . . I don't know what to call it . . . script? She recalls shooting a cannon. She supplies considerable fabulation detail about this gun, its sound, its effects, and so on, and reports she still hears it in what appear to be hypnagogic states."

"A cannon, huh?" says Kasdan, grinning. "That sounds like your department, Mickey."

"Yes, but sometimes a cigar is only a cigar"—Lopez laughs—"as the master tells us. Go on, Lorna."

Lorna turns to the last page of her sheaf. "Taken together, the scores don't conform to the typical abnormal, if that's not an oxymoron. In fact, I don't believe I have ever seen a pattern quite like hers, and I've done a zillion of these."

Lopez says, "So what's the bottom line here? Is she or is she not competent under the rules for section 12(f)?"

"She is not," says Lorna. The certainty in her voice even surprises her. "These results, combined with my observations of fabulation, delusional voices, and extreme resistance to talking about negative aspects of her past, are indicative of a defendant who cannot cope with reality, and cannot aid in her own defense. I recommend that she be remanded to treatment."

"Howie?" Lopez, with an inquiring look.

"I disagree. She knows where she is," he says, counting off on his fingers. "She knows what she's accused of, she can answer questions rationally; my position is that she's ready for trial."

They both look at Mickey Lopez, who leans back in his leather chair and bridges his hands judiciously under his nose. "Well," he says after half a minute of breathing silence, "I am inclined to agree with Lorna. Test scores are clearly abnormal, but the delusional voices are the clincher for me. I had a truly fascinating conversation myself with Ms. Dideroff on the subject of angelic and demonic voices and how to distinguish one from the other. What I don't want to see is a trial, with the pressure mounting, and all of a sudden she's standing up in the courtroom, saying, 'Yes, Jesus, what is it?' I do not wish to have to explain to Judge Pakingham how such a thing happened. Let's get her into Jackson, look at her for a while, see how she acts. There's no rush, is there?"

"Oh, hell, Mickey," says Kasdan brusquely. He checks his watch and rises. "Go for it! And you can include me too. I don't feel strongly enough about it either way to be the odd man on this. Meanwhile, I'm out of here. Got a lab meeting." He waves blithely to both of them and is gone.

Lopez too checks his watch. "I must go too, my dear. I'm sorry to have to throw you out into the street."

"Yes, the freezing cold," says Lorna, standing and putting away her papers.

Lopez also rises. "It's good to see you again. I miss you."

"Really. I didn't know analysts were supposed to miss their analysands."

He shrugs. "It is the case that some people are dull and some not, and it is inherently more interesting to talk to the interesting ones. If you don't tell the board, I won't either. How have you been getting on?"

"Okay. Living life. Doing my work. You know."

"Attacks? Dreams?"

"I'm fine, Mickey," says Lorna in a tone that closes this line of conversation. "But I'd like to ask a favor?"

"Which is . . . ?"

"I want to continue with this patient."

"With this Dideroff? What do you mean, continue? In what capacity?"

"I want to be on the treatment team. In fact, I want to be the primary. Under you, of course."

A judicious pause. "You're not qualified as a therapist. Technically."

"People a lot less qualified than me see patients every day over there. Student social workers? Interns? It's called supervised clinical experience."

She makes herself meet his gaze and relaxes the muscles of her face, to let the persona sag somewhat, trying to show him that this is not some neurotic tic but an honest and reasonable professional proposal, that she is not manipulating or trying to presume on their past relationship.

He says, "This is important to you?"

"Yes. I've been in practice for nearly six years and I've never seen MMPI test patterns like that. For one thing, she's showing frank religious mania without any indication on the mania scale. The readings on scale nine are highly unusual in themselves, and combined with the aberrant sexual orientation . . . I mean it's practically unique. We could get a paper out of this, the two of us. A new syndrome."

Lopez listens calmly to this, nodding slightly. When she finishes he says, "And also . . . ?"

She feels a blush starting on her neck. He used to give her that in therapy when she was weaving one of her elaborate gilded verbal curtains to shield the embarrassing lump of true feeling. Nor does she cop now. "Mickey, for crying out loud, it's professionally *interesting*. Isn't that enough? You just said it in reference to your practice, and it's the same for mine. It's at least a change from deteriorated schizo street people or shitheads trying to fake psychosis, which are the only two flavors I get on a daily basis. C'mon, Mickey. *Puh-leeze?*"

He grins and lets out a small laugh and throws his arm around her shoulder. "All right, all right! As you know, I'm a sucker for infantile behavior, which is why I'm such a crappy psychiatrist. I'll call Jackson NP after we get the remand. And I intend to supervise too, so don't think there's going to be any funny business! Now, scram! Out of my office!"

"Yes, Doctor." She bends to kiss him on the cheek and leaves.

In her car, she sits with the door open, the engine roaring, and the air conditioner pumping chilled air at her face, a familiar maneuver of South Florida. She is sweating even more than the heat and humidity require, and she can feel the thump of her heart. She closes the door and lets the car chill down. Her face dries. She slips out of her suit jacket and directs jets of air at her armpits, holding the sleeves of her jersey open for that purpose. She tells herself she should feel great, that she's just rolled rat bastard Kasdan, faced him down, marshaled her data, won Lopez's support, successfully lied to him about her psychic state, and rolled him again on the access to Dideroff. A red-letter day then, so why is she sitting here burning gasoline, with her hand on her heart, trying to count the beats, fearing tachycardia, fearing slipping into the kind of anxiety attack that would have her sitting paralyzed in the car for hours. She checks the fuel gauge—good, three-quarters. Once she had run out of gas racing her engine in a Dadeland parking lot, so now she is careful to fill up often. She has a much higher scale seven score than Emmylou Dideroff. A tendency to obsess. Anxiety attacks. No, no, no, she is *not* going to have a fucking attack in Mickey Lopez's parking lot. She shoves the gearshift into reverse, and the car shoots back, jumping the curb that protects a planting island, and performing a neat left-side taillightectomy against the trunk of a maleleuca tree. Cursing wildly, she slams the car into drive and shoots out onto Ponce de Leon.

On Dixie Highway she takes careful deep breaths. Manufacturing calm. When things are spinning out of control the trick is to control what you can, and you can always control your breathing, as her old panic attack coach used to say. Unless you're crazy, which she is definitely not. Or not very. Ill perhaps. Why does she sweat so much? Incipient Type 2 diabetes? Her grandfather had it. Although she tests her urine sugar almost daily. Some obscure hormonal imbalance? Or sexual deprivation? Oh yes, there was no doubt that Kasdan still turned her on, albeit in a faintly disgusting way.

Still the tension is undeniable, irritating, and she should take care of it herself, like a modern woman, but this she finds difficult to do. Lorna is not depressive (MMPI scale two score = 53), but she can make herself suicidally so by seeking sexual release without another human in attendance, and it has to be a man too. Others of her acquaintance are not so particular, she knows. Betsy Newhouse, her other best friend besides Sheryl Waits, wants often to discuss dildoes and vibrators and is always threatening to buy one for Lorna. She has a shtick in which she enumerates all the ways in which a vibrator is superior to a man. Lorna has heard many variations of this, and she finds it tedious, but she is a good friend, and besides, no one is perfect, and Lorna is no bargain herself.

Lorna arrives at her house, a stuccoed ranch in South Miami, enters it, and cranks up the window air conditioner in the living room, pausing a moment to stand in front of a chill blast. The living room is simply furnished—a Bahama sofa covered in beige Haitian cotton, a glass-topped coffee table, several canvas butterfly chairs in pale lemon, a cotton rug on the hardwood floor. Lorna's taste in painting runs to witty surrealism, and there are several pictures on the walls, all bought at art fairs in Coconut Grove. She goes into her bedroom and takes off all her clothes. It is cool in the bedroom because she runs the AC continuously from May to November, twenty-four/seven. Into the bathroom then, where she takes a quick, tepid shower and turns her eyes away from the black mildew springing from the tiles and the ceiling. A Guatemalan lady comes once a week, but she does not do mildew and neither does Lorna.

Naked but for a yellow towel, she goes into the kitchen and makes herself a gin and tonic, with a whole Key lime from the tree in the backyard, and drinks half of it down. Gasping a little, she returns to the bedroom and dresses in a light cotton shirt and bermudas. Then she goes into her office.

Lorna is a freelancer who works out of her home. The office is the largest room in the house, assembled by knocking out the wall between the second bedroom and what locals call the Florida room, a kind of enclosed stone-floored patio separated from the back garden by glass jalousies. From her desk she can look out through these to the croton bushes and yellow allamanders of the backyard. She sits in her swivel chair and enjoys this view, and the sound of birdsong, sipping her drink.

It is a strong one and she has not had anything for lunch. In a few minutes the buzz comes on. She relaxes and feels her face start to numb up. Doctors now recommend a drink a day as being good for the heart, she recalls (for she is an assiduous reader of medical advice), and drinks some more, enjoying the slosh and knock of the ice cubes against her teeth. She feels now the pleasant sense of accomplishment that eluded her upon leaving Dr. Lopez's office. Howie has been put in his place, an alliance with Lopez on a case, a professional opportunity to explore what could be a new species of craziness, maybe even a suggestion for a whole new subscale for the MMPI-2. That would really make her name in the world of psych testing.

Musing thus, she casts her eye around her office and finds it good. She has a large modern birch desk, an almost new computer with all the accessories, an expensive desk chair with lumbar adjustments, and lots of books. Except for a swath of wall devoted to diplomas and professional certifications, all the wall space is taken up by bookshelves. Lorna buys her clothes (nor are there many of them) on sale, takes few vacations (and these to the cheaper nearby islands), drives a six-year-old car. Her only luxuries are medical examinations and books. She has over four thousand volumes, and she has read them all, some of them twice. There is a teetering stack on a side table, books she has read but not shelved. She is about to stand up and shelve them, a practice that gives her a keen pleasure, when she notices that the light on her answering machine is blinking. She punches the button. The mechanical man in the device tells her she has three messages.

Betsy Newhouse's light voice: "Kiddo. Your reminder call—four-thirty at the gym. Be there or be pear." Beep. "Hi, it's me. Nice seeing you today. Give me a buzz. I'll buy you a salad." Kasdan, the rat bastard. Beep. An unfamiliar but pleasant voice says: "Dr. Wise, this is Detective Paz, Miami PD. I was the arresting officer in the Emmylou Dideroff case, and I'd like to talk to you about her. You can reach me anytime on my cell phone." He gives a number and hangs up.

Lorna reaches for the phone and starts to dial this number, if only to stop herself from calling the rat bastard *instantly,* then stops and hangs up. She has to think about this for a moment first. Paz is the cop Sheryl was talking about, the voodoo one, the potential date. She knew he had the arrest on Emmylou, but what could he possibly want with her?

Then, like a shark fin on a night ocean, a thought breaks the surface of her mind. The story about a new wrinkle in abnormal psych was enough to convince Mickey Lopez, and was a good story to tell herself, and might even turn out to be true. But that is not the reason she very much wants to (and, she just now realizes, is positively *driven* to) continue with Emmylou Dideroff. She now realizes, with a feeling that mixes wonder and dismay, and includes a funny hollow just below the belt line, that she has no idea what this reason is. Suddenly she is terrified, nothing to do with the case, she is convinced that there is someone else in her house. She freezes, listens. Someone breathing, a heavy rasping sound . . . or is that the air conditioner? Now she is in full panic mode, heart pounding, sweat springing freely. The sense of an alien presence is undeniable, it's in the room, it's right behind her. Her heart feels like it's bursting through her ribs. She lets out a gasp and spins around in her chair. Nothing.

It takes her the better part of an hour and two Valium to feel herself again. A panic attack, maybe a little fallout from the tension of the earlier meeting. So she tells herself, speaking aloud in the empty house. Her hands have stopped shaking now, and she picks up the telephone.

Jimmy Paz felt his cell phone vibrate against his hip but ignored it, allowing the voice mail to pick it up. He was standing in the auditorium of Miami-Dade Community College in a long line of people, all of whom were carrying copies of the same book. They were all waiting to get their copies signed by a pale young woman seated behind a table on the stage. The woman had marvelous corkscrew curls of red gold that glittered like a nest of Slinkys under the stage lighting. Her features were sharp and her eyes small and a little too bright, but she had a broad sensuous mouth. A few minutes ago she had finished reading from her poetry.

He arrived at the table and handed her the slim volume. She looked up, gave him the same nice smile she'd given to the fourteen people ahead of him, and said, "What should I write?"

"Whatever you want," he answered.

She wrote. He picked up the book and turned to the title page, where she had inscribed: *Come up to room 923 at the Grand Bay tonight at about eleven and I will fuck your brains out. Best Wishes, Willa Shaftel.*

"Do you write that kind of thing in everyone's book?" he asked.

"Of course," she said. "That's how you get to be a best seller."

"Then I better get in line right now," he said and, waving, took his leave.

Willa Shaftel had been one of Jimmy Paz's three main squeezes for a year or so, back when she'd worked as a librarian in Coconut Grove. Then she'd left and gone to Iowa on a writing fellowship, and when the first winter hit she'd spent three weeks in Miami, most of it with Paz and most of that in bed. During that time she had inveigled the story of how Paz had caught the Voodoo Killer, as well as details about the various ancillary characters attached to the story, and she had written a fairly successful novel about it, and no longer had to work in libraries. She came during the succeeding winter too, staying for six weeks this time, during which they saw each other nearly every day. Paz had never been deeply into fidelity, but after that he had found himself unwilling to look very hard for alternates. He'd even spent some long weekends at her tiny apartment in Ames, Iowa, a place nearly devoid of Cuban coffee.

Now he thought about her mouth. She really did have a most excellent mouth, and a hot skillful tongue, and she was the most actual fun to fuck of any woman he had ever known. He thought this might be the basis of a relationship more serious and permanent than any he had engaged in before. And she had spent a year in Spain studying Lorca and spoke a peculiar but elegant form of Spanish. No breasts to speak of, but she got along fine with his mother. All in all . . .

By this time he was out of the building facing the main plaza of the campus, which was tricked out in decorations and awninged booths for the book fair. Avoiding a mime, he found a little coffee bar, ordered a café con leche, and took out his cell phone. The voice mail service had a number of messages on it, only one of which was worth replying to just now.

"Dr. Wise? Detective Paz here. Thanks for returning the call."

"Uh-huh. Why . . . I mean, excuse me, I mean what can I do for you, Detective?" said the voice. Nice voice, he thought, husky, but a little slurred. And somewhat breathless. A few predinner cocktails maybe?

"This is about Emmylou Dideroff. I was the arresting officer on the case."

"Yes, you said."

"Well, she's writing a confession."

"That must've made your day."

"Not really," said Paz, starting to get a little annoyed. "I mean if she's crazy, the confession doesn't do anything for us. But it wasn't, I mean it's not a regular confession. She asked for a bound notebook, the schoolroom kind, not a spiral. I got her four of them at Staples. She wants to write down all her crimes, she says."

"She's delusional," said Lorna. "As a matter of fact, she mentioned a confession in our interview, but in any writing she does it's going to be hard to distinguish fantasy from what really happened."

"Just what I thought," said Paz brightly. "That's why I called you."

"I see. And why me specifically? I mean there are a zillion shrinks in Miami, and a lot of them are on government payrolls already. And I guess you know I'm not a psychiatrist."

"Yes, Doctor, I know. I'm a detective. The reason is I wanted someone independent, not an employee of the criminal justice system. So I happened to run into Leon Waits because I yanked one of his troopers for the detective squad, and he was giving me heat over it, and I remembered that his wife was some kind of therapist and I asked him could I call her and get a recommendation, and I did and the first name she came up with was you. And then I checked the file and found you were on the case already. It was magic. So the question is, will you do it?"

There was a pause on the line and what sounded like a sigh. "Do what?"

"Just read what she writes. Help me figure out what's what from a psych perspective. We'll get you a rate from the department. I cleared it already."

"Okay, right, but what I don't understand is why you're so concerned with Emmylou Dideroff. I mean is this something to do with clearing the case? Getting a conviction? Because if that's the situation, then I'm not sure I—"

"No, it has nothing to do with the murder we got on board now."

"Then what does it have to do with?"

"Are you using a cordless phone?"

"Yes, why?"

"And I'm on a cell. I don't want a guy who ordered some electronics off the Internet listening in on this. We can talk at the party."

"What party?"

"Tomorrow. At Sheryl and Leon's. You're coming, right?"

She laughed for what seemed to him no particular reason, quickly stifled.

"How did you know?"

"I told you, I'm a detective," he said. "See you there."

# Seven

"Do you have any brains left," she asked into his ear, "or shall we continue?"

"No, I think you got the last neuron," said Paz. "And let me say that was quite a performance. Don't they have fucking in Iowa?"

"I wouldn't know," said Willa Shaftel disdainfully. "All I do is read and write. No, I tell a lie. Writers are horny creatures, and I have dabbled, but one has always the sense that they're collecting material, and that your every spasm is going to wind up in some novel."

"As mine did in yours, I couldn't help noticing."

"Oh, yeah, but that wasn't serious. It was just to make a shit-load of money so I could escape from the poet's poverty ghetto." A long sigh. "My God, I haven't been truly *nailed* like that in a coon's age." She stretched luxuriously and picked several of his chest hairs from her exiguous breasts.

"My pleasure," he said. "Anyway, you did good writing. I liked that line about the herds. 'There are openings in our lives of which we know nothing.'"

"'Through them the belled herds travel at will. Long-legged and thirsty, covered with foreign dust.' Yes. Did you actually read the whole book?"

"Yes, but the words don't stick in my mind the way they do when you say them. It's because I'm still in touch with the primitive oral tradition."

"As you so amply demonstrated this evening," she said. "Is this paradisical or what?" she asked the world. "He's not a wuss, packs a rod, and likes my poetry. A ten." She laughed and hoisted herself up on an elbow to look at him more closely. He had a more sober expression on his face than she was used to seeing there.

"Something the matter?" she asked.

"No." Meaning yes. "I was just thinking about something you said once. You were going on about how great I was, like you just did, one of your complimentary litanies . . ."

"Complimentary litanies is good."

"Yeah, all about how I was polite but not a sensitive New Age man, buy a girl champagne, show her a good time, a great lay, albeit with a penis of only moderate size, and then you said there was a forty-foot-wide state highway sign over me that read DON'T GET SERIOUS, or something like that."

"Yes, DANGER! HEARTBREAK AHEAD. I remember. It was the night of one of the murders, when I went out to the crime scene and got you in trouble."

"Uh-huh. Well, I was thinking that I should take down the sign."

"Really."

"Yes, and you remember something else you said around back then, about Afro-Cuban-Jewish babies. When you were leaving for Iowa?"

"Ye-es?" Cautiously.

"Well, we should have some."

Her mouth dropped momentarily and then she laughed. "Jimmy Paz, are you *proposing* to me?"

He swallowed. Most of the blood seemed to be gone from his forebrain. "In a manner of speaking. The fact is that for, what is it now, fourteen months, you've been my only, I guess you could say, girlfriend. I think about you a lot, and not just lustful stuff . . . anticipation. And I've been thinking, okay, if not now, when?" He paused to check out her face. Paz was a professional judge of facial expressions, but he couldn't quite read hers now. Her eyes were wide, bright, and sharply focused, and there was a faint rosy blush on her cheeks. Romantic fascination? Or horrified traffic-accident fascination? He added, "I mean I didn't get a ring or anything. I wanted to sound you out first."

"That was wise," she said. "But then prudence has always struck me as one of your virtues." She groaned softly and wriggled half-upright, so that she was leaning against the head-board. "Gosh, I'm a little stunned. I had no idea. I mean, I thought we were great fuck-buddies and all, and now this. But it's not just *time*, is it? Not just, 'But at my back I always hear . . . '"

"'Time's wingéd chariot hurrying near.' No, not completely. I changed, more than I thought I had, since that summer, you know, with the killings. I used to—I mean this can't come as a surprise to you—have multiple girlfriends."

"Yes, I recall, having been of their number."

"Right. Three, four, five at any one time, up front about it and all, no sneaking, and either it was right for them or not, but I played it pretty straight, and I don't think anyone got hurt. Fun and games for healthy young adults, right? But since . . . what happened and all that, I don't know. I tried to, like, get back on the circuit, but nothing doing. I couldn't . . . I mean fun and fucking and fun . . . I started to feel like a jerk, like one of those assholes out on the Beach, forty-eight, on their second peel job, with the Tom Jones shirt and the gold chains. That's not me. So what is? And like I just said, the more I started thinking about that, the more I started thinking about you."

"And why me particularly, from out of the thousands? Now's the time for any litany of compliments you may have prepared."

He shrugged. "I don't know. I like you. We're funny together. You got your own life, you wouldn't be hanging on me to make you feel like a real person. Some of the people I work with have wives like that." He paused and added, "My mom likes you."

"Oh, *there's* a selling point!"

"Laugh if you want, but Margarita is a great judge of people. Plus you're not *like* her."

"No, I'm not. Continue . . ."

"You're smart as shit. You tell me poetry out of your head. I love your hair. And your skin. And your mouth. You have the hottest mouth in the world. And, finally, I believe I can say without fear of contradiction that we are sexually compatible."

"Mm. Of course, it's easy to be sexually compatible when there's nothing else on the table." Ten seconds later, without warning, she expelled a loud sob and then began to cry woefully.

Paz sat up in bed and held her while she trembled and

dripped tears and snot down his chest. "What's wrong? What'd I say?" he kept saying, but for once she couldn't find the words.

A little later, when she had gone to the bathroom and washed her face and dressed in the hotel's white terry cloth robe, she sat down on the edge of the bed and said, "Well, that was unexpected. I'm sorry."

"No problem. Let me guess. You like me, but not enough to marry me, and you didn't want to hurt my feelings. I'm assuming now it wasn't tears of happiness and we're going to rent the hall."

"No and no. No hall. And no, it's not about you at all. Oh, how to explain this so it doesn't sound like total lunacy? Come on, Shaftel, use your vaunted word power! It's like this: I don't have a heart. No, that's wrong, I have, but not one like you have. Not like regular people."

"Like the tin woodman?"

"Almost. The part that in normal people is occupied by living in a couple, loving, having children, making a home, is consumed by what I do. I fall in love, I have affairs. Hell, I'm in love with *you,* if it comes to that. You're my absolutely favorite man in the world right now. But it doesn't *mean* anything, Jimmy. Because I'm never going to *be* any different than I am now. All the growth and change is going to be in connection with the poetry and not within a couple. It's a little like being a nun, the kind that gets bleeding palms. And, you know, I'm on my super very best behavior when I'm with you. You haven't seen it working, when it's really voracious, when I stop washing and combing my hair and talking to people, and I eat cold chili out of a can. I'm talking weeks here. I'd kill a baby, I really think I would, just leave it in a car or in the bath and forget about it, like you read about."

"What, that's a rule, poets don't have kids?"

"Few do, and the ones they have are generally sad ones. It's probably not as bad for males. They can have *wives.* You're not a wife. Shit, I don't know, maybe it's the ghost of Sylvia Plath. Or Virginia Woolf . . ."

Paz stared at her. Virginia Woof? Fuck Virginia Woolfe! She was *rejecting* him? Fucking blowing him off? Smash her face. Smash her, break her nose, knock out her teeth, this fucking fat, white bitch this fucking *gusano* maggot was rejecting *him?* Stick his gun up her fucking *cunt* . . .

"Jim*eeeee!*" A high wail, a shriek.

Somehow Willa had slid off the bed and was now cringing in the corner of the room, on the other side of the night table. Her face, normally pale, was skim milk blue, except for heavy red marks around her neck and her eyes were rimmed with tears.

"What!" he cried. "What's wrong?"

"What's *wrong*? Jesus Christ, Jimmy, I thought you were going to kill me. It was like fucking Jekyll and Hyde. You grabbed my neck and you had your fist all balled up and cocked and you had an expression on your face . . . it was like something out of my goddamned *book*." She rose shakily to her feet. "I guess you're back to normal now, ha ha. What happened? A little problem with handling rejection?"

But Paz had no desire to return to badinage. He felt a wash of self-contempt, mixed with confusion and not a little terror. He started grabbing up his clothes and jamming his limbs into them. He was sticky and badly wanted to take a shower, but it didn't seem the thing to do just then.

"I'm sorry," she said. "I drove you literally crazy."

He stopped and looked at her. "No, I'm the one should be sorry. I don't know what the fuck just happened, but I don't think I should be alone with you right now. I'll call you," he said, picking up his jacket. He started for the door and then made himself stop and give her a nice hug.

"Shouldn't we sort of talk about this?"

"Nah, I don't think so. Sorry."

"The search for Miss Right begins immediately?"

"I guess." He embraced her again. "No hard feelings, Willa," he said into her hair. "You'll send me your next book."

"I'll do that," she said to his back and the closing door.

Paz went to his car and sat there for a while, watching his hands tremble. Gradually this passed as the rationalizing part of his mind, an industrial-strength unit, reinterpreted what had just occurred into something more normal, a mere flash of anger, mistaken by a hypersensitive and overimaginative woman as being something weird and alien. This done, he fell into a desperate numbness. It had simply never occurred to him that he would get turned down. Willa liked him, she'd said so, they got along fine. Everyone *knew* that girls wanted a permanent hookup, just like everyone knew that gravity sucked. Meeting the contrary was like observing an object falling upward. He noticed the yellow poetry book on the passenger seat. Suddenly seized by fury again, he grabbed it and flung it into the dark. Two minutes later he cursed himself, went out into the night-deserted street, and picked it up again. It was lying open, face-down, its bright yellow cover looking like a painting mistake on the yellow traffic line. He stood there in the middle of South Bayshore and read the poem on the page that had fallen open:

> *"Nothing lasts"*—
> *how bitterly the thought attends each loss*
>
> *"Nothing lasts"*—
> *a promise also of consolation*
>
> *Grief and hope*
> *the skipping rope's two ends,*
> *twin daughters of impatience.*
>
> *One wears a dress of wool, the other cotton.*

Paz felt a chill that was unconnected with the freshening bay breeze. He didn't like it when books fell open with meaningful messages showing. Even more irksome was that he actually felt consoled by reading it. He got back in his car and drove to his apartment, where he made himself a stiff drink of freezing vodka and lime. He changed into cutoffs and a sweatshirt and sat in a lawn chair in his backyard, chewing on the taste of the drink, dozing fitfully while the soft Florida night passed away.

When the sun was fully risen and he could no longer pretend that sleep was a possibility, he hit the bathroom, and afterward he pulled on a pair of checked pants from the restaurant service and a pair of greasy boots, and walked around the corner to Calle Ocho, where he had a café con leche and a fruit tart at his usual little no-name joint, and read the *Herald* and smoked a short, fat, strong, black cigar. Then he went across the street and opened his mother's restaurant.

There was something entrancing, he thought, about an empty restaurant early in the morning, rather like looking at a beloved but aging mistress at about the same time of day. You could see the scratches and wear that candlelight would obscure in the hours to come, but the revelation just added to the intimacy; no one else knew this side of her. He went into the kitchen, donned a tunic, a plastic apron, switched on the oil-splashed kitchen boom box. A samba band came on loud, Martinho da Vila, "Claustrofobia." Paz, bouncing a little on his toes, used his keys to open the meat reefer, walked in, came out with a whole round of beef, the entire boned hip of a steer. At the sink he stripped off the purveyor's thick plastic integument, washed the blood off the meat, dried it, and slapped it down on the butcher's block set against the wall between the two standing refrigerators.

If you sell a lot of beef in a restaurant, then the difference between profit and loss on those items is portion control, and at Guantanamera portion control was Jimmy Paz. Paz sharpened his favorite knife, licked the back of his left wrist, shaved a swipe of hair off with the blade, wiped it carefully away. Now he proceeded to turn a thirty-two-pound full round into (ideally) 102 *palomilla* steaks, each one weighing within a speckle of five ounces.

Paz sliced without obvious effort, peeling the red wafers off the mass, weighing each, and tossing each into a steel pan. This work took absolute attention if one were both to keep one's thumbs and make a buck, but made little demand on the higher functions, and from an early age Paz had used portion control to let his mind roam free. He belonged to that small fraternity of extremely bright men who have no patience at all with academics, from which is drawn most of history's entrepreneurial billionaires as well as those responsible for the physical maintenance of Western civilization: carpenters, masons, firefighters, soldiers, cops. Like most autodidacts, Paz had an original rather than a disciplined intellect, and much of what composed it had been put there across the pillow by a long skein of brainy women, the only sort he liked to take to bed.

His thoughts: how dumb could he have been, nearly twenty years of selecting from just that restricted set of women who *declined* to pursue permanent arrangements, and he's surprised when one of them turns him down, hilarious really when you considered it, what a jerk; possibilities of love, romantic love as against love that lasts, how to transit; *jerk,* Christ!; elective affinities, Goethean phrase whispered into his ear by German grad student white-blond Helga, idea that linkage of romance between two people was as natural and irresistible as chemical bonding, sodium and chlorine, no, not Helga, Trude, Helga was the Danish geologist, marine oolites, radiocarbon dating thereof in shallow seas, he'd taken her diving down at Pennekamp, should get the boat hauled and scraped soon, should *go out* in the boat sometime, find a girl, maybe run across to Bimini, where to find the time?; like a nun she said, with bleeding palms, stigmata, abnormal psych, varieties of religious experience, William James, skeptical acknowledgment of the reality of same, Beth the sociologist, not a believer but agreed with James's rejection of the "agnostic veto" insisting on rationality in decision imposssible to decide on rational grounds. Nature of faith, why can't he jump, given what he's seen, given his mother . . . and the crazy woman, Dideroff, or not crazy, those *eyes,* no, didn't happen, sleep deprivation, and the shrink, Wise, nice voice on the phone, and Sudan, Emma the geographer, the Sudan, sahel, savannah, ecotypes, ecotopes, dry, seasonal rains, thorny growth, the acacia, the baobab, something too about a civil war, she'd had to cancel a winter field trip, check that out . . .

He finished cutting and took the twenty-ounce cast-iron toothed mallet down from its hook above the butcher block and pounded steaks, making each one a quarter of an inch thick with just the correct number of blows, and afterward throwing each one into a bucket of the house marinade—garlic, lime juice, salt, pepper, and a bouquet of herbs whose composition was known only to Paz, his mom, and God. He pounded, pounded to the samba beat, and found (for this is why he had come in to do this task) that, as always, the work tenderized his heart along with the *palomillas.* Just before nine Rafael, the prep cook, came in and started parboiling a hundred pounds of potatoes, saying not a word to Paz, as he understood as well as any man the meditative aspects of pounding *biftek.* The kitchen grew warmer, sweat dripped from Paz's face, and he pounded the drops into the meat. His mother, demonstrating the process in the cramped steaming hole-in-the-wall kitchen of their first restaurant, twenty years previously, had said that Paz sweat was the real secret ingredient in their *palomilla.* Paz had believed it as a boy and believed it now.

The last steak dropped into the bucket. Paz washed and put away his knife and his mallet, stretched, doused his head under the sink, dried his face on a towel, and when he put it down there was his mother, yellow pantsuit, hair in its afternoon turban, a flowered one, hands and wrists ringed with pounds of gold.

"What's wrong," she demanded.

"Nothing's wrong, Mami," he said.

"You didn't sleep last night. You come in here, where I usually have to drag you, and you cut and pound out a whole round of beef. And"—here she waved her hand around his head, around the aura that she claimed to be able to see, jingling her many golden bracelets—"you're all cloudy and brown. So don't tell me nothing's wrong. It's some woman, hmm?"

"If you know, why do you even have to ask?"

"What happened?"

"Nothing, I told you. I just kind of broke up with Willa."

Mrs. Paz faced the heavens and jingled her hands at the uncaring gods.

"I will *never* have grandchildren. This is my fate. And there is something else . . ." She passed her hands through the air, as if trying to net a vapor. "An influence, a curse? God forbid! No, not a curse, but something heavy, dark . . ."

He turned away from her abruptly and covered the motion by taking off his apron. "Cut it out, Mami! You know I'm not interested in that kind of stuff."

"No, you're not interested, but it is interested in *you*. I tell you again, you have to be washed."

"No washing. I told you, I'm fine."

"Your woman left you, you're not fine, my son. And here I was so sure you were going to ask her to marry you."

"I did. She told me no."

"What! You said you loved her, that you could not live a moment more on this earth without her, and she said . . . what?"

"I didn't say that, Mami. I said we got along great together and we should, you know, make it formal, permanent. And she said no thanks."

"Of course she said no, you *besugo*! *Zoquete!* Don't you know that women like to hear that you love them?"

"Actually, I do know that, but I guess it turned out that I didn't. Sorry."

Cesar, the chef, walked in, picked up the vibes, decided he had forgotten something in his car, turned on his heel and vanished.

Paz had always had a hard time meeting his mother's glare, especially since, as he had observed from an early age, when Margarita was out of temper she seemed to increase alarmingly in size. She was a broad-shouldered woman, well muscled from years of heavy work, nearly as tall as her son, teak-colored, with elaborately processed and braided hair, glossy as licorice, still stunning in a harsh way at fifty. Now she towered over Paz (so it seemed to him) like a Latina Godzilla, and her nostrils were flaring preparatory, he knew, to reciting the tale of his failures, starting at age four. He therefore felt immense relief when a tingle at his belt line informed him that he had a cell phone call. He whipped it out and punched the button.

"Sorry, Mami, I got to take this. Police business."

"Don't give me police business when I'm talking to you!"

Paz headed for the rear of the kitchen with a parting mumble: "Why don't I just give you a sperm sample, you can forget about marrying me off."

"What! What did you say?"

He ignored this and scooted out the rear door. In the parking lot, he leaned against his car, put the phone to his ear, and heard the voice of his new partner, tentative.

"Jimmy? Morales. I'm not disturbing you or anything?"

"No, I explained this, man—you *can't* disturb me, I'm your partner. You got something I need to know, then any hour of the day or night is cool. I could be getting a piece of ass, I got to take your call. And the same the other way around."

"I mean what you were saying about a sperm sample? I thought . . ."

"No, that was just my mother. What've you got?"

A pause here. Then Morales said, "Okay, I checked out David Packer off of the motorcycle license. He's had the bike for a year and change, no violations. I called the credit bureaus, like you said, and they got nothing on him."

"What do you mean, nothing?"

"I mean there's no credit history on a David Packer, SSN 092-71-9116. He must pay cash."

"Do you believe that? A middle-class-looking guy, owns a

boat and a twenty-eight-grand motorcycle, never had a credit card? What does the phone company say?"

"Pays the minimum by check, no long-distance calls. The bank says he gets a U.S. government check for $2,467.18 deposited every month, and various checks from brokerages quarterly. He's good for about fifty grand a year, but he owns the boat and the bike free and clear, so he's doing all right, I guess."

"I guess. You call that passport bureau number I gave you?"

"Yeah, and that was another funny thing. I couldn't find out if he has a passport or not. I gave the girl on the line his information and there was a long hold and then she said she couldn't release that data, it was restricted and she gave me a number to call, her supervisor. Floyd Mitchell."

"And what did Mr. Mitchell have to say?"

"I couldn't get him. The phone just rang, no answering machine or anything. So I called the State Department locator and asked for a Floyd Mitchell, and they said there was no such person there. So I called the passport number again and the same thing happened, and I told them all about no Floyd Mitchell, and then after about ten minutes on hold, a guy came on and said he was Floyd and could he help me."

"And did he?"

"Not much. He said the computer was messed up and they couldn't extract the information I wanted, but if I left my name they'd get it to me when the computer got fixed."

"Yeah, Florida'll be underwater by then. Well, well. A man of mystery, old Dave. What about the other guy?"

"Oh, he was no problem. John F. Wilson, aka Jack Wilson, bought the business about two years ago. Before that he worked as a chief mechanic for Empire Boat Livery in Hallandale, eight years; before that he was in the navy. Credit's good, he pays his bills on time, owns a house in the Gables and a two-year-old Lexus. Plus the truck."

"He worked for Empire," said Paz. "Well, what d'you know?"

"You heard of it?"

"Oh, yeah. It belongs, or belonged, to a guy named Ignacio Hoffmann. Ignacio had a fleet of Cigarette boats, which he typically did not rent out to Dad and Johnny to go fish for snapper off Fowey Rocks. Did a lot of night work out in the Straits."

"But he's not still in business?"

"No, the feds busted him, must've been three or four years back. One of his people ratted him out, they got him on a federal indictment, he paid his million-dollar bail in cash, and took a hike. Interesting. I bet Wilson bought his business for cash."

"I don't know," said Morales. "I could check."

"Hm. Hell, what does it matter? We're not interested in Hoffmann or Wilson except where they connect to Emmylou. You do any good with all those business cards?"

"Yeah, he visited one of them the morning of the day he got it. I called but the guy was out."

"Just hold off on that until I get there. We'll go see him together."

"**O**kay, what do we know about this guy?" Paz asked when they were in the official Impala and heading east on Flagler. Morales was driving while Paz took his ease, like a prince, and smoked a cigar. Paz was pleased with himself and looked at his new partner benignly.

"He's in the oil business," said Morales. "The spot market, whatever that means. Our guy had an appointment with him the day he died. Seems okay, a citizen."

"But an Arab."

"That's not a crime."

"So far. No, but it's another ruffle on a shirt that's a little too fancy already. I wanted him to be a Cuban-American or a white-bread Presbyterian. A Jew would've been okay too. Our vic's an Arab on a federal watch list, the last person we know he saw before getting whacked is an Arab. . . ." He shrugged. "It's probably nothing."

"Could I ask you something?" said Morales, after a pause. Now they had turned onto Second Avenue. Traffic was heavy, but they were in no rush.

"Ask."

"What the fuck is going on?"

"Be more precise."

"I meet you by accident and a couple of days later I'm a homicide detective. My lieutenant knows diddly-squat about it. I go into the squad bay and everyone treats me like I got a contagious skin condition. Then you get me working on a case I know is closed. Is that enough to start? This is our building here."

"Park it in the bus stop," said Paz. "Okay, I was wondering when you would get around to asking. You're in because I needed a partner. Oliphant's orders, and I pulled some strings of my own. Why you? Why *not* you? First, while you haven't done anything particularly brilliant, you haven't fucked up either, and I liked the way you handled yourself at the crime scene. You didn't puke and that scene was fairly puke-worthy. A small thing, but what you might call a sine qua non for a homicide dick. No heaving. It fucks the crime scene and disturbs the witnesses, if any. Also, you followed my lead at the scene without me having to write it out in big letters and pin it to your shirt. You'd be surprised at the number of guys who can't do that. Finally, I kind of like giving orders to a white Cuban. That enough on your first question?"

"Yeah," Morales snapped.

Paz didn't answer immediately. He was staring at the side mirror.

Morales said, "What's up?"

"Nothing, I thought I saw something. I'm getting paranoid in my old age. And you're pissed, but I'm being truthful with you. I'm modeling the right behavior. Lie to your wife, your girl-friend, your mother, whatever, but never lie to your partner. Get mad at him if you want, but don't lie. Okay, next question. A kid patrolman with no apparent clout gets a high-visibility, high-prestige appointment. What do the other members of his new organization believe? Think!"

Morales thought for a while and then a look of dismay came onto his face. "They think I'm a rat?"

"Half of them do, given this is the Miami PD. They think IA is putting a mole into the bosom of the homicide unit. The other half is trying to figure out who you know, who're you connected to, what faction you're from, so they know if they should kiss your ass or kick it. Also, you're *my* partner, so that adds a little extra salsa to it, guys are going to give you grief just because you're with me. They don't much like me on the fifth floor. It hurts, but I try to live with it." He smiled, and after a brief hes-itation, Morales returned it.

"Okay, I can live with it too. Now tell me why we're working on a closed case."

"Because we've been told to. And the case may not be all that closed. You understand what I'm saying?"

Morales nodded vigorously. "Packer is wrong, Wilson is wrong, the victim's on an FBI watch list, the suspect is nuts, and this Arab in the oil business. Too many ruffles on the shirt."

"You got it. Speaking of which, do you have any money?"

"You mean *on* me?"

"No, in the bank. Like a couple of grand you can spare."

"I guess. Why?"

"You need to get some serious clothes. I'm wearing a fourteen-hundred-dollar suit and three-hundred-dollar shoes and you're wearing a piece of shit looks like you got it for first communion. What does that say, if someone looks at the two of us?"

"You like clothes more? I'm cheap?"

"No, it says I'm on the take and you're not. I want us both to look dirty."

"You want people to offer us bribes?" said Morales.

"See, I was right about you. You look like a choirboy, but you have a devious mind. Exactly right. Since I've been working solo I had three people offer me money. Best way of breaking a case ever invented. The guy's got money in his hand, you got it on tape, it's like his dick is hanging out of his pants. Prosecutors love it. After this, we'll go shopping."

The building was a ten-story brick near the Metro elevated route, white marble/black glass with a coral stone fountain in the lobby. Michael Zubrom had an office on the eighth floor fronted by a teak door on which raised bronze letters told the passerby that Polygon Brokers, PLC, would be found within. The reception area was small, with a glass gate for the receptionist. Zubrom himself, who came out to greet them, was a short, compact, olive-skinned man of around forty, with a fine head of dark hair, a beaked nose, and a look of knowing more than he ever said. They showed their badges and followed him in.

His office was messy, a place of work rather than a stage for acting successful—framed maps of the world on the wall, with pins in them, bookcases full of technical reports, drooping piles of printouts, and a rack of television monitors, four in all, silently flickering. They sat on dusty chairs, and Mr. Zubrom sat behind his cluttered desk, peering at them from between a computer monitor and a tall stack of oil industry journals.

"So, the police," he said. "I have to tell you at the start that I really don't know very much about this Sudanese." His voice was slightly accented, a familiar one.

"Excuse me, sir," said Paz in Spanish. "Is it possible that you are Cuban?"

A little smile. "No, I'm Mexican," he answered in the same language, "actually, Palestinian-Mexican. This is a branch of my family's Mexico City office."

Paz switched back to English. "And what was Mr. al-Muwalid's business with you on the day he died?"

"He sold me some oil."

"Like a sample?"

"More than that. Do you know what the spot market in petroleum is?"

"Not really," said Paz.

"Well, it's simple in concept, complex in practice. Perhaps police work is the same? Let me try to explain the concept at least. Oil is a valuable and fungible commodity. A barrel of sweet light crude, let us say, is the same in a tank in Dubai, on a ship in midocean, in a pipeline in Russia, and the rights to these barrels are traded just like currency. I come from a family that is fluent in Arabic, Spanish, and English, and so we can deal with most of the people in the world who have oil to sell."

"Why Miami?" asked Morales. "Why not Houston?"

"Good question. For that matter, why not stay in Mexico? The answer is that sometimes it's better that nobody knows your business. In oil towns everybody is looking to see who is visiting who, who's in town from Venezuela, the Gulf, Norway, Nigeria. In Miami, this little hole-in-the-wall office, it's better for privacy, for certain deals that require discretion." Zubrom's eyes kept flicking from Morales to his array of screens.

"And al-Muwalid had that kind of deal?" asked Morales.

An elegant shrug. "Mm. You understand that the spot market is abstract. We bid and contract for, you could say, only chips, markers, as in a casino. Promises to deliver at a certain price. But occasionally we have a situation where someone is selling to us a specific lot of actual petroleum, and this was the case with him. He said he had eleven thousand barrels in a tanker at Port Sudan. He had the papers, the clearances from the government there, so I did the deal. Oil is fungible, as I said, it's all one big pool more or less. Just a moment, please."

He looked at his screen and tapped his keyboard. "Sorry. There is something in Singapore I have to attend to."

Paz said, "Mr. Zubrom, what you have to attend to is us, right now. You were probably the last person to talk to the victim before he was murdered. He might have been murdered because of something that happened in this room. Maybe we should go downtown. . . ."

This remark obtained somewhat more of the man's attention, although they could see he was straining his peripheral vision to keep track of the flickering numbers and the feeds on the Bloomberg and the set tuned to CNN. "No, please. And I really don't see how that could be. It was a very simple deal from my standpoint. Let me see what I paid. . . ." He punched some keys. "Yes. Twenty-nine-dollars-forty a barrel, base price, less commission, less fees, less insurance and so on, made $303,533.76, which I had transferred to a numbered account at the ARPM bank. In Jersey."

"Where in Jersey?" asked Morales.

Zubrom gave him a peculiar look. "Not the state. It's an island in the English Channel with loose banking regulation."

"Anything else?" said Paz. "Any indication of what his plans were, other appointments?"

"No."

"Any mention of a woman named Dideroff?"

"No. Really, Detective, I am in the middle of my business day. . . ."

"What else did he say, Mr. Zubrom?"

"Well, we did not exchange small talk. He was not a pleasant fellow, I am afraid. But many of the people in the oil business are like that. Especially the Africans, if I may say so."

"And why is that, sir?" asked Paz genially. "If I may ask."

Zubrom seemed taken aback by this question. He licked his lip and stammered a little. "They . . . they . . . I don't mean to be offensive, Officer."

"That's all right, Mr. Zubrom, I'm not an African. Go on. They what?"

"They lack . . . lack the idea of public property. If a man controls something, it is his own, like his shoe or his house, his and his family's, or clan or tribe. The nation is just a figure of speech. Now, my own nation is corrupt enough, but we have a sense of limits. We have our commissions and bribes, but we don't think that our oil is the personal property of the petroleum minister and his friends. I think in Nigeria, in Sudan, they do think that. I believe this Mr. al-Muwalid had connections that were able to divert a quantity of crude to this tanker, so he could sell it for himself, which he certainly did. But you asked what we talked about. After the deal was over, he relaxed a little. I gave him a drink. He gave me a tip."

"A tip?" said Paz.

"In a manner of speaking. He asked me what would happen if a new strike was made, an oil field say fifty times larger than the Widha and Kordofan and Adar Tel fields combined. These are the main Sudanese fields, you see. I told him that it would not have an immediate effect on the spot market, for the reason that it is still difficult to get oil out of Sudan. The oil is highly parafinized and requires heating, the pipeline through Khartoum is small, and almost all the oil is in the south, where it must be moved through the middle of a civil war. But as I said to him, a find of that magnitude might—"

"What are we talking about here," asked Morales, "Saudi Arabia?"

A patronizing smile. "Of course not. Saudi is in a class by itself; it has no serious rivals as far as reserves are concerned. Do you understand that at this time Sudan is a *tiny* producer? Reserves of perhaps point six billion barrels. I mean tiny compared to Libya, with nearly thirty billion proven and Iraq . . . who knows about Iraq these days? Anywhere from one hundred twelve through to as much as two hundred twenty billion barrels. So I said to him if you multiply point six by fifty you are in a class with Libya, and that is a very serious class, and if that were to happen, it would create a change on the geopolitical level, never mind in the spot market."

Another shrug, a hand gesture partaking of both the Middle East and Latin America, acknowledging the futility of expectations. "Perhaps. Depending on the quality and cost of production and so on. I told him I had not heard of any such find and he said, Oh, it is there, we know it is there, but we don't yet have the proof of it. He meant data for the oil companies, so they could begin development work. He was somewhat full of himself then, talking, I don't know, how he was going to be a key figure in the future of Sudan, if he could get the data on this field, and he knew someone who knew where it was, right here in this city. This is why he required this money, you see, for expenses, to hire people, to look, you know, hard people."

"For protection, you mean?" asked Paz. "He felt threatened?"

"I believe he did."

"Who by?"

"You know, he didn't say. We were not best buddies. He took a call on his mobile while he was here and left immediately after. In something of a rush as I recall. That is totally all I know about this man." He looked desperately at his screens. "Honestly, gentlemen, this is ruinous. I am losing money by the minute."

They thanked Mr. Zubrom and left.

In the car, Paz said, "That was good. You did good, you picked up his eyes."

"He was looking at me," said Morales, somewhat uncomfortably. "He hardly ever looked at you, even when you were talking to him."

"Uh-huh. A black guy and a white guy show up together, and nine out of ten people are going to assume that the white guy is in charge, even when the black guy is wearing Zegna and the white guy's got a JCPenney confirmation suit on. Life isn't fair that way, and it gives me a bad attitude sometimes, which I intend to take out occasionally on your lily ass. In this line of work, though, it works pretty good. I can slide something in where they're not looking. An off-balance informant is the policeman's friend, as we just saw. So what did you make of all that?"

"I don't know. The vic had a hold on some serious cash. He had enemies. He was looking for something worth a zillion bucks. We know the guy wasn't a sweetheart off of that FBI thing the major told you about, plus what the suspect said. So . . ." He waggled both hands.

"So it looks a little less like a loony having a fit and clocking the vic on the head."

"Yeah. You think maybe she was set up?"

"Oh, I think she did it, but I also think she had some help. We didn't recover a cell phone off the vic, did we?"

"No."

"And Emmylou sure as shit didn't have one. She's got one built into her head connected to a switchboard in heaven. So that means . . ."

"There was someone else in the place," said Morales instantly. "He took the cell phone so we couldn't find out who called him at Zubrom's, the call that got him moving."

"Very good. Drive on."

Morales pulled away from the curb and headed north of NE First Avenue. "Where are we going?"

"Bal Harbour," said Paz, "take a look at some suits. I think you're a keeper, but I want to see how you clean up. After that . . . shit, there he is again!"

"Who?"

"Guy in a white Explorer with tinted glass. He's been following us. Make this next left. *Now!*"

Morales stamped on the gas and swept across the oncoming traffic into a left turn, leaving screeching brakes and angry horns in his wake. Paz swiveled around in his seat, expecting to see the white SUV make the turn as well, but it proceeded north with the other traffic. He felt Morales's stare. "Wait here," he said, "pull over, he'll go around the block." Morales did so and they waited. After five minutes' silence, Morales asked, "Did you get his plates?"

"No, did you?"

An uneasy pause. "No. To tell you the truth, I didn't even see what car you were talking about. A white SUV? I didn't spot it. Are you sure . . . ?"

"Fuck, yeah, I'm sure!" Paz was almost shouting. "You think I don't know when I'm being tailed?" Paz had a moment of rage so intense he thought he was going to have a stroke right there in the unmarked. Irrational. He was seeing things. It could've been a white Explorer, and maybe next time it'd be a hearse with a zombie driver or a circus van playing a calliope. First that thing with Emmylou, then the craziness with Willa, now this, and he'd realized now that he'd screwed up the interview with Zubrom, he should have pulled the guy out of there, taken him downtown, and sweated him some more, the guy was laughing at them, he knew a lot more than he'd said, if he had a decent partner instead of this asshole kid, he would've gotten a lot more . . . no, that was not him, not a line of thought that should have appeared in his brain. Morales was fine. He felt cold sweat start up on his forehead and back.

"Hey, Jimmy—you okay?" Paz looked at Morales, at his pale and worried face.

"Yeah, it's nothing, I'm a little . . . just go, drive."

A little *what*? Paz asked himself as they rolled. A little crazy? Crazy he could deal with, but not the other thing, not the . . . the word *possession* floated into his mind. He skittered away from that and took refuge in the forms of old prayers and grasped certain objects hung about his neck. By the time they got to where they were going he felt nearly human again.

The next seven years went peacefully by for the de Bervilles. Georges's affairs prospered. He had cannily observed that the world of the mid-nineteenth century had a lust for illumination, and that whales could not possibly supply all the oil required. He therefore began to procure and sell kerosene and also invest in the illuminating gas companies that were then getting started throughout Europe. By 1870 Paris was being called the City of Light, a good deal of which light was being produced by Georges de Berville et Fils. Georges bought a large stone mansion in the most elegant district of Metz. The little house at Pony was sold and replaced by a substantial château, Bois Fleury, at nearby Gravelotte.

The children prospered as well. Alphonse, despite his youth, was if anything more canny than his father, as well as owning a charm that his elder could not match. He had been given responsibility for negotiation with the suppliers of petroleum. In 1869 he traveled across the Atlantic to America, where he soon became conversant with American ways of business, and met many of the leading figures of American industry, including the young John D. Rockefeller, who took an instant liking to the French youth, going so far as to bring him into his family circle, a rare honor.

Meanwhile, Jean-Pierre had entered St. Cyr. He had always loved horses and excitement and desired a career in the army. As for Gerard, the youngest boy, he had received a call to serve the Church during his education at St. Arnulf's, and was by the year in question living at the seminary in Montigny. Thus only Marie-Ange was left at home to care for her father, although she was a day student at the convent of the Sisters of Providence, located just down the Rue Richelieu from her family's elegant home. We know from her school records that she was a student of no great distinction, except in languages, where she excelled. At this time she was near fluent in both English and Italian; German she had, of course, spoken from childhood, along with most of the citizens of Metz. What sort of girl was she then? In answer, we have from this period some letters written by Marie-Ange to her mother's sister, her beloved Aunt Aurore, who lived in Paris. In one of these, she writes:

*I confess my heart is torn between my desire to serve Christ as a nun and my love for my dear father, and my sacred obligation to him. He has been so good to me and has suffered so much! He wishes me to come out in society and go to balls like other girls do, and after that to marry, the poor man! How I wish I could oblige him, but I cannot. I do not care for balls, and, whatever may come, I shall never marry.*

It is clear from this that the vocation of the Bd. Marie-Ange de Berville came early and strong.

—FROM *FAITHFUL UNTO DEATH:*
*THE STORY OF THE NURSING SISTERS*
*OF THE BLOOD OF CHRIST,*
BY SR. BENEDICTA COOLEY, SBC,
ROSARIAN PRESS, BOSTON, 1947.

# Eight

The
## CONFESSIONS
of
## Emmylou Dideroff

### Book II

*It is strange to be confessing to you instead of to God, but then I always thought it strange to confess to God, especially in writing. If God exists, He clearly must know the evil you've done without a spoken word, much less a written one. Still, penance is a sacrament. You have to confess, although they call it reconciliation now. The act of speaking is necessary to reconcile us with God and restore the sinner to His grace and friendship, although it is little used now and the confessional booths are either gone from the churches or stand empty. I missed all that, coming late to the faith, but you being a cradle Catholic should understand, if the cop in you hasn't chewed all that up by now. I hope not. I am confessing to the Christ in you, you know, even if you don't believe in it, still it works, although I think it is better if you are open to it. I know you are open to that part of life, if against your will.*

*St. Augustine says in a late work that he wrote the Con-*

*fessions to excite his mind and affection toward God and he (modestly) admits that the book continues to have that effect upon its readers. He also wrote it to turn away scandal when they wanted him for bishop, and his enemies pointed to his misspent youth, deep in sex and heresy. It has been four years and around eighteen weeks since my last confession, an old-fashioned face-to-facer with Father Manes in the tin-roofed church at Wibok. If I'm uncertain about the time it's because time flows differently in south Sudan and we don't keep your calendar.*

*No, I can't get into that yet, in confessing it's important to keep to a strict chronology, as sin breeds upon sin. Sin is a vector, you know, not a scalar. It's not a <u>load</u> of sin, it's a velocity, either downhill or up. To return to God from a life of sin you have to retrace your steps, plot the back azimuth, undo the evil. In theory. In practice I'm not sure you can. For most people they think it's themselves, they're pursuing their good, oh, I'll just take this little bit of money, oh, I'll just take this girl to bed, and on and on, I mean all that's just superstition, the smartest thing the devil ever did was convince people he don't exist, but some of us can see him plain, can't we, can feel him working in us, like watching a bug crawl up your arm, I know <u>you</u> can, Mr. Policeman, I know you can feel him hanging there just behind your shoulder, giving you thoughts you think you shouldn't have and dreams too I bet*

*Avoiding again, it's so much easier to look at other folks than your own self.*

**A**nyway, I zoomed over to Oystershell Road on my bicycle, following the dim pencil of my little headlamp, lucky not to be run over on the way, hearing distant sirens. Hunter was counting money and he came to the door of his trailer with a sawed-off Mossberg twelve hanging down his leg. He let me in, and I saw stacks of bills, mostly tens and twenties, piled on the drop-down table, and a duffel bag open on the floor where he was tossing the counted stacks. I was pretty calm, considering, as I told him what had gone down at Gulf Avenue, omitting my own contributions. His response was to say holy shit a bunch of times and then go back to the table and ask me if I wanted to help him count up. Hunter was hard to believe sometimes.

I said we have to get out of here, out of Caluga, now, tonight, this minute, and he said no way are you fuckin' crazy, and I told him what Orne Foy had said about Ray Bob being paid off and they would find out and he didn't have protection anymore and if the cops busted his stupid trailer, which they would in about a half hour on account of looking for me and the cops knowing I was connected with him, he would go to Raiford and spend the next twenty years of his life getting fucked in the ass by big niggers. He sort of stood there with his mouth hanging open, so I turned on the spigots and said all about how much I loved him and wanted to get out of this shitty place get to a real city and have a life, a real apartment and do clubs and concerts and nice clothes and I would help him, etc., etc. The real reason, of course, was that I did not want to be around when they sliced Momma open and found all those caps with no tranquilizers in them and figured it all out. I didn't think I had done any kind of real felony there, but it would not have been pleasant after that to be an orphan girl in a town run by the Dideroff clan and their pals.

Before long we were on his funky bed and he wanted to fuck me but I blew him instead because I didn't want to be all sticky and sweaty for the ride downstate. I recall thinking how dumb men were, it wasn't nothing to control them, it was like they all had like this TV remote in their pants, you could change their channel anytime you wanted. Except Orne, of course, or so I thought then.

So we were off to Miami me making Hunter drive slower than he usually liked to so as not to risk a traffic stop. I did make him go to a mall outside Orlando, parked there in the empty lot as the dawn broke, eating a takeout breakfast, waiting for it to open. I wanted to get me some decent clothes and makeup, so I could disguise myself and look older. We also stopped at a used car place and traded the pickup for a four-year-old T-bird and cash. I had to explain to Hunter that we were through being trash and no one was going to rent us the kind of place I wanted for us unless we showed some class. I was going to drive up to the rental people in our respectable car dressed in my respectable clothes and pay the rent with a check with our names printed on it.

I spotted a storage locker place from the interstate and made him pull off and I rented a locker to keep our dope and cash in and we drove into the city and checked into a Ramada. Hunter was cranky because I hadn't let him bring any dope along, but I made him clean up and we had a big meal at a Red Lobster nearby and then we bought some beer and I fucked him into unconsciousness. After that, I got the little book he kept the accounts in from his dope business and found Orne's number. It was hard to get in touch with him by telephone. You had to call a little grocery store near where he lived in Virginia and leave a message. He called back in a couple of hours though. I told him what had transpired in Wayland (edited) and my thinking and he said it was the right thing to do but to hold tight and definitely do not try to sell any weed in Miami and he would get back to us real soon.

The next day I dressed in my outfit, which I had copied from the mommies of the gifted and talented girls in Wayland, a little tan suit, a white linen blouse with no sleeves, a string of fake pearls and kind of expensive tan shoes, panty hose, and a leather bag, and enough makeup to make me look not seventeen. I took Hunter's cash ($12,580) and opened an account at a Citibank nearby, after which I drove to a real estate office and rented a furnished apartment in a town house out on Bird on the far side of the expressway, giving as my name Emily Louise Garigeau, which was not the name on my driver's license, but that was OK because I was a newlywed and the real estate lady cooed oh how lovely and said there were a lot of other couples just like us out in our development (West-

*field Lakes), so we would be right at home. I got us a
phone and turned the utilities on, although it used up a
lot of our cash for the different deposits, because neither
of us had any credit record or even a Social Security number. I got rid of all the paper with my old name on it and
took out a driver's license with the new one.*

*Well, there we were, a pair of high school dropouts from
the boonies living among the striving squares, guys who
ran Burger Kings, women who groomed poodles, mail carriers, airport workers, the people who assistant-managed
the big stores, Home Depot, Staples, and it hit me (but
probably not Hunter) that this was the life I was slotted
for, this was what girls like me were supposed to aspire to
if we kept our nose clean and finished high school, and I
knew right then it was not for me. I was a criminal in my
deepest soul, delighting in what was wrong. Getting
money would not be a problem, with all that dope in the
storage all just waiting for Orne Foy to tell us what to do
with it, and had some other ideas which I did not share
with Hunter like being a very very high-priced hooker if I
could learn how.*

*You can take the boy out of the country, as the saying
goes, and Hunter was a good example. He started slipping
bricks of dope out of the stash and smoking it around the
house, which was bad enough, but then he went and
parked near Palmetto Springs high school and began moving product. When I tried to reason with him, he cursed
me out and said if it wasn't for me he never would've had
to leave home, like he'd left some mansion on the hill and
was living in a shithole instead of the other way around
and when I pointed this out and told him I was going to
tell Orne he was selling weed without his say-so, he
punched me out, not that bad because I knew how to roll
with it and he was pretty stoned, but that was it for me and
Hunter. The next day I called Orne and left a message,
but he didn't get back to me until it was too late.*

*They don't like you selling dope around high schools in
Florida, at least not right out in the open. The cops don't*

*like it and neither do the other dope dealers. Someone
must've dimed us because two nights after I called Orne
our door crashed in and we were surrounded by cops with
lights and guns yelling and screaming, me with my bare
ass hanging out of a T-shirt on the couch in the living
room, and we were busted with felony weight.*

*They seized all our money and cars and stuff because it
was the produce of drug dealing and they discovered the
key to our storage locker and thirty kilos of primo
sensemilla dope. Naturally they wanted Hunter to tell
who his dealer was, but he didn't, because I will say one
thing for the Foys, they stick together. This pissed them off
no end, and even though they could clearly see he could
hardly tie his shoes they treated him like a major trafficker, and I guess he was headed for a long visit with his
daddy at the Union prison up in Raiford. I pretended to
be a little slow, which I knew how to do pretty well from
my days with the dumb kids, and gave my name as Emily
Garigeau, so as to avoid any connection with Caluga
County, and they figured Hunter was this big drug mastermind and all the stuff I had planned and accomplished
in Miami was me being some kind of robot obeying his orders. Juveniles don't get real trials, so I went in front of a
lady judge and cried a lot and got confused, and said I
was an orphan and when they asked me where I was from
I said it was a blue trailer in Alabama I didn't know the
town, ma'am, it was near a tree hit by lightnin'? They sent
me to Agape House, a residential facility in Dade County
for girls needing drug treatment or if they had behavioral
disorders. I guess they figured dumb was one of those,
close enough anyway. It was a Jesus place and we had to
sing hymns. I had a six-month sentence, but it was a
minimum-security facility, and after three days I was over
the fence and away in just the clothes I stood up in.*

In another letter we find:

> You will laugh, but in the dull warm afternoons I sit here in
> Gravelotte and imagine what sort of nun I shall be, if I ever
> get my courage up to tell my father of my intentions. As you
> know, I am far too stupid to be a scholarly Benedictine, and
> too nervous to make a good contemplative. The Carmelites
> would not have me with a queen's dowry! I think that what I
> would really like is to help the sick, as our Lord did. I have
> read with interest the reports of Miss Florence Nightingale
> and think it a shame that the English should be so far in ad-
> vance of us here in Catholic France, as it was we who in-
> vented the very idea of hospitals. I know that there are now
> some congregations of religious who do such work not in
> hospitals, but in the homes of the poor and helpless, and I
> think I would like that. I have a strong stomach and am not
> frightened of blood, or troubled by horrid smells. Would
> you be so kind as to look into the Institut de Bon Secours de
> Paris, and tell me what you think. Oh, and, although it is
> very wicked to ask this, would you please not tell Papa!!

It is not known whether Aurore Puyot ever told her brother-in-law
about these notions, but in any case, events were to overtake them all,
bring an end to Marie-Ange's girlhood in Metz and set her feet on the
course they were to follow for the remainder of her life. In August of
1870, while she sat penning this letter, perhaps in the gazebo at Bois
Fleury that overlooked the small river Mance, war came to her nation,
bringing its dread tide to her very doorstep.

From the start this war did not go well for France. The French
Army of the Rhine fell back through Metz on its way to Verdun,

with the Germans in pursuit. On the morning of the 16th of August, Marie-Ange was awakened by the sound of horsemen in the courtyard of the château. As she expected the arrival of her brother Jean-Pierre on convalescent leave, she ran down the stairs in just her robe and slippers, pausing at the door to throw on a blue uniform cloak of her brother's that was hanging there. Yet when she burst through the door, she found to her dismay not her brother's coach, but a troop of Prussian uhlans.

—FROM *FAITHFUL UNTO DEATH:*
*THE STORY OF THE NURSING SISTERS*
*OF THE BLOOD OF CHRIST,*
BY SR. BENEDICTA COOLEY, SBC,
ROSARIAN PRESS, BOSTON, 1947.

# Nine

Lorna follows Darryla Chambers down the Pine Sol–perfumed corridors of Jackson Memorial Hospital toward the locked ward run by the Division of Forensic Services. Darryla is a large woman, so large that much of Lorna's field of view is occupied by her blue scrubs, the broad back and shoulders, the spectacular rolling buttocks. Darryla the Gorilla to the wards, but this is because of her size and not, as far as Lorna knows, because of either her ferocity or the color of her skin. She is actually a gentle and caring person, who brooks, however, no shenanigans from her criminous lunatics. As she walks, Lorna continues her reflections on large women. Judge Packingham is large, larger than Darryla, really, a set of shoulders like a linebacker in pads, her face flat and pale beneath a ridiculous little gray perm, those black robes accentuating the hugeness. Packingcrate they call her around the courthouse, the usual cruelty. A few decades back she had worked for Janet Reno in the state's attorney, and they used to say that she was the box Janet had come in.

At the hearing the judge did the right thing, really the only thing she could have done given the agreement among the headshrinkers and the acquiescence of the prosecutor. Emmylou was deemed incapable of assisting with her own defense and remanded to Jackson for thirty days' observation. The defendant sat quietly during the twenty-minute hearing and answered in a clear voice when the judge explained to her what was about to happen. She seemed to Lorna at that moment the furthest thing from crazy.

That was the day before yesterday, and now Lorna is about to visit Emmylou for the first time. She catches up with Darryla and asks, "How is she settling in?"

"Dideroff? Shoot, give me a couple more like her I could get rid of half my staff."

"What do you mean?"

Darryla pauses to open a locked door with one of the large ring of keys she carries at her waist. She motions Lorna through, then follows, locking the door behind her.

"Spends most of her time writing in a school notebook. Besides that . . . well, the population always responds to new people, usually by getting upset. There's a new mix on the ward, in the dayroom, you know? But this time, it seems like she calms everyone down."

"She calms them?"

There is a nurses' station inside the door, and Lorna signs in on a clipboard.

"Yeah," says Darryla, "she reads them stuff from the Bible. And explains it, like it was the newspaper, not preachy or anything."

The dayroom smells of people and bleach, not unpleasant really, compared with some of the booby-hatch dayrooms Lorna has experienced; this is because the inhabitants are the dangerous rather than the incontinent type of nut, and many are not nuts at all, but mere criminals feigning madness. Darryla gestures and Lorna sees that Emmylou is sitting on a couch with a book open on her lap. Two women, one black and one white, are sitting on either side of her on the peeling vinyl, and the black woman is stroking her arm. Emmylou's lips are moving, but Lorna is too far away to hear what she is saying and something in the scene disturbs her so much that she does not wish to come any closer. She observes, however, that of the two dozen or so people in the dayroom, somewhat more than half are paying attention at varying levels to Emmylou, while the rest are conversing with the usual demons: some unseen, some on the screen of the television set hanging from the ceiling.

"You can use therapy room B," Darryla says. "I'll go get her for you."

Lorna leaves the dayroom and walks down the hallway. A smiling figure blocks her way, and it takes her a moment to recognize Rigoberto Munoz. Rigoberto has been cleaned up and looks as normal as deteriorated schizophrenic street persons ever look: only mildly nightmarish. The man grimaces involuntarily and says, "Hi, Doc." Lorna assumes a professional smile and they chat. Rigoberto is doing fine, is scheduled for release. To where? The man looks doubtful. He thinks his cousin in Hallandale will take him in. Lorna makes a winding gesture with her hand. "So that's okay now?" Rigoberto shuffles and looks embarrassed. "Oh, yeah, no problem," he says as his tongue shoots out and does an elaborate lip lick. Lorna is happy that Munoz no longer thinks his penis is being reeled into his abdomen by aliens, but she does not wish to know much more about his mental state or plans. It is not her job.

She excuses herself and enters Therapy B, which is a room about half the size of a high school classroom, containing nothing but chrome and plastic chairs in cheerful colors and a couple of Formica-topped tables. She sits and takes her notebook and tape recorder from her bag. In a minute or so, Emmylou comes into the room, dressed in a gown and a striped bathrobe and paper slippers. Lorna gestures to one of the chairs, and Emmylou sits in it. Lorna sees she is carrying the book she had in the dayroom; not surprisingly, it is a Bible.

"So you decided I was crazy," says Emmylou, smiling, gesturing to the environment.

"We decided you couldn't effectively help your own defense," says Lorna primly. "Like the judge said, you've been sent here for observation and treatment. How are you doing on your meds?"

"They make me sleepy and dull."

"We can have the dosage modified."

"To zero?"

"Well . . . I'll speak to Dr. Lopez and see if we can't get you more comfortable. Meanwhile, you seem to be adjusting well. You're writing, I understand."

Emmylou nods and holds up her Bible, and Lorna can see that there is another, slimmer book clutched beneath it. "Uh-huh. Detective Paz got me these notebooks. I finished the first one already."

"Well, I'm sure we'd like to read it. Darryla tells me you're reading to the other patients. I saw you in the dayroom."

"Yes, I like crazy people," Emmylou says. "They do less harm than the sane, and many of them are close to God. One of the hard things about being crazy is that people stop looking at you like you're a soul. And I touch them, and help them to pray, if they're possessed. Sometimes it works."

Lorna's throat is suddenly dry, almost crackly and painful. She swallows, wishing she had thought to bring a bottle of water. She thinks she is nervous because she has not done any real therapy in a long time, assuming that is what this is. Could it be that she fears the mad? No, nonsense, put that out of the mind! A little initial nervousness, which she assuages by fiddling with the recorder. She falls back on the good old Rogerian ploy, affirm the patient by repeating her statement. She says, "Possessed."

"Mm-huh. Of course, if I believe that, that's another symptom of me being crazy, right?" Emmylou has been staring down at her hands and the Bible she carries, as if anxious to return to the sacred realms, but now she lifts her head and turns her eyes full onto Lorna's. This is highly unusual. Crazy people do not go in much for eye contact. For an instant there enters Lorna's mind the thought that Emmylou Dideroff is the furthest thing from crazy, that it is the hospital authorities and the psychiatrists and the guards and the real estate tycoons who control the city of Miami, and the people in Tallahassee and Washington, D.C., running the government who are crazy; for an instant another world appears to her inward eye, a world as real as stone or bread. But just as quickly a lifetime's defenses against this world take charge, and although the hairs stand up on her arms and a chill runs down her spine, she is able to pretend that nothing has happened, that she is in command of the situation, she with her Ph.D. and her pass out of here and this woman is an uneducated redneck lunatic murderess. . . .

Lorna clears her throat and says, "So . . . you think you can exorcise other people just by touching them?" The *e*-word in invisible quotation marks.

"Christ can," says the other confidently. "That was the main kind of thing he did when he was among us, and he still does it. Sometimes he uses me, sometimes other people. But we can all do it our own selves, really, Christ is driving out demons from the inside of us all the time, or the world would be a much worse place than it is, if you can imagine that."

"Mm. But . . . you don't have a demon in you, do you?"

"Who says I don't?"

"I thought you were conversing with saints."

A stunned look appeared on Dideroff's face. Her mouth gaped and then suddenly and surprisingly she bursts into hearty laughter, which she quickly brings under control, wiping at her eyes with the heel of her hand. "Oh, Lord, I'm sorry. That just struck me so funny. Lord!"

Lorna has not joined in this laugh, although the valuable word *hebephrenia* now swims up out of her memory, and she scribbles it down, followed a second later by a question mark. "Would you like to tell me what was so funny?"

"Oh, it's hard to put into words. Just, really, you assuming that demons and saints can't dwell in the same person, or not even that, because it's pretty plain you don't believe in either saints or demons dwelling in folks and you were trying to, I don't know, catch me out with some kind of lawyer's trick, when it's just so plain that it's just the ones who are most afflicted by demons who get to be saints. What you said, to a religious person, it'd be like saying, oh, because you're sitting in the dark, that means you *can't turn on the light!*" Here she lets out a little giggle. "That's why I laughed. I'm sorry."

Lorna decides to forget everything but this apology. "Emmylou, I'm not offended. I'm just trying to help you."

"To . . . ?"

"Pardon?"

"You're trying to help me to . . ."

"I believe you're mentally ill. I'm trying to help you get better."

"So that I can be tried for murder."

"Well, yes, so that you can aid in your own defense. But it seems to me that you could develop a pretty strong presumption that when you committed the crime you're charged with, you were not legally sane."

"I don't see how that could happen. I haven't got a mental disease and I sure didn't murder Colonel al-Muwalid."

"Well, then who did, Emmylou?" Lorna snaps. "The invisible man?" Lorna felt herself blush. The damned woman has made her lose her clinical perspective, although she immediately excuses this as another result of being out of practice. To her surprise, Dideroff seems to be considering this rhetorical outburst as a legitimate question. Her face is grave as she answers. "Yeah, I've been giving that some thought, all right. It's my fault in a way. I thought I could carry it all myself, but he won't be carried. He's been waiting and waiting, I can see that now, he counted on my pride, and now he's away loose, doing his work."

"Who? Who's been waiting?"

"The devil, of course. And his minions on earth. Another sin to my score, I guess."

Lorna writes down "paranoid ideation" and "religious mania" on her pad.

"Minions?"

"Mm-huh. The spirit that destroys don't ever have much of a recruiting problem, and he don't tell me his plans. A little murder ain't nothing to him, but as far as the why of it, your guess is as good as mine. He'll wreck things here on earth for the pure fun of it, he likes when there's misery and despair and for people to give up on the Lord. Oh, my, that poor man probably hasn't got an idea what's happening to him."

Lorna was lost. Her pen stuttered to a stop. "What poor man?"

"Why, that policeman. Detective Paz. I felt him fly right out of me and stick to him and he saw it too, only he'll never admit it, that's the pity."

"Okay, Emmylou, let me get this straight. You think the, ah, devil that was in you jumped out of you and into Detective Paz?"

"Mm-huh."

"And that would mean he's no longer in you, right?"

Lorna is looking at the woman as she says this, and so she sees something remarkable happen. The person she has been talking to disappears and is replaced by someone else. The blue eyes turn from mild to icy; the very bones of the face seem to recompose themselves into something less, or more, than human. Lorna is familiar with the expression "it made her blood run cold" but has heretofore considered it a mere figure of speech, but it is actually, she now finds, a good description of what she now feels.

The new Emmylou says, in a quite different voice, one that seems to penetrate Lorna's head without using her eardrums at all, "It don't work that way, honey. My name is Legion." And she smiles, showing more teeth than Emmylou Dideroff actually has in her mouth.

This cannot be happening, Lorna thinks, and closes her eyes. It is all she can do to keep from screaming. When she looks again she sees yet another change come over Emmylou. Her body stiffens, she cocks her head unnaturally to the left, as if straining to hear something, or attempting to dislocate her neck. Her mouth opens, her eyes flutter rapidly, a blur of lashes. She stands, she reaches for something invisible to Lorna, and falls forward. Lorna catches her and now she does cry out.

To Lorna's surprise and relief, Mickey Lopez is not particularly exercised over the day's session with Dideroff, nor does he regard it as a failure. They meet later that morning in the office he keeps in the mental health center. Mickey is his usual avuncular, supportive self. "Okay, you moved fast, but she challenged you, and I think you did the right thing," he says after listening to the tape.

"I did?"

"Yeah, entering the fantasy, as if you wanted to participate in it, this cops-and-robbers game she has going, with the devil tossed in. But you can't get distracted."

"No." Doubtfully.

"Right. Look, my dear, there is an impairment here, and now we know it may have a neurological basis. She had an atonic seizure, yes? Seizure, religious hallucinations, we're now maybe looking at epilepsy with a focus in the medial temporal lobe, it's practically diagnostic. What you need to remember is *she* is crazy, *you* are not. Sane, presenting yourself as sane, you pose to her delusional system a serious challenge. You can regard that system almost as a person in its own right. It wants to survive, yes? When you push it, as you did here, it will fight back, or retreat from contact, which is what we just saw. The devil, or whatever, is chasing her, and she can't talk to you, so she checks out." Lopez leans back in his chair and bridges his hands, a typical gesture, but here in the plain institutional office and not his well-appointed shrink's lair, it seems thinner, more ticlike. Is Mickey as confused as she is? She rejects this thought. He continues, "So in these delusional cases, we must do two things simultaneously: one, we encourage the person to spin out their tale, we become confidants without ever actually validating the delusional system." An admonitory finger: "A subtle point. It separates the men from the boys in this business."

"So to speak," says Lorna. "And the other?"

"You tell me."

Lorna considers this for a moment, grateful for the show of confidence, if that is what it is. "Well, I guess to deal with, I mean, to try to locate the underlying cause, the lesion, or neurosis, or trauma, and help the patient work it through, using appropriate means."

She is rewarded with a smile for this conventional answer, which goes only a little toward relieving her of her doubts. Mickey was not there in Therapy B, did not see the woman's eyes. Or her teeth. He says, "Yes. Easy to say, difficult to do, of course. Now, the meds may help." He checked the file on his desk. "We have her on Haldol, two milligrams tid. How's she doing?"

"She complains of drowsiness."

"Yes, well that's normal the first couple of weeks. We should start her on Dilantin too, for the seizures. But she's social, not withdrawn?"

"Very social, apparently, the belle of the ward. She calms the place down, I'm told."

He chuckles. "Yeah, her and the Haldol. Anything else?"

"What if she won't talk to me anymore?"

"That's always a possibility, she's fitting you into her paranoid delusion. Let me know if that happens, and we'll up her dosage or try another med."

"I'm not sure that's indicated, Mickey. There's something about her . . . I don't know, it seems crazy"—here they both laughed—"but, you know what they say, even paranoids have real enemies."

Now Lopez's smile cooled. "So, what . . . you think she's coming off a genuine trauma? Some abuse?"

"Yes, and I'm concerned that we don't have a real file on her. She has no background, no relatives to talk to . . . I don't know, she seems so . . . *non*impaired compared to the typical NP remand, really centered and calm. . . ."

"So she's writing her life story for you, right? You'll read it and you'll come to a conclusion. If she's been to heaven and talked with the angels, that'll be one outcome, and if she was in with a gang of Colombian *drogeros,* that's another. Meanwhile, she's safe and warm and we're in no rush. You have to get your paper out of this, remember?"

Lorna does, with some shame. They talk technicalities for a few minutes and then Lopez says he has another meeting. As she leaves, he speaks: "One more thing, kiddo. Don't fall in love."

"In love?"

"Yeah, don't fall in love with the patient. Everyone knows about transference, but it works the other way too. Obviously something about this woman appeals to you. At some level, you don't really want to believe she's crazy, yes?"

A shrug. He says, "Just watch it is all I'm saying," and gives her a big, warm, Mickey Lopez–faux-Jewish smile.

After this, Lorna drives downtown and meets with a group of retail-chain personnel managers about testing programs that might reveal a propensity for dishonesty in potential employees. She is smooth and cool and much appreciated by the conclave of middle-aged men and women, and she wonders yet again why she does not restrict her practice to such bland services. The environment, an elegant office suite in a NE Fifth Avenue high-rise, is terrifically beige and has a great view of the bay. It is roach free, nor does it smell of Pine Sol, all of these features a nice change from her usual venues. Why, then? A last scrap of youthful idealism?

"Sheer dumb, honey-child," said Betsy Newhouse when Lorna puts the question to her lightly an hour later at their gym. "I keep telling you that the rich need good done for them just as much as the poor and they pay a lot better. I mean, let's face it—if they had anything on the ball, they wouldn't be poor." Lorna laughs in spite of herself, although not very vigorously, as she is struggling, as always, to keep up with Betsy on the StairMaster. This is one of the pleasures of the freelance life, the two women agree; they can come to the gym when they please, when it is empty. For Betsy, who is in real estate, this means access to whatever machine she needs to hone each muscle group to perfection, while for Lorna it means not having to strip naked in front of many women. Other than them there are only two men and a woman in the place, the latter being, delightfully, in far worse shape than Lorna feels herself to be.

"I have a social conscience," puffs Lorna. She is streaming sweat despite the artificial chill of the air-conditioning, and she imagines her face looks like prime rib. She casts an admiring glance at her friend, who is stepping easily, dry as a bone, her breasts solid as bisected baseballs in their spandex casing. Lorna does not wish to think about what hers are doing: a pair of pups fighting in a gunnysack is a phrase she once heard on the street in reference to a jogging woman (not her) by a couple of construction workers. Ever since, she has never been able entirely to expunge it from her mind.

"There's a procedure for that now," says Betsy. "You could have it removed along with a tummy tuck. Oh, listen, we have to go to De Lite after. They've got *pesetje* this week."

"What?"

"It's this great Albanian goat cheese, unpasteurized and zero fat. Zer-o." Lorna voices appreciation of the Albanian nation's cheesemongers and agrees to the date, although she wishes Betsy would not suggest surgical modifications quite so often. It reminds her of Rat Howie, and also of her late mother, whose body was whittled down to a nubbin by surgery of the noncosmetic variety during her last year of life. Surgery *not,* is Lorna's prayer, or would be, did she ever actually pray. Slow Lorna must keep on climbing the endless staircase (such a symbol of her life so far!) when Betsy completes her allotted generation of ergs.

After this climb, Lorna hits a few other machines, somewhat less vigorously than her trainer would like, and then waves to Betsy and motions upward. Betsy waves back and shows five fingers, meaning she will be along in a notional five. The dressing room is deserted, Lorna happily observes. Moving like a thief cleaning out a bank vault, Lorna strips, grabs a towel, and heads for a shower stall. With a towel wrapped almost around her, for she is too generously built for the stingy gym towels, she weighs herself, although she knows she is not supposed to do this every day, and is pleased to find that she has dropped a full pound since the previous visit, or perhaps a little more, as the towel must weigh half a pound at least. As she steps past the shower curtain, however, she catches a glimpse of herself in the mirror and sees not a figure that would have made Auguste Renoir fall to his arthritic knees in worship, but galaxies of hopeless lard. She does not cry in the shower, although she has before this, any number of times. She dresses, and she and Betsy go to eat. The Albanian goat cheese tastes like library paste and chalk, but Lorna is a good soldier and snaps up far more of it than Betsy does, without complaint. Zero fat.

Toward the end of the day, Paz got a buzz from Major Oliphant's secretary, requiring him to report forthwith, which he did, garnering several speculative looks from other detectives as he passed. The major was behind his desk, in shirtsleeves, drinking from his FBI mug and eating what looked to Paz like a churro. Oliphant offered coffee, which Paz accepted and got it in a cup marked with a Treasury seal and the legend THIRD ANNUAL COMPUTER FRAUD CONFERENCE, DENVER.

Oliphant gestured with the pastry and said, "You got me hooked on these things, Paz. These're not anywhere near as good as yours, though."

"They have to be fresh, sir. Thirty minutes out of the fat and you might as well use them to pack bearings."

"We could set up a fryer outside my office."

"Good plan, sir. I could be the departmental *churronista.*"

"You'd like that, would you?"

"I'm always ready for a new challenge, Major."

Oliphant chuckled, a dark organic sound. "Well, I called you in about an old challenge. The Trianon affair. Christ, it sounds like one of those things you learned in grade school, that caused the First World War, but I can never remember the victim's name."

"Jabir Akran al-Muwalid."

"Right. I got an interesting call from Washington today, a buddy of mine who shall remain nameless, passed on a heads-up about our case. Your partner talked to a guy named Floyd Mitchell recently? About David Packer?"

"Yeah, but he didn't get much out of him. Mr. Mitchell is tight with information."

"That may be because Mr. Mitchell doesn't exist, and that fact stays in this room. Mitchell is a cutout. Every major intelligence operation has one. A local PD calls asking for information on some name, like your guy did, and the girl brings it up on the machine, and a bell goes off and she goes 'Hold for Mr. Mitchell,' or Blake, or Fox, and the call shunts to the duty officer on the case and he spreads snow on the inquirer, and they hope he goes back to sleep."

"And are we going back to sleep?" asked Paz.

"Maybe we should. My guy there tells me this is high level. That call rang a lot of bells. Your Mr. Packer is one well-connected fellow."

Oliphant tossed his bad churro into his waste can, followed by the bag and waxed paper, nice swished shots, and then took a drink from his FBI mug. "National security is a funny business. I never had much to do with it in the Bureau, never much wanted to. Nowadays, of course, everyone running around with their head cut off, I guess every swinging dick is involved in it somehow."

There was a pause. Oliphant seemed to be making his mind up about how much to tell Paz about whatever this was about. Paz said helpfully, "What was it you did for the Bureau, sir, if you don't mind me asking."

"Oh, the usual. Bank robberies, kidnaps, fugitives. Bread and butter stuff. Taught at Quantico for a couple of years. I enjoyed that. Then I got interested in computer stuff and I headed up a special task force on kiddie porn. We busted a couple of major traffickers, which gave me a lot of satisfaction. Then I was deputy SAIC in New York, where I met the chief, and here I am. Things have changed, obviously, last couple of years, since the events in New York. And we, I mean the Bureau, is ill-suited to carry out the national security mission. In fact, the last time we tried it we made fools of ourselves, spying on movie stars while the fucking Russians were taking everything that wasn't nailed down. The reason is that we're trained to make cases, to collect evidence for criminal prosecutions. That's where the gold has always been, how you get promoted. Now you say you want us to stop things from happening, a whole different kind of op. Well, how the fuck do you do that?"

Paz had no idea. After a moment he asked, "So Packer was involved with the victim, and you learned he was a national security menace?"

"Huh? Oh, no, that's not the point. My friend wanted me to know that the people who put him on the watch list were kind of a peculiar outfit. You haven't come across any references to anything called the Strategic Resources Protection Unit? The acronym is pronounced 'serpu.'"

"No. What is it?"

"Well, strategic resources need protection is the idea. Chemical plants, pipelines, power grids. Transshipment terminals, especially petroleum terminals. If someone had something like six bombs in the right places—the Gulf, Saudi, Canada, Mexico, Nigeria, and so on—they could cut sixty percent of our petroleum deliveries off for months. It's a fairly vulnerable business, or so I've been told. Anyway, this SRPU has that job, both here in the States and overseas."

"That makes sense, then. The vic was in the oil business."

"Really?"

Paz related what they had learned from Michael Zubrom, including the odd business of the missing cell phone.

Oliphant said, "Okay, so this Zubrom suggested that the victim had secret knowledge of an oil find and . . . what? He was using diverted oil to raise money so he could develop it? That doesn't make any sense. I don't know a hell of a lot about it, but I always thought oil fields were developed by oil companies, and they spent in the multiple millions to do it. So a couple of hundred K is not going to make a dent in that. Besides if the Sudanese government knew about a big find, they'd be negotiating openly. I mean oil isn't like some kind of hidden treasure, with a map, $X$ marks the spot, you go down there with a truck one night and you're set for life."

"Oh, you're baffled too?" said Paz. "Good. I thought I was losing it. Plus, this new thing. The victim is on a watch list of an outfit that's supposed to protect let's say oil fields, refineries, from terrorists. Was he a terrorist? It doesn't look like it, unless that was what the oil sale was for, money to set up a terror network."

"It's something to think about. Did we find any money?"

"Not that kind of money. I got Morales checking wire transfers out of that Jersey bank Zubrom sent his payment to, but I don't have any high hopes. Those guys are pretty tight with their information, and they're not going to be impressed by a cop from Miami."

"No, they're not that impressed by the FBI either. I hate that you didn't find a cell phone."

"Yeah, me too. Among other things, it casts doubt on Dideroff's guilt, or at least suggests that she didn't act alone."

"Did she act at all?" Oliphant's tone had been speculative, collegial; with this last he was a boss again and staring directly at Paz.

He shrugged and answered, "Sir, you know what we know, except I arrested her and I saw something there. She could have killed him. For a couple of seconds she had that killer look. Whether she did or not . . ." Another shrug. "She's not what you would call a regular person."

"What about the giant confession she's supposed to be writing?"

"Apparently still scrawling away. I'm dying to curl up and read it."

"I bet. Look, I'm going to talk to Posada, get you both on this thing full-time. You need to find out more about this victim and our suspect, where they intersected, and we're no longer just interested in strengthening the case against Dideroff. I want to know the whole story if possible. Use what she writes, but don't stop there. I want her life story checked and cross-checked. Find out who our Arab was and what he was doing in Miami besides selling a shipload of oil. It can't just be that. He could have done that from anywhere. He was in Miami for a reason. He was after something and someone was after him, and he knew it, or he wouldn't have told your oil guy about getting some backup. Maybe he did get some backup—if so, find out what or who it was."

"Okay, sir, but would you like to tell me why we're putting a full-court press on something that looks a lot like a grounder."

Oliphant made an impatient gesture. "Oh, hell, you know damn well it's not a grounder anymore. You ever have a rat die in a wall? It doesn't matter how much deodorizer you spray, there's still that stink that sticks in the back of your throat. This thing has a stink like that. People are fucking with us, major players are playing us, and I'm goddamned if I'm going to be played. We need to go into the walls and find the rat."

Paz took a breath and asked, "Sir, this wouldn't have anything to do with why you left the Bureau?"

Oliphant stared at him so long that Paz was forced to drop his eyes. "That's really none of your business. But if anything from my FBI experience ever becomes relevant to this case, I'll bring it to your attention. Are we done?"

Paz stood. "Yes, sir."

Oliphant was still staring at him. "You getting enough sleep, Jimmy?"

"Sure."

"You don't look like it. You got red rims on your eyes and you yawned three times in the last half hour. Maybe you need to lay off some of that Cuban coffee."

"Yes, sir," said Paz, "maybe I do." He was in the hallway before he realized that Oliphant had steered the conversation away from revealing why the name David Packer had caused the security gates to slam down at the State Department.

# Ten

Lorna Wise lies in bed and considers her symptoms. It is Saturday, so she can lie in bed doing this for longer than she usually does. A scratchiness in the back of the throat. A twitching in her calf muscle. A sort of deadened area just above her left elbow. She blinks one eye, then the other. Perhaps a slight blurring of vision in the left, or maybe that's a bit of sleepy dust. Although, it's worrisome that it's the left one. The left calf muscle too, bad, speaks to central nervous system malfunction: an ischemia, a smallish brain tumor, the subtle onset of MS. As she lies, she palps her breasts, although she knows she should be upright, and although she will do it again when she showers. Probing for the tumor she knows is lurking, surely her fingers, so competent after all these years, can catch the nodule at the earliest possible stage and she can have the surgeon pluck it out. Although she knows that's not true, although she is by now a fairly decent amateur oncologist, although she knows there are cancers so treacherous that by the time they show a palpable tumor they have spread througout the body. Not the kind her mother had, however, her mother was carrying a tumor the size of a tangerine around before she went to the doctor. Why, Mom, why didn't you go to the doctor? Because I thought it was nothing. Because I hate doctors.

Lorna drops her breasts and sits up on the edge of the bed, experiencing a wave of dizziness and perhaps a slight nausea, the infallible sign of a brain wracked with metastases or else mere sickness and disgust at herself. Unlike Mom, Lorna happens to love doctors, occasionally in a sexual way, as with Rat

Howie, and for this reason has decided that her personal physician should always be a woman, and so it is. She suppresses an urge to call Dr. Greenspan, for she saw her only thirty-four days ago and does not wish to acquire a rep as a crock. For some reason, she thinks as she starts her Saturday routine, the first minutes of the day are always the worst, the times when she feels most fragile and afraid.

She breakfasts on grapefruit and health pills and coffee on the little patio in the back, surrounded by flowers and twittering birds. She receives both the *Miami Herald* and the *New York Times* every morning and reads both all the way through, except for the sports sections. The *Herald* is an excellent paper, but she does not feel civilized without the *Times;* the *Times* and the *New Yorker*, banners her dad flew, declaring that although he now lived in the New Jersey burbs, he had not surrendered to barbarism. And she likes the crossword puzzle, which she now does in twenty minutes, not as good as her dad but not disgraceful either.

After that, she sits in a sling chair, sipping the cooling coffee and recounting all the various tasks she has put off until the weekend and now must do or feel like a slacker. The phone rings, and she reaches for the cordless she has brought out with her and it is Sheryl Waits. Who asks if she is ready. Ready for what? It now turns out that Lorna's mind has erased the appointment she made with her friend to go shopping for a dress to wear to Sheryl's party, an actual party dress, which I don't believe you own one of, sugar, because you are not entering my domicile looking like bark. Uh-uh!

That evening Lorna shows up at Sheryl's party more than fashionably late in a scarlet spaghetti strap dress with a Saran Wrap cling and a built-in bra that offers her breasts up like twin servings of flan. The place is jumping, cars lining both sides of the street, people standing on the sidewalk and on the front lawn, holding drinks, lights strung among the branches of the pines and around the trunks of the palms on the property, light pouring from every window of the good-size split-level house, and thumping music.

She finds Sheryl in the kitchen taking a tray of fried chicken wings out of the oven. Sheryl screams how good she looks and requires everyone in range of her voice to see how good. Lorna says, "I hate you. This is the least fabric I've worn on my body outside a pool since I was four."

"You're such a fool, child! You look fantastic. Don't she look fantastic, Elvita?"

Elvita agrees she looks fantastic. Lorna mugs for them, a pulp temptress. Hilarity.

In general, Lorna is bored by parties, by the way people act when they are drinking, nor does she like dancing with or being pawed by strangers. At loud parties, she usually finds a quiet corner, sits down with a glass of white wine, and observes the various species at their social rituals, an ornithologist in a rain forest. But because it is Sheryl's party she feels obliged to be social. She circulates, sipping a wine and soda. Most of the people here are connected to the police, somewhat over half of them black, the rest a mix of Anglos and Cubans. As she expected, the men are standing about in clumps, clutching drinks in big plastic cups and talking sports or shop. The women are in clumps too, talking shop, shopping, vacations, clothes, kids, of which there are large numbers running underfoot and shouting in the yard. Some people are dancing under colored lights on the patio, to the Weather Girls, "It's Raining Men."

A man comes up to her, introduces himself as Rod, identifies himself as a friend of Leon's. He is muscular, hairy, a cop, has only small talk to offer; he stares at her tray of breasts. Another man, taller, Ben, with the kind of big Adam's apple she rather dislikes comes and joins them. He also stares at her breasts. She feels like she should be on a rotating platform, like a new model at an auto show. And another, Martin, younger and better looking, and what does he stare at? Not her flawless skin. They are all Miami PD and they engage in a joking rivalry, saying amusing bad things about one another to her, all of them eyeing her body. She can almost hear the saliva gurgle, the blood surging through their genitalia. This is it, then, sexual triumph: she finds she can't take it seriously, it's like thinking that a construction worker's whistle signals the start of a meaningful relationship. Yet she feels obliged to play, to bat back the slightly salacious repartee, to *simper,* for God's sake! And to sweat. A good thing about this outfit is that it doesn't come close to her armpits. A drink in a large plastic cup is placed in her hand and she drinks: sweet and very cold. Leon must be making his famous frozen daiquiris.

Somewhat of a blur after this. She dances with several men, feels several sets of genitals against her unprotected belly, several sets of hands on her ass. The dancing is to funk and disco, music she does not care much for. Then, suddenly, the music changes, a Latin beat, but unlike any Latin music she has heard before. It is layered, multivoiced, with rhythms that are incredibly complex yet still engaging of the groin area. Now she is dancing with a man who is leading her in steps she doesn't know but seems to be able to do fairly well, or perhaps that is a result of the rum. He has steady hazel eyes set in a face that's the caramel color of a Coach bag she owns. He is just her height in heels.

"What's this music?" she asks.

"It's a machine for the suppression of time," he says.

"Pardon?"

"Lévi-Strauss."

"Lévi-Strauss?"

"Yeah. Plays third base for the White Sox. How about those Marlins?"

"You're Jimmy Paz," she says.

"And how do you deduce that, Dr. Wise?" A grin now, small white teeth shining, like a cat.

"Sheryl said you were brainy. I don't think many men at this party would respond to a question with a quotation from Lévi-Strauss."

"Only those on the structural anthropology softball team."

"Of which you are a member."

"I am. Left *bricoleur*. We play ball, we down a case of cold ones, and sit around the locker room discussing *Tristes Tropiques*."

"Seriously, what is this music?"

"It's *timba*. A Cuban record, a band called Klimax."

"What are they singing about?"

"*Yo no quiero que mi novia sea religiosa*. I don't want my girlfriend to be religious. Speaking of which, how's our girl?"

"Oh, no, not shop! And here I thought you were dancing with me because you liked my dress," Lorna says, not really believing that she has let this slip from between her lips.

He flings her out and leads her through an elaborate break and then snaps her back close. He smells of tobacco, not a smell she is used to on the health-conscious men she tends to hang with. Not unpleasant, though. Spicy. He throws her out again to the beat and now he gives her a long appreciative look that she feels running over her skin like heat. He says, "No, it was mainly the dress. Mainly the nondress zones, to be honest. Creamy. It makes me wish I had a long spoon."

"I think we could use another drink," she says.

Somewhat later they are sitting side by side on a somewhat ratty Bahama couch in the Waitses' Florida room with that drink, Lorna's a second foolhardy daiq and Paz with some dark brown liquid on ice. Lorna sees Sheryl zoom by with a tray of nibbles. Sheryl spots the two of them and rolls her eyes while licking her lips dramatically. Lorna sticks out her tongue.

Paz catches this action but declines to comment on it. Instead he says, "So. What do we have?"

It takes a second for Lorna to recall what he is talking about. Then she hears herself talking, the words slow and only a little slurred. She listens to the person speak, as from a great distance. "Two interviews and one notebook full of writing. From the interviews, nothing much. She's a hard case, very smart, doesn't want to give anything away. There's a . . . I don't know how to put it, a split in her, somewhere deep. Her usual persona is mild, saintly, lots of religious references. But occasionally, if she feels pressed . . ."

"Out comes the spider woman," says Paz.

"You've seen it too? *Her,* I should say." Lorna feels a rush of grateful relief. She has not discussed this aspect of her client with Mickey Lopez.

"Oh, yeah. I saw something when I interviewed her after the arrest. A look in her eyes. That's when I knew we weren't dealing with the Little Flower."

"Excuse me, the little . . ."

"A saint, Teresa of Lisieux. I guess you're not Catholic."

"No. But I'm sure it's not simple malingering. I've seen a lot of that and it's fairly easy to tease out. We have tests that . . . anyway, not to get technical, but she's for real, there really is something bent in there. That confession you got her to write tends to confirm that. She had a horrendous childhood."

Paz listens as she summarizes the contents of the first notebook, professionally sympathetic, not particularly shocked; he has heard and seen worse. Studying the woman as she speaks, he sees something unsaid flickering behind her bland professional delivery, and he knows that she has seen the same kind of inexplicable transformation he'd seen himself. It wasn't just a look in Emmylou Dideroff's eyes, but what it actually was he cannot say, doesn't want to think about, and for damned sure is not about to bring up just now.

He says, "A double murder–suicide should be easy to check. So she sets up her mom to whack her stepfather and the little brother goes down too. Quite the sweetheart. But even though she has no problem spilling that, she totally denies tossing our guy off that balcony. How do you figure that?"

"She's not legally responsible for what her mother did. It's no crime leaving out a key and depriving someone of tranks. But clonking someone on the head and throwing them to their death is a different story. I think."

"So, you think we're being gamed?"

"No, she's not a psychopath. In fact she feels responsible for everything."

She sees the confusion on Paz's face, feels it in her own mind too. This is actually stupid, trying to discuss a case with a cop with her being half in the tank.

Lorna is finishing her second daiquiri now, and as she does, a young boy is standing in front of her with a tray of tall cups full of the same brew. He is dressed in a too-large maroon monkey jacket and has a clip-on bow tie loosely clutching the collar of his white shirt.

"Take another one," he says.

"Does your mother know you're dispensing liquor, young man?" says Lorna.

"She said I *had* to, that's how low she is. You want a daiquiri, Detective Paz?"

"I don't think so, John. I believe I would be contributing to the delinquency of a minor."

"Wimp," says the boy. "*We* the *po*-lice here," and turns to Lorna.

"C'mon take one, Lola, it's a party!" he says, taking the empty and placing a full cup on the wooden arm of the couch. He gives Lorna a frank once-over. "Lookin' fine, Lola. Dress is da bomb!" He slides away into the crowded room.

"Lola?" says Paz.

"My family name around here. One of the kids called me that when she was a baby and it stuck."

"It suits you. In that outfit."

"You think it's da bomb, too, hm?" She takes a sip of the new drink. She knows that if she finishes it, she will be really drunk, fraternity house drunk, as she has been careful not to be for some time. She decides to go ahead. Better to be completely incapable of speech than try to make sense of Emmylou Dideroff on half a brain. Also, she is sitting with a man who knows who Lévi-Strauss is. She drinks her drink so quickly that its chill makes her jaw ache, aware of Paz watching her, that little grin playing around his broad lips. She leans toward him, a little closer actually than she had planned, her breast squashing up against his arm. "How about another little dance, Detective?" she says.

She groans and pulls the sheet up against the morning sunlight. There is a dull pain behind her eyes, and her entire pharynx feels dry enough to crackle. It is painted thick with the particularly foul rotten-molasses taste you get when you drink a lot of rum. Her mind is perfectly empty, even for a moment or two void of her own identity. Memory returns in a slow trickle: who she is, where she is (her own bedroom), her current condition. She is hungover and naked. No, not quite, she is wearing the red lace thong from last night. There memory stalls. She recalls the third daiquiri and Paz and whirling with him around the patio and his insolent, examining grin, and then a blank. It is inconceivable that she could have driven home, so someone must have driven her. She can't recall. Did she have sex? She might have taken on the Dolphins' defensive line for all she knows. Sheryl calls, but Lorna has no dirt to give her, and they arrange for the return of Lorna's car amid a degree of girlish giggling that only increases the pounding in Lorna's skull.

An hour later, the car has been dropped off, she has showered (after confirming that the only pubic hairs clinging to her skin are those she grew herself) and eaten Advil and drunk half a pot of black coffee. She is lying in the lounge chair in her office, trying and failing to get interested in a recent novel. She is restless, wired, the sheaths of her nerves scraped raw by toxic ethanol metabolites, but at the same time exhausted, lacking even the energy to stroll through a fictive garden. She spies the school notebook on her desk, puts the novel aside, fetches it back to the lounger. Emmylou's confessions now sprout a shrubbery of Post-its. She thumbs through to one in particular, examines the page. Emmylou's writing is large and bold.

<u>This has happened to you too, hasn't it?</u>

Underlined, directed at the reader, at Paz obviously, some relationship established there already. Why? A Catholic thing? Exterior voices a common enough phenomenon, she knows, particularly in childhood, here we had an extreme case, the impulses of the id projected out and turned into an imagined figure, this shiny man. Why shiny? Some early visual hallucinations too, fading with age. Fascinating. There is a whole line of therapy that she can generate from this. Lorna goes to get a pen and her own notebook.

The phone now rings. Twice and the machine picks it up. A voice, distorted by the cheap speaker: "Lorna . . . Jimmy Paz here, hope you're okay. Look, I need you to give me a call—"

"Hello?" She has flown across the room and snatched up the receiver.

"Oh, good," says Paz. "You survived. I'm not going to ask you how you feel."

"That's very considerate of you. I assume you got me home last night. I'm sorry, I don't usually act like that."

"Like how? Get drunk at a party and have fun?"

"Did I have fun? I can't remember."

"You were laughing a lot. That's usually an indication."

"Well, it was nice of you to take the trouble." A little pause here, both of them in the embarrassment of forced intimacy, waiting for the other to make the first move, which eventually Paz does, saying, "I hope you don't mind about me getting that dress off you. It looked uncomfortable to sleep in. I didn't realize about the top. The no-bra aspect."

"That's okay."

"I kept my eyes closed the entire time, I want you to know."

"That was very considerate of you. Was it hard?" Guffaw, shared. "No, I mean was it difficult getting it off. . . ."

"Not at all. It was like skinning a mackerel."

Lorna thinks this is the sexiest thing anyone has ever said to her. She tries to think of a rejoinder, but all she can do is breathe stupidly into the mouthpiece, like a telephone tormentor.

"Look, um, another reason I called is I need a favor."

"Sure, what is it?" she asks.

"Could you, like, come over to my place?"

"You mean now?"

"Yeah, if it's no trouble. I'm in sort of a jam and you were the only one I could think of to call."

"What kind of jam?"

"Um, it's hard to explain over the phone. It'll just take you a minute."

Lorna agrees right away. He gives her the address and tells her where a key to the back door is stashed, under the near-left foot of the picnic table. He thanks her warmly before he hangs up. She dresses in haste, the crisp look today, khaki shorts and a white shortsleeved shirt, like a camp counselor. She drives to Little Havana, SW Nineteenth off Calle Ocho, lets herself in, feeling a little odd but not uncomfortably so. Anticipatory, even.

"Jimmy?"

"In here. The bedroom."

She follows the voice. Jimmy Paz is lying in a brass bed, covered from the waist down by a light quilt and showing from the waist up an impressive expanse of buffed musculature coated in smooth dark golden skin. Gold chain and crucifix too, and another small dark object on a thong. That was strange and a little exciting in a scary way. Lorna can almost feel her pupils expand.

"Thanks for coming," he says. "I did something really dumb." He wiggles his foot, and she sees that it is fastened with handcuffs to one of the bed's pipes. "I had the key right here on the table, and to be extra sure I didn't lose it I had it inside my watchband, right? So, of course, I wake up in the middle of the night and the first thing I do is check the time, and the key kind of hooks on the band and skitters off across the floor. Over there." He points. "Can you locate it?"

She can and hands it to him. He unlocks the cuffs.

"Thank you." He gives her the grin. "Free at last, free at last, great God almighty . . ."

"And so on," she says. "Well, it looks like my work here is done."

"Time for play, then. You doing anything today?"

"I'm free more or less except for some errands. What were you thinking of? It can't involve alcoholic beverages."

"Of course. Yet numerous teetotal experiences are available here in Miami, it being the sun and fun capital of the world. Do you like the water?"

"To drink?"

"To float upon. To dip into. The sea. Boating."

"You mean sailboats?"

"No, I mean a Cuban workboat with fish scales all over it. We could run down to the reef, throw a line over, get lucky maybe, catch some redfish."

"You know all the good places, I bet."

"Some of them. You up for that?"

"Sure, if I can go by my place and get some stuff."

"I'll come with you," he says, "or I would if I could figure out a way to get dressed with you in here."

"I'll close my eyes," she says. And she does, nearly, while he slides naked and truly terrific-looking from under his quilt and pulls on a pair of faded cutoff jeans and a black T-shirt that says GUANTANAMERA COMIDAS CRIOLLAS on it, and a baggy plaid cotton shirt with the sleeves ripped off over that. Then he clips on his pistol and slides a shield wallet into his rear pocket.

He catches her stare. "Regulations," he says. "Does it bother you?"

"I don't think so. But I never spent any time with a man who had a gun."

"You did last night, with about fifty of them."

"I mean consciously. It must be weird."

"You get used to it," he says shortly and leads her out.

They take his car, a Datsun Z of a certain age, in sun-faded orange. At the curb in front of her house she tells him that she'll just be a minute. As she opens her front door she stops for a second as it strikes her that her hangover is quite gone, and more interestingly, that she has not had a hypochondriacal, neurotic, or self-conscious thought since the minute Paz called her. She feels terrific, in fact, better than she has in ages. She is arranging her beach bag in her mind as she turns the key and enters her front room. She needs a tube of industrial-strength sunblock and a towel, and yes, she intends to wear an electric blue bikini she purchased on Antigua and has never summoned up the nerve to wear locally.

She barely sees the man before he clubs her aside with his fist and races out the front door. Paz is leaning against the driver's side of his car, staring contentedly after Lorna, and so he has a perfect view of what has just happened. The man trips slightly on a little rag rug Lorna keeps inside her front door, and when he is halfway down the path, just building up speed again, Paz is already leaning over the top of his car with his Glock out, yelling, "Freeze, freeze, police! Get down!"

The man slows, startled, staring. Paz sees that he is a thin Latino man dressed in satiny black warm-up pants and a black tank top with *Heat* written on it in red cursive letters and big white Air Jordans, with his head wrapped in a shiny black cloth. Maybe twenty-something, Paz figures, and he's got a dark flat object in his hand that Paz can't quite identify, because he is focused on the man's face, and all of a sudden he can see what the man's going to do and ice enters his belly. He fills his lungs with air to shout again.

The man's right hand snakes behind him and comes out with a dark angular shape that could be anything, a toy, a knife, a Walkman, but Paz doesn't wait to see what it is. He fires twice, and the man sits down at the head of Lorna's walk in that cutstring-marionette way of shot people, with dark leaking punctures above and below the *a* in *Heat*. Paz rushes to the man, sees he isn't breathing, plants his mouth over the blood-filled mouth, feels the sparse hairs that rim it. He pushes down on the sternum, blood squirts up between his fingers.

"I called 911," says a voice behind him. Lorna, smart lady. He keeps working, although it is clearly hopeless. His prayer now is that it was a real gun in the guy's hand, although he can't see one when he lifts up his head to breathe. What he can see is a small school notebook standing on the sidewalk, its spine perkily upward like a tiny house. It's exactly like the ones he bought for Emmylou Dideroff.

Remarkably, we have a vivid description of that scene from the viewpoint of the uhlan captain, Manfred Ems von Frisch, recorded in his memoir, *To Paris with the Thirteenth Uhlans* (1889):

> *Suddenly there appeared before us a pretty girl of about fourteen, tousled from sleep, and dressed in silk slippers and a French cavalry cloak. She presented a remarkably calm mien, as if finding lancers in her yard before breakfast were a common occurrence. I saluted her and said, in French, "Little miss, have you by any chance seen the French army?" To this she answered, in good German, "I am surprised that you dare to ask me such a question, sir, for you make me choose between polluting myself with a lie and betraying my country. No gentleman would place a lady in such a position." I was somewhat taken aback by this sally, and irritated at being made to look the fool in front of my troop. Therefore, I said to her, "The exigencies of war, mademoiselle, preclude such nice distinctions." She replied, "I must differ with you there, sir. War or peace, there is no excuse for rudeness. Your king would not approve, nor would your mother, I believe."*

A better exhibition of Marie-Ange's spirit and fearlessness could not be found! Ems von Frisch further reports that she offered him and his men refreshment and fodder for their animals, but gave no information whatever. After the Prussians left, Marie-Ange dressed hurriedly and ordered the coach to be prepared. She intended to travel with speed to Metz, as she knew that her father would be frantic for her safety when he heard that the enemy had crossed the Moselle.

The road east from Gravelotte was jammed with advancing

French troops and local people fleeing the battle, whose guns could already be heard to the east and north. The coach was forced off the road by an artillery train, and while they waited, Marie-Ange heard the sound of a woman crying. She got out to see what was the matter and found a farm cart in which were lying a man and two children, covered in blood. The woman stilled her tears long enough to explain that they were from Villers-au-Pois and that their farmhouse had been taken over as a strong point by French soldiers. While the family hid in an outbuilding, a Prussian shell had scored a direct hit upon it, with the present sad results. Immediately, the girl abandoned her original plan, loaded the wounded peasants into her coach, and drove back to Bois Fleury.

—FROM *FAITHFUL UNTO DEATH:
THE STORY OF THE NURSING SISTERS
OF THE BLOOD OF CHRIST,*
BY SR. BENEDICTA COOLEY, SBC,
ROSARIAN PRESS, BOSTON, 1947.

# Eleven

The
## CONFESSIONS
of
### Emmylou Dideroff

### Book II

*This never happened before first you detective and now this doctor. It's not like him to show and then I fainted I probably scared the poor woman half to death. I don't understand it, he doesn't usually manifest like that, usually it's just a little tickle, like tickling a trout until practically asleep and you can grab it up, a little tickle, hey that girl, that man, looks so fine, who would it hurt, the wife the husband doesn't have to know, the money was just sitting there, I'll give it back, can't you shut the goddam kid up and so on, so something important is happening around you all, like in Bible times, unless we're all of us as crazy as*

*It was night when I took off, with nothing but the shorts and shirt I was wearing and a denim bag full of makeup and spare panties and my bra, which I had slipped off, and I popped open the first two buttons on the shirt. I walked over to the first big street with traffic on it and hitched a* ride with some old guy in a Buick. We drove around for a while talking, him staring at my tits at every stoplight. He was wasting time, so when he offered what do you like to do as a conversational gambit I said I liked to suck cock at twenty-five dollars a pop. Which I did behind a Phillips station on 112th Street, my entrée into the profession. I got about six more rides that night, tending northward as I did, and had the last guy drop me at one of those crummy old-fashioned motels, just a line of low concrete buildings and a fizzing neon sign in peach and blue TUD R COURT VACA Y.

I worked out of that motel for the rest of the week, making pretty good money. It is easy to accumulate reasonable sums at whoring if you are not blowing it on drugs and if you have no pimp or kids. The worst thing about this time (and I really thought that was the worst thing, God forgive me!) was that I had nothing good to read and Miami is so spread out I couldn't get from where I was to a good secondhand bookstore and they won't give you a library card without proof of a permanent address. I could've asked one of my tricks to drop me at a mall with a Borders, but for some reason I never did. I could recollect pages of things I had read, of course, but that's not quite the same thing, is it? I was forced to read wire-rack garbage from the local 7-Eleven store, science fiction, thrillers, westerns, romances, although I read them faster than the book company truck could refill the racks. It's hard to be a street prostitute with advanced literary tastes.

The third week I was on the street I got picked up by a man in a new black Cadillac Eldorado with gold-plated trims. He didn't say anything but just started driving pretty fast, east on the highway, and when I asked him what he thought he was doing he said shut the fuck up bitch so I did. He had the same dank stink of evil that Ray Bob had, except he wasn't making any moves to hide it, far from it, he was proud of it, it was his stock-in-trade. When we got off the highway, he started in talking about what all he was going to do to me to teach me not to be whoring on his territory and when we got to his apartment in Lib-

*erty City he did all that plus some stuff he hadn't got around to threatening. I think he did more to me than what he usually did to a regular kid because I wasn't scared of him particularly. All he could do in the end was to deprive me of my life, which I didn't think was worth much, although at the time I sort of regretted not ever making it with Percival Orne Foy. Jerrell Robinson was his name. He isn't hardly worth describing, about as individual as one of a school of sunnies, whipped up by the movies and the street, nothing in his mind but More.*

*Anyway, the usual pimpish workup of an amateur, nothing I hadn't done before except for the ass-fucking, which was quite painful, and the shooting up with heroin, which made me sick as a dog but tended to dull the pain. I did not get addicted, strange to say, except physiologically, and that amounts to twenty-four hours of discomfort, nothing I couldn't handle. I'm not an addictive personality, it turned out. I pretended to be, though. He got a deal of pleasure out of making me beg for my next shot. What gave me pleasure was thinking of how I would kill him.*

*I say that now, but when I really try to recall how I felt, day to day, I draw a blank. Maybe I didn't have any feelings at all. I know that I lived a good deal of the time outside my body, in a waking dream fed by books. Some sweating pig would be on me and I would be floating through an English garden chatting with elegant ladies and gentlemen, or landing with a roar of white fire on a new planet. There is a level of not caring what happens to you next that is difficult to describe to people whose lives are governed by expectations and entitlements. One good thing was that Jerrell put me in one of his whore apartments so I had an address and could get a library card.*

*I was actually a very good whore. I never stole, either from the johns or from Jerrell. He had me in a two-bedroom hole on NW Thirty-fourth Street with two other girls, Marlys and Tammy, both lily teens like me, but genuine junkies. They stole all the time, stupidly, fruitlessly,* and on an average of once a week he would whip both of them with wire coat hangers. Then he would whip me, if anything a little harder than he did them, because he couldn't find my loot or my dope nor could his imagination expand to contain the notion of an honest whore, as if he had come across dry water. This was part of the plan, of course. Then he would usually fuck me in a particularly degrading fashion and then fall asleep. Part of the plan, as well.

Jerrell had a rival pimp named T-bone Carter. T-bone prided himself on being a cut above the ordinary piece of street shit, and in fact he was somewhat more intelligent than Jerrell, although this was not an epic feat. He drove a Mercedes rather than the Cadillacs the other street dudes had, and he dressed English style, always a nice suit and tie and handmade shoes for T-bone, and he liked jazz rather than funk. I knew some of his girls, and they said he was okay for a scumbag, light on the torture and easy with gifts and dope. A prince.

T-bone ran a poker game that Jerrell joined every Thursday, and of course he always lost, being a dumb shit, and blamed it on bad luck. Yet another aspect of my plan, but the core of it was Marlys, the stupider and prettier of my two roomies. I got Marlys scared of Jerrell, or more scared than she already was. I said he had killed girls just for fun. I said he told me he was pissed at her ripping him off all the time, that he was going to make an example of her for the other girls. I told her what he was going to do to her, and here my recent reading of crappy thriller fiction furnished the details. When I had got her sufficently petrified, I suggested that a way out might lie with T-bone Carter. Jerrell was scared of T-bone, I said, and T-bone would get a kick out of stealing one of Jerrell's best earners.

I happened to be in Jocko's Tropical Lounge on Second Avenue, my usual hangout, and it was early, maybe four, and I was thinking about heading for my stroll, which was fishing the exits off 395 for squares going home to the burbs, when Jerrell came in fuming, having just heard the news. He slapped me around a couple just on general principle and to show the onlookers that he was still da Man. He had a drink and began whining about what he was going to do to T-bone, how he was nobody's bitch, and I took this opportunity to tell him that maybe T-bone was treating him like a bitch because it wasn't any different from ripping off his money at cards all these years, and how I had heard T-bone joking about it right here, and then I gave him some details of the way he'd been shafted, which I had cribbed from *Gambling Scams* by D. Ortiz, borrowed from the Miami Public Library. Jerrell got real quiet then and went out to his car and came right back and I knew just what he had gone out there for. He drank Courvoisier and 7UP, his favorite, for the next half hour, one after another, and then I had to go to work. It's a pity I missed it, because I would've loved to have seen the look on his face when he pulled his Colt Commander out on T-bone and held it in that stupid sideways way they all do now and pulled the trigger a couple of times. T-bone never carried a weapon, claiming that packing a gat ruined the line of his suit, but he always had a sidekick with him, and on this particular evening his boy was carrying a TEC-9. I heard that Jerrell was still pulling the trigger of the Colt when T-bone's boy shot him to pieces.

I was on the street after a trick, rinsing my mouth with Lavoris, when one of the girls told me the news, and I spat it out high into the air, a victory fountain yellow-green under the anticrime lights and then dancing my devil dance down NE Seventh Street heart on fire with demonic glee yelling and screaming, not knowing then that it was the squealing of an animal in a trap. The people I passed stared at me, probably thinking what's that ho so happy about. Shameful to me now, but if I have to speak the truth, the truth was that it was glorious to feel the strength of his evil hand in me.

I grabbed a cab for Jerrell's place. Of course I had made a copy of his house key too. During one of his after-torture snoozes I'd taken wax impressions in a little tin box

I got from one of my regulars, a car thief, who made the house key and car keys up for me in return for a couple of free fucks. That's how I got into Jerrell's glove compartment, so I could pull the firing pin out of his Colt, as Ray Bob had taught me to do during one of his famous gun maintenance and safety sessions.

But no cash did I find there. Either someone had beat me or he was carrying his whole roll or he'd lost it all at cards. There was a nice bag of blow, however, and some gold junk. I'm trying to think of what my plan was for after that. Get out of town was the first part of it, or at least away from the part of town where I was known. I had a fugitive warrant out on me, and it wouldn't take the cops long to figure out that Jerrell getting shot had to be an inside job. Maybe T-bone would be unjustly accused of setting it up, with me as an accomplice. I got into another cab and told the guy to drive south. I was thinking the Keys eventually, but I needed a little time to get myself together, so I told the driver to take me to Coconut Grove because I had heard that kids hung out there and I wanted to be a kid again, even a homeless kid.

As I recall, it was a Friday night a balmy evening and the streets were full. I got some strange looks, as I was wearing a silver threaded halter top and tiny pink shorts and white platforms. I went into a Gap and bought jeans, a couple of T-shirts, a shoulder bag, and tossed the whore garments in the trash. I washed the whore makeup off in a restaurant bathroom, dropping several years in the process. I was finished with whoring, or at least finished with it on the street level. I was not that gorgeous I knew, but I had technique and I was a good enough actress and I had a look some men liked. I did a couple of lines of coke in the Gap dressing room to improve my attitude and went out to see what I could turn up in the way of shelter.

I went to the park they have there down by the water, and there were plenty of kids hanging out to the sound of Def Leppard from a boom box. There were a couple of bicycle cops too, but they didn't give me a glance. I am a *good fitter-in. I went over to the raggediest bunch of kids I could find, looking for the telltale bedrolls and bags, was asked for spare change, handed over a couple of bills, got to talking to a gangly Mohawked and tattooed white boy holding a string leash attached to a black and white mutt. Tommy and Bo. Tommy had a girlfriend, Carmen, brown skin, buckteeth, dreads, bracelet tats on the wrists, heavily pierced about the face and navel. Told some plausible lies, learned the ropes on how to be a homeless teenager in Miami. Right now they were staying in a squat set up in an old commercial building on Douglas off Grand. It was scheduled for demo, but there was some legal delay and really nobody owned it. There were some bad junkies hanging there and guys, you know, looking to score young girls. And boys. But you could avoid them. They usually spent the night there, in the Market, as they called it.*

*I bought them both a meal at a fast-food place, and late that night we crawled through the chain-link and crossed the rubbled parking lot. It was a two-story concrete block building whose main distinguishing feature was a high square tower that held a water tank and had once displayed the logo of the defunct retailer. The main squat was a cavernous former drugstore. There were a couple of dozen people there sitting around candles, making it sort of like a cathedral, although one whose god had taken a hike. Tommy and Carmen were obviously well known. People petted Bo and talked quietly. There were smaller kids there, with parents and without. Carmen lent me one of her blankets and showed me how to make a pallet out of plastic bags and newspapers. Not the Hilton, but after all that had happened that day I found I was exhausted. I would have slept pretty well except I had shoved the bag with my gold jewelry down into my underpants, and every time I rolled over it woke me up.*

*In the morning I got on the Metrorail and took it downtown, where I found a no-questions pawnshop and got rid of Jerrell for four hundred and change.*

*Why these details? I am drifting, am I not? The tone is*

*drifting too, isn't it, the person I am now oozing back into the past, coloring the story with later experience. The voice problem again. Oh, Jesus, if you could just help me get out of my own way for two minutes at a time . . . !*

*Okay, back to the park, hook up again with Tommy and Carmen. Smoked some mediocre dope. Was offered crack but declined. Got hit on by two guys in their twenties, offered money too, I guess it showed, I mean what I really was, but declined that too. It was the world of no-plans, we were like pigeons pecking at bits and pieces. Restful in a way, much easier than whoring. A week or two or three passed like this. Then one morning Carmen said it was her birthday, sixteen, and cried. It turned out she came from a family that did not believe in parties, some religious nut thing, and she had never had one. So I did the first fairly selfless thing I ever did in my life—hey I got some money, I'll throw you a party tonight at the Market, and I did, cake and candles from the Winn-Dixie, KFC, beer on my fake ID. I don't know where it came from, maybe the first feathery light touch of my saint.*

*It was nice for her and for the kids I guess. I was pretty out of it because I started having bad cramps around four in the afternoon and they just got worse, and Motrin didn't do anything for them. I was bleeding like crazy too, not like usual at all. I started to think seriously about my plumbing, writhing there on my pallet, and realized that my cycle had been screwy for months, although I laid that to my career choice at the time. I should also say that, weirdly enough, while I was having sex with hundreds of men a week the idea that it would have some effect on my body never once crossed my mind, I was that young.*

*Anyway Carmen asked me what was wrong and I told her and she said I ought to go to the hospital and I said no way, for obvious reasons, and then Audrey, an older woman with two kids, said I ought to try the sister van, which was this nun who drove a white bread truck around where the homeless hung out and handed out medicine and did exams and never asked about anything. You're on the run, right? she asked, and I admitted I was.*

Tommy and Carmen half carried me to a parking lot on Dixie Highway off Douglas where an old white-painted bread van stood under the orangey anticrime lights surrounded by a small group of homeless patients. I was dripping blood down my pants leg, so they let me through first. The van's interior was brightly lit off the idling engine and held a gurney, a metal stool, shelves, and cabinets. The proprietress was about forty, smooth brown skin looking darker against a white head cloth with red piping across the brow and under the broad forehead black serious eyes behind steel-rimmed glasses. Something wrong with her face, the right side drawn up in a funny way, so that it looked like a smirk but there was no smirking in the rest of it, the opposite really, deep serious. Gray dress, white apron like a restaurant cook, a chain with a heavy silver crucifix on it, a pin at her breast, another lighter chain around her neck with something small and brassy on it. She looked like she weighed ninety pounds wet, but her grip as she helped me on the gurney was like a jockey's. She slammed the door on the interested crowd. Trinidad Salcedo, my very first Blood Sister.

Off with the jeans and underpants, soaked red. Temperature taken, blood pressure. I was weeping with pain. She looked, probed gently and at length. A smell of antiseptic and a sting. More pain. I howled. She was between my thighs, busy. What's wrong with me? Her head rose above my belly. How long have you been pregnant? Are you nuts? I'm not pregnant! You were, she said, you just had a miscarriage. More antiseptic, stick in the arm, a tiny cylinder filling with red. Wave of nausea. Take these. Pills. I swallowed, asked for another glass of water. I pulled up my bloody jeans.

What's your name? I gave her Emily, and she introduced herself. You in the life? No small talk from Sister Trinidad. A lie leaped nimbly to my lips but a sudden and unfamiliar impulse batted it away. Yeah, I said, but I quit. Good girl, she said, and it wasn't until that very moment that I realized that it was true. She handed me a bottle.

*You have crab lice. This is insecticidal shampoo. She gave me a photocopied list of places where I could get a shower.*

*There was a knocking on the van door. She opened it, and there was an old deteriorated piss bum with a gash on his forehead. She ushered him in and motioned me into a corner of the van. I sat on a padded chest and watched her work. She talked to him more than she had to me, she knew his name, apparently not the first visit. He stank, and I wondered how she could stand to touch him, and felt obscurely jealous and then felt angry with myself for giving a rat's ass.*

*Stitched and bandaged, he left. A couple of more customers then, mostly first aid, but one baby too, the mother a little older than me, speaking Spanish, frightened. The nurse seemed to have forgotten me. I may have dozed.*

*Her hand on my shoulder, face close to mine. I have to move to my next stop, she said, and asked me if I had a place to stay? I said I did. I asked her if she was a nun. She said she was a sister, she explained that nuns are sisters who live in communities, which she and the others of her order did not, and told me the name of it, which meant nothing to me. I don't think we had any sisters or nuns in Caluga County. She waited for me to go, but for some reason I was reluctant to leave her presence, no not for some reason, no this was the Holy Spirit making his first little chip at the ashes impacted around my heart. I said what do those letters mean, pointing at her badge. It was a gold cross on white enamel with a red bleeding heart in the center and on the arms of the cross U V I M and around the gold rim*

S N S B C * F A M

*She said pointing this means Society of Nursing Sisters of the Blood of Christ and Fidelis ad Mortem, and these letters stand for <u>ubi vadimus ibi manemur</u>. I asked what it meant and she said it means faithful unto death and where we go there we stay. I must have looked blank be-*

cause she explained that it meant that when they decided to go someplace and take care of people, they stuck with their patients even if it meant the sisters had to die. I asked whether any of them had ever died, and she said only about a hundred or so. In Miami? She let out a surprising guffaw then hid her face in her hands, a strange sort of oriental gesture, and begged my pardon. No, in other countries. We specialize in helping people hurt by wars, she said, and asked if I wanted to go to the hospital. I said no and asked her why she was here there wasn't any wars in Miami except dope wars and she said she was taking a break, this was like a vacation for her.

I had a lot more questions, like what was that little brass angel she wore around her neck, but although she wasn't looking impatient or anything I could feel her vibing me out of there. She handed me a package of thick sanitary pads. Take care of yourself, Emily, she said, and God bless you. She looked at me and I could feel that she could see through me just like I thought Ray Bob could that time, but instead of seeing all the bad she was just seeing the good. It surprised the hell out of me at the time since I didn't think I had any in there. Then I was outside thinking that aside from Percival Orne Foy she was the most interesting person I ever met.

# Twelve

They put Paz on administrative leave while they investigated the shooting. He didn't think it would be much of an investigation, because they had the guy's gun, there was a civilian witness (Lorna Wise) backing up Paz's story to the letter, and the victim was a well-known local scumbag named Amando Cortez, Dodo Cortez to his friends and the police, who knew him as a head breaker and enforcer for the dope people. He had a pair of murder arrests on his sheet, both of which he had beat at trial, and a thirty-six-month jolt for aggravated assault/attempted murder. He was also a whiteish Cuban and so could be shot by a cop of any color whatever without hysteria breaking out.

Paz was spending his first day of administrative leave with Lorna Wise, who had also taken the day off, and had called him early and then turned off her phone. He was surprised to have been thus called, but he had driven over, and now they were sitting in her little terrace out back under a mango tree, drinking iced tea together like old friends, which they certainly were not, but there was something working there, under the surface.

She asked whether he was in any trouble, and he explained that it was what they called a good shooting, and why.

" 'A good shooting,' " she said. "What an expression!"

"As opposed to a bad one, the old lady shot in the back because a cop was under the impression that she was a crazed felon with a shotgun about to attack."

"Does that happen?"

"In Miami? More than it should. We got a bunch of detectives on trial now for running sort of a death squad, whacking bad guys they didn't like. How are you feeling, by the way?" He had noticed a crinkling around her eyes, as if she were going to cry.

"A little numb. I never saw anyone killed before. I never even saw a dead body, except for my mom." She took a long, deep breath. "I guess you have, though."

"Lots." He paused and smiled slyly. "Would it be more comforting if I said you never get used to it or if I said oh, yeah, after a while it stops bothering you?"

"How about the actual truth?"

"Ah, the truth! Okay, the truth is, it depends on the condition and type of the corpse. A three-year-old kid's been in a cardboard box for a week in August is rough, and a fresh gangbanger with one through the ear is no big deal."

"What about killing people. Does that depend too?"

"I'm not sure on that one. I only ever killed two people, including your guy."

"The other was that voodoo one."

"Yeah, that one," said Paz in a tone that closed the subject like the hatch on a sub.

He drank some tea and said, "So. We need to discuss a little. Off the record, for starters. I noticed you policed up that book your guy dropped. Emmylou's notebook."

"Yes. And please stop calling him 'my guy,' like we were dating."

"Sorry. Anyway, the notebook. Technically, that's violating the integrity of a crime scene."

"Is it? I noticed you didn't say anything about it to your colleagues. Technically, isn't that abetting the violation of the integrity of a crime scene?"

He twitched his eyebrows like Groucho. "Yeah, we're a couple of felons together. Meanwhile, are you going to let me read the thing?"

She put her iced tea down on the picnic table and walked off. Paz watched her body as she did so. Paz was an ass man, although he was amusedly conscious of how banal that preference was in a man of his culture. There it was, however, and it could not be denied that Lorna Wise had a terrific butt, although she had no idea of how to display it. In fact, he did not think he had ever seen a woman less at ease with her body. He studied her also as she came out of the house toward the little patio. A Gap dresser, naturally, khaki bermudas and a light blue T-shirt, wonderfully convexed. Paz did not mind a decent rack, the absence not a deal breaker for him as it was for some men, more of a nice-to-have, but clearly their owner did not agree. It was like she was trying to cross her shoulders over them. Peculiar, but interesting in a way.

"What?" she said, noticing at last. "Do I have egg on my shirt?"

"No, you're egg free," he replied and gestured at the notebook. "There it is. Do you mind if I read it now?"

"Not at all. I have some things to do around the house. Take your time."

He did and it wasn't easy, a little battle between his detective's urge to seek out and absorb all evidence and his personal desire never to have anything more to do with Emmylou Dideroff or any of her works. He had hoped that it would be a regular confession, a list of facts, of crimes committed, not something so intimate, not something directed at him, Paz, as if he were a literal confessor. He felt as if she were looking into him in that hideous way she had in the interview room, *something* looking at him through her. He made himself finish it and then leaned back and closed his eyes. He was going crazy, getting undeniable now, it was affecting his work already, and now this flesh-crawling nauseated feeling as he read the notebook, he was going mad, or else . . .

His mind skipped a little, like a scratched record. He was going mad, or else . . . or else it was . . . Paz's well-oiled circuit breakers popped. When he opened his eyes again, Lorna was sitting across from him, in the warm mango-scented shade.

"So, what do you think?"

He blinked and sat up. She said, "You were sleeping. Was it that boring?"

"No, I was just thinking," he said, rubbing his face.

"No one will ever admit that they're asleep, except when they're in bed. I wonder why that is?"

"You're the psychologist, Lorna. You tell me."

She let this pass, pointing to the notebook. "Any conclusions?"

With some effort, Paz reinhabited his cop persona. "No, but I'm dying to hear the rest of it. Any chance of us doing a full-scale interrogation at this point?"

"On a mental patient? Look, this has to come out as it comes. She gets extremely hostile when you press her on stuff that's outside the stream of the narrative. She seized the last time I pushed her."

"But she's playing with us. I mean you picked that up, right? You got that whole cornpone peckerwood thing, and there's what sounds like an educated woman looking over her shoulder and making wiseass remarks, and then there's the religious nut quoting St. Augustine. It doesn't make sense. It's not anything like a real confession."

"No, but you're not looking at an integrated personality here. We all agree that she's seriously deranged."

Paz got up abruptly and paced a few times across the flagstones, then turned to face her, pointing. "Say I give you that. Say it's sound and fury, she's traumatized, whatever, multiple personalities—"

"I didn't say multiple personalities. . . ."

"Well, whatever—deranged, like you said. The key thing here, the *key* thing, is what's *not* in that book. Hm?"

"The dog that didn't bark in the night."

"That dog." A quick grin. "Which is, there is absolutely nothing there that would make anyone take the risk of doing a B and E to get it. An armed burglary, which is very rare. Burglars are almost never armed. I mean why risk it—the whole point of burglary is in-and-out, nobody sees you."

"There's the sexual stuff."

"You mean for blackmail? No, the perp is dead, and I can't see old Ray Bob's family wanting to protect his good name after all these years. Okay, there's the Foy dope dealing too, but I can't see that either. She could say she bought smack from the governor, it's not probative, it don't mean anything without concrete evidence. It could be the ravings of a lunatic, no, it *is* the ravings of a lunatic. So why is it maybe worth killing for?"

"You think it's connected to . . ."

He rolled his eyes. "Well, hell, yeah! The vic, the Arab, comes to town, he sells some oil and talks about a huge oil find, it's going to change the world oil situation, and he also says he's hiring muscle, he's scared of something. Then, of all the people he could possibly meet in Miami, who does he run into but our girl Emmylou, who has a reason to whack him, and who gets found in his place after he gets slammed on the head with an auto part out of her truck and tossed off his balcony? You think that's a coincidence?"

"It could be," she says weakly.

"No way. My boss said it, and it's true. Somebody's playing with us, and . . . hm." Paz stopped and stared off into the middle distance for a long half minute. Then he pulled a cell phone out of the pocket of his jeans. "Excuse me a second," he said and called up a number. He walked a small distance away and turned his back.

"Yo, Tito, it's me. Yeah, I'm good. Look, man, I want you to do something for me. Get the package on Dodo Cortez, tour his usual places, talk to his known associates. No, this's got nothing to do with the shooting; the shooting is cool, but I want to know what he's been up to recently, his source of income, who he was working for. I especially want to know if there's any connection whatever between him and Jack Wilson. No, don't go see Wilson. No, we'll go see him together. Just get all the background you can. Are you following me here? You know why I want this, right?"

"Right," said Paz after a longer pause. "Good man. Get back to me at my place tomorrow, on the land line, not the cell. Okay, take care."

Paz sat down across from Lorna, his face more serious than it had been. "Lorna. Look, here's the thing. I don't want to freak you out or anything, but it just now hit me: I don't like that they sent Dodo Cortez on this."

"Why not?"

"Because he's not a break-in artist at all. He's a shooter. You would've been home that morning if I hadn't called you and asked you to come to my place."

A small gasp from Lorna. "What, you think he would've *threatened* me? But I don't *know* anything."

"Yeah, but *they* don't know that. All they know is that she's writing stuff down and you're her therapist. People tell stuff to therapists. Maybe she told you the thing."

"What thing? *What?* Oh, God, this is ridiculous! It's like some movie . . . secret messages, guns, people getting shot. No, thank you, this is *not* part of my job, this is *not* happening to me." She looked away from him. "I'm sorry. This is starting to look like a mistake on my part. I mean an interesting case and all, but, ah, I can't have this kind of stuff, threats and bloodshed. No, I'm sorry, that's not me."

Nearly a minute slipped by in silence. Then Paz said, in a neutral voice, "Okay, you can pass the case on to somebody else. I mean, I think we can reduce the risk to . . . whoever, but if you can't handle it, you can't. I'll keep this notebook and we'll make arrangements to get any others she produces."

He picked up the notebook. He said, "If you do decide to drop out, you'll let me know who the new man is, okay? Nice seeing you again."

He started to leave.

Lorna finds herself up on her feet, the metal chair scraping the flags with an unpleasant violent noise, and she hears her own voice saying, "No, please, stay. I didn't mean it that way."

She knows she did mean it that way. The new man. The new *man.* Did he do that on purpose, is he that manipulative? Doesn't matter; she's manipulated. He cocks his head a little and gives her a searching look, connecting, not staring at her tits this time; she'd thought Oh, no, not another one of those, and now she sees he's not, although she doesn't know quite what to think of his eyes on her body, and here they're in the middle of a desperate professional conversation. The strong light through the mango tree renders a camouflage pattern on his tan face and lends glitter to his odd light eyes. She is frightened of him, there's a voice in her head saying *Stupid stupid crazy you're crazy get away from this stupid crazy. . . .* It's a voice she knows well, her father's voice, and these were and are his favorite expressions for anything outside the pale of his rationality. *Don't be stupid, Lorna! That's crazy, Amy!* The dead mom. *Don't be crazy, Amy, there's nothing wrong with you.* Was that something he actually said? Or something she imagined him saying. No, *focus,* Lorna . . .

The cop is still looking at her, but now there is a tiny wrinkle on his smooth forehead. "Are you okay?" he says.

"Yes, I'm fine."

He grins impudently. "No one will ever admit they have a problem, except when they're bleeding. Why is that?"

She can't catch her breath and there is no strength in her legs.

She goes down hard into her chair, and again that scraping sound.

After clearing her throat, swallowing some tea, she finds her voice. "I'm sorry, really. I guess it all just hit me at once. There was a . . . a killer in my house and you shot him dead right on my sidewalk." She cries, not hysterics thank God, just a slow ooze of tears. She dabs delicately with a paper napkin, careful of her eye makeup.

"Oh, good, finally!" he says.

"What is that supposed to mean?"

"It means it's okay to come apart a little when something like that goes down. They have therapy programs for incidents, people who're involved in violence. Christ, you of all people should know that. I've been watching you, after it went down and now today, and I'm thinking where does she keep it and how is it going to come out? And here it is. You looked like you were about to keel over just then."

"I was," she says, but she knows it's not just post-traumatic stress working here. There is deep stuff stirring, stuff that Mickey Lopez never got to in over two years of therapy, she thinks, and then quickly excuses Mickey, it's all her fault really, but now some combination of Emmylou Dideroff, and violence, and this strange man on her patio, attractive and repellent at the same time (*That body! That gun!*), is working on the toxic sludge, raising clouds of fear, of excitement. She does not choose to explain this to the cop. She takes a number of deep breaths, attaining control. The tears dry.

"Uh-huh, and about continuing with Emmylou, you still want to pull out?"

"No!" Too vehement. More calmly, she says, "I mean, no, I don't think it would be good for her to . . . change therapists at this point."

She has to look away from him, for even to her own ears it sounds like sanctimonious bullshit. The moment passes. He sits down.

"Fine. Good. And now that we got that settled, I have to say I thought you showed a lot of class in this whole deal."

"Class?"

"Yeah. Guy knocks you down and there's a gun battle outside your house, you don't run around in circles screaming, you calmly call 911 and then you calmly hide the vital evidence, and even though you're scared right now, you decided to do the right thing. And you got a nice smile. Thank you."

She feels like an idiot, grinning as she now is, and he is grinning too, that thin cat grin with the little lights in his eyes. "And there's more," he says, "truly the coolest thing, is that you didn't ask me even once what I was doing handcuffed to my bed."

"Well, we psychologists are trained to discretion."

"You didn't want to embarrass me."

"You don't strike me as someone easily embarrassed."

"Trained to perception too. Cool, discreet, perceptive: that's a nice trifecta."

She laughs, not a maidenish titter, but a real laugh of pleasure. It is pleasant being tossed compliments by this attractive man, and she understands that these compliments are not mere sexual flattery, but the honest assessment of a potential comrade with whom she may be about to go in harm's way. He really wants her to know what he thinks of her. It is unutterably refreshing and unlike any experience she has had with a man before. Some beaming here, and then this moment passes too.

"So," he says with a brisk clap, "I owe you a boat ride. We could get some food and beer, run over to Bear Cut and have a picnic, get some fishing in. You up for that?"

She is. She goes into the house and dons the blue bikini without examining herself in the full-length mirror, and puts shorts and a Hawaiian shirt over that, and plops a canvas beach hat on her head. In his Z car they head north, and in the region known as Souwesera, he cuts into a strip of stores near the tan bulk of a rent-a-locker storage operation and enters a tacky-looking Cuban joint to get their picnic. She sits in the warming car, looking at the storefronts through her sunglasses, slowly translating the signs in Spanish, wishing she had paid more attention during her single year of the language. She feels ridiculously content, the only little cloud being that at some point in the afternoon she may have to take off her shirt and shorts and stand revealed in this insanely revealing bathing suit.

It is well that she has stopped giving a shit, although she wonders why this is so. Perhaps a brain tumor in the rostral portion of the frontal lobes. As it grows, she will lose more and more inhibitions until she is putting out not only for her colleagues, but also for everyone, jail guards, this fat guy sitting in front of the Cuban joint in the wife-beater undershirt and the black cigar, or patients, maybe even Rigoberto Munoz, tardive dyskinesia and all, and just as she thinks this, who should appear within her field of vision but Rigoberto himself. He has deteriorated since the last time she saw him. He has his own wife-beater undershirt on, with an open dotted seersucker shirt over it, both filthy and torn. He is mumbling, grimacing, sticking his tongue *all* the way out and otherwise demonstrating that he is off the meds. He is attempting to correct this by self-medicating via a forty-ounce malt liquor clutched in a paper bag, and yes, he has spotted her, although she is now crouching low in her seat and pulling down on the brim of her beach hat.

He grins horribly and waggles his tongue. "Hey, Doc," he calls and bellies up to the car, giving off a mighty stench: the beer train has crashed into the vomit factory.

"Hey, Doc, hey, I gotta job."

"That's wonderful, Rigoberto."

"Yeah, hey, I gotta a job onna fish boat with, hey, you know my cousin Jorge? I gotta job with him cleaning fish up by, uh, that bridge, what you call it? The fish boat."

In case she does not know how fish are cleaned, he demonstrates by taking a thick-handled, black-bladed knife out of a belt sheath and waving it in front of her nose.

"Them, hey, them people are back, Doc," he says. "You know they talkin in my head again. They say to do bad things but I don't listen to them no more, uh-uh. Like you said, um. Where you goin' in the car, hey?" Waving the knife. She watches it, semihypnotized, feeling the smile straining at her lips.

Then Paz is there, with an arm around Munoz's shoulders, gripping hard. *"Oye, Rigoberto, mi hermano, ¿qué tal?"* he says, walking the man away from the car. There is a brief conversation in rapid Spanish, and the lunatic shambles off. Paz has taken the beer away, which he flings neatly into a trash barrel.

He returns to the car, places a paper bag and a plastic bag of ice onto the backseat.

"You know Rigoberto?" she asks.

"Oh, yeah, me and him go way back. He was one of my first collars when I was in uniform. He didn't scare you, did he?"

"No, me and Rigoberto go way back too. But you get credit for another rescue."

"I don't know about rescue. He's pretty harmless if you don't set him off."

"Yes, harmless for a violent paranoid schizophrenic with a big knife. But the amazing thing is I was just this *instant* thinking about him and here he is."

"Plate o' shrimp," says Paz, tooling out of the lot and onto Twelfth Avenue.

"Pardon?"

"Plate o' shrimp. *Repo Man?* The movie?"

"You lost me."

Paz puts on a drawling accent. "Say you're thinkin' about a plate of shrimp, and all of a sudden somebody says 'Plate o' shrimp' or 'Plate of shrimp,' just like that, out of the blue. No explanation. No point in lookin' for one either." In his ordinary voice he adds, "A little later in the movie you see this sign in a restaurant: 'Plate of Shrimp $2.99.' It's a classic."

"It sounds like it. I'll have to rent the video."

"I got it at home, we can watch it later."

"You're a full-service operation, Paz."

"We don't cash checks," says Paz.

Paz's boat is a twenty-three-foot locally built plywood cabin cruiser with a planing hull and a 150-horsepower Mercury outboard. It is painted fading pink on the topsides and chipped dirty white below, and is called the *MA TA II* according to metallic stick-on letters applied to the stern. Lorna is completely charmed by it, having spent more time than she really wanted to on large, spotless doctors' yachts where you had to wear special shoes so as not to mar the teak deck and got yelled at when you pulled on the wrong goddamned rope. Nothing seems to be required of her on this vessel, so she arranges herself on a padded locker at the stern and sits like the Queen of Sheba with a cold Miller as Paz arranges their departure and heads down the Miami River, under the bridges, past the little boatyards and moored boats, the downtown towers and the highway full of cars full of people who have somewhere to go, but they are free for the day, and when they leave the river's mouth and clear Claughton Island, he opens it up. The boat sits up on its plane like a well-trained dog, and they are off on the sparkling blue bay, headed south, and a weight she didn't know she was carrying lifts off her.

They fly under the causeway, and he veers left and cuts the motor to a burble and steers into the shallows. They coast, and when they are in two feet of water he heaves the motor back and tosses out an anchor. They float off a little beach backed by a line of mangroves and Australian pines waving and casting moving shadows on the sands. As it is a weekday, there are only a few blankets laid, Cuban matrons sitting and the tan children dashing about, their shrill calls like those of seabirds.

They wade ashore with their beach burdens. They spread their blanket, Paz's blanket, none too clean unfortunately, but while she can detect no absolutely shameful stains, she cannot help wondering how many on this very blanket. He removes his garments and proves to be wearing a minuscule black French bathing suit. She forces her greedy eyes away from that zone and focuses instead on his chest. There's that crucifix and that walnut-size brown lump on its thong. Before this, she has never consciously socialized with a man who wore a crucifix, although she has seen boys in high school who did. They usually spent a lot of time in shop. To distract herself from this memory, she asks, "What's that around your neck?"

He touches the crucifix. "This? It's a symbol of Christianity. You see, many centuries ago, God came down from heaven, and by the power of the Holy Spirit . . ."

Laughing at her. "I mean that other thing."

"Oh, that! That's an *enkangue*. A charm in Santería. You know what Santería is, right?"

"Vaguely. What does it charm?"

"It wards off zombies, among other things."

"Have you been much troubled by zombies?" she asks archly.

"Not that much, recently," he says, "but when I got it they were pretty thick on the ground."

He does not seem to be joking, but he has to be; maybe there is something Cuban that she isn't getting. Looking around, she says, "I can't see any. It must be working."

"QED," he says and smiles at her.

They eat their sandwiches and drink cold Miller twelves. Paz takes out his cell and makes a call but gets no answer. Lorna doesn't ask whom he's calling, but hopes it is not another woman. She realizes she knows nothing about this man, that he might, in fact, be the kind who would be capable of lining up a date while on a date. If this is a date. She becomes by degrees a little depressed, and this makes her desire food. Ordinarily she doesn't care much for Cuban fare, finding it fatty and crudely spiced, but when she bites into this sandwich she experiences deliciousness. The roll is absolutely fresh, the two meats succulent and tasting of the grill, fresh pepper, and anise, the cheese is real unprocessed Swiss, the pickles add just the right astringency, without that awful sweat-making rush.

She makes a spontaneous mmm of pleasure.

"Good sandwich?"

"Incredible!" she says around a wad of it.

He tells her about the sandwich, how it is the best Cuban sandwich in continental North America and why, how his mother found Manny Fernandez in his little shop years ago, how she encouraged his instincts toward perfection, how this sandwich became the featured item on the lunch truck she had before the restaurants, how her reputation spread, how Cubano construction and landscaping workers would drive miles to where she was parked and bring dozens of sandwiches back to the job site, how they prospered enough to buy their first little place.

She liked the way he told it, funny but without the mockery or resentment that many hard-knocks immigrants threw in. Then he said, "What about you? What's your perfect Cuban sandwich?"

Lorna prides herself on being a good listener, a useful trait, considering the sort of men she has chosen to be around most of her life. One of the reasons she picked clinical psych was that people told you about their lives and did not wish very much to know about yours. So there is not a ready spate, her Cuban sandwich does not spring instantly to mind. He gets her résumé therefore, together with the usual set-piece anecdotes about college and grad school and internship, but nothing deeper, and a number of the fibs she uses to ward off any efforts to dig. But she expresses her desire to find out what makes people tick, why they were so different, one from the other, and to learn if skilled interpretation of standard instruments can ferret out their secret pain. He listens. To her surprise, he asks informed questions, she warms to her subject. She began this outing with a number of expectations about what would transpire, but a lively discussion about the operational differences between nonparametric and parametric statistics was not one of them. She draws in the sand with a stick, the normal curve, the equations and tables that analyze variance. . . .

There is at last a silence. "Getting hot," he says. "Let's have a swim." He walks to the water, wades in, and dives below the surface with barely a splash. She pulls off her top and shorts. She has prepared herself with two beers, but this is always a sticky moment for her. She walks toward his head, now floating above the shimmering surface, slick and glistening like a seal's. He watches her with an appreciative smile as she enters the water; she feels his gaze settle on her, and she hurries her steps to submerge her body. The water is tepid and has an oily feel, as if megagallons of bath oils have been added to Biscayne Bay.

They bob together, in chin-high water, touching briefly, then floating away like flotsam. She thinks it must be the beer, this voluptuous languor she now feels, she has not been out on the water since the breakup with Howie Kasdan, who now passes across her mind. If Howie were here, and he never would have come to so plebian a beach as Bear Cut, he would be swimming laps, making her swim laps too, coaching her, deprecating her style.

On the beach someone turns a radio up, music and a woman's voice singing in Spanish. Paz turns to her and says, in a conversational tone, "She sang beyond the genius of the sea, the water never formed to mind or voice, like a body wholly body, fluttering its empty sleeves; and yet its mimic motion made constant cry . . ."

For a moment Lorna thinks he is translating the lyrics of the radio's song, but after a moment she doubts that the sentiment is one ordinarily expressed on Cuban AM's Top 40.

". . . caused constantly a cry, that was not ours although we understood, inhuman, of the veritable ocean." A grin after this and a gesture to the Bay, its sky, its littoral.

"What's that?" she asked after an astonished pause.

" 'The Idea of Order at Key West,' first stanza," he replied, "by Wallace Stevens. A friend of mine always used to recite the whole thing whenever we were out on the tropic seas."

An unexpected little stab of jealousy here. "So you weren't an English major."

"Nope."

"Not psych?"

"Not anything."

"Everyone has a major. Where did you go to school?"

"Archbishop Curley High."

"I mean college."

"I didn't," he said.

"Really? But . . . how come . . . I mean . . ."

"How come a dumb-ass high school graduate cop can converse about clinical psych and spout modernist poetry?"

"I didn't mean that."

"You did, but I don't take offense. I have smarts but no patience for sitting in a classroom or taking tests. I resent tests. I have a good memory for what I hear, and I've picked the brains of a lot of smart people, mainly women. I get books recommended. Sometimes I even read them. I use a dictionary for the big words. You could say that I went to the University of Girl. For example, before this afternoon I didn't know what Wilcoxon's signed rank test was, and now I do. But to be honest, I'm a mile wide and an inch deep. I don't really know anything, alls I have are these bits and pieces, like one of those birds that collects shiny things, what d'y call 'ems . . . ?"

"Magpies."

"Magpies, right. And that's okay in a way because it turns out that knowing a little bit about a lot of stuff is handy if you're a detective. Because there's really only one thing I have absolutely got to know."

"Which is?"

"How to read people," says Paz and shifts slightly in the water so that he is facing her, with the sun at his back and the dazzle of it coming off the water and forming a bright nimbus about his head.

He says, "Can I ask you a personal question?"

She feels a pressure in her chest. An infarct? That Cuban sandwich? She takes a deep breath and another. "Sure," she says.

"Why do you walk like you do?"

"What do you mean?" she asks, knowing very well.

"All slumped over with your shoulders rolled forward. Is this embarrassing? I mean you didn't have some kind of tragic childhood disease?"

"No." Floods of shame.

He slips behind her and puts his hands on her shoulders. His fingers probe, pull, gentle but insistent. "What is this in here, concrete?" he says. "Just relax, okay? Let me do this." His left arm slides around the front of her and rests just above the line of her breasts and he pulls her into the pressure of his thumb, which now seems to be penetrating her body in a way that is both pleasant and slightly frightening. His hands move to the muscles around her neck. His thumbs press and move an inch, press and move on. It's not at all sexy, but it's not clinical either. She has been massaged before but nothing like this. She feels waves in her flesh. Control is slipping away, control she did not really know she was exerting. But now she exerts.

He feels the resistance and stops. She drifts a little away and says, "What was that?"

"Shiatsu. Your ki is blocked up big-time."

"Thank you." Coldly. "Did you learn that at the University of Girl?"

"I did." Now she swims away from him, feeling anger. She is not sure she wants to join that faculty yet. She leaves the water and starts walking back to where they have left their blanket. She feels strange in her body, and at first she thinks it's only because she's been floating in salt water for so long, but then realizes that it's not the usual heaviness and imbalance you get when you leave the support of the sea but its opposite. She feels lighter and more balanced on her feet. She is not slouching as much, her shoulders are back, her breasts seem to have filled with air.

They lie on the blanket at a respectable distance from each other. She has no idea what to say to him now. He is lying back with his eyes closed, a rolled towel behind his head.

"God, I'm really tired," he says.

She starts to rub sunblock on her skin. "Take a nap," she says. "Would you like me to put the handcuffs on you?"

"You've been dying to ask, right?"

"Busted."

"The reason is because I'm a somnambulist." He tells her about the egg-woman nightmare and his wanderings.

"Interesting. You're being told that anonymous sex with eggheads is a room with no outlet. A closed hell."

He laughs and says, "So no more sex with eggheads is the prescription for restful nights?"

"Oh, I think eggheads are fine. It's the anonymity you have to watch." Their eyes meet now and there is a silence that becomes uncomfortable. She looks away first.

"Have you tried pills?"

"No. Pills won't help. What it is, to tell you the truth, I was sort of knocked out of the real world for a while. And some of that other . . . stuff stuck to me."

"You mean that voodoo business?" Her eyes go to the thing around his neck.

"That voodoo business, yes."

"But you don't really, I mean *really,* believe in all that."

His eyes open and his stare is flat and baleful. "I don't know what I believe anymore. But I'm not as ready to call it bullshit as I used to be. And I got news for you: Our girl Emmylou in your nuthouse, she's been there too. I can always tell."

His eyes close again. A small cloud covers the sun now, and a little chill wind like a wraith speeds along the beach. She feels a shiver pucker her skin.

By the time she finishes with the sunblock, Paz is breathing deeply, fast asleep. She is actually glad about this, as she needs time to think. Lorna does not care much for violent amusement park rides, but she has been on a few, and this is what it feels like when the roller coaster is towing the car up the first steep slope: anticipation, and the desire to flee, and the expectation of the screaming rush of descent. She works on her breathing.

She lies back and turns her face toward him. His skin is four inches from her mouth and out of nowhere comes an intense desire to lick it, and the thought that it will taste like caramel. Now she actually smells caramel coming off him. Synesthesia? No thank you! She sits up, astounded, and says stern things to herself. It's ludicrous, she hardly knows the man, and with all those other girls, probably has three or four on the string right now, she absolutely does not need this after Rat Howie. . . .

As if propelled by something other than her mind she jumps

to her feet and goes to the water's edge. She looks out at the cut. There is a large white cabin cruiser moving slowly across her field of view. There is a man on the rear deck. He wears a ball cap, and now he removes it and wipes his face with a bandanna. He is very pale and his hair is flaming red. He replaces the hat and raises something black to his face, a long tube of some kind. A telephoto lens, she can see the glint of the glass as he trains it in various directions. He is at it for an oddly long time. She looks around to see if there is any spectacular wildlife behind her, but there is nothing but mangroves and pines and a few gulls. The red-haired man turns to whoever is running the boat, and in the next moment the engine roars as the boat shoots away. It does not occur to her then that he has been photographing her and Paz and Paz's boat, because why would anyone want to do that?

All that morning long the Prussian General von Steinmetz sent waves of young soldiers up the steep ravine of the Mance, where they were cut down in droves by the rifles of the French. Walking wounded began arriving at Bois Fleury shortly after Marie-Ange had settled the stricken peasants in her own bedroom, and when she saw these wretched men and realized that there would be many more in the same state or worse, she sprang into action with her characteristic energy and resolve. Marshaling the household servants and the farm workers, she had the carpets rolled, the furniture moved, lamps and candles arrayed, and pallets made of straw and the linen of the château. Maids were set to turning tablecloths and napkins into bandages. In short order, the German regimental surgeons learned what she was doing and set up their dressing stations in the grand ballroom.

Having seen to everything at the château, and having placed her steward in charge, the intrepid girl assembled some farmhands and wagons and made for the battlefield itself. There she directed the gathering of the helpless wounded onto carts and sending them back to Bois Fleury. She herself crawled through the thickets by the banks of the Mance to find wounded men caught there and then commanded terrified laborers and the few soldiers not engaged in the fighting to help drag them out while shells exploded and bullets snapped through the branches. By late afternoon, she had donned a cook's apron and wound a large white damask napkin cloth around her head, but besides that she remained in the clothes she had put on that morning, under the cavalry cloak. Her house slippers were by then cut to rags and filthy, and a Prussian officer made her put on ammunition boots taken from the body of a French drummer boy. Those who recalled that dreadful day later described Marie-Ange as being everywhere at once, comforting the sick, collecting the wounded, lashing her people to greater efforts. Here she showed for the first time the remarkable powers of organization that would serve her well in later life. One Prussian officer reportedly remarked that "had this girl been our general instead of that old lunatic Steinmetz, half these poor devils would be walking still."

Toward the end of the battle, the Prussians brought their heavy guns to bear and blew the French lines to pieces, after which the stream of wounded pouring into Bois Fleury were French and not German. Of course, these were cared for equally with their enemies, and dying men of both nations had as their last earthly vision the sight of a young girl's face, full of compassion, framed by a white headdress spattered with blood and a white cook's apron. Thus was born in the ranks of both armies the legend of the Angel of Gravelotte.

—FROM *FAITHFUL UNTO DEATH:*
*THE STORY OF THE NURSING SISTERS*
*OF THE BLOOD OF CHRIST,*
BY SR. BENEDICTA COOLEY, SBC,
ROSARIAN PRESS, BOSTON, 1947.

# Thirteen

Paz got his shield back a week after the shooting, not a record for a shooting panel, but still pretty fast. Paz detected the hand of Major Oliphant in this and wondered whether he finally had a rabbi in the department, also whether he liked this or not. Lieutenant Posada, from whom he collected his shield and his service weapon that morning, was his usual morose self. He slid the items across his desk with the élan of a convenience-store clerk delivering a package of chewing gum, together with the information that the major wants to see you. Paz had never done a bad deed to Posada and didn't know why the head of the assault and homicide unit disliked him. It could have been mere race prejudice, or the natural enmity of some dull people for some smart ones, or something more political. It did not keep Paz up nights. Tito Morales was standing in the squad bay when Paz left Posada's office, and he got a thumbs-up and a grin from his partner, but not from any of the other detectives.

Oliphant poured him a ritual cup of coffee and sat him in a comfortable side chair. Paz noted that his cup was marked with the seal of the FBI Academy at Quantico; perhaps meaningful, perhaps not.

After the shortest possible interval of pleasantries, Oliphant said, "So, does it connect up?"

Paz was pleased with the shorthand. His old partner used to do that too, jump over the details and express the thought that two equally smart cops ought to have been thinking at a particular juncture. Cletis would say stuff like "Where was the key?"

and Paz would almost always know what key and where the key should have been, even though no one had mentioned a key before. He said, "It has to, sir. Dodo Cortez got no business burglarizing a South Miami home with a gun in his pants. He was a shooter, basically, and more than that, he worked for Ignacio Hoffmann, who also employed our suspect's current employer, Jack Wilson."

"Hoffmann?"

Paz recalled that Oliphant was still with the Bureau when Ignacio had his non-day in court, so he explained who Ignacio Hoffmann was, the dope running, the bail jumping.

"Interesting," said Oliphant, "but of course I wasn't thinking of that aspect."

"No, it's an extra. The real connection is between our original killing and someone burglarizing the home of Emmylou Dideroff's psychologist. So I'm thinking, what's the prize? Why kill a guy, why burglarize a shrink? The answer has to be information. Someone wants to know something they think our suspect knows and they're willing to use violence to get it."

"You're saying they pressured the victim to tell something, it went too far and they killed him?"

"Maybe, but I have a feeling al-Muwalid was a rival for the same information. I've gone over my notes and talked to my partner and I think we had him wrong. He was hiring muscle around town and we assumed that he wanted to protect himself. What if he was hiring them to look for Emmylou? The oil guy he met, Zubrom, actually told us he was looking for someone, and I ignored it because I was only thinking about danger *to* Muwalid, not that he might be a danger to someone else. I mean, *he* was the one who got whacked. So the odds are that whoever killed Muwalid sent Dodo Cortez to find whatever it was Emmylou might have told her therapist."

"I thought this Dideroff woman killed Muwalid."

"That's the official position."

"But you no longer believe it."

"I'm not sure what I believe, Major. It all depends on who Emmylou D. really is. People think she knows something, but does she know she knows it? Is she a player playing cagey? Or is she a victim?"

"What does she say in that confession she's writing?"

"Not much. A lot of childhood memories and religion. We're awaiting the later installments."

Oliphant swiveled for a moment and sipped thoughtfully from his own FBI mug. "It doesn't work."

"I know," Paz admitted. "The hole in it is that if they thought Emmylou knew something, why didn't they just snatch her up and put the irons to her? Why all this rigmarole with framing her for Muwalid and going after the confession? Well, one possibility is she doesn't know what she knows. She's already been tortured once. Maybe that was their first shot at trying to get it."

"Tortured?"

"Yeah, the docs say she's got recent dislocations in both shoulders and whipping scars on her back and soles of her feet. Burns too. So maybe they think that in a situation she feels is safe, with a therapist who's got no interest in any secrets, she'll let something slip."

"It's plausible," said Oliphant. "Barely. So . . . next move?"

Paz had prepared for this question, of course, and he answered fluently, although with more confidence than he actually felt. Since the early passages of this affair he had caught glimpses of a brewing chaos, weirdness, conspiracy in high places, international crap, the stench of Africa again. It was important to have a tale to cling to, as children do, and now he spun it out.

"Basic fact: Emmylou Dideroff, if she acted at all didn't act alone . . ."

"Because of the missing cell phone."

"Right. There's no cell phone. Next fact: my partner talked to the late Dodo's associates. About a week before the murder Dodo got a phone call that excited him. Apparently Dodo has not had an organizational home since the Hoffmann gang went down, but now he's talking about steady work. He was seen a couple of times by two different people getting into and out of a silver Lexus with a big Anglo guy at the wheel, always at night. According to the regulars at the lounge he hung out in, Dodo's talking big, he's got more money to spend."

"You're starting to like him for the hit on the Arab."

"And Jack Wilson, who drives a silver Lexus. Look, Wilson knew that Emmylou was in the vicinity of a particular machine shop at a particular time, because he sent her there. There's a phone booth across the street from this machine shop. We know that Muwalid got a cell phone call in Zubrom's office and he took off like a bullet after it. Maybe the call said something like we have your information, go to such and such phone booth and wait. That second call both shows him to Emmylou and sets up a meet in his hotel room. He goes there, followed by Emmylou. Emmylou parks the car and begins her search for Muwalid's room. But Cortez already knows the room. He picks up the connecting rod from Emmylou's truck, goes to Muwalid's room, kills him, dumps him over, and leaves. Emmylou arrives and is waiting like a patsy when we walk in."

"Or Emmylou and Wilson are in it together. Maybe she fingered Muwalid for Dodo."

"Then why wouldn't she take off?" Paz asked. "Why was she waiting there praying, or whatever?"

"A deeper game? She wanted to be locked up in a nuthouse for some reason?"

"That's pretty deep. Although, given that it's Emmylou, we can't rule it out."

"Get more facts," said Oliphant.

"Fine. The main fact I need is, do you know anything about the guy who owns her houseboat, David Packer, the man of mystery?"

"Why would you think that?" A little glaring here, which Paz ignored.

"Because you were with the feds and the feds are involved in this in some way, unless you think it's a coincidence that the guy who rented Emmylou her domicile has got the State Department covering up for him when a cop calls for information. I got the sense that there are calls whizzing back and forth between that phone there on your desk and Washington, D.C., and there's a bunch of you watching me to see what I'll turn up, like a bunch of kids watching an ant on a sidewalk, maybe poke it with a stick once in a while. Because if that's the case then, with all due respect, sir, fuck it."

They played eye games then for what seemed like a long while to Paz. He had been thinking about this aspect of the case, the week off duty had given him plenty of time to think, and about what Oliphant had said the last time they'd discussed it, and how unsatisfactory it had been even then. He had called David Packer a dozen times during that week and got his answering machine and left a message, but had not been called back. No big deal, it was not a crime to leave town, but still. . . .

"Not whizzing," said Oliphant, "I wouldn't say whizzing. But I've gotten some calls. And made a few. And the fact is that you're going to have to let me be the judge of what I can and can't tell you, and the reason for that is that people I respect are feeding me information that they've got no legal right to release to me, they're putting their jobs and pensions on the line."

Oliphant leaned back in his chair, lacing his hands across his midsection, which to Paz looked about as soft as a steel-belted radial. "Let's talk a little more about the intersection between national security and the work of the FBI. We're interested in bad guys in that area just like we are in O.C., mail fraud, computer crime, and so on, and obviously the best way to penetrate the bad guys is to turn a bad guy. That's how we got the Klan and the mob. Not so easy with terrorists, because the kind of terrorists we're mainly interested in nowadays are pretty impenetrable by your average FBI-type person. So we look on the periphery. Terror cells need services like any other organized body. They need false IDs, they need money moved, they need transport and weapons and ammo. And there are, naturally, all-American scumbags who will supply this stuff for a price."

"So you penetrate the scumbags."

"We do. But you can see the problem. In order for your penetratee to work effectively, he has to continue with his scumbaggery, for which he now has effective immunity, because he's been doubled. He keeps selling, let's say, fake IDs, and even though he lets us know what he's doing, we are still not going to pick up all the evildoers he's selling to, because these guys are not dumb, they can figure out that if everybody who bought bad paper from old Charlie got busted, there must be something funny going on with old Charlie. And there you have the great conundrum: you're licensing guys to commit criminal acts, in the hope that you can prevent even greater criminal acts. It's inherently corrupting. Inherently."

"So what do you do?"

"Well, it depends on whether you believe in our system," said Oliphant. "If you believe that justice under law is essentially weak, then you'll bend the law until it breaks. You'll have killers and rapists and every kind of human garbage on the payroll of the United States. And you'll stop some terror and some will take place anyway. If you believe that justice under law is inherently strong, then you won't license criminals. You might use them or squeeze them but you won't fucking protect their criminal acts. And the result of this is that you'll stop some terror and some will take place anyway. Will you have more victims? Unclear. I tend to doubt it. You can stop ninety-nine percent of terror attempts just by taking your thumb out of your ass, like we could've stopped nine-eleven if we hadn't been having turf wars and snoozing in our deck chairs. The rest of it is like lightning strikes or traffic fatalities, it's part of life in any open society, get used to it, not that the attorney general is ever going to get up on the TV and say that. But if you play it straight, at least you won't have blowback, you won't have impunity, you won't have the corruption of law enforcement."

"This is why you left the Bureau," said Paz; a statement, not a question.

Oliphant shot a hard look over, but Paz met it, and after a bit the man nodded. They were in a new country now. "A guy in New Jersey snuffed a teenager he was fucking and we gave him a pass because he was buying air tickets for some al-Qaeda types. Maybe coulda-been al-Qaeda types, I mean they didn't even fucking know! This was a high-level decision, by the way." He pointed to the ceiling. "Very high. I thought of blowing the whistle, but I decided that at the end of the day . . . at the end of the day I'm not a whistle-blower, not that I couldn't respect someone who was, but it wasn't me. So I handed in my papers instead. My sad story, now you know, and if I hear it from anyone else, I'll make sure you spend the rest of your career guarding the concession stand at the Orange Bowl."

A long uncomfortable silence followed this remark. "And yes, I am a fucking fanatic on this issue. And why?" Here he pointed to his face. "This. People like you and me, the law is all we got going for us. Corrupt as it is, unjust as it is, without the law we'd both still be chopping cotton."

"Chopping sugarcane in my case," said Paz.

"Chopping whatever, but not in a suit and tie in a nice office, with authority over white folks. No fucking way."

"That was very inspiring, boss."

"Fuck you, Paz," said Oliphant without ill-humor. "I wasn't trying to inspire you, I was trying to illustrate why I've been getting phone calls from pissed-off guys."

Paz didn't budge. "So who in the federal government is hiring bad actors? No, let me guess. David Packer?"

"The name came up. He was in Sudan, I hear. He was employed by SRPU. And now he's here. And you are not to fuck with him."

"Why not?"

Oliphant's face took on a harder expression. "Two reasons. One is that I just told you not to and I'm the fucking commander of this organization. The other is if Packer yells to the people he reports to, all kinds of shit is going to hit the fan, and the helpful calls from Washington will dry up, and a big chunk of federal law enforcement will stop hunting bad guys and start looking for who leaked it. So follow up on Wilson, follow up on Cortez and your suspect. Find out who killed Muwalid and why. That's your job. Go do it."

It was a dismissal. Paz got up and left and flagged Morales from his desk in the squad bay. Out in the parking lot, Morales asked, "What did the major have to say?"

"He said you're looking sharper since you got some decent suits. He likes the Fendi."

"Really."

Paz told him really. Morales said, "Holy shit."

"My thoughts exactly," said Paz, getting into an unmarked Chevrolet. "Let's go see what Jack Wilson has to say for himself."

But when they arrived at Wilson Brothers Marine they found not Jack but a smaller, stouter version, who greeted them at the door to the shop with an air of relief.

"That was fast," he said. "I just called it in a couple of hours ago."

"I'm sorry," said Paz. "You're . . . ?"

"Frank Wilson. You're here about the missing persons report, right?"

"Who's missing?"

"Jack, my brother. You're not from missing persons?"

"No, homicide," said Paz.

"Oh my God!" said Wilson and paled beneath his tan.

It took them a few minutes in the little office to straighten it out. Jack Wilson had not been seen for nearly a week. His car was gone, he did not answer repeated pages or cell phone calls, he hadn't deposited a couple of large checks made in payment for work. Frank, it turned out, was the technical guy, Jack took care of the business end, although he knew his way around a marine diesel. Frank seemed anxious to talk and they let him. He assumed the cops knew that Jack had worked on Cigarette boat engines for some shady characters and made no attempt to hide this, but he assured them that all that was in the past. No, there had been no large withdrawals of money from the company account. No, he hadn't heard of anyone named Cortez nor did he recognize the photo they showed him. They left after half an hour of similarly fruitless questioning.

"That was a waste," said Morales when they were back in the car.

"No it wasn't," said Paz. He got on the radio and made Jack Wilson a wanted man, giving the specifics on his vehicle. Then he said to Morales, "Jack Wilson took off right after Dodo Cortez showed up dead on the evening news. Probably not a co-incidence. Assume he was running Dodo. A well-known hit man tries to steal a piece of evidence connected with our suspect, and that leads to the thought that maybe the suspect's been framed, that the well-known hit man did it. He knew we'd ask around and pick up on the connection between him and Cortez. He tried to keep it dark but he didn't bother to get an old beater for his meetings with Cortez, and a new silver Lexus is going to catch the eye in that neighborhood. Speaking of which, let's take a look at Mrs. Dodo. You know the address, right?"

"Yeah, Second and Fifteenth. I told you I already talked to her. She's uncooperative."

"I'll use charm," said Paz. "Go."

It was the kind of Miami neighborhood where the front lawns are used to park cars, meaning that the small houses are occupied by large numbers of recent immigrants, not necessarily in the same family. The small concrete-block-stucco house formerly occupied by Dodo Cortez had a patchy lawn with no cars, indicating a slight elevation in social status. Paz told Morales to wait at the front door while he looked in the windows to check out the grieving widow. From the side of the house he was able to see through partly open blinds into the living room, where a woman lay stretched out on a Bahama couch. She was dressed in a sleeveless orange blouse, a pair of black panties and one shoe, which hung like an ornament off her toes. The television was on, a Spanish soap it sounded like, but the woman was not watching it. Among the clutter on the nearby coffee table he saw a burning candle, several glassine bags, a bent spoon, and a hypodermic needle, all of which explained the woman's stunned lassitude.

Paz went back to the street. He told Morales, "Give me two minutes and then pound on the door and yell 'Police, open up!'" He then went around to the back of the house. It took very little time to wiggle a glass jalousie pane out of the rear door and pop the lock, and by the time Morales made his demonstration, he was moving through the kitchen and was in plenty of time to keep the woman from flushing her heroin down the toilet.

After a lot of noise and some weeping, the two cops had the woman settled down and handcuffed on the couch. She said her name was Rita and she didn't know nothing, and hadn't done nothing and they planted that dope and she wanted her lawyer. She looked about nineteen.

"I told you," said Morales.

Paz smiled and spoke to the girl in Spanish, sitting down next to her on the couch, as if they were about to go on a date, the usual cop endearments, he wanted to help her out, he'd be happy to go away and leave her with her dope, provided she gave a little, helped them out, they were murder cops, not narcs, they could care less about her habit. And then he sketched out what would happen to her if not, the heroin looked like felony weight; maybe they could fatten up the bag, if not; the state's attorney really wanted to clear this murder that her boyfriend had pulled off, and so did they, and so they would put her *under* the jailhouse on the dope charges, if not. And it wasn't like she was ratting Dodo, Dodo was dead on a tray in the county morgue and he didn't give a shit, and so on in a calm voice in soft Spanish, like he was talking her into bed.

A long silence and then, "So what do you want to know? I don't know shit about Dodo's business, you know?"

"He ever mention a guy named Wilson?"

"Wilson? No, not that I heard."

"How about Jack. Big guy, blond hair like a surfer, drives a silver Lexus?"

"Oh, yeah, Jack—him I know. He came by, picked up Dodo a couple of times."

"Good. You want me to take the cuffs off?" She nodded, and he did. Some further questioning and it became clear that she was telling the truth. She could connect her boyfriend with Jack Wilson, but that was all.

Paz said, "Could we check out his stuff?"

She nodded glumly and led them to a bedroom, rubbing her wrists.

The room was small and paneled in cheap imitation white pine. It contained a bed, unmade, a dresser, a bedside table, a TV on a metal stand, a color reproduction of Jesus, framed, and a large closet with mirrored doors. The two cops searched the place carefully, going through the pockets of all the clothes and checking the undersides as well as the insides of the bureau drawers. They took their time; the woman got bored. She asked, "Can I go back and watch my program?"

"Yeah, go," said Paz, and then, "Hey, wait: what's this hole in the paneling from?"

"Oh, that's from Dodo. He used to hit the wall when he got mad. He was going to get it fixed."

Paz brought his face close to the wall, then took a penlight out of his pocket and shone it into the space between the walls. His arm disappeared into the void up to the shoulder, and when it came out there was a white garment in his hand. It was a waiter's monkey jacket with the seal of the Trianon Hotel on the left breast and a plastic nameplate with LUIS stamped on it on the right. There was also a small, dark brown stain on the right cuff.

L orna has been feeling out of sorts for a week or so and thinks she may be coming down with something. Also, she does not know whether she is falling in love with Jimmy Paz, and so she has decided not to think about it. Low key, take it easy is her current mantra. Conversations with Sheryl Waits, which have heretofore acted as the analytical retort of her emotional life, have proven unsatisfactory. She does not seem to want advice or a sympathetic ear. Sheryl is too pressing, too avid for this to be a success, or rather a success in Sheryl's terms. Give Sheryl any encouragement at all and she is offering consumer reports on bridal salons. Lorna hasn't mentioned Paz at all to Betsy Newhouse, whose interest in Lorna's emotional life is limited to a casual "getting any yet?" whenever they meet. She has twice turned down invitations from Betsy to go out with the less attractive pal of one of Betsy's current squeezes, and this has caused remarks and comments about keeping a stock of new batteries for the vibrator.

In fact, Lorna has not gotten any from Paz. She has received three fairly chaste if sincere kisses from the man, one on each of their three dates: the beach outing, a dinner at a Chinese-Cuban restaurant, and an evening of dancing. All of these have been pleasant, but no one is talking about buying a ring. She wonders sometimes if he likes her at all, and as soon as this thought crosses her mind, well-oiled valves open automatically and her mental pool fills with all the reasons why Jimmy Paz is not quite suitable. A high school graduate? Please! Lorna has an album of set pieces in her mind representing mating satisfaction. She wishes to admire his brains and his career, with, naturally, equal respect for *her* career; she wishes masterly decisions to be made as to lifestyle, vacations, dwellings, but with due consideration of her tastes; she wishes a healthy sexual relationship, in which he will take the lead but not do anything perverse or disturbing; she wishes to be carried away but also to stay in more or less the same place; she wishes for coziness and comfort, doing the *Times* crossword puzzle on Sundays, but also for unpredictability and excitement; she wants fidelity, but not tedium.

Yes, Paz comes up short in many of these areas. She can't imagine him doing the *Times* crossword puzzle. Or sitting through the ballet, not that she frequents the ballet, but still. . . . And then there is the whole gun and violence thing, which is faintly disgusting, and she is not sure she will ever be able to expunge from her mind the sight of him actually slaying a human being right there in front of her house, never mind that he probably saved her life.

On the other hand . . . there is the memory of his hands on her body, and his body, its controlled stillness, the violence perfectly contained. She considers the Zen-like simplicity of his life. She reflects on how many of the men she has been with have been putterers, nudges, how Rat Howie had to have a particular brand of wood-strawberry preserves, or he couldn't eat breakfast, how often he would send food back to the restaurant kitchen with elaborate directions for the chef, and the whole wine thing, the yacht thing . . . although he did finish the Sunday *Times* in less than half an hour, and Paz's eyes, she had never seen eyes like that on a man, interested eyes, interested in *her,* and then a guilty thought but no less real for that, an end to a certain kind of liberal naggery, because if your man was black then that was proof, wasn't it? Yes, probably he didn't like her that much, but then he *had* called her three times in one week, although that might have been cultivation for business purposes, but . . . or maybe she was simply going crazy, sinking into the early stages of erotomania, she'd end up parked outside his house slashing the tires of his real girlfriend's car. . . .

She laughs out loud, since if she is crazy she is certainly in the right place. Many of the people in the locked-ward dayroom would, like her, be conversing with the unseen (but out loud) were they not stupefied with drugs. Or nearly so: a big white man looms over her, about forty, ginger hair in outflung wisps like a circus clown's. On his doughy face he wears the tight-lipped staring visage of the paranoid psychotic. "Are you laughing at me?" he demands.

Professional calm kicks in; this guy needs to have his meds cranked up a little, she reflects automatically, and puts on her bland-but-caring expression.

"Not at all," she replies. "I just thought of something funny."

"Liar," he says in a hoarse whisper, but she slips past him and notes that the powerful Darryla and Ferio, the dayroom orderly, have picked up on the interaction. They begin to drift a little closer to the big man. Not her problem in any case.

She spots Emmylou off by herself in a corner, scribbling away in one of her school notebooks. When Lorna greets her she looks up, startled, like someone who has just awakened, and when she sees who it is, out comes her church-painting smile.

"I see you're still writing."

"Yes. It's an interesting process. Painful, but interesting."

"Why painful?" Lorna pulls up a plastic chair and sits facing her. She is a little frightened, she finds; she has not quite extinguished the memory of what she saw the last time, what appeared before the woman's seizure. She hopes this session will involve only psychology and that she can steer the discussion away from the weird stuff.

"Inhabiting the former self," Emmylou says. "Recollecting feelings I had, seeing things through my former eyes. I wish I was a better writer, but then I think, no, it's a confession, not a novel, so I have to leave out most of the stuff that sets up what I was feeling at the time, people mostly, but also the air of a place, the essence of the other people, the way Flaubert and Dickens do. I'm afraid it makes pretty dull reading. Although I have to believe the truth can't be dull, since it partakes of God. I just pray I can make myself do it. I finished another book. Would you like to take it?"

Lorna takes the proffered notebook and says, "I don't think you have to worry about your writing. It's very clear and vivid and not dull at all. And conscious. It's really amazing, considering . . ."

"That I have no formal education? Higher education. Plenty of the lower kind, though."

"Yes, and it's remarkable that you're able to write about that material so . . . dispassionately," Lorna says. "Most people, it would take years of therapy to be able to confront all of that abuse, but you seem to have no trouble. That speaks to a lot of psychological toughness. It's a good sign."

"Not that good, since I seem to be locked in the loony bin."

"Well, clearly you do have some problems. My God, who wouldn't after what you've been through?"

The woman gives Lorna one of those searching, discomforting looks. She says, "Dr. Wise, I know you want to help me and I appreciate it, but we might be getting ourselves all crosswise, if you're looking at my life from that point of view. You're thinking of all the bad things that happened to me as traumas, leaving psychological scars that grew into a mental disease, which you think I have. I look at them as afflictions sent by God to attract my attention to him. Can I tell you about a dream I had once?"

"Yes, of course, but I'd like to continue our session in the therapy room."

"Oh, this won't take but a minute," Emmylou replies, and her gaze shifts away from Lorna's face. Lorna follows the look and sees the big man who confronted her in the hallway standing by one of a row of folding wooden bridge tables set up for card playing and the working of jigsaw puzzles. The man is standing over a small woman working a puzzle. His shoulders are hunched and his fists are clenched. Darryla and Ferio are standing a dozen feet from him, watching.

"I dreamed I was getting a guided tour of heaven?" Emmylou says. "I was wearing a jumpsuit and a hard hat and my tour guide, he was an angel, of course, but he looked just like a regular man, dressed the same as I was, and we were in this giant building, kind of an industrial shed like in those boring old movies they used to show us in high school, how they make paper or ice cream. And there was this big huge machine in it, whirring and clanking away, and there was a conveyor belt coming out of one end of it, and on the conveyor belt were rows of golden bricks, but softer: they looked like giant Twinkies, row after row of them, and when they got to the end of the conveyor belt they fell off of it. I looked to see where they were falling to and I saw that there was a big hole in the floor there and through it I could see clouds and blue sky and the earth far below. I asked the guide what the Twinkie things were, and he said they were blessings, and I remember thinking, in the dream, how marvelous is the Lord showering all these blessings down on us. Then we moved on, across an alley and into another big huge shed with the same kind of machine cranking away, the same conveyor belt, the same giant Twinkies falling down, and I said to the guide, 'Oh, these are more blessings,' and he said, 'No, those are afflictions,' and I said, 'Oh, but they look just the same as the blessings,' and he said, 'They *are* the same!' Excuse me . . ."

Emmylou rises while Lorna sits there dumbfounded a little by what she has just heard, and then the dayroom is shaken by a roar. "I knew it! I knew it!" shouts the big undermedicated psychotic, and now he has pushed over the jigsaw lady and snatched up the folding table, scattering like snow the tiny bits of a view of Mount Shasta. He holds the table over his head, bellowing, and smashes it down on the floor. Darryla and Ferio close in warily, Darryla pressing some kind of electronic device as she does so. The man smashes the table down again, and this time the wood shatters and he is swinging one of the table legs, which has a long, sharp screw and jagged splinters sticking out of one end of it. The man is now bellowing in tongues, incomprehensible. The table leg whirs like a fan as he swings it around his head. Now his direst paranoid fantasy becomes flesh as half a dozen orderlies and nurses rush into the dayroom. They *are* all out to get him!

Darryla talks soothingly as Ferio circles around to get behind the madman, but the madman sees him and strikes at his head with his club, and Ferio goes down with a cry, holding his forearm, grimacing in pain. He is gushing blood from a long cut on the top of his skull. Darryla rushes the patient like a linebacker, hitting him in a low tackle, and he goes over onto his back, striking repeatedly at Darryla with the butt of the table leg. One blow connects with her skull and she rolls off him, stunned.

Now the rest of the inmates have joined the fun, screaming, tossing things around, getting into fights and in the way of the reinforcements. Lorna is frozen in place, standing by her chair. She sees the madman and his blood-spattered club, he is on all fours now, roaring like a bear, and there is Darryla, blood pouring from a wound in her temple, trying to rise. Ferio is struggling to his feet, but it is clear that his arm is useless.

And suddenly Emmylou Dideroff is crouching in front of the madman. Lorna sees her mouth moving. Saliva drips from the madman's mouth. Emmylou places a hand on either side of the man's face, and then from his open mouth issues a sound Lorna has never imagined coming from the vocal machinery of a human being, a roar-scream-howl-sob of such intensity and pitch that for an instant everything in the room seems to freeze.

Emmylou falls away from him, down on her back, Lorna can hear above all the other racket the clunk of her skull against the linoleum, and she goes into what looks like a grand mal seizure. Lorna starts moving now, but Darryla is there before her, fitting the padded tongue-depressor she always carries into Emmylou's champing frothing mouth. A drop of blood falls from Darryla's head onto Emmylou's forehead. Lorna swallows, fearing that she is going to faint.

Meanwhile, the psychotic is swarmed by many orderlies, although he has quite ceased to struggle. Lorna happens to look at his face and sees that it is the face of a confused man, a fellow caught in an embarrassing situation that he hopes will soon resolve itself, but the madness has gone from his eyes. Nevertheless, a hypo is slammed into his butt, a gurney is fetched, and he is strapped down to it and rolled away.

They shoot up Emmylou as well, and the spasms disappear into deep sleep. After she too is rolled off on her gurney, Lorna finds that her limbs are trembling uncontrollably. Instructed by the movies that violence is of long duration, balletic, and easily followed, she is unprepared for the way it really is. From the first psychotic roar to the takedown, perhaps forty seconds have elapsed. A heavy hand lands on her shoulder and presses her into a chair. "You okay, dear heart?" asks Darryla. "Look at me. You all right?"

Darryla is holding a gauze pad to her own temple. It is soaked in blood, as is the front of her green scrubs. Lorna locks eyes with the nurse, nods, and then a wave of nausea rises, with cold sweat breaking over her face. She drops her head between her knees until the worst passes.

"Wow, I wasn't ready for that," she says. "How are *you*?"

"Oh, I'll survive," the nurse replies, and her face creases up in a grin. "I been cut, bruised, abused, and misused, dear heart. Just another day on the lock ward."

"I don't think so," says Lorna. "What happened? Who was that man?"

"Oh, Horace Masefield? Horace killed his wife some years ago, mashed her up with a meat cleaver. It was a big deal on the TV, the Hialeah Hacker. He did five years up in Chattahoochee, and he got out all cured of his mental disease, and then he married a woman who probably didn't pay much attention to the local news and guess what? He used a hatchet this time, which is why he's here. He's carrying a load of Haldol that'd stun a Brahma bull, but like you just saw, he still got his attitude going."

"But what *happened*, Darryla?"

"Oh, that. Well, dear heart, I got my *PDR,* and my *DSM,* and I attend the Sunset Park A.M.E. church on Sundays, and that all's what I believe in. If we was living in Bible times, I'd say we just saw an unclean spirit driven out, but that ain't what I'm going to put down on my violent incident report form. Uh-*uh*!"

Now a searching professional look. "You sure you're okay? You want some water? A Valium?" Lorna tells her no; with a final grin and a hug, Darryla lumbers off to her duties.

Emmylou's notebook is still clutched under Lorna's arm. She gathers up her stuff and the bag that Emmylou has left, and drops this last off at the nurses' station on her way off the ward. As usual, she has a review session scheduled with Mickey Lopez, who, the moment she walks into his office, asks, "What happened?"

She collapses into a chair and has a little weep, which she thinks is allowable in the circumstances, and after some heavy Kleenex work she describes the events in the dayroom, but she cannot bring herself to convey the part that Emmylou Dideroff played. Or seemed to play, for by now the concrete sense memory of what she saw has fought against her belief system and her training, and has predictably tossed in the towel. It *could not* have happened like that, therefore *did* not. She says instead that their patient had another epileptic fit in response to the violence, and Mickey nods sagely and says that such a thing is not unusual and actually a confirmation that there is a physical trauma at the root of Emmylou's problems. They agree that an MRI scan is warranted and discuss for some time how this is to be paid for under the labyrinthine budgetary relationships among the university, the hospital, the county, and Medicaid.

Now she summarizes the information in the first notebook and then adds the material from the morning session. She has saved the dream, the best part, for last. Mickey focuses on this description, nodding, making encouraging sounds. This is, after all, his meat. He asks, "So, what do you make of this?"

"A coping mechanism? She can't really admit the emotional effect of the trauma she was subjected to, so she lays it off on the will of God. She's got guilt feelings too about the death of her mother and the little boy, so she . . . so if blessings and afflictions are really the same thing, she can resolve both the guilt and the trauma. She's suffered, she caused suffering, but it balances out, and it's all God's fault anyway."

Mickey nods, smiles. "Mm, yes, a good reading. And also I think some of the problems we have with this kind of sexual abuse are on the guilt side too. The little girl is being rubbed, the feelings of pleasure are genuine, she's got Daddy all to herself, and this especially when the mother is cold and rejecting, as we have here. You would agree?"

Of course she agrees, even though at some deep level she does not believe a word of it, she does not believe that Emmy-lou Dideroff fits into the standard psychological paradigm, much less its Freudian province, but what else does she have?

Mickey Lopez is regarding her closely, and the expression on his face is turning from collegial to therapeutic. "Speaking of trauma, you don't look so good."

"I'm fine, Mickey."

"You're twitchy, and you got no color in your face. You want a Valium? A Xanax? Half a milligram, you'll relax. . . ."

Everyone wants to dope me, she thinks, I've seen something I shouldn't have seen and they want me to go back to sleep, and then, Oh, great! Paranoid ideation, just what I fucking need on top of the obsessing and the hypochondria, and she really does feel a little flu-ish. . . .

"No, I just need a break," she answers, forcing a smile. "I'll go home and take a shower. I'll be fine."

Outside the building she makes a cell call, leaves a message, and by the time she has returned to her car, Paz is ringing back. She tells him she has the next notebook and he tells her he'll meet her at her house.

She gives herself over to driving, pretending that she has just learned how and has to consciously will every action: red light means stop, so foot off the gas foot on the brake press gently, glide. . . .

Paz is there when she arrives.

He takes the notebook, locks it in his car trunk. He says, "You doing anything right now?"

"Not really, but you know, Jimmy, I'm wiped. I just want to go and lie down."

She turns away from him, her door is a blur ahead of her, but now he reaches out and holds her by the arm. "What happened?" he asks, and she pivots neatly and puts her face against the hollow of his neck. And without her planning in any way for this to happen, now it all comes out, the full story: the demon face earlier, the maniac today, the violence, Emmy-lou, the dream, and the casting out of the evil spirit, especially that part because she knows somehow that Paz will understand this, that it will not scare him or make him think she is nuts herself.

And he is the first significant person of the day who does not offer to tranquilize her. Instead, he hugs her for a sufficient time, and she is proud of herself for not blubbing against his nice suit, and then he says, "Let's go for a ride. I want you to meet my old partner, Cletis. He's good on this kind of stuff."

# Fourteen

The
## CONFESSIONS
of
### Emmylou Dideroff

### Book III

*What passes for goodness among us fallen humans is generally not much more than a mutual picking of lice from our fur, and a suspension of our desire to eat each other up, it is only social goodness, like the nanny telling the docile child what a <u>good</u> little boy. We must be good in that way, not killing stealing lying, so as to help us accumulate more of the world's riches. Only God is really good, and only those who allow God's reflected glory to shine out of them can be accounted good on earth. I didn't know that then and so I was confused by my encounter with the nurse Sister Trinidad Salcedo. In a strange way (can you say this?) I was innocent of good. I was like a sexually pure girl from way back, a Victorian, say, who understands that there is something being hidden from her, because she is not totally isolated from society and she sees the signs all around her, the giggling factory girls, the innuendos, the looks of men in the street, and observes the* *behavior of her peers. She is curious, let us say, she feels cheated and incomplete, perhaps—what is this horrible thing I'm supposed to avoid that the world takes for granted, that the world thinks is the most important thing? So with me good was my forbidden fruit. I was attracted to it, and repelled at the same time. For if good was a fraud, like Ray Bob's churchgoing, then I was just fine, a beast like the other beasts I now hung out with in the Market squat. But if not, if the world <u>wasn't</u> just Grab and Fuck, then*

*Then the world could not be borne. I say this now, knowing what I know now, but then it was not even a thought, just a psychic itch, a feeling of vague discontent, expressed as annoyance and short temper. I was reading stuff too, stuff I couldn't understand too well because I didn't get it and it pissed me off, how could glorious brilliant me not get everything on the page? I recall that when I read my Russians I had to put down Crime and Punishment because I couldn't understand why the asshole turned himself in, what was that <u>stuff</u> going on in his head, what confession and repentance meant. I mean I knew the words and their formal meanings, but the underlying thought had no grip on my savage mind.*

*Nevertheless, I read all the time. I had my whore-address library card and I was a frequent visitor to the Coconut Grove library in Peacock Park. Books was my street name by then. Hey, Books, whatcha reading? I would read to them sometimes, mainly books that had been made into movies, they ripped these off from stores or found them on trash piles, the kids especially, barely literate but they knew about Star Trek and Star Wars and Harry Potter. They couldn't afford the movies but they wanted so much to be included in the great American media dream.*

*The life of the homeless: not much to say here, unromantic, dirty, violent in spurts, softened by drugs, sex, and booze. I could handle it pretty well, but what I really wanted was to get together with Orne Foy, and I didn't know how to do that. I had his number and I called him* from time to time, but he had nowhere to return the call. I tried giving him a phone booth number, but that got too frustrating, waiting there all day and going crazy when someone would come in and use it.

I also tried to attract the interest of Sister Trinidad, but no luck there either, I had imagined nuns were always trying to make you holy and get you to go to church like the church ladies in the Amity Street church back in Wayland, but apparently not, she seemed not to care much about that, only healing the bodies of the homeless, and that in a distracted manner, like her eyes were focused on another place entirely. She didn't chat, she was close with information, she wouldn't tell me what the brass angel meant and I didn't like the way she looked at me like I was nothing in her eyes or like I had made a mess like a little kid and she was waiting for me to get hip to it so I could clean it up. I sensed that I bored her, which was insufferable. We can forgive bores, but never those who are bored by us as La Rochefoucauld says in my Quotation Book.

So one day when she hadn't given me the treatment I thought I deserved as queen of the universe I went back to the Market in a bad mood. I decided to do some coke to cheer me up, I still had most of the bag I took from Jerrell's place. It was daytime and the main squat was pretty cleared out except for the people sleeping off a drunk and the regular junkies and who should I meet there but Tommy and we did a number of lines together and then it seemed like a fine idea to go to one of the offices upstairs and have a fuck the poor dumb shit. I put it in his mind, an act of pure evil.

After that he was crazy for me, strange because Carmen loved him and would do anything for him, but men are like that I have found. He would send her off on errands for him, get him some food he had to have or cigarettes or out to panhandle and as soon as she was gone up to the offices, filthy places full of junk and broken glass and plaster dust and stinking of piss and cats, another romantic affair for Emmylou.

*It was the plaster dust that gave us away, she spotted it on my back and she must have been smarter than I gave her credit for or maybe she was just smart about this one thing, because she came in on us while we were doing it and threw a screaming fit, and I cleared out for the rest of the day. To say the devil made me do it is now a joke, but I recall wondering all that day why I did such a foolish and uncalculating thing to a girl who had never done me anything but good, who had probably saved my life, with a man I didn't particularly care for. But you know what I'm talking about now, Detective, you don't think it's such a joke.*

*It was getting dark by the time I got back to the Market and there were TV lights and flashing cop lights and bright beams from firetrucks pointed up at the tower above the Market where I could see Carmen up there, and a fireman on a ladder it looked like he was trying to talk her down. And the whole neighborhood was out, the usual idiots yelling jump jump, with the TV cameras pointed at us all to show the people at home how depraved we were on the street. A woman I knew told me Carmen'd been crying all day and getting any drugs she could into her, smack, crank, PCP, acid, whatever was around and I said if she jumps off she'll probably fly but no she stepped into the sky just as the fireman was reaching out to her from his ladder and fell in the usual way and the woman gave me a look like she just stepped in dog shit.*

*Trini Salcedo was there too, in her van, and I went over and started talking to her, and before I knew it I was telling her the whole story about me and Tommy and Carmen. She listened and after I was finished asked me why I was telling her this and I realized that I didn't know why and she said well you might want to think about that and she turned away and went back into her van and I recall it pissed me off considerably, me confessing and all and she just turned her back instead of I don't know what all I expected, but* <u>something</u>*. If I had a weapon I swear I would have just murdered her then.*

*I headed back to the Grove. I recall being angry, fuming, cursing on the street like a crazy person, but I can't recall what my anger was about and maybe I didn't know even at the time. What had I expected the nun to do? Forgive me? I wasn't really conscious that there was such a thing or that I needed it. Another feather touch from Him, a baby's tug.*

*Because I was angry I did something dumb. Homeless was getting old I decided a bunch of sick losers and why was I hanging out with them anyway? Tommy acted like it was all my fault and bad-mouthed me around the Market as much as he could, like he was a baby in the big city I had seduced. I thought it was ridiculous, like high school, but I also noticed people avoiding me. Meanwhile, I still had maybe eight ounces of really pure coke left, which was running then at about two hundred a gram. Cut that in half for wholesale, and I figured I could score a little over twenty grand, enough for me to start a serious new life and so I put the word out on the street that I had half a pound of blow to sell and a couple of nights later I woke up to a kick in the ribs and a couple of guys standing over me, where's the product, bitch. I guess I had counted on the people who lived there to give me some kind of warning, which we usually did for one another, but at that point I realized that the community such as it was had booted me out on account of what I'd done with Tommy, high school or not. Maybe they still believed in true love, I don't know, or maybe it was Tommy who had set me up, revenge on the temptress.*

*I made a racket anyway, because there were often cops and social work types hanging out there and I saw flashlights go on and candles. The men cursed and beat at me and finally one of them slugged me on the head with something hard and I went limp. I wasn't entirely unconscious, so I knew when they carried me out and tossed me in the back of a SUV. It was new, I could smell the new car smell and the cologne and sweat of the men. The problem with SUVs becoming fashionable among gangsters is that they don't have trunks for jobs like this, but gangsters usually don't think in such practical terms. They had me squashed down in the footwell of the rear seat. One of the men had his big Nike on my neck and the other two were in front. They were arguing in Spanish, with the man in the back putting a word in from time to time, and after we'd been driving for a while the driver yelled mierda and I heard the screech of brakes and a heavy pressure jamming me forward then a crash a tinkle of glass and two explosions as the airbags in front deployed. Maniacal cursing from the driver. The foot was off my neck. I could see it twitching above me along with its mate because the guy in back had flown over the front seats and crashed into the windshield and I wriggled upright and reached for the handle of the rear door. I heard the sound of the front doors opening and then a string of little pops like firecrackers going off that I knew weren't firecrackers. One of the men groaned. The back door swung open and there was Orne Foy with a smoking machine pistol in his right hand. He reached out his other hand and pulled me out of the car. My head hurt real bad and when I touched where the pain was I felt a hot tender lump bigger than my thumb where they'd whapped me. I could hardly stand up so he threw his arm around my waist.*

*He said I been looking for you and I asked him how he'd found me and he said you were on television and I've been hanging around that squat for days now, nobody told you? No nobody did. He said he'd decided to search the place at night and had come by just as they were taking me out God had sent him as I now know but luck is what I thought then. I looked around. The SUV was jammed up against a power pole with its front stove in and two men were lying all splayed out dead with lots of blood flowing in black runnels under the anticrime lights and the front windshield was all blown to pieces with bullet holes so I guessed the third guy had never got out of the car. We were on Douglas between Grand and U.S. 1 and not a car in sight. A red Ford 150 Supercab pickup with* oversize tires and a large dent in the quarter panel was standing there and we got in and drove away. It was pretty clear what had happened, he'd chased down the kidnappers and forced them into the power pole. Orne never talked about it after and I didn't ask him, some kind of instinct that he didn't like to talk much about operational details. At that point I was flying from the adrenaline and the relief and contented to go anywhere in the world in this pickup truck with Orne Foy the first man who ever killed anyone for me but not the last by far, oh no, may Christ have mercy on me.

I passed out as soon as the truck took off, lying on the bench seat in the back of the Ford cab, and when I woke up just after we crossed the Georgia line on 95 I was lying in the backseat of a Chevy Suburban. I checked to see if it was still him driving and it was so I drifted back into sleep. I didn't ask any questions. I was so tired of knowing stuff and having to figure out what to do next.

It was a fourteen-hour drive all told. When he stopped for gas and food in Valdosta I took a handful of aspirins with my Coke. I wasn't hungry, nauseous in fact, and returned to the backseat and heavy sleep. When I awoke it was late afternoon and we were off the interstate on a two-lane blacktop in mountains heavy with summer growth. I had never been in mountains before. I was hungry now and said so and he said we'll be home soon. At this word I was filled with a feeling of happiness such as I hadn't known for a long time, not since my daddy held me before I could read. The devil can gin up all the sweetest things to turn us from God. But it is true sweetness, not false, because it _is_ of God, although we don't know it. Satan himself got nothing in his pockets God didn't put there.

We left the blacktop after a while and began to climb a steep gravel road, switching back and forth past ravines full of honeysuckle and deadfalls choked with kudzu and on the ridges tulip trees, mountain ash, dogwood, pin oaks, hickory not that I knew all the names then it was all a blank to me before I studied the land. We went through *a swing pole stretched across the road with a sign on it* KEEP OUT PRIVATE. *He asked me to get out and close it behind us and when I did I heard him talking into a portable radio. Then up an even steeper road with the big V-8 straining in four-wheel and when we rounded this one big slatey boulder Orne stopped us and shouted and in a couple of seconds a man in camo gear holding an assault rifle appeared like magic out of the brush. Orne introduced me, Wavell this's Emmylou she'll be staying with us. He nodded and disappeared back where he came from. We crossed a wooden bridge over a little bubbly branch and then we were in the place. Orne said this is Bailey's Knob, the last piece of free America. It was like a little town, old houses and a couple of small trailers, smell of wood smoke and a deeper animal smell, which I recognized too well. Pigs I said sniffing and he said no just pig shit. I got out of the truck and suddenly the pain came back in full force the light was too bright and then it shuttered out to black like an old-time movie fade-out.*

*When I woke up I was in a small room, in a big old-fashioned high wooden sleigh bed, the dark lit by a yellow glow from a bug light outside the window. My head hurt so much it was making me nauseous and showing sharp colored lights every time I moved it. When my eyes adjusted I saw there was a woman in the room with me, small, slight with some kind of white headdress on that covered all her hair. I thought of the sisters in Miami and I said are you a nurse? But she didn't answer and I asked where's Orne? But she didn't answer that either she just looked at me and smiled in a funny way. She had a long nose and strange long eyes like willow leaves. I asked her if I could have an aspirin or codeine and some water, but she just sat down on the bed and took my hand or that's what I recall happening but then I must have blacked out again and then I woke up again and the woman was gone and so was my pain.*

*I felt well enough now to rise from the bed and leave the room. There was a narrow hallway outside and I stood still*

for a moment and tried to get the feel of the place. It reminded me of Gran's house, that smell of dust and old
paint and cooking you get in a wood house that's been
around for a while silent now except for the usual creaks
and the wind outside and crickets. I could almost have
been in Wayland except for the cool of the night and a
kind of sulfur smell and a distant rumble of some engine.
I found a bathroom and used it, washed my face and tried
to straighten out my tangled hair, what a mess, bruises
and smudgy rings under my eyes. Then I followed the light
out to the front room.

Orne was lying on a cracked brown leather couch reading. I could just see the top of his yellow-haired head and
the book's pages and his feet in gray socks up on the other
armrest and I just felt so good watching him that I didn't
say a word just looked around. There was a square enamel
stove over in one corner of the room and a big scarred
table and some chairs and a rag rug on the floor, a fire-
place and a mantelpiece, an old rocker with a quilt on it,
and the rest of the room was all books, thousands it
seemed like, on shelves covering every wall from floor to
ceiling except for where the windows poked through. And
everything was neat as a pin, no clutter, the floors swept
and mopped, and no books jammed anyhow into odd
spaces in the shelves like they were at Gran's, more like at
the library.

I took a step and a plank creaked and up Orne shot like
a snake, on his feet and the book gone flying a .380 tight
in his hand. Shit he said and took a couple of deep
breaths and put the little pistol in his pocket and he said
I'm not used to other people in the house at night and I
felt glad because it meant he didn't have a girlfriend. He
asked me how I felt and I said fine and asked him who the
woman was who tended me. He looked at me funny then
and said there was no woman it was I tending to you and
no one else. And we agreed it must've been in a dream. He
said I had been out more than twenty-four hours and he
had been worried and if I hadn't got up pretty soon he was

going to take me down to the community hospital in Bradleyville.

My stomach growled just then astonishingly embarrassingly loud in the quiet room and we both laughed and he said come on we'll get you fed. He had a big pot of stew, venison, we ate a lot of venison on Bailey's Knob, the deer were swarming in the state forest and God knew we had plenty of guns and no respect for the hunting laws, although I didn't learn that until later. He warmed some up and watched me eat like a hog, tipped back in his chair drinking a glass of murky beer. I had some too, malty and bread-tasting, homemade like most of the stuff we fed on. I asked him what the throbbing noise was and he said the generator, we're off the grid here.

The question foremost in my mind then—actually the next foremost, since the first was when I was going to get into bed with him—was why he had come looking for me but I didn't know how to say it, but then he seemed to read my mind and said the question and answered it. He'd been looking for a woman, young, trainable—he didn't actually say that but that's what he meant—bright, capable, and he thought I was the one. It was time for him to start a family, past time really but he had been so busy with his Work. Capital letters here because that's what it always sounded like when he said it. I had heard some of this when he came and talked to me at Hunter's place but now it all came out in a spate, me listening while I ate and nodding agreement. The great collapse was not far off, they were running out of time to prepare, the Bastards had ruined the world with their money and manipulations and thought control and there would be a blowup pretty soon, engineered plagues and nuclear war and anarchy, just like in those African countries, all the assholes thought we were immune but no and we had to prepare. Billions would die as the control systems collapsed and all those people who only knew how to manipulate symbols, who thought that symbols were real and thought the food came from a supermarket and energy came from the walls and water came from a tap and wastes just vanished by magic, they'd be helpless. The only people who'd survive would be the ones who understood the Real Stuff, who weren't moral cowards whining to a dead god, no, after all the loser and dirt people were swept away we would found a new race and its foundation stone would be the people that the Bastards had disdained as white trash. Why? Because they were the best stock in the world, the descendants of Vikings and warrior Celts and Teutonic tribes, they'd come here with nothing and built here in these mountains the only decent civilization that had ever existed in America yeoman farmers proud and independent, free of social garbage from Europe and Africa and Asiatic hordes, until the Bastards had come to the Appalachians and destroyed everything decent with their commodity capitalism and their man-eating coal mines and now they were eating the land itself ripping mountains apart in their greed turning everything on the planet into money well let the Bastards try to eat their money and their fucking data when the day of doom arrived!

He wanted me to appreciate the funny part of it—the triumph of the trash paid for by dope that the Bastards needed because their miserable money-grubbing lives and their dead god couldn't give them anything to live for, no decent food, no decent air or water, their heads full of TV crap concocted by Jews, no decent sex, their manhood dried up by the gray lives they had to lead to make the money they thought they need to buy the garbage the Jews and the faggots told them they had to have to be men . . . and on and on like this it must have been hours, and it made perfect sense to me as an explanation of the shittiness of the world although to be frank I had kind of lost focus when he mentioned decent sex. Although you might have thought that given my experiences in that line I would've been off the whole thing but you would've been dead wrong there because you know while all of that was going on from age nine I had only one thought in my head that I was holding on for someone who would make it all turn out right who would redeem my fouled body with blazing passion and wipe the stains away, redemption through sex a common American trope and I did not need any Jews or faggots to put it there either it is in the air of my native land.

I finished eating and he was still talking away, few are made for independence it is the privilege of the strong, Nietzsche, oh, my, could he wail on Nietzsche, pages of it in his head, his gospel, him and the two Toms, Jefferson and Paine, and he was still talking as I took my bowl and cup to the sink and washed and still talking when I turned around and he only ran down a little when I ripped my T-shirt off and yanked down my pants so I was jaybird naked and jumped up on him wrapping my legs around him and grabbing his still talking mouth with my mouth, but he shut up for a while after that and I made him fuck me on the cold enamel of the kitchen table.

As I reflect now I have to say that in all the time I was with him he never said he loved me nor did we exchange many words of tenderness. We lived with each other like fierce beasts an occasional snarl a cuff of the paw and then all submerged and forgotten in blazing sex. I believe many people live in this way and some of them write songs about how great it is and I thought it was great too I thought that was what love _was_. I love him still. If he walked through the door right now I might give it all up and follow him, I can't be sure, my faith is so weak really it needs a bodyguard of saints. God will judge not me.

The next morning I got the tour. Bailey's Knob was not a commune or even much of a community. It was a company town, Orne being a CEO straight out of Ayn Rand and the business was the growing of high-grade marijuana. I guess that the people who lived there more or less believed what Orne believed about the government, they were all some kind of survivalist type of person, but I never saw much organization aside from the guard roster, which everyone accepted as a business necessity. It wasn't a Christian Identity center or any other kind of center and I

doubt whether any of the people I met knew who Nietzsche was or cared. They were all lanky, pale people with
light hair and tin-pail eyes, the children and grandchildren of miners tossed off their land by the strip mines or
unemployed by the deep mines closing down. They had a
grudge sure enough and guns and they weren't going to
send their kids to the town schools where they'd learn to despise who they were, like I had. They had no use for the
kind of America they saw on TV, they didn't understand it
and didn't want to. Not big fans of diversity but not exactly fascists either because while they respected Orne
there was no cult of personality going on that I could see.
They mainly wanted to be let alone, and if Orne gave
them the opportunity to support themselves and their families they'd give him a wary loyalty and most of them believed that the world was really going to crash just like
Orne said, or maybe they were just hoping it would and
didn't want to be left behind. The Foys, it turned out, were
originally mountain people from around here. Most of
them had lit out for north Florida and become the depraved tribe I had grown up with but some of them stuck,
and Orne had come back and with money that came from
no one knew where, had bought a whole mountain's worth
of busted coal mines and ruined streams and piles of spoil
and started his business.

The heart of the operation was Caledonia Number
Three, which was the name of his coal mine, in a gallery
two hundred feet down inside the mountain. We took a
cage elevator down, and it was not dark as a dungeon at
all but full of blazing light from Gro-Lux lamps in long
rows shining down on tables covered with long rubber tubs
in which grew dense green marijuana plants over eight
thousand of them at various stages from seedlings to
harvest-ready. A team of women was moving up and down
the line, tending plants, fertilizing from shoulder tanks,
pinching buds into plastic pails, snipping and trimming.
Orne said they regularly tested different plants for yield,
part of the breeding program. Then we went to the pro-

cessing center in a side adit where some other people men
and women and young girls were stripping the buds from
harvested plants and tossing the leaves and stems into a
hopper, for later chopping and processing into low-grade
weed and some were compressing buds into bricks with a
hydraulic rammer. They wore masks so they could remember what they were there for and not work the whole day
stoned from the fine intoxicating dust that hung yellow-
green in the air and coated every surface. I got a buzz from
five minutes in the place.

They had a shipping area too where they packed the
bricks in shrink-wrap and loaded them into cartons. Orne
moved bulk around the country in regular trucks and private planes just like UPS. He had a computerized billing
system and inventory control. As a cover operation he
bought crafts—dolls and quilts and rag rugs—from local
women and shipped those out to mail-order. It explained
the boxes going out air freight and washed the dope
money.

He was moving tons of the stuff right out in the open
like that and never a sniff from the cops, because according to him the cops and the DEA were set up to catch
dummies really, not smart people like Orne or Kaczynski
the Unabomber, a local hero, unless they're betrayed by
someone close to them. In another gallery of the mine he
had the armory and we took a look at that too. He had
every kind of weapon, pistols, rifles, machine guns, mines,
rocket launchers, boxes of shells and ammunition, plus
other military hardware like radios and generators and in
another room stores of food and water for when the nuclear destruction came and they had to all sit it out down
in the deeper tunnels where the radiation couldn't follow.
The electricity to run the place they generated from
methane that came from a digester fed on hog manure
from North Carolina and he also had a little steam generator that ran off of coal, but that wasn't hooked up yet.
We cooked with the methane too.

So I began my life on Bailey's Knob. Everyone was

*friendly to me in that reserved, formal mountain way, except for a couple of the younger women who had their eyes cocked on Orne and were mad that I had got him instead, but nothing too bad. The whole place ran on kin spirit, they were all Randalls, Warrens, Wendells, Coles, more or less related to one another and to the Foys, because you couldn't run an operation like that with just hired help. Any one of them could've blown us but none of them ever did and I will not blow any of them now by supplying names. The other thing about the Knob was no TV. There was no reception of course because of the mountains and no one wanted a satellite dish. They listened to the radio and made music themselves, like in the olden days, or watched movies on VCR. I thought it was real restful, not to have people blaring at you from commercials every night and besides it left more time to read. And no phones, no ringing to distract you, to bring news from the outside no electrical bane or boon interrupting life. No phones no taps, was Orne's rule and he wouldn't have one on the place. The pay phone outside the grocery in Tiptree was our only contact with the outside, and Orne paid the salary of a girl there all she did was answer the phone and take messages for him. Once or twice a day she'd ride up the mountain and deliver the messages and every couple of days or once a week Orne would go down there and make calls.*

*I was there two years and four months and in that time I guess I read every book in Orne's library. There was all of Nietzsche, naturally, and near everything that anyone had ever written about him biographies and such, and some other philosophy and political science and economics, as long as it didn't say anything good about religion or welfare or socialism. Besides that, most of the shelves were taken up with history and military history and how-to books, and reference works, so that when the world collapsed we could construct civilization again, but leave out the parts Orne didn't like. There were no novels. Orne thought that fiction was a waste of time, and no poetry ei-*

ther except one book called the 500 Top Poems, some guy collecting the most anthologized poems, and Orne thought that was good enough, plus the complete works of Shakespeare. He also had a nearly complete collection of field manuals for the U.S. Army and a complete Loompanics catalog, all kinds of books on how to be a terrorist at home or change your identity and all.

Right off he taught me the business. The trade in domestic marijuana is much larger than most people think. In California it's second only to grapes as a cash crop. I don't know about Virginia, but I guess we were right up there with apples. Slade County hadn't produced so much income since the Caledonia shut down. The prime sensemilla we grew went for over $200 an ounce on the street and paid us around forty dollars or $1,280 a kilogram and we shipped between 400 and 500 kilos a month so an income of half a million per. Figure 70 percent for salaries and overhead that's still a lot of money and all of it went into gold, because Orne didn't want to have his money in data when all the computers went to slag. Once a month he'd go to Roanoke and hire a private jet and fly around his distribution area, collecting his take and converting it into one-ounce ingots, maple leafs, Krugerrands and when he had enough he would bury them around the property in gallon jars. He used a mil-spec GPS receiver and took a digital photo of the burial site and then he stored the photo in encrypted form along with the GPS coordinates on his little solar-power Argonaut ruggedized laptop. I learned how to do that too.

Besides this work, my time was my own. When I got sick of reading, I walked the land with map and guidebook, learning the trees and plants, sometimes with Orne, who knew it like his own face, and sometimes alone. They had built a watchtower on the rocky crest of the Knob and we would sometimes go up there and view our eight hundred acres. From there you could see the growing blanket of the state forests and watch it turn from green to golden and red and also the blighted areas where the coal companies *were carving the tops off mountains and also St. Catherine's Priory, lodged against its own hill, Sumpter Ridge across Crickenden Hollow from Bailey's Knob, a set of blue-gray boxes among the trees. Orne pointed it out to me and said maybe they would sack it like the Vikings did when the end came. It was in my first autumn there that I saw snow for the first time, and was also for the first time cold in a cold wind and felt what it felt like to be hugged warm by someone else.*

*I'm sorry, you're not interested in my delights, although it's the case that the devil has a whole bag of them. Not like in the horror movies where the devil's always obviously nasty, yellow eyes shooting flames from fingers making people fly into the walls, oh no he is as nice as pie and truly solicitous of your comfort. It is God who makes you cringe and hide your face and suffer pangs of torment, and flings you against the wall, not that I knew that then, and not that you know that now, but I pray you will learn.*

*What else? We played a lot of paintball, all joining in after work and on weekends, war with two teams or sometimes escape and evasion with three or four trying to get through and the others trying to keep us out. We took turns being commander. Most of the guys and some of the women had been in the service, so it was a pretty tough league and at the beginning I was usually killed fairly soon. I never got particularly good at being the commander, which is kind of strange, considering what happened later on. We did a good deal of shooting too, pistols rifles of all kinds machine guns rocket launchers. We had a 60 mm mortar and I got to shoot that and we also practiced making booby traps and blowing things up. Orne had the whole place packed with explosive devices and in case of a raid he intended to seal the mines under tons of rock, hopefully with all the narcs inside it. We tested these demo charges in unused tunnels. There is so much blasting in those hills from the mining that no one ever noticed our noise. I liked blowing things up, there is a luxurious thrill that goes through my body when I release a shot. Orne said I was a dab hand at it.*

*I didn't meet Skeeter Sonnenborg until I was there for well over a year, in fact on October 10, 1989, because he had been away in some far corner of the globe, although I had heard a good deal about him from Orne and everyone else. Ol' Skeeter. Remember that time when ol' Skeeter run his motorcycle through that wedding in Boonetown? Or started the goat racing? Or got drunk and brought a girl back to his place having forgot he already had a girl there he just asked to marry him? Skeeter was the best buddy. On that morning I was lying in bed with Orne and about to either get up or do it again, when we heard a crackling of gravel and then the potato-potato-potato sound of a Harley-Davidson exhaust and Orne lit up a big grin and said damn it's Skeeter back again. We got out of bed then and I was just looking around for something to put on when the door kicked open and there was Skeeter in his riding leather and his Nazi helmet. He ran his eyes over me and said nice tits honey and then jumped on Orne and they wrestled and whooped and punched each other down on the floor until Orne got him pinned in a hold and he hollered enough.*

*Well there is often a problem with the girlfriend and the best buddy. With Skeeter around Orne seemed to lose about twenty points of IQ, not that Skeeter was dumb far from it. He had gone to a fancy prep school name of An-dover or Hand Over Your Money Daddy as he always called it and spent some time at the University of Pennsyl-vania before he dropped out in '73 and joined the marines, which is where he met up with Orne. They didn't want to miss out on the war. He was obscure about where all he came from, allowing only that his daddy was a plu-tocrat and he didn't have much to do with his people. That was strange to me, since among Orne's kind you just didn't leave your kin no matter what kind of low dogs they were but there were a lot of rules that didn't seem to apply to Skeeter, including him making fun of Orne's philosophi-cal ideas. Skeeter didn't believe in getting ready for the End of the World, nor strictly speaking did he believe in* getting ready for the day after tomorrow. Or that's how it seemed, although in fact he was a perfectly competent businessman. What he did was sell weapons. He lived in Kelso, Virginia, which was about fourteen miles away on the other side of Sumpter Ridge, where he ran an outfit called The Gun Nut. This was not just selling Remingtons and Colts to the locals. He was an arms dealer on a fair scale, and he traveled all over the world buying and selling lethal hardware. He was the first person who ever talked to me about Africa, but I have run out of pages so here ends the third book.

Shortly before the surrender of Metz to the Prussians, a frantic Georges de Berville shipped his daughter eastward to what he imagined would be the safety of Paris. Marie-Ange arrived in the capital on the second day of September, but within three weeks the city was besieged by the enemy. She lodged with her Aunt Aurore at first but soon gained admission to the Institute of Bon Secours as a postulant. Called *gardes malades*, these women were devoted to the care of the sick, both rich and poor, in their own homes. All through the terrible winter of 1870 Marie-Ange worked ceaselessly in the poorer quarters of the Left Bank, bringing food, coal, and medicine when she could, bought from her own pocket at siege prices, and toward the end, when there was nothing to be had at any price, she brought a cheerful face and a comforting word.

Paris capitulated in January, but the agonies of the city were far from over. In March, the people of Paris revolted, and the revolutionary movement known as the Commune took over the city. During this time, Marie-Ange was working in Neuilly, which had been heavily bombarded by government forces. When the Commune began to arrest priests and religious, she merely changed her clothes, dropping the habit of Bon Secours and resuming the costume that had served her well in the Battle of Gravelotte.

That spring, the government forces advanced irresistibly, and the Communards were pushed back to a few heavily defended bastions. In the last week in May, Marie-Ange found herself in a wine cellar in Monmartre, where she had established a dressing station with no medicines but wine and no bandages but old sacking and the torn-up garments of the dead, washed in vinegar. By May 23, surrounded on all sides, subject to a ferocious cannonade, the Communards in the strongpoints of Monmartre lost heart and began to drift away. Her companions urged Marie-Ange to flee as well, for she could do nothing for the dying men and women in her charge, besides which, the attacking troops were shooting every rebel they encountered. She had almost been convinced of the futility of her plight when, as she later wrote, "all at once I became aware of a Figure at my side, the Blessed Virgin, who said to me, 'As I did not desert my Son at the foot of the cross, remain faithful to your charges, for these too are beloved of Christ.' So I composed myself for death with a good heart, although I was saddened that I would never more see my dear papa or my brothers short of our glorious reunion in paradise."

Then she heard a final fusilade and the door crashed down. The soldiers made to bayonet the helpless wounded, but Marie-Ange threw her frail body in their way, and cried, "Soldiers of France! Are you not Christian men? In the name of Christ and his Blessed Mother, have mercy!" Despite this plea, it is likely that Marie-Ange de Berville would have been killed in that vile cellar, had not the Providence of God brought Lieutenant Auguste Letoque to the spot at that very moment. This young officer was a close friend of Jean-Pierre de Berville and had often been entertained at Bois Fleury. Striking the rifles away with his saber, he shouted, "Fools! Would you slay an angel!"

—FROM *FAITHFUL UNTO DEATH:*
*THE STORY OF THE NURSING SISTERS*
*OF THE BLOOD OF CHRIST,*
BY SR. BENEDICTA COOLEY, SBC,
ROSARIAN PRESS, BOSTON, 1947.

# Fifteen

They drove north and then east for hours into a part of Florida where Lorna had never been. When they left the highway they seemed to enter a different world, one that had nothing to do with the jaunty vacationland image the state tried to project. Driving on two-lane blacktop bordered by murky canals they passed burning fields of sugarcane stubble and slowed often behind mesh-sided trailers piled high with cut cane. Once they passed a stake-bed truck full of standing cutters, men and a few women, scarfed against the dust that covered their clothes, that whitened their plum-black skin.

"My fate," said Paz as they drove by, "although these are Jamaicans, not Cubans. They fly them in for the cutting season. Americans won't cut cane."

"How does that make you feel?"

"About Americans not cutting cane? It's a national scandal."

"No, about escaping your fate."

"Duh, I feel good, I guess," said Paz.

Lorna felt herself blush. "I didn't mean——" she began, but he cut her off. "No, that's okay, but I have to admit that once in a while I grab my machete and chop an acre or two just to keep in practice, in case you all decide equal rights was a bad idea. How about you? Did you escape your fate?"

"No, I'm solidly in the groove. My daddy designed me to be a bright little thing and accumulate academic honors and gain a respectable profession requiring a Ph.D. and do the *Times* Sunday crossword puzzle in less than twenty minutes."

"Twenty minutes is pretty good," said Paz. "I do it in about three."

"You don't!"

"Yeah, I just leave it for a week and then they show you how to fill it in. It takes no time at all."

"Laugh if you want to," she said, laughing, "but it's an important part of my pathetic teacup of self-respect. My brother, Bert, feels like you do about the sacred puzzle, though. He escaped *his* fate."

"Oh, yeah? What was he supposed to be?"

"A famous research scientist M.D. discovering the cure for cancer. It turned out he liked girls and money instead. He's in bonds in New York, does fairly well, I think: nice apartment, a place in the Hamptons. He's on his third wife, because I guess the first two were not quite vapid enough to suit his refined tastes. Fortunately, Daddy had a spare child. Unfortunately, a girl. Fortunately, much more academic talent than Bert. Unfortunately, not enough to get into medical school. Fortunately, just enough to snag an Ivy League Ph.D., so she can be introduced as my daughter, Dr. Wise."

"So the cancer cure is pretty much out?"

"Afraid so. My sad story. What a stench! What *is* that?"

"Sugar refineries. Like a herd of brontosaurs got drunk on rum and puked up. We'll be out of it soon. Here's a point: as sad as your story is, you don't have to breathe this in every day."

"I'm not going to get any sympathy at all from you, am I?"

"No, although if I contract cancer I might be fairly pissed off at you. And your brother. Speaking of fate, this guy we're going to see, totally designed by nature to be a police detective. Mozart, Michael Jordan, that level. Probably cleared more felonies than anyone else in the history of the Miami PD. And because of a situation outside his control he gets the boot."

"What happened to him?"

Paz told her the story, the official one, about how Cletis had been driven crazy by African-style witch doctor drugs, and then she wanted to know more about the famous Voodoo Killer case, and he supplied more of the official version.

She said, "Why does your voice go all funny when you talk

about this? It's like you're one of those brainwashed Korean War POWs talking about how they did germ warfare."

"You detect prevarication."

"My stock-in-trade. What really happened?"

"You wouldn't believe it."

"Try me."

"Okay. There's a tribe in Africa that can do real sorcery. They can give you dreams, become invisible, create zombies. They can create psychedelic drugs in their own bodies and make you see anything they want you to see. An African-American went over there and became a witch, and then came back here and started eviscerating pregnant women to get the power he needed to destroy America and we couldn't stop him worth a damn. And the spirits exist."

She laughed. "No, really."

"See? I rest my case." Then he changed the subject to Cletis Barlow in his prime, his amazing feats, his peculiar beliefs, his kindness to Paz. "I'd still be, as the saying goes in the department, chasing niggers up Second Avenue if he hadn't dragged me into the detectives. I had a couple of nice collars, but no one was looking to promote me to detective. The ethnic politics of the Miami PD are a little weird. So I owe him a lot."

"A father figure."

"You could say that."

"And the actual father? Not on the scene?"

A long pause here. Lorna thought that Paz was ignoring the question and she felt a small pang of regret for having asked it. They drove out of the sugar regions and into a pleasanter country, green pastures occupied by humped white cattle staring stupidly from behind wire fencing.

"The short version," said Paz, after clearing his throat, "is he's a rich white Cuban. He loaned my mom the money to get her started in catering, and used her ass as collateral. I was the product. He does not have paternal feelings. When I got a little famous around that case and was on local TV a lot, he took his family on a world tour, lest anyone make the connection."

"That's really sad. I'm sorry."

"Yeah. But, *amor fati*."

"Pardon . . . ?"

"*Amor fati*. Love your fate. A friend of mine used to say that. The secret of happiness."

Lorna did not respond to this, as she did not wish to explore the source of the Latin tag, whom she suspected was on the staff of the University of Girl. She looked out the window. Soon they turned off the blacktop onto a gravel road and off that onto a narrow dirt track between rows of dusty pines, past a sign reading BARLOW Registered Charolais, and into a yard containing a red-painted, tin-roofed farmhouse with a wide screen porch, a barn, some outbuildings, and a tall, rangy woman in her early sixties, wearing a tattered straw hat and an apron.

Paz got out of the car and into this woman's warm embrace.

Introductions then: Dr. Wise, Edna Barlow, Paz slipping the doctor in there, Lorna wondering why. She shook the woman's hand, which was hard and strong, and looked into her face, which was plain, strong, seamed, tanned, a stranger to the spa, obviously, and equipped with sharp blue eyes. Lorna wore her formal face, as she did with people who might be offended by advanced ideas. She felt like she had walked into a 1930s movie.

They sat on the porch, which Mrs. Barlow called a veranda, and drank sweet iced tea from clunky glasses. Paz and Mrs. Barlow chatted about what he'd been doing and what they'd been doing, and the doings of the three junior Barlows (college, the marines, high school basketball), and although Mrs. B. attempted to bring her into the conversation, it was awkward, leaving Lorna wondering what she was doing here. She caught Edna looking searchingly at her several times and wondered what that was about.

A white Dodge pickup came dusting into the yard, and proved to hold Cletis Barlow and his sixteen-year-old son, James. More greetings, but apparently men didn't hug chez Barlow. Lorna thought Cletis Barlow had the meanest face she ever saw on a man, the face of the leader of a lynch mob from central casting, except there was a nice person living inside it by mistake. It was all scars, lumps, bad teeth, and wrong angles, and the eyes were the color of a washboard.

They got a tour of the rancho then, the two guests in borrowed rubber boots moving gingerly among the big cattle in the barn, swatting, but not too obviously, at the many flies. Paz was trying to sense the mental status of his former partner;

Lorna felt like she was on a school trip, a feeling enhanced by James, who seemed fascinated by her, although he called her ma'am and told her more about Charolais cattle than she wanted to know.

An early supper is the custom here. Through a manipulation that is proof against all of Lorna's psych skills and feminist principles, she finds herself in the kitchen with Edna, preparing snap beans and tomatoes from their garden and peeling potatoes. Lorna realizes that she has never actually peeled a potato. At home she was an honorary boy, the children were called in to a laden board, the mother never requesting her daughter's help. Message: This girl is for higher things, Dad things, feminism clearly not applying to Mom, although Dad talks a good game, and just as clearly she has fallen into a time warp here in south-central Fla. Who peels potatoes? Lorna's entertainments are infrequent, and at those few that involve spuds, she bakes them, and while they bake she dispenses wit in the living room.

Edna is watching, incredulous. Finally, she speaks. "Honey, I believe you haven't peeled many potatoes."

"Not even one," admits Lorna, and now she can put down the peeler and apply paper toweling to her wounds.

"Well, sit yourself down then. I only asked you to be sociable," says Edna, who now stands by the sink and with rapid flicks of the instrument causes the skins to practically leap off the pesky tubers.

Lorna feels obliged to compliment the woman on this skill, which she does and then feels unutterably patronizing, so adds a personal slamette. "I'm not very domestic, I guess."

"Well, you being a doctor and all, I figured you had enough to be doing. I just drug you in here so the boys could talk by themselves."

"Are they telling secrets?"

"I don't know, but they do like to get off alone. The two of them're real close, and Cletis has missed it something awful, although he'd never say a word. Anyway, I can't abide a man in the kitchen. It gets me all nervous."

"But if you feel that way, you get stuck with all the cooking and serving. And the cleaning up."

"Well, I wouldn't say 'stuck,' exactly," says Edna. "There's enough work to do in the world and I don't see why it can't be divided up so's we all know what we're supposed to do and get good at it. I believe the Lord intended it that way. I've changed truck oil, and greased bearings, and run farm machinery, and hauled feed. Who d'you think ran this place while Cletis was off being a policeman down south?" She holds up the peeler. "Honey, if you think this is hard, you try castrating a bull calf. No, thank you! Which is why I thank the good Lord for men. Although they can be a trial. How long have you known our Jimmy?"

The unexpected out-of-context question of the skilled interrogator. Lorna feels suddenly off balance. "Not long at all. We're working on a case together."

Edna seems a little disappointed in this answer, so Lorna adds, "He seems very good at what he does."

Here Edna turns on her an unexpectedly radiant smile. "Oh, my, yes, he is. Oh, but we think the world of Jimmy Paz. He's just the sweetest thing!"

The sweetest thing was at that moment in a sagging wicker chair on the porch vaguely wishing that Cletis had not added total abstinence to his skein of virtues. Paz wanted a drink and a cigar. He had told Cletis what Lorna had told him about the events in the locked ward, and was now relating what he knew about the Muwalid murder; it was tough going, Paz fearing that any moment Cletis would interrupt with a question about whether Paz had performed some action that might have broken open the case, which Paz had forgotten to do, and now it was too late. But when Cletis did stop him, it was about a detail from the first interrogation of Emmylou Dideroff.

"She said *what*?"

"She said it would be an honor to be executed unjustly, like Jesus."

"Well, well. If that don't beat all! I'd sure like to meet this woman."

"Yeah, the two of you'd get along real well, putting the pope to one side for a while."

"You think she was serious?"

"I guess. That was the saint part talking, though. There's another part in there that's not so nice."

"That don't signify," said Barlow dismissively. "There's demons in us all. Go ahead, what happened then?"

Paz finished his tale, adding the business about Wilson and Packer and Cortez and the material from the first volume of the diaries. After that, Barlow thought for a while, leaning his ladderback chair up against the side of his house and chewing on a toothpick, staring into space. Paz knew better than to interrupt him at this juncture.

They were called to supper.

Barlow let his chair go forward with a thump. "It don't work, Jimmy," he said. "I can't say for sure without seeing this girl, but she didn't do it. The frame's too obvious and sloppy. I think she was telling the plain truth. She was set up and she just walked into that room like she said. They knew you'd be up, and they knew you'd find her, and the murder weapon, and they knew you'd believe she was crazy. Uh-huh, I see you're confused. That's cause we always look at the victim, why was he killed, who were his enemies, what was he doing in the twenty-four hours before he died and so forth."

"Boys!" from the house. Barlow opened the screen door. Paz followed him in. "And . . . ?"

"It ain't him, it's her. She was why he was killed. He was just a convenience. They wanted her, not him. Well ain't this nice!"

The table was spread with food, steaming platters of mashed potatoes oozing butter, chicken-fried steaks the size of hubcaps, chunks of corn bread, enough bean salad to flatulate Orlando. Barlow went to wash up and Paz drew Lorna aside.

"And did you help cook all this?" he asked.

"Oh, right! I was put in a corner like a porcelain doll while Edna did all. She considers herself lucky not to have to castrate bull calves too."

"You disagree, obviously. I hope you gave Edna the full feminazi treatment."

"I know you're loving this. In fact, I personally *would* like to castrate bull calves. According to any number of my boyfriends I've been doing it figuratively for some time."

"You shared that point with Edna, of course."

"What is this, some kind of test? You've brought the whole University of Girl through here to bounce them off Edna?"

Paz thought about this. With some surprise in his voice he

said, "No, you're the first one." Lorna did not know what to say to that.

They sat down, Cletis at the head of the table, and he said grace. Lorna had heard grace said at the Waitses' house before this, but it was a routine, with one of the children rushing through it. But here there was a silence before, and Cletis Barlow really seemed to be communicating his thanks to God. As always, Lorna was faintly embarrassed. She looked over at Paz, who seemed to be in a trance. Grace concluded, she turned to the food. She was unfortunately not at all hungry, although she had been too upset by Emmylou's fit to think about lunch. There was something wrong with her gut, and it was an effort to get down enough food to avoid insult. The Barlows, who obviously ate such meals all the time, were all lithe and gnarly as vines. Maybe God kept them thin. It was a possibility. Paz was eating like a machine. Bright chitchat was apparently not expected at the Barlow table.

Paz was eating hard so as to avoid unprofitable mental excursions. Of course it was the girl, or woman, Dideroff, and not the hapless Sudanese official. He had discussed that very thing with Oliphant, but as one of a number of baffling possibilities, and had Cletis still been his partner, they would have nailed it the first day, and of course Cletis would've taken one look at the woman, had a nice talk about Jesus and the saints, and come up with the right answer in about six minutes. He had to talk to Cletis some more, but not just now; Barlow placed a Chinese wall between home and work, not that it was his work anymore, but still. . . .

The clattering of cutlery and other eating noises slowed. Mrs. Barlow urged further consumption. They tried, faltered, failed. Mrs. Barlow sighed, observed they would just have to throw it away, and stood up, casting a meaningful eye on Lorna, who felt herself pulled to her feet by tidal prefeminist forces. She began to help clear, although when collecting Paz's things, she was inspired by his self-satisfied grin to pour a little iced tea onto his lap. Oops! He had the nerve to laugh.

Dessert was pineapple upside-down cake sweetened fully as much as the laws of physical chemistry allowed and thin sour coffee. Talking was apparently allowed during dessert. James was on Lorna's right, and he told all about his recent Boy Scout trip. He was an Eagle and an assistant scoutmaster. Lorna had never sat next to a Boy Scout before. Waves of wholesomeness wafted from him, and he blushed whenever Lorna spoke. Then Cletis said, "Lorna, Jimmy here tells me you saw a lady drive out a demon."

Now it was her turn to blush. "I'm not sure what I saw," she said.

"I take it you don't believe in demons."

"I don't believe that's the cause of mental illness, no."

"What's the cause then, would you say?"

"A variety of things. If you're talking about frank psychosis, schizophrenia, most authorities believe it's a chemical imbalance in the brain."

"And what causes them?"

"Genetics in some cases, maybe environment; it's not clear. They used to think it was bad families, but they don't think that anymore."

"Hmm. So what's your explanation of what you saw?"

"I don't know. It all happened so fast. I might have been confusing what I observed after the orderlies sedated him with what happened just before, when Emmylou was touching him."

She saw a look pass between Barlow and Paz, a sly smile from the former, and on the face of the latter an expression that could have been embarrassment.

"Yeah, you might've been confused. Witnesses sometimes are. But what're you going to think when you go back to that hospital and find what's-his-name, Masefield, is as sane as you are?"

"That's really unlikely."

"But just suppose."

"Well, in that case, I'd have to put it down to spontaneous remission. It's rare but it does happen." She paused. Everyone was watching her, not like a gang of inquisitors, but like a family watching to see baby try something new. "But I still wouldn't believe in demons."

"Well, that's interesting. So you're closed off to any way of accounting for what your eyes see and your ears hear, except where it fits into your kind of explanation, even when that explanation doesn't make a lot of sense. Spontaneous remission? Why, that sounds like a fancy way of saying 'Heck, it beats me!'"

"It beats believing in demons," snapped Lorna, her temper rising.

Barlow said, " 'For as the heavens are higher than the earth, so are my ways higher than your ways, and my thoughts than your thoughts.' Isaiah, 55:9. Let me tell you a story, explain where I'm coming from. One time there was a wild young man. He cursed, he drank, he committed acts of violence and fornication, he broke every commandment but number six. He hadn't killed anyone yet, but that was just because he hadn't met anyone who he thought wanted killing. Well, one day that changed. He'd run a load of moonshine down from Georgia for this fella, and the fella had paid him some money and promised him more at delivery. Well, he delivered it all right, but the fella said he didn't owe him nothing more, and he just kind of grinned and passed looks around at all the men who were there waiting to get their liquor, and our young man couldn't do a thing, on account of the fella was armed and so were all the other men, they were that kind of men. So he was angry as a kicked-up nest of hornets and he goes running back to his truck, and takes his sixteen-gauge shotgun down from the rack and loads it up and he's got his hand on the door on the way to murder, when he sees that he ain't alone in that pickup truck. Lord Jesus is sitting right there on the passenger seat, looking just like a regular man. And Jesus looked that young man in the eye and all the love and forgiveness in the world flowed into him and he heard the voice of Jesus say, 'Son, put up your weapon and go on home and sin no more.' And he did. Well, that's a true story and that young man was me, praise the Lord."

James and his mother murmured, "Praise the Lord," and Barlow added, "Well, what do you think of that?"

Lorna said, "I'm sorry, this is really very difficult for me. I don't want to offend your religious sensibilities . . ."

Barlow grinned at that. "Oh, we're used it it. 'But we preach Christ crucified, unto the Jews a stumblingblock and unto the Greeks foolishness,' First Corinthians, 1:23. Go on with what you're going to say. We won't bite."

Paz said, "No, but after they clear the table they're going to hold you down on it and torture you with hot irons until you convert."

"Yes, and I believe we'll need the extra-large size irons for her," said Edna, deadpan. "James, why don't you go get them ready in the torture room."

"Aw, Ma, do I have to?" whined James. "I *always* have to do the tortures."

There was laughter then, in which Lorna joined, but uncomfortably. At the parties she normally attended, people like the Barlows were the butts of jokes, and while she saw the irony in thus having the tables turned, it was not particularly pleasant. So she spoke with more asperity than she otherwise might have. "Yes, well, no offense, as I said, but we would regard what you experienced as an hallucination brought on by stress. Blood pressure rises, adrenaline and other hormones are released, these have an effect on the medial temporal lobe and you hear voices and see visions. We can reproduce the same effects in the laboratory with electrical stimulation."

"And does it make you happy to believe that?" asked Barlow, fixing her with his colorless eyes.

"Happy has nothing to do with it. It's the truth. It's the way the world is. We just have to live with it."

"Hm. Well that's a point of view. But just because they figured out how the sun works, and just because they can build a bomb that works the same way, that don't mean that there's no sun in the sky, does it?"

While Lorna was thinking about this, Barlow said, "Jimmy, if you don't mind, I'd like to take a look at those confession notebooks you've got. I might come up with something, since I don't guess I'm going to get to see this woman."

Paz said, "If it's okay with Lorna. They're her property. I'm just guarding them."

Lorna assented, not without some secret irritation at the irregular aspects of this case, although she was happy that the theological discussion seemed to be over. The line between what was confidential therapeutic material and what was a public legal document had become hopelessly blurred, and it annoyed her. She grabbed up the dessert things somewhat roughly and stalked into the kitchen.

"I'm sorry we were such teases," said Mrs. Barlow, after five minutes of Lorna's stiff face and short answers. "It's just what we always do with Jimmy. I guess it's something of a family joke. I hope you weren't offended. That's the last thing we meant to do."

Lorna felt close to tears, for unknown reasons, which made the feeling worse. "Oh, it's not that. I've felt a little nuts ever since I met this woman. And I *asked* for it." Here Lorna unburdened herself about the various oddities of her relationship with Emmylou Dideroff, all of it pouring out into the steamy kitchen air.

"Y'all're being led to something," said Mrs. Barlow.

"But I don't *believe* in any of that!" Lorna wailed.

"You know, it don't much matter what you believe. You heard Cletis's story. Whatever y'all say about brain chemicals, there was a real change there and it came out of nowhere. I knew Cletis Barlow before that and I can tell you. He was the wildest boy in Okeechobee County and that includes the Indians."

"Were you going out with him then?"

"Oh, heavens, no! My pa would've had my skin if I'd even've looked at Cletis Barlow. We were hard-shell twice-on-Sunday church people. But I did look anyway. I guess I was sweet on him from third grade. When he showed up at our church afterward and got saved, I declare I nearly fainted with thanksgiving."

"What did you like about him? I mean before."

"I liked the way he moved. And if he was wicked, he wasn't mean wicked, if you know what I mean. And to tell the honest truth, I reckon I just couldn't love a man who wasn't a little bit dangerous. Could you?"

Again Lorna was at a loss for words.

Paz spent the next hour playing horse with James at the backboard nailed to the barn. He got creamed, a first, and felt cranky and old. Again he wished for a drink of something other than iced tea. Cletis was on the porch, in his chair, with the two notebooks on his lap.

"Slowing down, Jimmy?"

"He's getting taller. What do you think about our girl?"

"I'll tell you, son, I don't often lust to be back on the job, but here's one makes me feel like an old lame hound on a frosty night when the coon is out. She won't talk to you at all?"

"No, she says the devil's in her and it'll make her lie unless she writes it all down in order."

"I'll believe that. But she'll lie in writing too. Just once, maybe, hoping it'll slip by them."

"Them?"

"Sure, whoever's behind all this. Whoever's got your Major Oliphant from the FBI so agitated. Anyhow, you ain't going to find the bottom of this in Miami."

"No? Where, then?"

"Where she's been. Up to Virginia where she stayed, talk to those nuns of hers . . . but they're not going to let you do that."

"You think?"

"Heck, no! She didn't kill that Arab, but you got a dead man they can stick with it, which is always real handy, and you got this Wilson fella as the mastermind. That's as far as it'll travel. Kind of a shame, to tell the truth. I'd sure like to know what all got it moving."

Paz said that he'd like to know it too. He went into the kitchen to say good-bye to Edna and collect Lorna. He found Edna alone.

"So, when's the wedding?" she asked.

"Edna, I just met the woman. You know, you should get together with my mother."

"What makes you think we ain't getting together already, plotting and cackling and praying for your salvation and a mess of grandkids?"

Paz laughed, but a little uncomfortably. "Stop it, Ed, you're giving me the willies."

"She likes you. I can tell."

"She's a pleasant colleague is all. I brought her up here because she had a weird experience and because I was coming up anyway because I wanted to talk to Cletis. How's he been?"

"He pines a little, but the place keeps him busy enough. Oh, here you are!" said Edna brightly, in just that tone that informs the newcomer that she has been the subject of discussion.

"Whenever you're ready," said Paz, and then, "Just a second . . ." because he felt his cell phone vibrating in his pocket. He stepped into the hallway to take the call.

"Where are you?" asked Morales.

"North of the lake. What's up?"

"You need to get back here, boss. Jack Wilson's car went into a canal off Alligator Alley. It looks like there's a driver in it."

"Oh, terrific! What's the location?"

"It's just west of the Miccosukee line."

"I'll meet you there in an hour or less," said Paz and gave his young partner a complex set of instructions on how to deal with the state police and those of Broward County and the Indian tribe involved.

Lorna has assembled a number of witty remarks about the visit to the Barlows, about how it was like an excursion to one of those attractions, common in the Northeast, that purport to show us how our ancestors lived. Only ten miles more to Pre-Modern Village! She also wishes to needle Paz about the religion business. She is a little ashamed of the way she behaved earlier, nearly blubbering about what she thought she had seen in the locked ward. She is papering this over, layer upon layer of logical denial and explanation, and she wants Paz in on it, to defend the threatened paradigm. Paz is cool, she thinks, he is slightly cynical and funny, and she imagines this attitude will help. If not, if he actually buys into the malarkey, then she assures herself that she's not interested.

Except she can't get out of her head that remark about dangerous men. Lorna has been careful to avoid dangerous men. Dangerous men are violent and stupid and tend to be male chauvinists, so she has always thought. Romantic is okay, preferred actually, but that only means a certain savoir faire, the ability to discuss the films and books of the day, the correct liberal ideas, and of course professional brilliance, the ability to take the risk of an unusual academic stance, to write a controversial paper.

But not anything like this, right now, which is driving down the center of a two-lane blacktop road at ninety miles an hour with the siren going. Now there is no lagging behind the trucks, now they whip around the trucks and play chicken with the oncoming traffic. Lorna has heard about pissing in terror but has never actually experienced the urge. Night falls in the theatrical manner of the tropics—a blush of red in the west and then black velvet, especially here in the lightless Glades—the world vanishes except for the headlights of Paz's unmarked police car, the fearful beams of the near misses in the northbound lane, the red glow of swiftly overtaken taillights. The siren is boring into her brain, her muscles ache with the continual tensing for the crash. Paz has explained over the noise that he has to get to the crime scene to exert some control, even though he will have no official standing. The importance of this is lost on her, she thinks he's crazy, she hates him. He is smoking a cigar, she can see his face in the red glow of its tip. She decides to hate that too, unhealthy, disgusting. . . .

Now they head west on Alligator Alley, blasting through the official no-toll gate and accelerating on the ruler-straight freeway. Lorna has never traveled above one hundred miles an hour in a car. She finds it is almost like flying, the thumping of the wheels is now absent. Suddenly she is beyond fear; sinking into an almost sensual passivity. She slumps into the corner of the seat, her thighs lolling open.

A cluster of flashing lights appears ahead. Paz slows and pulls onto the shoulder, nosing among a cluster of police and emergency vehicles. He says, "Stay here, this won't take long. Are you okay?"

"I'm fine," she says. He vanishes.

She is not fine. She is shaking. It is stifling and humid with the car AC shut down, and her throat is raw with thirst, she has a headache and feels, really, quite ill. Despite this, and the damp heat, she sinks into a light doze.

She is awakened by the slam of the car door. Immediately afterward, the engine starts and a grateful frosty breeze dries the sweat on her face. Paz's face looks grim as he moves the car off the shoulder. State troopers are controlling traffic, and they are able to swing back onto the eastbound highway.

"What happened?" she asks.

"What happened is that our main suspect just got himself killed. This is probably the guy who hired the guy I shot, who was probably the guy who actually killed al-Muwalid. So we're screwed, plus I called my major to report this and get him to use our chief to grab hold of the body, car, and contents, but apparently that's not going to happen. The murder took place on an Indian reservation, so the FBI has jurisdiction, and apparently they don't intend to cede it. In fact, the FBI is now showing a keen interest in the whole case—the Sudanese, Dodo Cortez, and Jack Wilson all getting killed seems to have lit up some kind of light on the big board in Washington. Anyway the feds are in it. Oliphant is pissed as hell, but I can't see that he can do much about it."

"What about Emmylou?"

"Unclear. There're these new antiterror laws, which seem to let the feds do pretty much what they please. Maybe they'll name her an enemy combatant and disappear her."

"No, seriously . . ."

"I'm being serious. I wish I wasn't. Oliphant is sure taking it that way. He pointed out that Emmylou essentially belongs to the state's attorney, who belongs to the governor of the state, who happens to be the president's little brother. I don't think the state's attorney will put up much of a fight if they want to grab her up. Shit!"

Lorna feels a chill that has nothing to do with the air conditioner. Her modest and controllable life seems to have come apart. She seems to be involved, even if only peripherally, in something huge. Murder. International intrigue. Governors and presidents. She wishes none of this had happened. She wishes for it never to end. And there is something else happening to her. She is going into the most intense sexual heat she can readily recall.

They arrive at her house. She says, "Would you like a drink?"

"Oh, Jesus, would I!" he says.

Inside, she turns on the living-room AC, but the house has been sucking in heat all day and it will take some time for it to cool down. She makes two huge rum and tonics. They sit together on the couch and drink as if it were Gatorade, then catch themselves doing it and giggle.

"Want another?"

"I'm game."

She brings out the cold-beaded tumblers and says, "You know, I'm dripping sweat out here. Aren't you?"

Paz is nearly sweatless as always, but he agrees, yes, sweaty. She adds, "This time of year there's only one cool room in the house."

He follows her into the bedroom, which is like a meat locker. He perches carefully on an armchair. She says, "I feel like I have grease and slime all over me. I'm going to take a quick shower." She does so, lickety-split. It might've been the fear, or the violence, or him, but she feels no need to resume her clothes as she returns to the bedroom.

When Georges died in 1889, all the family except for Alphonse were amazed at the size of the estate. De Berville et Fils was the largest refiner of kerosene in Europe and controlled the gaslighting companies in most French cities. Its founder had also owned, through his Rockefeller contacts, nearly 7 percent of the stock of the Standard Oil Company of New York as well as large holdings in other petroleum firms. Alphonse inherited the business, and Jean-Pierre was given stock and property worth many millions of francs. But two of his children were in Holy Orders and could not own significant property. For them, Georges had established a trust, named Bois Fleury after his beloved country estate, to "advance the cause of Christ through works of charity." Into this trust he placed all the Standard Oil stock, and gave his son Father Gerard de Berville the responsibility for managing it.

It took nearly two years for Marie-Ange to put her plans into effect. Gerard had been as supportive as she might have wished: funds would not be a problem. But her superiors in Bon Secours and especially the anticlerical government officials to whom she applied were adamant that the idea was absurd. In that era, respectable women working at nursing was itself a suspect notion, but for such women to also travel unescorted into war zones? The idea was preposterous.

While affairs were at this stand, she went on with her preparations. An organization was formed, and young women were recruited into it. Most of these were tough, working women, from the mines around Lille or, like Otilie Roland, from the working-class quarters of Paris. A life of dedication to the sick, possibly at risk of death, was less daunting to such women than it would be to those more delicately raised, although the first twenty members included the daughters of a count and of a senator of France.

From the very start the order was established on military lines, and here the foundress was inspired both by her brother the colonel and her brother the Jesuit. She also recalled the ill-discipline of the Commune's defenders. Her recruits would not melt away when danger threatened, and would meet death gladly if need be. During this time too she designed the habit of what she hoped would one day be a religious order. The sisters were to wear essentially what she herself had worn at Gravelotte: a gray dress in cotton or wool, a cook's apron, a simple white linen scarf tied behind the head, high-laced ammunition boots, and a blue cavalry cloak.

—FROM *FAITHFUL UNTO DEATH:*
*THE STORY OF THE NURSING SISTERS*
*OF THE BLOOD OF CHRIST,*
BY SR. BENEDICTA COOLEY, SBC,
ROSARIAN PRESS, BOSTON, 1947.

# Sixteen

**P**az was having another nightmare, only this time he knew, in the peculiar way of lucid dreams, that he was having one and wished to get out of it. He was at a crime scene, some horrible crime, the atmosphere of horror hung in the air, all the worse for being unnamed. He was interviewing two little girls, both about seven. They were on the street, twirling a jump rope between them. He wanted them to stop twirling, but the thought came to him, as it does in nightmares, that they would tell him more if he started jumping himself, and so he did, faster and faster, the little girls smiling now, their eyes empty of joy, and he noticed that one of them wore a dress of wool, the other of cotton. . . .

He opened his eyes and discovered where he was: in Lorna Wise's bed, with the AC chilling the room enough to make it cozy under her duvet. He recalled the previous night. Very nice, and now he was awake, unless, of course . . . the thought rippled his belly and broke sweat from every pore. He turned his head slowly. The blond locks of Lorna were on the pillow next to his. He could hear the gentle sighing of her breath. He brought his nose close to her head and sniffed. Herbal shampoo. He sniffed lower down, at the warm wafts from beneath the quilt. Essence of girl, the world's most entrancing fragrance. Had to be real, dreams don't have smells, he recalled hearing that somewhere; on the other hand he could be off the charts in some way, and that neat little head could now turn around in an unnatural fashion and exhibit a grinning skull or a dog's muzzle saying "Surprise!" He could feel his heart knocking in his chest and then he thought to himself, just in passing, no, if this wasn't real he would go to his mother, let her do what she had to do, and if that failed he'd check out of the job, let the shrinks play with his head, because he couldn't stand it any-more. He sincerely believed that people who carry weapons ought to have a firm grip on reality.

Such were Paz's thoughts as he breathed in Lorna Wise as if sucking oxygen from a mask. Minutes went by. She murmured, stretched, and rolled over. It was, he observed with vast relief, her regular face. He thought he had never seen such a beautiful face, although he had actually seen plenty, and in just such situations. He sat on the side of the bed and stared at her for some time until his eye beams stirred her awake. She opened her eyes, saw him, started to smile, and then, observing his expression with a trained eye, she knitted her brow and said, "What?"

"Nothing."

"Something. Did you have a nightmare?"

"Yes, a strange one with characters out of a poem. I thought I was still in it. Did you ever have one of those, when you wake up and you're still in it?"

"No, I never have bad dreams. And as your personal therapist I have to tell you that there's only one sure cure known to med-ical science."

"And what would that be, Doctor?"

"I'm afraid you'll have to lie on top of a naked woman for a certain period of time."

"No, no, not that!" cried Paz, although he began the therapy immediately. "How long do I have to?" he asked after the nec-essary slippery adjustments had been accomplished.

"Until the naked woman says to get off," said Lorna.

Lorna is now floating in the most pleasant phase of postcoital hypnopompic semisleep. She is awake enough to realize that she is not lying in the dreaded wet spot for a change, and not awake enough to start obsessing about the future of her rela-tionship with Jimmy Paz, a nearly perfect combo, promoting cosmic well-being. He is not in bed just now, but that's all right too. She slips back into dreamland, surfacing only when the sound of clinking crockery and silver intrudes. Paz is entering the room with a tray, upon which is the container of her Krups coffee machine filled with sloshing blackness, assorted jugs, mugs, napery, and utensils. The delightful smell of coffee and fresh baking arises from the tray. Paz places it on the side of the bed. He is naked except for a pair of slight black Hugo Boss underpants.

"What is that?" she says, sliding herself up to a sitting position and pointing.

"It's a plate of magdalenas," says Paz, taking one. "You didn't have rum so I had to use cognac. They're not bad, though."

"Oh, well, the hell with it, then. You expect me to eat magdalenas without rum? What kind of girl do you think I am? God, this is beyond delicious."

"Are you thinking of your great-aunt's house in Combray yet?" asks Paz.

"Oh, he reads Proust too? Or is that something you picked up from one of the many?"

"From Willa Shaftel, as a matter of fact. We were watching a rerun of a Monty Python, the summarizing Proust contest? And afterward she actually summarized Proust for me during the rest of the weekend."

"Uh-huh. You know, bringing up previous girlfriends all the time can get old real fast."

"As can needling me a little every time I say something you figure is beyond the normal range of a dumb cop."

"Oh, are we having our first fight now?"

"Yes, and now it's over. Have another magdalena."

She did and said, "This is well worth seventeen additional hours on the StairMaster. Where did you get them?"

"I made them." As he pours coffee.

"Wha . . . you *made* them? In *my* kitchen? You carry a madeleine pan around with you?"

"No, I used yours. It was in the back of the closet outside the kitchen. It was still in the box. It must have been a present."

"It was. From my brother, in whose fantasies I am ever a baker of cookies."

"Well, I broke it in for you. I hope you don't mind."

"I certainly do mind! Never *ever* break in a madeleine pan in my house again! Christ, this is strong coffee!"

"Weak," says Paz. "It barely sticks to the spoon."

Lorna eats another madeleine and falls back against the pillows with a sigh. She feels, to be honest, a faint nausea, but otherwise so good that she decides not to pay any attention to it. "I really wish something interesting would happen to me. Having terrific sex and then being brought breakfast in bed by beautiful naked men morning after morning, I mean, sometimes I want to scream with the tedium of it all."

"Humor me," says Paz.

"You're really gay, right? That's the catch."

"I'm afraid so. I have to pretend to love women so the guys down at the police station don't make fun of me." They laugh, but in the midst of it Lorna feels the first twinges of real life. The devil speaks into her inner ear: Yeah, this is great, but you know you'll go out another couple of times, fuck like minks, have fun, conversations, and then he won't call for a day, three days, a week, and then, desperate to know what's happening, you'll call him and leave a half-dozen increasingly irritated messages and then he'll call and it'll be, what? As from a stranger.

Paz senses the change. He says, "I'll clean this up," and picks up the tray.

"No, leave it," she says. "I'll do it."

Lorna is nearly overwhelmed with the urge to say something nasty and disruptive of this thing that seems to be developing, far too nice for the likes of her. As she fights against it, there is a beeping from Paz's jacket where it hangs on a chair: the first bars of "Guantanamera." Thank God, she thinks, something tacky at last.

Paz answers the phone. There is a lot of listening interspersed with gnomic utterances from Paz. Lorna rises, slips into a light robe, takes the tray to the kitchen. It is spotless and smells of coffee and sweet bakings. As she rinses the dishes she feels tears well in her eyes and recalls feeling the same way when she was with him on the beach at Bear Cut. No, she thinks, this is too cruel, my heart won't take this. As if her body agrees, she feels a bolt of sharp pain through her middle, a kind of pain she does not recall ever having before. Sweat breaks out on her face and back. It passes, and for the first time in a while the old fear returns. Something wrong, something wrong inside. Again she suppresses the thought.

She goes back to the bedroom and hears the shower going, so she drops the robe and joins him. After some fooling around with soapy skin surfaces, he sighs and says, "I have to go to work."

"The phone call."

"Yeah, my partner. The autopsy on Jack Wilson found a blood alcohol level of point three six."

"My God, that's paralytic."

"Yes, and they also found traces of Nembutal. Plus an empty bottle of cheap vodka in the car. The feds are treating it as an accident, and Broward County is going along. We were lucky to get as much as we did out of them."

Paz turns the shower off. She senses he is somewhere else already.

They dress in silence, he much faster than she. Paz is in her study, looking at her books and possessions with his consuming policeman's eye when she emerges from the bedroom in one of her bland suits.

He says, "Listen, are you going to see Emmylou today?"

"Yes, I want to check on her condition. Why?"

"Could you ask her something for me?"

Lorna hestitates. "A police question, you mean."

"Not really. I just want to know who connected her with David Packer."

"Jimmy, I really can't help you in your investigation. It's unethical."

"Okay, no problem. You going to find out if she did the cure on what's-his-name?"

"That's not very likely, is it?"

He looks at her without answering for a while, then crosses the room and embraces her. "You have any plans for Sunday evening?"

She did not. "We'll go have dinner at the restaurant. You should meet my mother."

"Uh-oh."

"No, she's a charming woman," says Paz. "Everybody loves Margarita."

Frank Wilson lived in a condo, a modern eight-story building off Le Jeune in the Gables. When Wilson let them in, Paz could see that he had been crying. His eyes were red and his face seemed to have fallen away from the bone, gone spongy. He kept dabbing at his nose with a wad of tissues. Paz thought it was a strange reaction, but then he'd never lost a sibling, or had one. Wilson collapsed onto a leather couch. He neglected to offer the two detectives seats, but they took them anyway. Both pulled forth notebooks. The tan meshwork drapes on the big picture windows were tightly drawn, and Wilson hadn't switched on any lights. The room was consequently dim, which made it hard to observe their informant's face.

"It's like a kick in the gut, this is," Wilson said. "I still can't believe it. It's just so not Jack."

"What isn't, sir?" asked Paz.

"Oh, drinking, driving . . ." The voice trailed off.

Morales asked, "He drink much vodka, Mr. Wilson?"

"Couldn't stand the stuff," said the brother. "He thought it tasted and smelled like rubbing alcohol."

The two detectives considered this for a moment and then Paz asked, "How would you describe your brother, Mr. Wilson? What kind of man was he?"

Wilson sat up a little and stared at Paz. "What kind of . . . I don't understand. This is a traffic death in Broward. I mean why does a Miami cop want to know that?"

"Well, sir, as I guess you know, Jack was peripherally involved in another case and we're just trying to tie up the pieces on that. Also . . . we think your brother's death might stand further investigation. You say your brother had no head for liquor and hated vodka, so, ah, you could ask what he was doing with a point three six blood alcohol and an empty vodka bottle in the car."

Wilson goggled at him. "What . . . you think someone killed him? They forced him to drink all that vodka?"

"That or they knocked him out with Nembutal and ran a nasogastric tube into him."

Wilson gaped and stammered, "But that's crazy! Who would do something like that?"

This was of course the very question that now engaged Paz and Morales. They were driving to Jack Wilson's domicile, having obtained the keys from the brother, along with a description of the late Jack's character. A little wild, bored with the business, a ladies' man, a good conscientious mechanic, if a little too ready to party after hours. On the assumption that Jack Wilson had been murdered and that no one was going to let them near the case, not the tribe, and not the FBI, then the whole thing had come to more or less a dead end. Wilson had been the last thread that led from al-Muwalid's murder. Whoever had arranged that killing knew how to cover their tracks. Paz shared with his partner the observation that Cletis Barlow had made, that the point of all this was not the Sudanese but Emmylou Dideroff, and that all this bloodshed was designed to draw from her something that she knew.

Morales said that it sounded far-fetched, but what did *he* know, Cletis Barlow was the great detective. Paz detected a little envy here but let it go. He might have agreed with Morales about far-fetched, had he himself not traveled personally over even farther fetches, but he declined to mention this now. They arrived at the Wilson house, a small, tile-roofed Spanish colonial over Coral Way not far from the Palmetto Expressway. Jack Wilson had fancied a nautical theme: signal flag upholstery, marine landscapes on the walls, captain's chairs around a hatch-cover table in the dining room, ship models in a glass display case. "Everything looks shipshape," said Paz. They laughed, but everything actually did. Wilson was something of a neat freak, in his home if not his personal appearance. He liked Peg-Board, and where the pots and kitchen implements hung on one of these, he had painted a silhouette of each implement under its hook, lest one be hung out of place.

They tossed the place rapidly, Paz with the skill of long practice, Morales learning as he went. Paz took the master bedroom and got a little shock off what he found there; Morales searched another bedroom fitted out as a den or home office and was intrigued by what he didn't find. His partner called out to him, and he walked into the master bedroom, where he found Paz staring at a brightly painted statue. It was nearly two feet high and depicted a haloed woman in a gold dress and a red cloak holding a sword and a chalice, which rested upon a vertical cannon.

"Somebody's been through the place," said Morales.

"Yeah, they have," Paz agreed. "They were real neat about it, though. How could you tell?"

"There're no personal papers in that office aside from a

folder full of paid bills. No address book, no files, no Rolodex, no personal mail. No diaries with an entry that says 'I'm scared shitless that $X$ is gonna get me.' He's got a big wooden desk with two file drawers, both practically empty, but you can see from the dust marks that they were full of file folders at one time. There's a fancy digital phone that can store twenty numbers, but they've all been cleared, and you can see where he had a little list, maybe about which buttons called which people, taped to the desktop, the wood is unfaded and there are tape marks. Someone took the trouble to rip it off."

"Very good, very interesting," said Paz. "It goes with the rest of the picture. Someone is clipping connections, the connections that lead up from Jack Wilson to whoever was running him. There's something strange here too. First of all, the clothes in the drawers were all jumbled around. Someone had been through them because the rest of the house suggests neat, and they weren't neat. So that confirms that they were searching for some physical object or objects. What is the most interesting absent physical object in this case?"

"Muwalid's cell phone."

"Right. I'd bet that's what they were looking for. The other thing is that." He pointed to the statue. "You know what that is?"

"A religious statue?"

"It's a Santería cult figure, Santa Barbara, aka Shango, the *orisha* of thunder and violence. That's not supposed to be in a regular straight-up white guy's house."

"I don't know, people collect all kinds of weird shit."

"True. But he's also got this." Here Paz held up a double-bladed axe made of wood, painted red and yellow, from which depended a string of red and white beads. "This little axe is an *oshé*, the symbol of Shango, and the bracelet is an *eleke*. You only get an *eleke* at an initiation, when you're made to an *orisha*. Also, you notice that sweet smell? That's *omiero*. They smear it on objects and people during ceremonies. No, this isn't a tourist item. It's a working shrine. Wilson, or someone he knew real well, was involved in Santería."

"You know about this stuff?"

"More than I would like," said Paz, putting down the axe. Suddenly there was too much spit in his mouth. He said, "Are you hungry, by the way? I only had some cookies for breakfast."

A little startled by this change of subject, Morales replied, "I could eat, yeah."

"We'll swing by the restaurant," said Paz. "My mom'll make us something."

Lorna drives to the hospital and wonders yet again if she is in love. No, that's crazy, the man is delightful, sure, but also a completely unreliable womanizer, he has the whole act down, the charm, the showing off the new sweetie and so forth, the mom even, but even as she thinks this she knows she is making it up and feels hollow and helpless, as if caught up in a current. Circling the drain, she thinks cynically and laughs.

Speaking of circling the drain: the first person she meets when she passes through the locked ward is her old boyfriend Howie Kasdan, M.D. As always when he leaves his office and ventures into the clinical world, Dr. Kasdan is wearing a long white coat, from the pocket of which peeks a stethoscope, although to Lorna's knowledge Dr. Howie has not checked for heart sounds in a long while. He has his foot propped up on a chair and is writing on a clipboard braced against his knee, but he notices Lorna despite her usual camo costuming and flashes his caps at her.

"Lorna! Hey, you look great. You look like you dropped some weight."

"Thank you, Howie," says Lorna coolly. "What brings you into actual patient contact?"

"Oh, one of my drug test subjects, paranoid schiz, just went into a complete remission. It could be a real breakthrough. I mean this guy is like *normal*? He wants to know what he's doing in a loony bin. I mean he only chopped two of his spouses into wife stroganoff—"

"Wait a minute, this isn't Horace Masefield?"

"That's the guy. A friend of yours?" More caps.

"I was there when he went ballistic. I actually saw him remiss. What kind of drug is this?"

"It's called traxomonide. It's a completely new approach to brain chemistry, operates directly on the SEF2-1 mutation, which shows increased allele frequency in schizos. It codes for a helix-loop-helix protein that we think may have a significant role in—"

"How big is your N, Howie?" Lorna asks.

Kasdan frowns; he is not often interrupted in his expositions. "A hundred ten. They're here, and in Chatahootchee, and in a couple of other sites."

"Have there been any other remissions like this?"

"Not that I know of, but we just started the study, the drug's barely reached therapeutic levels. I wanted to get Masefield scanned as soon as possible, and I know we're going to see changes. I'm totally pumped about this."

Previously, Lorna would have been pumped herself at the prospect of fame and fortune represented by a new mental health drug even at one remove, but not anymore. It isn't just that she no longer cares for Kasdan, nor that she has less faith in the chemical model than formerly. No, it is learning that what she had witnessed had probably been an artifact of some new dope and not . . . what? Something rich and strange. It is like learning that Mom and Dad were really Santa Claus. It makes her sad, and she knows it has something to do, in a confusing way, with what is going on with Jimmy Paz.

"Lorna?"

"Hmm?"

"Something wrong?"

"No. Why?"

"You looked like you were zoning out there. Are you still on medication?"

"No."

At that moment Lorna feels a rush of weakness pass through her body, so that she nearly staggers and has to touch the wall for balance. Sweat oozes on her brow and lip. "I have to check on a patient," she says. "Nice seeing you!" And she hurries off on wobbly knees.

What was *that* all about? she wonders as she inspects herself in the staff bathroom mirror a moment later. She looks pale, and more than that, she feels fragile. The nice oily-in-the-limbs feeling from this morning has quite vanished, and she recalls that blast of pain at the kitchen sink. And now this. Could it have been long-suppressed repugnance of Howie? Unlikely. A return of the panic syndrome, from which she had been remarkably free of late? Possibly. She sits on a plastic chair and takes deep breaths. She palps the lymph nodes in her neck. Are they larger, more rubbery? She can't tell. She washes her face and reapplies makeup. Something is still not right.

On her way to Emmylou's room she passes a doctor's scale. Lorna has never weighed herself in public before, but now she steps on it and shoves the little sliding weights around. She has dropped seven pounds. She tries to convince herself that it is the exercise kicking in and fails. A little knot of fear starts spinning in her belly. She thinks of the old cliché, even paranoids have enemies, and there's one for hypochondriacs too. She leans against the wall and uses her cell phone to dial Dr. Mona Greenspan, but when the secretary answers she breaks the connection. This has to stop, she tells herself, there is nothing wrong with me, I am not a crock, I do not have cancer.

Emmylou Dideroff is sitting up in bed reading her Bible. She looks up when Lorna enters and smiles. Lorna says, "Haven't you finished that book yet?"

"I keep hoping it'll turn out different. Ever read it?"

"In college. As literature. How are you feeling?"

"Everyone asks me that and I tell them I wish they'd stop making me take all these pills. I can't stand being this dopey."

"It's the Dilantin, probably. They don't want you to have another seizure."

"It wasn't a seizure. I'm not epileptic."

"I was there when you had it. It looked like a seizure to me."

"Everyone in a Santa Claus suit ain't Santa, as my daddy used to say. He uses our bodies. I mean God does. What else *is* there? People don't understand that, they think it's all airy-fairy special effects, but we're meat; not *just* meat, but mainly so."

"So what do *you* think happened, Emmylou?"

"It just seemed like the right thing to do, to touch him. And the demon came out of him. It wasn't me, of course, but the Holy Spirit. In professional exorcisms, they use teams, half a dozen people sometimes and it can take days. You don't know about this? Well, the church keeps it dark for obvious reasons, but you can still get an exorcism done. Anyway, God decided that Horace Masefield had been crazy long enough and I was going to be the instrument of liberation. Nearly broke me doing it, but it wouldn't've been the first time." She smiles and taps on the Bible. "I guess y'all can sure tell me apart from the Son of Man when it comes to the exorcist business. You don't believe a word of this, do you?" She seemed pleased with that for some reason.

"No, I'm afraid I don't. It turns out that Mr. Masefield was taking an experimental antipsychotic drug. It just happened to take effect at that time."

Emmylou is grinning at her. "And I just happened to throw an epileptic fit at that very moment, even though I never threw one before."

"No, actually, you have a history of fainting spells. And anyway, coincidences happen." Lorna feels the falseness in these words, even while she clings to their validity.

"Yes, they do," the woman agrees. "Just some damn Eskimo again. There's a whole Congregation at the Vatican devoted to distinguishing between the coincidental and the miraculous. Of course, you would say they're all superstitious nuts." She held up the Bible. "God speaks to us in Scripture, and through our inner voice, but he also speaks to us through a conspiracy of accidents. George Santayana said that, and he was at Harvard." She stretched and yawned. "Mercy, but I'm tired of this place! And I don't want any more drugs."

"They're supposed to help you," says Lorna, wondering whether she'd heard correctly. Damn Eskimo?

"No, they help y'all. I don't fit into your mold of what a person's supposed to see and believe, so I'm crazy, and if crazy, I have to be drugged. But I'm not crazy, as you very well know."

At these last words she casts her gaze directly at Lorna, they lock eyes, and once more the pins that support Lorna's view of the world and of her own place in it soften and bend. She is the one who breaks eye contact. She is sweating, her heart flutters. She struggles to fit this experience into a familiar box. Hypnotic elements. Her own physical condition, low energy, stress, prone to brief hypnagogic episodes, Emmylou's the crazy one, not you, and so on, until she was again in possession of herself and is able to speak.

"Emmylou, even if you assume that, um, spiritual forces are involved here, it still doesn't make sense. Why did God wait for just that moment to cure Horace. Why didn't he cure him before he murdered two women? Why not before he hurt a couple of people right here on the ward?"

Dideroff waits a moment before answering, a peculiar look

on her face, like a maiden aunt just asked by a child where babies come from. "Well, you know, *why* is not a question we like to ask of God. It opens the whole issue of theodicy, and you know Milton wrote a zillion-line poem about justifying the ways of God to man, and I'm not sure how successful he was except to make people admire Satan." She taps the Bible again. "And there's Job, of course. I'm sure you're familiar with *An Answer to Job* by C. G. Jung. Have you thought at all about my dream with the giant Twinkies? It's relevant, don't you think?"

Lorna says, "Of course," spontaneously, but she is thinking about Milton and Jung. She has heard the names, naturally, but has not read the referenced works. It almost never happens that psychologists working in the public sector meet as clients people smarter or better educated than they are. The thought passes through Lorna's mind that this skinny woman on her loony bin bed, this high school dropout, is brighter than Lorna herself, and certainly more widely read in the Western canon. She realizes that she does not know what *theodicy* means. The woman is looking at her expectantly, but Lorna's mind is completely blank.

Emmylou rescues her. "I think it was triggered by a line from Weil, actually. I mean the dream."

"Vay?"

"Yes, Simone Weil. You know who she was, don't you?"

"Oh, sure," Lorna lies.

"Well, she says that the pure love of God means being exactly as grateful for your afflictions as you are for your blessings. It's an interesting way of looking at the world, isn't it?"

Lorna is recalling the dream interpretation she'd cocked up for Mickey Lopez. "Yes, if bad and good outcomes are the same, then you're off the hook aren't you?"

"Off the hook?"

"Yes. You can relinquish the unbearable responsibility for having done bad things. If bad things and good things are both randomly distributed by God, then there's no need to grow, to take responsibility for your acts. I mean, wouldn't that be another way of interpreting that image?"

"You think I'm trying to *avoid* responsibility?"

"On a certain level. I think you're retreating from what

you've done, from what's happened to you. And I don't blame you at all."

Emmylou leans back and lets out a sigh. "*Ok anhier ok yin.*"

"Pardon?"

"Dinka. It means 'I'm lucky to be with you.' It was an illustration, meaning you don't understand my language and I might as well be talking Dinka. I'm sorry, it's been a long time since I've had a conversation with someone with no religious sensibility at all. Look . . . oh Lord, how can I express this so you'd understand? Okay, God is omnipotent, and good, but there's evil in the world, bad things happen, and they sometimes happen to good people. How to explain this? Well, we're advised in the strongest terms not to try, but putting that aside, and also putting aside pure materialist atheism for a second, how do you live in a world like that? Y'all can be like the Buddhists and say it's all an illusion, no good, no evil, break free of all attachments, and then if y'all make it, return as a bodhisattva and dispense compassion. There's fatalism. You see it in Job, in the classical world, the Stoics, and it survives pretty well intact in Islam: God knows, we don't, shut your trap and drive on, don't whine, it's ignoble, and so on. Not a stance that would appeal to us improving Americans, so what we do is to whine a *lot* while drugging ourselves into insensibility with work, sex, money, actual drugs of course, and the illusion that we can live forever. Most of us live terrified, desperate lives and die like dumb animals in places like this. On the other side, we have what Weil said about the greatness of Christianity being not that it provides a supernatural relief from suffering, but a supernatural *use* for it. Say you have every good thing. Then you thank God for the honor of being able to serve the poor and wretched. Now say everything is taken away from you, you're crushed like a bug. Simone calls it *malheur,* the last extremity, nothing left of your personhood at all, sociology has failed, medicine, economics, politics, all the usual dodges are futile, but on the other hand you're a tissue paper away from God. Lose everything, get everything and more, unimaginable graces. Blessed are the poor in spirit. You can't lose."

Only some of this got through to Lorna. She had been trained to discount the content of what the insane had to say, and to examine their speech only for the evidences of pathology or to find some entry for the insertion of a therapeutic remark. She now does so.

"Well, if suffering is so great why did you devote your life to a nursing order? I mean, why relieve suffering at all, if suffering brings you close to God?"

"Because it's a commandment. It's also a paradox, but if you're impatient with paradoxes you need to stay away from Christianity. Atheism is so beautifully simple, like a kid's drawing. I can see why you're reluctant to let it go. I certainly was when I was at St. Catherine's."

"Which is what?"

"It's a priory of the Society of Nursing Sisters of the Blood of Christ. It's in the Blue Ridge, the Virginia panhandle, right close to where I was staying. You'll read about it in the notebook I gave you, my first sight of it. What all happened there is in the next one, and all the stuff about Africa."

Dideroff falls back against the pillows and closes her eyes. "I'm sorry, it's the dope. Have you cured me enough today? I really need to drift off."

Lorna puts her notebook and recorder away in her canvas attaché case, making agreeable noises to hide her distress. She has never had a session like this with a patient; yes, occasionally you draw a therapeutic blank, but this one was completely out of control, almost as if the patient were therapizing her!

Dideroff opens her eyes and smiles. "Sorry for the two-minute theology, it's a bad habit of mine. St. John of the Cross warns against it as an impediment to spiritual progress. Don't forget the notebook. I just finished another one. I never thought it would take so many pages. But one more ought to do it." Dideroff indicates a school notebook on her nightstand; Lorna picks it up and starts to leave. She pauses at the door, feeling a certain resentment now, a need to exert control. She says, "Emmylou, do you want me to do anything about your houseboat? I'd be glad to go talk to your landlord if you want to keep it."

"Oh, thanks, but I don't think it'll be necessary," says Dideroff.

"I'd like to live on a boat sometime. How did you manage to find it?"

"It was offered, and the price was right. I didn't hardly have a dime when I got here, and Mr. Packer said a good tenant was valuable to him and he'd let me stay there until I got on my feet. He got me the job at Wilson's too."

"So he was, like, an old friend?"

"Oh, no, a Samaritan. I just happened to run into him in the airport lounge. I'd never seen him before in my life. And it turned out we had some mutual friends."

Feeling a little slimy, Lorna checks through ward security and takes the elevator to the lobby. There, instead of descending to the parking garage, she goes to the staff cafeteria, where she orders an iced tea. She sits alone at a table and reads the notebook rapidly, taking no notes. She calls Paz to tell him about it and arrange its delivery into his safekeeping, but his cell phone is busy. She leaves a voice mail message. She feels better than she did a little earlier, although her hand ever rises to caress the lymph nodes under her jaw. Rubbery. She tells herself it is a mild infection she is fighting off. On the elevator, she becomes aware of a mild itching on arms, back, and thigh. That was it: the other night out in the Glades, mosquitoes bit her and she is having a small reaction to their bites. It's happened before. Stop worrying, she tells herself, but her heart still pounds so.

She walks toward her car. She is nervous in parking garages and holds her case under one arm and her keys ready in the other hand. Just as she reaches her car, a man steps out from behind a pillar. He is wearing a plastic Porky Pig mask and carrying a large hunting knife. She hands over her bag without giving him any trouble.

# Seventeen

### The
# CONFESSIONS
### of
### Emmylou Dideroff

### Book IV

*It seems like all we did that winter was talk, the three of us in Orne's living room around the hot cube of the stove occasionally tossing in a chunk of oak and pulling out of our mouths some idea, cut to size, quartered, aged, and dry like the wood. It was mostly me and Skeeter who talked, which I found strange because Orne had always been the biggest talker I knew, but he seemed content to sit sipping home-brewed beer or corn liquor and listen to us chop logic.*

*Topping was what our conversation was mainly about, I have to say that even though Skeeter was supposed to be Orne's best pal he was mean to him in a sly way that for some reason Orne didn't seem to resent, always putting him down about things of the mind. He was hard as blazes on old Nietzsche because he knew Orne had sort of built the whole structure of his life on that philosophy, and Skeeter had got pretty good at tearing it down. Nee*

*Chee, he would say, how can you take him seriously? He never made any money and he never got laid. What the fuck good is his philosophy if he never made any money and never got laid, when the point of his philosophy was you ditch God and then you're the superman and you can do what you want, and here's superman Nee Chee wandering around Europe jerking off in low-end hotels collecting cheap soup in that stupid mustache. And more like that.*

*So I am drifting again. This is not the important material. The important thing was that Orne was fading away from me that winter. I thought it was because I couldn't get pregnant and Orne was a planning man and a planning man don't like it when his plans go awry even in a small detail like that. I said I could go to a fertility clinic I looked up in Roanoke, but he said no because he didn't trust doctors. He had a couple of theories about them too. It never did occur to me that every time I wasn't there Skeeter was tearing me down to his best buddy, but I didn't find that out until it was much later and didn't matter anymore.*

*So one day he was off on one of his trips without even a farewell fuck like we used to and near as soon as his dust had settled on the road the best buddy was trying to get into my pants. And I wouldn't let him and it really peed him off, because we were not what you would call a moral bunch, a point he made a good deal of. I mean why not? What's a fuck between friends after all, why is it different from borrowing a truck or a tool, he would say, Orne won't mind, you want me to ask him? In fact, I can see he's trying to get rid of you already, and listen, darlin', I wish I had a dollar for every time Orne and me switched off girlfriends, I mean what is your problem?*

*On the other hand . . . I guess that besides being tedious and all it was also interesting to be courted that hard, something you kind of miss in the whore business, and Skeeter was an interesting man aside from him being a bandy rooster type with the shaved head and the tats, although built up from lifting weights. He really had been to all those places, buying and selling weapons, and occa-*

*sionally he would seem to forget about his seduction routine and just go on about Abidjan and Mombasa and Nairobi and the mountains of the moon and the Andes and slipping planes into secret airports at night and the sweating faces of desperate men shining in the light of flares.*

*So one day, Orne still gone who knew where, Skeeter said to me I have to go see a Depot of the Damned and would I like to come and I said what's that and he explained about how army units accumulated stuff that they weren't supposed to have and the officers and NCOs lied about it and hid it during inspections in some truck or other and that after a while the stuff got too conspicuous and they had to get rid of it, no questions asked, and Skeeter supplied the disappearing service. He was a pilot, did I mention that? We flew down to Georgia in a Cessna and he wore me down so I let him fuck me in the back of the plane just to get past it and to get back at Orne too and it turned out to be my very last voluntary fuck as I shall tell.*

*It is real hard to practice evil unless you are a hypocrite, and lie to yourself about what you're really doing. I have seen a lot of evil men in my time and Skeeter Sonnenborg was one of the few I met who didn't lie in that way—he was bad and gloried in it—and another good part about him I have to say is he didn't hold a grudge, he was not that flavor of evil. He bought me a big box of fudge at the airport and stuck his business card from the Gun Nut onto it with a note that said anytime, babe, and boy was it stupid I mean <u>fudge</u> but it touched me because I had not experienced much in the way of gifts without some immediate payoff expected.*

*Orne got back the next day and he was colder than he had been before he left. The problem with living like fierce beasts is that not much talking goes on and if your credo is an individualism so extreme that intimacy feels like oppression then there's not much you can say anyway. Do you want me to leave? Do whatever you want. So I moved*

*my quilt and pillow into an empty room and cried my lit-
tle eyes out for a couple of nights, hoping he would hear
and come in or relent or something, but no. After about a
week of this, I came out to the kitchen one morning to
make some coffee and there was a girl there younger than
me fussing with the coffeemaker, Sharon her name was,
and we sat down and had a civilized conversation over
coffee and sweet rolls and she told me that she was carrying his child and I could stay as long as I wanted she
didn't want to kick me out or anything.*

*I thought about killing the two of them Sharon and
Orne and then myself, really thought hard about it for
days, the devil in me painting a pretty picture of how it
would feel the look on his face and such, but in the end I
just didn't, God was directing me to a different fate. I did
want to kill <u>something</u> though, and so one dawn I dressed
up in a heavy winter camo jacket and overalls and my
good boots. I took Orne's Jarrett 280 with the Swarovski
PH scope, which nobody but him was ever supposed to
touch, and my Buck knife and a pack frame and rope, and
headed out to get a deer. As I walked out of the place
someone was playing a banjo and singing*

> *Up in the Blue Ridge mountains
> It's there I'll take my stand.
> A rifle at my shoulder
> A six-gun in my hand.*

*Our theme song you might say.*
*The place we usually hunted from was a little knob
overlooking a meadow that ran down to the banks of Crit-
tenden Run, the little stream of the holler that our mountain overlooked. There was good cover on the knob, and
the deer would come down to water, and in the spring the
bucks would use the meadow for their joustings. I got comfortable in a little scoop of ground full of the season's
leaves that we'd covered with a camo tarp and from
where I could look out from under a laurel bush at a view*

*of most of the meadow and the stream. Through the scope I could see deer tracks in the sandy shore on my side of the stream. I loaded up and waited and before long a buck and a pair of does came down to the stream to drink. I put the crosshairs on the buck and as always when I hunted thought of Ray Bob, how he had taught me not to try to keep the cross rock steady on the target but to control its waver, moving it in tiny circles and slowly squeezing your trigger at the same time in coordination so that when the round went off the sight picture would be just right. Where I come from we are not sentimental about edible animals. The buck raised his lovely head from the water and stiffened, only his ears twitching, and I dropped him with one right behind the eye.*

*An hour later I had him gutted and skinned out and a haunch bagged and tied on to my pack frame, when I heard the first shots, which I didn't pay any mind to, and then a whole lot more, automatic fire in volume and then the whole face of the mountain shook and there was a whomp of noise and I started to run up the trail. I thought it had to be an accident one of the demo charges must have gone off and I thought of all the workers in there crushed and dead. I honestly never thought that he had set them off on purpose that the Knob was under attack by the law until I came off the trail onto the gravel road and I saw it was full of SUVs with government markings. Men were crouched down behind cars, and some of them were shot and bleeding and there were bullets cracking over-head and they were returning fire. Two of them spun around and looked at me, they were like space aliens in gas masks and helmets. I guess they thought I was one of the defenders. I had a rifle in my hand, and it didn't occur to me to throw it down. Instead I turned and ran and one of them shot me in the back and I fell off the road and down the side of the mountain rolling and rolling until I crashed and disappeared into a big patch of laurel.*

*It was dark under the leaves and stank of rot and that peculiar laurel smell. I had wound up facedown, with the heavy pack frame pressing me into the cold earth and the little hard laurel stems. I didn't move for the longest time. Gradually the firing died down. There were other explosions, but not as loud. I could hear sirens too and truck engines and the sound of people talking urgently on radios. The pain from my back wasn't so bad, more of a pressure hard to tell from the weight of the deer meat where it bore on the frame and pressed it into my own flesh, worse were the little laurel spikes, there was one that felt like it was going right through my breastbone to my heart. I thought I would die there in the laurel but I didn't yell or anything, I just tried to think if Nietzsche had said anything about death and came up pretty blank except it was ignoble to worry much about it.*

*I drifted off, or maybe I fainted, and when I woke up it was dark and quiet with the patter of freezing rain on the leaves above my head. And cold. Which seemed to wake me up. The shiny man was there I could see him in the glint of the raindrops and he was telling me all about how I would get eaten by animals and beetles and turn into a skeleton and wasn't it sad, poor Emmylou, and this made me so angry I shucked out of the backpack and struggled upright and then the pain really hit me.*

*I crashed along downhill for a while stumbling and falling the rain heavier now the Run where I crossed it up to my thighs and of course I slipped and fell and rose coughing soaked to the skin and thought if I could just lie down a second and rest I would feel better but the nurse said not here not here child go ahead go just a little farther. The nurse from before when I was alone that first night in Orne's house, with the willow-leaf eyes. I didn't give a thought to how she had got there it seemed so natural that she was there I could see her white headcloth shining although the clouds were low and heavy and there was no moon showing. But it glowed.*

*The nurse was speaking now but in a language I couldn't understand, I mean I couldn't understand the words but I could extract their meaning she said God has brought you this far child now you must go the rest of the way yourself and I said I don't believe in God and that's when I knew I was dying and that this was a dream.*

*Then I was warm again and floating up around the ceiling of a long white room and thinking oh this is what dead is. I could see close to my head the rough texture of the plaster and the light fixture and the white paint flaking around where the chrome of the fixture was attached it said KayBee Electric Inc. Decatur GA on the base plate and looking down I saw a row of hospital-type beds empty except me and bango it was morning and I was on my back in the bed not dead but feeling like it and a brown woman in a white headcloth and apron was taking my blood pressure. Our eyes met and for a moment I thought it was Sister Trinidad Salcedo in Miami and maybe all that happened since I last saw her had been a dream, but no, no such luck, she said well you're back with us, how are you feeling, and I said the traditional where am I and she said this is the infirmary at St. Catherine's Priory and I'm Sister Mercedes Panoy. Who are you she asked and I said I was Emily Louise Garigeau. I said, you're a Blood Sister aren't you? She gave me a funny look and asked if I were comfortable, which is what nurses say when they want to know if something hurts like hell and when she said it I realized that my whole back was in agony shooting pains radiating all across it from my left shoulder blade. I said no my back hurts and she went away and came back with a couple of red-and-white capsules and a paper cup of water.*

*I spent the next week in an oxycodone haze. I learned I had been shot through the shoulder blade but that my meat-filled pack had reduced the force of the bullet, which probably saved my life. When found, I was suffering from hypothermia and a raging infection, as well as from an immune reaction owing to the deer meat that had been forced into my wound. No one asked me how I had been shot and I didn't volunteer. I was in a facility of the Nursing Sisters of the Blood of Christ as I had surmised, actually their central training facility in North America.*

When I was well enough to walk around, after about ten days, I took myself to the little dayroom they had there and read the Roanoke Times. The story was still getting play, a massive raid on a marijuana-growing empire international criminal white supremacists, six officers and an unknown number of criminals had been killed in the shoot-out and explosion, including Percival O. Foy, the mastermind. There were protests from the usual idiots, the Feds had blown up the innocent victims and oh how awful armed militia in our state Virginia is for lovers ban the guns.

So that was the end of Orne Foy, blood and fire, the death of a Nietzschean hero, as he wanted. I discovered I had no tears for him then although he was the first being I loved, loved in the sense that I wanted his good more than my own. He of course did not believe in that kind of love at all and looking back I see that God gave him to me to make the first crack in the armor of my self and only a tool as hard and as merciless as Orne could have held the edge that did it. I believed in him too, in his nonsense, his apocalypse, and also I see that now as my introduction to the _act_ of belief, and also practice in loving the fairly unlovable, my darling racist killer. "I have done that says my memory; I cannot have done that says my pride and remains adamant. At last, memory yields."—Nietzsche. But not for me, I am denied even that.

I had to believe the nuns knew all about where all I'd come from but no one said a word nor did I see an official, which was fine with me. I did see a lot of Sr. Dr. McCallister, a dry old bird who was the surgeon who pulled the slug out of me and also head doctor at the priory. She informed me among other things that I had probably stumbled into the best place in eastern North America outside a big city ER to get a bad GSW treated. So I considered myself lucky, although as I now know luck had nothing to do with it. The doctor asked me though how I had happened to find the priory through the rain and dark and with such an awful wound and so I told her about the woman who had led me to their gates. I said that one of *the sisters must have been out and found me lying in the rain but she assured me there had been no such person. She asked me to describe the person and I did—the white cowl framing the face, the long thin nose and those eyes. She stared at me strangely, but said nothing.*

*I was a slow healer and required a good deal of painful therapy to regain movement in my arm and shoulder. Joining me in physical therapy was Margaret Chitoor, a postulant aged eighteen. She had been operated on for a club foot. From her I learned something of how the Society recruited its members. Chitoor was not her family name but the name of the place where she had been found by a missionary. She had been thrown on a trash heap to die as an infant, an unwanted girl, a useless cripple. She laughed when she told me this, as if a little joke had been played on baby her. She said many female babies were thus disposed of, in India and other places, and the Society was able to save a tiny fraction of them, to be raised in its priories around the world. Of these, a substantial number volunteered at age eighteen for service with the organization that had saved their lives.*

*I confess Margaret irritated me no end. I resented her cheerfulness under pain. I myself howled and cursed at our physical therapist, a stocky woman with a crew cut and a face like a bulldog. I was vile to her and would have begged her forgiveness later only she shipped out before I became sane. I was vile to Margaret too. She would pray at night and I would mock her prayers. I quoted from Nietzsche to destroy her faith, like any village atheist. The Christian faith is from the beginning sacrifice: sacrifice of all freedom, all pride, all self-confidence of the spirit; and at the same time enslavement and self-mockery, self-mutilation, and on and on, but oddly enough the words of a nineteenth-century brilliant middle-class syphilitic philosopher cut little ice with a girl who had been saved from a garbage pile. She looked at me like I was crazy, quite properly, and said oh Emmylou you mustn't talk that way it makes me sad to hear you talk that way, and I* heard her mention me in her prayers. I wanted to kill her. I would've too. I would have killed them all for their goodness if I had the means.

Impotent, I fumed and was sarcastic, sarcasm being the last refuge of the impotent and I nursed my contempt for the sisters. They were most of them maimed in some way, except for Sr. Dr. McCallister, most of them rescued from third world hellholes and trained to be sent back to third world hellholes to die for Jesus. I thought it was the very essence of insanity and said so often and loud.

It took me nearly two months to heal enough so I could move without pain. I was taken on increasingly longer walks, first around the infirmary, then to the refectory for meals, then around the grounds. The priory consisted of four three-story buildings made of gray local stone built around a quadrangle. In the center of the quad was a statue of a woman holding a wounded man, which they told me was of St. Marie-Ange de Berville, who had started the Blood Sisters long ago. Two wings of the building were dorms and one was offices and the chapel and the other was the services wing, which was where the refectory and the infirmary and the library were.

The Society felt about poetry pretty much the way Orne did and mostly they had religious books and medical and nursing texts, but they did have a fiction section full of classics. I read all the novels. No one suggested I read the others. I was out of hospital gowns by then and wore what everyone else wore when they weren't on nursing duty—what they called <u>bleu de travail,</u> French mechanics' one-piece jumpsuits, a souvenir of the Society's origins in France. I was sitting in this outfit in the dayroom reading Daniel Deronda when Sr. Mercedes came in and said that the prioress wanted to see me. I said I'm busy, at which she took the book firmly from my hand and said the prioress wants to see you <u>now</u>. Well I had heard plenty about the prioress. They called her the Rottweiler and she ate human flesh when she was in a good mood. Mercedes said comb your hair it's a mess, and I said fuck you and walked out.

*I had expected her to be a big square-jawed warhorse like Sr. Dr. McCallister, six foot tall and breathing smoke. What I found instead was Jette von Schwerigen, a small, spare elderly lady in the full habit of the Society sitting in an armchair, reading. When she saw me hesitating at the door of her office she gestured me closer with a finger and pointed to a chair opposite. She picked up a file and perused it. Her office was plain, whitewashed, a desk, low bookshelves, a large wooden table clock on a wooden file cabinet, some framed photos, the only wall decoration a large crucifix. She looked at me until I became uncomfortable. Sharp blue eyes behind gold-rimmed round glasses. Gave a little sigh, said Emily Louise Garigeau, what are we to do with you?*

*A slight barely noticeable accent. I recall I wondered what a German woman was doing running an American operation. I said I wanted to split and she expressed concern for me, where could I go no clothes no money and I said I'll manage because I was thinking about all those jars of gold coins, and I could call up the maps in my head pretty well. She told me the cops were after me, she knew about the dope business and said my picture was circulating, was on the TV, some federal agents had come nosing around the priory. I asked her why she didn't turn me in and she said that wasn't any of her business and then she said tell me about this woman you met, who cared for you when you were injured and led you here.*

*So I described the mystery nurse, her face, her cowl or whatever, the prioress nodding, asking questions. Then she opened a book she had on a table next to her an art book red cover with a color picture of a man with arrows sticking out of him and I read the title upside down it was Medieval Italian Painting. She turned to a page and reversed the book and handed it to me. There was a picture of my nurse looking down, a close-up three-quarter view in color you could see the tiny cracks they have on old paintings.*

*A chill raised the hair on my arms and I felt sick come up my throat a little. The picture had a caption, detail from St. Catherine by Andrea Vanni, San Domenico, Siena.*

The prioress said the artist who painted that was a friend of Catherine of Siena and he did that from life, that's what she really looked like. And that's what you saw, isn't it? I take it that you have never seen that painting?

I snapped the book shut. I said I don't know what you're talking about and she said young woman, you appear to be under the protection of a saint. I understand you don't believe in God and all that nonsense, and I said yeah, right, and she smiled and shook her head. Do you know that there are perhaps thousands of people on their knees at this moment praying for some sign from God that will reward them for their faith and perhaps they will never receive one, and here are you, who does not believe at all and you have such visitations. What do you make of this, hmm?

I shrugged. I said I must have seen the painting in a book somewhere and forgot, though the lie curdled in my mouth. It was a hallucination, I said, I was sick.

The prioress did me the courtesy of ignoring this remark. She said I have always thought that the Holy Spirit had a sense of humor and this is one more evidence of it. So, we return to the question of what you will do. I assume you don't wish to end in prison.

No. Sullen now. My eyes were traveling around the room not wanting to look at her, but the place was so plain and bare that nothing held the eye except the crucifix which I was not going to look at it creeped me right out. There were books in a low glass-fronted case, no help there I couldn't see the titles and one of the photos, the one in an oval silver frame, was a photograph of a man in uniform. I didn't recognize the man but the uniform was a famous one.

I asked her are you any relation to General Hanno von Schwerigen? Children who have been raped have a well-developed ability to change the subject.

Her eyebrow tilted and she glanced at the photo and

*said it was her dad and asked me how I knew the name, and I said I have an interest in military history. He commanded the Twenty-second Panzer in Normandy. It was in that John Keegan book about the battle.*

*But she was clearly as skilled as I in the opposite direction. She said, But you are the subject of our conversation here and not my father or long-ago battles. She told me that I was well enough to do work, and that I had the choice of leaving, and they'd give me clothes and a little cash, or they'd find me something to do. She said their rule is a modification of the Rule of Benedict, work and prayer.*

*I said I was an atheist and she said fine, it's an old and respectable faith. Some of my best friends are atheists. I've worked with atheists who are better Christians than I will ever be. Then she said, be that as it may, you shouldn't try to ruin the faith of those who have faith because if it is truly of God then it is a waste of your time and in any case it's impolite. She said manners are important in a community like this one, so if you stay, you can't do it anymore.*

*Now the interesting thing here was that the shiny man was in plain view out of the corner of my eye, just past my left shoulder where he usually hung out not saying anything but sending out his get-out-of-here vibe like he'd done after Momma got herself killed and with Hunter when he went all stupid, and I was about to say well I guess I'll leave then, when I noticed that the prioress was staring over my left shoulder and I got it into my head she could see him too and this scared me worse than anything I'd been through up to now. I froze like a dead man and the minutes just ticked and I noticed the sound of the clock suddenly loud in the room and somehow time stretched then going from ticktockticktock to Tick. Tock.      Tick.*

*She broke the silence first. She said I don't want to influence you unduly, but here is something to think about. It is clear that God is speaking to you through his saint — why we don't know. He certainly never spoke to me that way and I have been a religious fifty-three years. And He has led you here, also we don't know why. So let us say you have a certain talent for seeing things usually unseen. I suspect you have also heard from the other side, yes?*

I said I don't believe in any of that shit! My voice was up and warbling nearly out of control. She said *then you are insane. Do you feel insane?*

I had to think about that. I'd been around crazy people enough, my momma and the street people in Miami and I knew in my heart I wasn't like them. Crazy people were kind of helpless when you got right down to it, and I wasn't that. So I had to tell her no.

This seemed to make her happy. She said *something interesting has decided to happen to you, we won't presume to say what it is, but this is probably where you are meant to be. St. Catherine brings you to a priory named for her?*

Coincidence, I said like a good little materialist. To my surprise, she laughed. For a little lady she had a deep laugh almost like a man's. That's when she told me the Eskimo story, which I will write down because it's important for you.

A pilot walks into a saloon in Alaska and the bartender says, oh Fred we have not seen you in church recently. Where have you been? The pilot says, I don't go to church any longer. I have lost my faith. The bartender says, but why? The pilot says, last month I crashed my plane in the wilderness in the mountains and I was trapped in the wreckage. I prayed to God to get me out but nothing happened. Day after day I am praying, but nothing. I decide that there is no God and I am going to die and there is nothing after death. This is how I lost my faith. So the bartender says, but you <u>did</u> escape from there. You are here and alive. And the pilot says, oh, that had nothing to do with God. Some damn Eskimo wandered by and pulled me out.

That wasn't why I stayed, that story. But after she told it she said, *and another thing, my dear: there are no men here. Sometimes it is nice to take a vacation from men, yes?*

*Yes, indeed.*

*Thus I began my life in religion, God had found me and pinned me in this little corner, forcing holiness down my unwilling throat. In doing so I entered a strange place, strange even among religious foundations. The religious life is dying in the rich countries as everyone knows. The era of huge foundations is over, there are few vocations anymore among young girls, priories and convents are filled with the old and dying and their caretakers. St. Catherine's was not like that, and this was because of the peculiar nature of the Bloods. This I learned from three books that I got from Sr. Marian Dolan, who was the sub-prioress and in charge of the lay sisters. The books were Faithful Unto Death, which was all about how the order got founded and how great Marie-Ange de Berville was, and then a book by her, The Formation of Nursing Sisters, and a little thin one, The Rule of the Society of Nursing Sisters of the Blood of Christ, which she also wrote. The reason why they had young nuns and oblates is that they recruited from those they raised from childhood in foreign countries and also from some they rescued from the streets. Girls are still human garbage in much of the world and they grab a few from that great dump.*

*Sr. Marian was a woman in her fifties with a rock jaw and thick round steel-rimmed glasses, who wore her coif low on her forehead, so she looked a little like a motorcycle rider in goggles. Sr. Marian seemed always to be leaning into the wind of her passage. She told me I would be considered a lay sister as long as I chose to stay. St. C.'s did not have guests, held no retreats. Everyone in the place was a member of the community and worked. She asked me what skills I had, and I said whoring, stealing, and helping run a dope business. Also I could shoot and ride a horse. I thought I would shock her, little did I know. She wrote something down and then said we usually start new people in maintenance. It's simple, healthy work, and it will give you a good idea of how we live. Or there's the kitchen, if you'd prefer that. I said how about nursing, I thought you were all nurses. She said nursing was for professed sisters, they wouldn't put the others through the training, and she didn't think I had a vocation for it, did I? Well, I sure didn't, the whole bedpan and sticking needles business freaked me out and I didn't want to work in the kitchen either, so I told her whatever, acting bored.*

*There were about a dozen of us in the maintenance crew. Six were Filipinas, plus the Indian girl Margaret, and the rest were various types of lowlife who had wound up in the hands of a Blood, a couple of whores like me, a suicide attempt, some real young runaways. The head of us was Sr. Lorette, who looked about ninety but was spry. I recalled what the prioress had said about talking down the religion and I was pretty good about that, I mean who gave a rat's ass about what any of them believed, as long as they didn't try to foist it on me. Still it wasn't that comfortable being around them all. The Filipinas were cheerful and devout and chattered among themselves in their bubbling language. They were all orphans who had been rescued from various horrible fates in their homeland. The others were converts and zealous in a particularly annoying way, talking about Jesus and the saints as if they could contact them whenever they wanted. None of them seemed to be contacted by saints against their will as I was, although I didn't discuss that with anyone.*

*The work wasn't that hard, as work, but I grudged it, and that made it wearing. Despite my so-called eidetic memory I find it hard to recall what was going through my mind at the time. A lot of anger, mainly at myself for having screwed up my life, and at all the people who had let me down, my daddy by dying in that stupid way, my gran for not figuring me out in time, my momma for marrying a pedophiliac hypocrite, Ray Bob for being one, Foy for blowing himself up, and also at the people at the priory for being so bone-stupid they couldn't even see how dumb and worthless I was, and all this shot out in all directions like sparkler sparks, but black, and especially at the people who were the sweetest to me, Margaret and Sr. Lorette* mainly, but anyone who happened to come in range of my tongue. I wanted a fight, but no one would fight with me. One time I was up on a ladder in the infirmary changing a lightbulb, and as I took down the globe, I saw that it said KayBee Electric Inc. Decatur GA on the base and I remembered my first night there and how I'd seen that floating up along the ceiling and I dropped the globe and didn't tell anyone about it but it shook the shit out of me. I started volunteering for work outside after that, felling trees and clearing culverts.

Occasionally I would see her, standing away at the edges of my vision, and once as I opened the door of my truck she was standing quite close, close enough to touch. She never said anything, although I shouted at her and used vile language and threw rocks, like a maniac, at Catherine of Siena. I feared I was going to be crazy like my mother, and I think that one of the big reasons I stayed at the priory was that if I was out in the world and people saw how I acted I would get arrested and they would check my fingerprints and that somehow (I wasn't too clear on this but it was a terror nonetheless) I would end up back in Doc Herm's rest home in Wayland and the Dideroffs could do what they liked with me.

Aside from that and everyone hating me (as I believed) life at St. C.'s was pretty fine. The Bloods are not an ascetic order, about the furthest thing from as a matter of fact. They feed themselves well when they can get food. The Foundress has a whole section of her book on recipes, how to make daube for 250 and so on, navarin of lamb, blanquette de veau, coq au vin, soupe à l'oignon. They baked their own bread too, and croissants. I never had food like that before or since. Bd. Marie-Ange thought that life was hard enough and they were all going to die fairly soon, and that God had given us all these good things like food and wine to enjoy and we should enjoy them. Over the entrance to the refectory there was carved a saying from St. Teresa d'Avila—"When it's time to pray, pray; when it's time for pheasant, eat pheasant." We had wine with our meals too, except on Friday (when we ate only soup and bread) and during Lent. The order was liberal in some ways and conservative in others, like that, or maybe they were on the other side of that whole liberal-conservative thing, but I didn't know anything about that then. I guess they liked their traditions was the main thing, like the habits and the French words they used for different things. _Goûter_ for the snack they served in the refectory around three. _En principe_, when you were going to do something a little outside the rules: en principe, it's not allowed, but. And _débrouiller_, of course, but I should say about that later because that was connected with Nora Mulvaney.

And _rappel_. Every Sunday we had rappel, which meant the entire population stood in lines marked on the pavement, the sisters dressed in their coifs and cavalry capes and us lays and postulants in our bleu de travail and berets and the little old prioress standing straight as a flagpole in front of the big bronze statue of the Foundress as the Angel of Gravelotte giving a drink to a wounded peasant lad, and then the subprioress, Sr. Marian, would say, in French, here are 120 (or whatever the number was) souls at your service and also how many sick or absent there were and the prioress would say I thank you, sister, my service to God and His people, we are faithful unto death. May the Lord have mercy on us all. Come my children to the house of the good Lord. With which she would turn on her heel and march into the chapel, with the sisters following and after them us lays. They say that in the old days in Europe they used to have drums and bugles at rappel, but they don't here. What they still do is the youngest member of the company stands at the church door facing out and ready to give the alarm in case any dangers appear, which happened in Algeria a long time ago, some bad guys snuck up on a bunch of Bloods and patients and killed them all. I didn't understand this because what were they going to do except get killed whether there was warning or not, and I asked one of the professed about it and she looked at me funny and said, they could have escaped.

She said, the point isn't to die, the point is never to abandon. Oh my, she said, we run like rabbits all the time carrying our patients on our backs, and laughed.

Actually it wasn't just one of the professed it was Nora, and I see I am anxious to get to her part of the story so I will move on.

Well, the thing was I refused to go to church and after a while the prioress sent for me. She didn't beat around the bush any either. As soon as I walked into her office she said, Emily, listen to me. This is a religious community you are in. We all work together, we all eat together, and we all attend church together on Sunday. This is the rule and if you wish to remain here you must follow it. I don't demand that you acknowledge the creed or participate in worship, but your presence in church is required. Perhaps you will tell me why you object so strongly to this. And I said in the nastiest way I could that I despised her religion I thought it was disgusting to worship death, a dead man, that you had to be crazy to think that the world was run by a God who was good, that Christianity stifled life and health it was fit only for terrified slaves, and that the idea that it was okay to be miserable now in hope of some fantasy of reward after death was the worst idea that anyone had ever come up with. I went on for some time.

She said I see you've studied Nietzsche, and I agreed that I had and she smiled and said, I too, he is lovely in the German, a great artist. Unfortunately he is what happens when a spirited little genius is raised by a bunch of pious church ladies. Nietzsche probably never met a real Christian in his whole life. They are extremely thin on the ground at the best of times. So forgive me if I say you don't know what you are talking about. I said that I still thought it was stupid and that she was stupid to insist that I park my body in a certain place at a certain time even though nothing would be going on, and that I would hate and resent every second of it and she said, it's important where the body is, and you can never tell what will happen in a church. Besides, she said, it is the rule and you should *try to follow a rule for once, as breaking them all has not appeared to have done you much good in life. Then I got really angry, like I hadn't since that time with Ray Bob when he was going to arrest Hunter and I called her a lot of foul names at the top of my voice and went into a kind of state and before I knew it the whole story of the very Christian deacon baby-fucker Ray Bob leaped from my mouth in tongues of flame plus some extra stuff about pervert priests and nuns that I had gathered from the recent press and also from some pamphlets that Ray Bob had around the house about the Scarlet Woman of Rome.*

*She took it all in as if I was telling her about my summer vacation, nodding, and then she said, yes, this is what I imagined. Let me say two things. First, you have observed that the church is corrupt, and I don't mean just the Catholic Church I mean the church entire, for it is all the same in every splinter, and I agree, because you know it's partly a human institution and as such subject to the ruin of this world, and the more so as it has from time to time exercised power and power tends always to corrupt. So for nearly all its history the church has been run by gangsters, sometimes by literal gangsters, but almost always by egotistical power-hungry men without the slightest interest in following Christ. They may admire Christ and think he is very great, but that was not what Christ was after, you know, not at all. One of my countrymen once wrote that the church is the cross on which Christ is crucified every day, but then he said also that Christ cannot be separated from His cross, which means that in addition to being a seedy club of somewhat dull men wearing funny clothing the church is also the eternal, perfect, and mystical Body of Christ, which is why we women bother with it at all, and why we give our lives to it and count ourselves fortunate. You don't understand this now, but perhaps later you will.*

*I said something or started to and she said be quiet for a moment please. And I did, and she said, next, as to you and this story you have told me: you have been cruelly treated and betrayed, your childhood has been stolen. The world is oftentimes une pâtisse' émerdée, a shit pie, but this is known, this is boring. The only interesting thing is how we use the suffering that is inevitable in life. Believe me, I understand what you have been through.*

*I said you have no fucking idea.*

*Do I not? she said. Then listen. In the winter of 1945 I was fifteen. My father had been arrested and executed in the July plot against Hitler, as perhaps you know, since you seem to be familiar with history. My two brothers had by this time been killed on the eastern front, and we were in a farm cart trying to get out of East Prussia before the Russians got us, my mother, my sister Liesel who was three years younger than I, and me. We failed in this and ended up among hundreds of refugees trapped in a ruined factory and when the Russians found us they raped every woman. Us three they tied to pipes naked and we were raped an uncountable number of times for two days and two nights. My sister was raped to death. I saw a couple of drunken Russians throw her out the window like a sack of garbage. In her whole life no one had ever said a harsh word to her, and so she died. My mother hanged herself the next day. I wandered for some weeks trading my body for food and cigarettes to whomever would buy. Then the Bloods found me, a group of German sisters, and naturally they had all been raped too. The interesting thing was that we never complained about what had happened to us because by then we knew very well that our people had done far far worse in Poland and Russia. So we suffered silently like dogs.*

*I remember that line very well although I'm not as sure of the rest. I am making it up the way we do in our minds, when we play back our memories. We've been taught by the voice-overs in movies. But I recall that about suffering silently like a dog, I recall it in my heart.*

*She went on and told me how she had walked with these sisters to the west, then they were joined by others who had been released from concentration camps where* the Nazis had put them. After the war was over a small group of them from all over Europe gathered in what had been a Blood priory in Rottweil in Germany. She said I saw all these women who in many cases had suffered worse than I had, lost everything, been tortured, ruined in their health, and all they could think of to do was to help others, and I was insane with rage I wanted to scream at them why why how can you believe in a God who allows such things, death, torture, rape, the slaughter of little children? And this woman, Sr. Magdalena, one day came up to me. She had been in the retreat too, they had nailed her naked to a farm cart so that any soldier who came by on the road could have her, like a public latrine. And one day she said to me you have to forgive them, they didn't know what they were doing. And I lost my mind when I heard these words, I attacked her right there, I spat on her and scratched her face. But she threw her arms around me and soon we were wrestling on the floor, and she pinned me down and put her crucifix in front of my face, this crucifix in fact—and here the prioress held up the one she wore, held it in front of my own face—this very one. Then, she said, Sister Magdalena showed me the scars on her hands left by the Russian nails. Look look you stupid child she shouted at me what do you think this is, a joke, a fairy tale? I was crucified and I died and now I live in Christ, blessed be His name. And you! Don't you see you are a corpse too after what was done to you and the true life is waiting for you to pick it up. But you will not, no you clutch the death to you like a child with her rag doll. Only forgive them now and you will be able to forgive yourself for not having died with your family and live again in God.

So that was the prioress's tale, or the important part of it anyway. Eventually God touched her heart and she stayed with the Bloods as they pulled themselves together after the war, and later she became a sister herself. She explained that the women who were there then, the survivors of the catastrophe in Europe, were called Rottweilers and

I said I thought it was because you were mean as a bad dog and she laughed and said there is yet another thing on which you were misinformed. When I left I heard the shiny man say well you really told her off. I am still using my childish name for him. I should say Lucifer now, but that sounds like something in a movie, with the special effects and the funny eyes.

You know that despite my tough front I really have a very weak mind, my brain is a vessel in which anything can be poured and I will tend to buy it. My poor parents left me so hollow. Unfortunately, there is no drain valve. So the prioress's words stayed with me against my will and I pondered them in my heart, like Mary in the Gospel.

I agreed to go to church and I did. I stood I sat I knelt I crossed myself with the others I made the responses and I sang. They wanted an outward show, I said to myself, I would give them the outward show, but inside there would be no change. The priest was Father Munch, a small elderly man with shiny fake teeth. He arrived in procession, he proclaimed the Gospel, produced an anodyne homily, said his magic words over the bread and wine, and drifted away. I sensed he wasn't all that comfortable at St. C.'s. I've heard that at regular convents priests are petted and doted over, but the Bloods I knew always treated them like union plumbers—they had the package and the ticket so they got to do the job, but that didn't mean you had to like it. Poor man, and I can't help believing he felt unappreciated, getting up before dawn and driving over slick winter roads up the mountain from Bradleyville to say mass for a bunch of hard-faced women who'd spent their lives dodging bombs and death squads and had no doubt they could carry off the whole thing a lot better themselves. And probably had too, as I found out later.

After some weeks I found it was hard to keep my mind off of God during mass. I had heard the Bible words before and they fell like they say on deaf ears but my body was moving in the ritual ways and even though I mocked I was doing it and slowly it got to touch my pondering heart. Now in this ecumenical age we're not supposed to speak against the charisms of all the different shards into which the church has shattered yet I can't help feeling that no other church would have seized me as this one did. I am a fleshly creature and the Catholics work through the body in all things more than the others I think. The Bloods spend much of their lives amid really horrible ugliness and so when they have a chance as at St. C.'s they pour it on—processions, incense, banners, choirs, organ. I had never heard music like that, being a cracker barbarian, only the clunky hymns they sang in Wayland, so Palestrina and Mozart and Schubert hit me like a brick on the head, the opposite really, it knocked me _awake_ in a way I hadn't imagined before. Several times I cried despite myself.

As I say, I started to pay attention, and when poor Fr. Munch held up the bread in his shaky hand and said this is the Lamb of God who takes away the sins of the world the thought started in tickling my mind what if it's _true_. And then the denial. Once I found myself shaking my head from side to side and people looked. Otherwise everyone left me alone, another Catholic habit. I'm sure if they came over to me with urgings and tracts like in Ray Bob's church I would have bolted like a hornet-stung horse, but that was also God's work I believe. It might not work for you, you might go for fire-breathing Baptists, or cool Congregational light, what do I know except what grabbed me?

I did a lot of reading that winter, in the bad weather, no longer the novels but works I could barely understand, the Gospels, Augustine, Origen, Aquinas, St. Teresa, Chesterton, Rahner, Küng. The Catholic Encyclopedia devoured in a week, what was I looking for, permission or ammunition I don't know, but it helped in the pondering. I call myself a rebel, but really I can't bear to be a dummy about anything, and so I am easily bidden to the lamp. The sense then of roads being closed off, a feeling of exhaustion. The "Hound of Heaven" is not much of a poem but it was one of the 500 and lodged there in my brain and dripped down into my heart, I heard the steps beating behind me now, all things betray thee, who betrayest Me, but I was too cowardly I needed a friend of the heart like the prioress had Sister Magdalena to pull me the last gap over the titanic gloom of chasmed fears.

It was a Monday, I recall, March the seventh, when I first met her. On Mondays we all gathered at the toolshed, really a big garage where they kept the tractors and pickups and mowers and all the tools. It was a clear morning, not too cold, and I was carrying a large thermos and a box lunch from the kitchen because I figured I was going to be out in the woods. As I approached the doorway I heard laughter, the modest tittering of the Filipinas mixed with the American yawps of the other women and also one laugh I hadn't heard before, loud free and rich. I walked in and there she was sitting on an oil drum, a woman maybe ten years older than I was, her legs crossed and only the left boot hanging down beneath her apron. She was telling a funny story in Tagalog and then translating it into English for the others, something about a man in a Mindanao village who fell in love with his buffalo and wanted to marry her and what the priest had done or not done. She had an Irish accent. Tagalog in an Irish accent is apparently extremely funny, the Filipinas were bent double.

I couldn't follow the story because I was staring at her face. It wasn't that she was beautiful in the usual supermodel way, I'm no oil painting was one of her sayings, but she <u>was</u> like an oil painting, a painting of a queen from olden times, except that her face was covered with freckles, which I think those old masters usually left off. She had red hair, the true metallic copper kind which grew in tight corkscrews on her scalp and heavy red gold eyebrows and deep-set green-hazel eyes. I guess I took in all this when I first saw her in the toolshed, but it wasn't the physical that blew me over. It was like the first time I saw Orne Foy, the sense that this was someone off the charts, the source of

*light in any room they might enter. I don't know what it is.
Total ease and confidence? The fancy word is charisma
but what is that except a label? She had it and he had it
and I don't, but I vibrate to it like a string to the right note,
and what I wanted more than anything since Orne died
was that she look at me and like me.*

*But not until later. My first feeling was resentment: who
does she think she is, casting all that light was my first
thought for in my wickedness I saw women as adversaries
and men as tools. I felt my jaw tighten as she looked at me
still laughing and beckoned me in and held out her big
freckled hand. It engulfed mine and she held it warm and
said Nora Mulvaney. You must be Emily.*

*What it was, Sr. Lorette had to go into the hospital and
Nora happened to be there to help plan some meeting of
Blood bigshots they were holding at the priory in the
spring and she agreed to run maintenance for a while, a
typical Blood solution, even though she was on the staff
of the Mother General she could still ply a rake so to
speak although she couldn't really with that leg gone. The
next day she was there at dawn when I came to get the
truck and said she wanted to ride over the land with me it
had been years since she'd been here. We drove up the
mountain she singing a song in Gaelic like we were going
to pick flowers tra la la, and it took all my grit to keep from
being charmed. She had a scent too, like fresh bread, it
filled the cab. Then she said, So you're the atheist dope
lord, or dope lady I suppose. What's that all about, mm? I
didn't answer. She said, Meself I haven't ever had the
pleasure of atheism, being a born Cat'lic and dope makes
me sick up, give me a pint anytime. Me father now, he was
the atheist, he thought the Church was the curse of Ireland, only exceeded in ignominy by the goddamned Brits.
I was seven before I figured out that you could refer to the
inhabitants of the UK without that particular prefixial
adjective. It was me mother was the religious one and I followed in her path. Maybe it was self-preservation, you
know, because he was a consuming man, me father, he ate*

*people up. Although a great man in his field, him being a consulting neurosurgeon in Dublin, don't y'know. He's married to a woman a year younger than me. Me mother died of acute pancreatitis brought on by drink and I suppose by the way he treated her, I would say like a dog, but we had a dog, Raffles, a big stupid setter, and I never heard him raise his voice to the creature. He waited a dacent six weeks before he married his girlfriend. In his worst nightmares he couldn't imagine a more terrible fate for his bright little girl than becoming both a sister and a nurse, the lowest of the low. We don't talk. I've got a brother too, Peter. You know what he does? I said a bishop and she let out that laugh. Almost as good, she said, he joined the British army and not even as an officer. Serving in the ranks, although he's now a sergeant-major. We do talk, Peter and me, and don't we work black conspiracies against Mister Himself?*

I was out of the truck by now and filling my chain saw with gas. She was leaning against the tailgate. She went on, about how she went for a nurse in Ireland, and then joined the SBC and was taught the special skills that the SBC teaches right here at dear old St. C. and then went out to the Philippines where there was a terror war going on in the southern islands, and then she was replaced by Filipinas and they sent her to south Sudan, where she would be still if not for her leg. *She said I trod on a wee land mine, chasing some little kid, and the funny thing was the kid ran through the mine field without a scratch and Nora that great clod of a woman gets herself blown up.*

That was the first time I ever heard the words wee and trod used in speech. It was like being in a book, with her, a delight, but I didn't let on.

*I see you're fascinated by me sad story,* she said, *but I just thought we'd start off a little more even, since I know all about you.* I said you don't know shit. And she said oh, dear, but I do, I do. I know some things you probably don't know yourself. For example, you're a cradle Cat'lic too. I said bullshit! I am not! Oh, yes you are, she said, *baptized*

*in Holy Family Church in Gainesville, Florida, U. S. of
A., age one month eight days, all done proper. Your father
brought you. I stared at her. She went on, see here darlin',
you may think we're a bunch of dotty women but the SBC
has one of the finest intelligence services in the world. The
Jesuits are older but we've got more money. Do you think
we'd let a person in here unless we knew absolutely everything there was to know about them? It's the money, you
see, the Trust. You know about the Trust do you? I said I
did but I thought it was all lost in the war. She laughed at
the thought. Oh bless you it'd take more than a world war
to break the Bloods there are deep deep vaults my darlin'.
No, we kept most of it and it's grown since, although we
did have to bail out the Holy Father when he got in a bit
of a jam over that Banco Ambrosiano thing back in the
1970s. The Holy See was bankrupt and we stepped in as
good daughters of the church, us and the Opus Dei. If
not, believe me, darlin', we'd all be making tea for bishops.
As it is, the money lets us do as we please, and we're the
pope's favorite little nursie girls, that and the fact that we
die so uncommon frequent. It makes it hard for them to
crack down, d'you see, the church still having a soft spot
for holy martyrs. Jim De Bree is sort of our unofficial
motto. I said I didn't understand and she said it was
French je me débrouille, it means something like making
things happen in ways that don't bear strict scrutiny. Then
she said, So when a little wench shows up on the run from
the law and half-dead at our biggest priory spouting atheism and declaring visitations from St. Catherine of Siena,
eyebrows go up, chins are stroked in Rome. Jette is no fool
as you'll have learned, and she thinks you're something
rare. Not a spy, nor a fraud at any rate. What do* <u>*you*</u> *say
you are?*

*I said I didn't know. I was confused and scared and
starting to get weepy which I definitely did not want to do
then, and she took a step and put an arm around me and
said then we'll have to help you find out, mm?*

*The touch was what did it electricity of goodness or*

something stranger because without any warning I was hysterical. I literally collapsed in her arms, soaking her crisp white apron with snot and tears. I had no idea really what I was crying about maybe it was the nature of the touch, communicated on some level way down below. I never got touched like that, even when I was a little kid, my mother never did and neither did the men, and I never had a real friend, it was a touch erotic but not sexual a rare thing in this world saying we are all miserable wretches together here is some comfort. Darlin' she said there there over and over, Daalin' in her accent. She said, let's go on back but you'll have to drive on account of I'm a foot short. That got me turned from crying hysterically to laughing hysterically until my belly was tight as a washboard.

That was my conversion as it turned out. C. S. Lewis said he was converted on a motorcycle ride to Whipsnade, and St. Paul was knocked off his horse on the way to Damascus and as for me I rode down the mountain in a pickup truck, with Nora Mulvaney at my side she was humming "Stór Mo Chroí." Simple as that, I got in the truck an unbeliever full of theology and when I got out in the garage I was Catholic.

I was at St. Catherine's for seven months and three days after that. Joy is very simple and does not require much art in the telling I think pain and struggle are more literary. I became more or less her driver and confidante. Neither Lucifer nor any saints or angels made a further appearance in that time, having accomplished their mission or so Nora said and also she said the devil's a good Cat'lic too when all's said and done, he does the job required and he loves the church, by God, _you can't get him out of it!_ Oh, Christ, I loved her, and I had a time distinguishing between that and the love I owed to God, although maybe it comes to the same in the end.

That Easter we drove into Roanoke and a moon-faced eunuch for the kingdom of heaven oiled a cross on my brow and I was confirmed and took communion for the first time. I wish I could say that it was transcendent, but it was not. Nora was my sponsor of course, and she gave me a rosary, which I still have but have rarely used. I am not the devotional sort—I think you have to be born into all that, or at least I would have had to be. But it made her happy. While we were in Roanoke I saw Skeeter Sonnenborg on his Harley, like a noisy ghost from my past life. He drove by us with his straight pipes ripping the air apart. It gave me a start because I thought he was dead with most of the others. I didn't say anything to Nora about it or to anyone else, but then I got real paranoid and bugged her to hurry back to St. C., but we had to drop some packages off at the post office, and there was my face on the wall with the other wanted criminals. Like an idiot I stood staring at it with my mouth open and when I turned away there was a middle-aged woman looking at me and I saw her gaze flick back at the picture on the wall of the notorious cop-killer and drug kingpin Emily Garigeau. I got out of there fast and back to Nora, who said not to worry darlin', we'll arrange something, je me débrouillerai, and with that she found a phone and made half a dozen calls and we drove not back to the priory but to eastern Virginia near Arlington and put up in a house there with some other sisters. That night Nora helped me dress in the full habit of the Bloods, which I wasn't even entitled to wear, and someone delivered a passport with my picture in it, but in the name of a sister killed in Colombia. Nora said, we keep the passports of our dead and keep their deaths quiet for just this purpose. We often have to get people across borders and we débrouillons when necessary, you understand? Yes, I did indeed.

The airport was no trouble on either end. This was before our current terror times, and in any case no one ever looks at a nun. Two days later we were in Rome.

By early 1914 the Sisters had established priories and other facilities in nearly every western European country and had also established themselves in the United States (Baltimore, 1908) as well as in the Philippines, Brazil, Mexico, and Chile. The training facility in Nemours was flourishing, as was the language institute directed by Claire de Roighy-Brassat in Rome. These were expensive undertakings, but the flow of money into the Trust was unceasing, tied as it was to the burgeoning value of petroleum in the new century. The general war everyone had dreaded began in August of that year. Marie-Ange startled her companions by declaring that "now it is my turn," and resigned her post as Mother General, in favor of Otilie Roland.

She appointed herself in charge of operations in western Europe. She chose Lille as her headquarters, a city she knew well, and by late August refugees were already streaming in from the border areas affected by the German invasion and from as far away as the Belgian front. She established her chief hospital in a school near the cathedral, and went about organizing medical relief for the refugees. Those who observed her in these days said that she seemed to have recaptured her youth, exhibiting an energy that belied her fifty-eight years.

By the first week in October, they could hear the guns of the approaching Germans. Marie-Ange seemed to be everywhere at once, offering encouragement, even lending a hand with the terrified patients. Among them was Msgr. Matteo Ratti, an Italian scholar who had been wounded in Louvain on August 26, when the Germans destroyed the university and the lovely old city. Now they seemed to be doing the same to Lille. From October 11, the artillery fire was almost continuous. When shells began crashing into the cathedral itself, Marie-Ange ordered the patients moved to the school basement. According to Msgr. Ratti, the Foundress was helping a novice transfer him to a stretcher. He recalled saying to the terrified girl, "Don't worry, God will protect you," and her superior saying, "Whether God protects her or not, she must do her duty. Kindly lift his feet."

Those were her last recorded words. At that moment a large shell exploded in the room, and the ceiling came down. Hours later, Ratti was rescued from the rubble, unhurt. As her final conscious act, Marie-Ange had thrown her body protectively over her patient. Lying thus she had received a splinter of steel through her valiant heart.

—FROM *FAITHFUL UNTO DEATH:*
*THE STORY OF THE NURSING SISTERS*
*OF THE BLOOD OF CHRIST,*
BY SR. BENEDICTA COOLEY, SBC,
ROSARIAN PRESS, BOSTON, 1947.

# Eighteen

**P**az hardly ever brought his male Cuban friends to the restaurant, and his mother (whom nothing escaped) had often remarked on this: What, you're ashamed of me? But it wasn't that at all; it was because of what was going on now with Morales. The young detective was eating *zarzuela,* what the Cubans have instead of bouillabaisse, served out to him from a pan the size of a bus tire by the proprietress herself. An observer would have been hard-pressed to derive from the scene which of the two men was the beloved son and which the stranger, or rather the observer would certainly err, for Morales was getting the royal treatment, with Mrs. Paz dropping the most succulent marine tidbits on his plate, while leaving Paz to scoop for himself from what was left. Within twenty minutes of sitting down at the special banquette reserved for her most favored patrons, Mrs. Paz had sucked from Morales his entire life history and that of his immediate ancestors. It turned out that Morales lived with his mother, that his two older sisters were both married with children, that he himself was engaged to be married (picture exhibited, to sighs of admiration from Mrs. P.), that he was taking courses at Miami-Dade University on the road to a bachelor's degree. Paz had not known much of this, and he found himself wishing that Morales had a secret life as a violent pedophile. As this love fest progressed, the mother shot him numerous little looks: See, this is what a good Cuban son is like!

Paz only picked at the marvelous food, as a way of getting back at her, but of course this was just another indication of his inadequacy, for Morales was putting it away with both hands. Eventually the young man had to stop, when the constraints of physiology trumped even the will of Margarita Paz. Having consumed a mass of prime seafood about the size of his own head, and at the point of tears, Morales rose from the table and repaired to the men's.

"You know, Mami," said Paz, "I think it's a felony to make a police officer explode in public."

"That's a nice boy," said the mother, ignoring this. She gestured and a waiter made the debris vanish. "It's a shame his sisters are married already." A deep disappointed sigh. Then to the attack: "You ate like a bird. Something's wrong with you."

"Nothing's wrong, Mami. It's the middle of the day. If I ate like he did, my brain would shut down."

"What, he hasn't got a brain?"

"He doesn't need one as long as he's partnering with me. Look, Mami, I need to ask you a favor. . . ."

"No, you look bad, son of mine. First you kill that *brujo,* and just the other week you shoot someone else. Don't you know you have to be washed after something like that?"

"I'm not going to your *ilé,* Mami."

"Of course not, you know everything, why am I even wasting my breath?" A red-nailed finger pointed at his eye. "Also you have a new woman," said Mrs. Paz. Sweat popped out on his forehead and the *zarzuela* did the fandango in his belly. "And of course you're ashamed of your old mother, you don't bring her to meet me. I know the spirits are angry with me, what other *reason* could there be to be treated like this—"

"Mami, on Sunday. I've invited her to dinner on Sunday."

"Mm. I'll make *langosta a la crema.* And what is this favor you want from me?"

"I need to talk to Ignacio Hoffmann."

She looked away. *That* was unusual. "He doesn't come in here anymore."

"Mami, I know he doesn't come in here anymore. He's a fugitive. Look, I got no interest in the man or in causing him any grief. I just need to talk to him."

"What makes you think I can find him?"

"Come on, Mami. Ignacio practically lived in this banquette for years. The seat is still warm from his ass."

"Watch your mouth!"

"And besides, you *have* to know him. He's *omo-orisha*." This was a guess. Paz didn't know whether Hoffmann was a devotee of Santería, but the altar at Jack Wilson's house had suggested the connection. Where would an Anglo like Wilson have picked it up if not from his former boss? And he knew his mother knew anyone who was at all prominent in the cult.

Now the eyes came back at him, full force. He made himself meet their mighty rays. "I'll think about it," she said.

"Mami, it's part of a homicide investigation. I'm asking you nice, but the fact is every citizen has to help the cops when they ask them to."

She held out her hands, wrists together, golden bracelets dinging softly. "So arrest me."

"Mami, come on . . ."

"I *said* I'll think about it."

Paz was about to say something about time being critical, but at that moment his cell phone rang. He glanced at the screen. "This is the girlfriend. I'm going to ask her to marry me and have four grandchildren for you right now."

"Oh, you're so smart!"

"Hello, Lorna. *What!* When? Calm down, Lorna. Porky Pig? Are the cops there yet? Uh-huh. Okay. Okay, let me talk to him. Yo, Jerry . . . yeah, I do. No, this is part of a homicide investigation. Right. You got anything on the guy? Yeah, Porky Pig, I heard. No vehicle ID? Uh-huh. Look, can you do me a solid? Have someone drive the vic over to me. I'm at Nineteenth and the Trail . . . yeah the restaurant. Okay, great, I owe you a meal. No, I'll take the statement and we'll handle the complaint. Yeah all the paper too. Thanks, Jerry. Put the vic on again."

After some soothing words, Paz clicked off the phone and explained to his mother what had happened. "See, you don't even have to wait until Sunday," he said.

"Not hurt?"

"No. But it's no fun getting mugged."

Mrs. Paz examined her son closely and waved a hand, as if to indicate something floating around his head. "You're worried now. I think you like this one."

"Yeah, it's true, I like this one, and I think I got her into a world of trouble."

"If you were in the restaurant business or you had a nice profession you wouldn't be getting women into trouble."

"Thank you, Mami, that's helpful."

"Don't be sarcastic with me, Iago."

Morales came back to the table at that point, picked up the new vibe, and looked searchingly at Paz, who directed his own gaze at the big fish tank. Mrs. Paz, however, gave the young detective a radiant smile and said, "You have room for some flan, yes?"

"No way, thanks, Mrs. Paz, really. . . ."

She gestured to the hovering waiter. "Two flan," she commanded.

This was delivered, and Morales was induced to consume some, after which Mrs. Paz left to attend to other customers.

"I can't finish this," said Morales as his stared at his flan. "I'll die."

"Okay, but if you don't you're not the perfect Cuban son. My mom's got a lot invested in you now, and she's going to be pissed if you don't finish every rich spoonful. Alternatively, there's a pain-in-the-ass job you can cover for me."

"Anything," said Morales.

Paz explained what had happened to Lorna Wise. "Jerry McLean caught it, but he's not going to break his balls on a mugging with nothing much taken and no one hurt. Grab the case from him personally, do a thorough canvass of the area, try to find anyone who saw the guy getting away, his vehicle, whatever."

"I'm on it," said Morales, and slid from his seat. "Porky Pig, huh? You think that's significant?"

"It could be, Tito. It could be Elmer Fudd trying to send us a message. Or Bugs himself. You'll find out. Go!"

Ten minutes later, Lorna Wise was deposited in front of the restaurant Guantanamera by a police car, where Paz, who had been waiting for her under the awning, snatched her up and embraced her. She looked terrible, he thought, pale, splotchy, her makeup tear-ruined, and she trembled. He wanted to shoot someone.

Inside, she went straight to the bathroom and was in there for so long that he almost called one of the waitresses to go in and check on her, but eventually she emerged, looking somewhat more put together. He ordered coffee for her and a plate of *torticas de Morón*, but she touched neither.

"Look," he said, "I know you're shaky and I'm sorry as hell that this happened, but I have to ask. Did you get a chance to read the notebook before it got taken?"

She nodded.

"Okay, then you need to tell me what, if anything, in it was relevant to the case. Your memory is fresh now. . . ."

"Yes, I understand. But I don't know what's relevant and what isn't, it's just more amazing adventures of Emmylou." She gave him a summary of the third notebook and added, "It's a continuation of her sad story. She seems to have caused another killing, run off with a survivalist dope lord, and got herself shot. No secrets that anyone would want to know about, that they would shove a knife in someone's face, unless it's the gold. . . ."

"What gold?"

"This dope lord she lived with buried pots of gold all around his mountain. She knows where they're hidden."

"And some guy in Sudan came looking for it? That doesn't make any sense."

"Although everything else make *perfect* sense," she cried, her voice breaking at the end.

He made soothing sounds and patted her hand, but she pulled it away and dashed off again to where the restrooms were.

Lorna retches, bringing up little. This is the second or third time today. It may be, she thinks, a nervous reaction to what happened, or something to do with being truly ill. She washes her face, stares at herself in the mirror. She thinks of extinction, that this very face will grow thin and hollow-eyed and yellow as the cancer takes over its body and then waxy on an undertaker's slab being made up to look natural, and then be reduced by flames to nothing at all, a few grains of dust. She feels her neck and armpits again, as she does every hour or so now, and finds the same rubbery bulges. Diagnostic for lymphatic cancer, as are the sweats and the weakness, the itching and the weight loss. She has not heard of nausea being a symptom, but it is entirely possible that her gut is involved too, that the thing sneaked up on her, despite her precautions, and all the watchful diets and exercises, the too-frequent doctor's visits. Strange how she knew from an early age that she was doomed in this way, perhaps even before her mother succumbed, maybe the cells tell us, Don't count on long life, sweetie, the genome's deeply fucked. What does she feel now? She consults her heart, finds an odd relief, not to have to worry anymore, death the end of neurosis at least, she is one with the kamikazes, the suicide bombers, an unearthly calm. A certain interest in religion, although that could be due to her current immersion among the snake handlers and speakers in tongues, still perhaps it would be even nicer to die thinking that a loving Jesus was set to carry you off. To where? She has never thought about eternity before, discovers she has no idea what it means. Also an urge to cry, to cry and never stop. Also an urge to find a drug, to turn off the mind entirely until the end. And other urges, surprising ones.

She puts her face together and goes back to the restaurant again, suppresses the nausea occasioned by the food smells. A large woman in a flowered yellow pantsuit and a lot of jangling gold jewelry is standing talking to Jimmy Paz, who politely rises as Lorna approaches and introduces her to his mother. She receives a long look and returns one. It strikes her as amusing that she and Mrs. Paz are almost exactly of a height and, allowing for the twenty-year age difference, have virtually the same figure. This makes her smile and feel crazy, and amazed that she can still find humor in things. Mrs. P. smiles too, slides into the banquette and pulls Lorna down next to her. After the obligatory commiseration about the mugging, and a capsule biography from Lorna, Mrs. Paz compliments Lorna on her hair and other features, then adds, "You know, you look like a serious woman. I admit I'm surprised, this son of mine, he's always bringing around these, what you call them, *esqueletas* . . ."

"Skeletons," says Paz.

Lorna finds herself laughing. "Not guilty," she crows.

"*Sí, sí,* I can tell you are a serious person," Mrs. Paz continues. "You have a head on your shoulders, a profession, and I have to say, although it sticks me in the heart, my son is not a serious person."

"Gee, thanks, Mami."

"See, like that, always with the sarcastic remark. You want to know the truth? I think you could do a lot better."

"I do too," says Lorna, deadpan. "But you know, I can't help myself, he's so pretty."

Mrs. Paz looks at her son. "He's not bad," she admits grudgingly. "Not what you would call ugly."

Paz looks ostentatiously at his wristwatch and stands. "Well, this is so pleasant, but I got to go to work. Lorna, I'll take you home unless you think you can do better thumbing on Calle Ocho." He embraces his mother, kisses her cheek. "Mami, always a real treat . . ."

"I need you for lunch tomorrow."

"No can do, Mami, tomorrow I got my day job. Speaking of which, are you going to get me with Ignacio or not?"

"Come to the *bembé* tonight," says Mrs. Paz. "Then we'll see."

"Mami, please . . ."

"I mean it, Iago. I have to consult the *orishas* about this and you have to be there."

This is in Spanish, and in the dialect of Guantánamo, so Lorna cannot follow it. But now the mother turns her eye upon Lorna and says in English, "And bring her too."

She sails off to greet some favored patrons. Lorna says, "Bring me where?"

Paz explains about the Wilson connection to Santería, and who Ignacio Hoffmann is, and his connection to the case, and what a *bembé* is and how his mother has him over a barrel here, because all the leads have run out and Hoffmann, if he can get to him, is the last link, the last person who might know why someone like Jack Wilson would have been interested in killing a Sudanese in the oil business.

"And why does your mom want me to come?"

"Why does my mom want anything? I don't try to figure her out anymore. But it might be interesting, part of the tour de wacky superstition I seem to be taking you on."

"This is like voodoo, right?"

"Not exactly. My mother, you should know, is a big deal in Santería."

"What does she do?"

"She gets help from the spirits," says Paz, "and gets ridden by the *santos* when they come down to earth." There is an astonished pause.

"You believe this?"

Paz shrugs. "No, but I've seen weird stuff happen." Lorna senses his discomfort and declines to press him further.

They arrive in front of Lorna's house. Paz asks her if he should pick her up later.

"For the voodoo jamboree? I'm game. Why not? Will they foretell my future?"

"Maybe. I've never been to one of these either, so what do I know?"

"Really? So we'll lose our Santería cherries together."

"Yeah. Okay, I'll pick you up around eight. Will you be all right?"

"I'm fine, Jimmy," she says. "Can you come in?"

"No, I got to get back and follow up on some things."

"That's a shame," she says and leans over to kiss him.

Paz thinks it would be a simple good-bye deal, but it is not. She grabs his head and plants her open mouth on his. Steam is generated, his tongue receives a fine chewing, she hikes up her skirt and throws a thigh into his lap. He feels her smoking crotch grind against his leg.

After some time, he feels obliged to pull away and looks at her. Her pupils are unnaturally huge, nearly erasing their blue surround. "Jesus, Lorna," he says, croaking a little, "give me a break here. I'll have to change my shorts." Her mouth now attacks his neck with small bites.

"Stop, Lorna," he insists, feeling stupid, and moves her firmly away. He examines her face. If he didn't know she was sober he would have said she was drunk. She sags back in the passenger seat and lets out a long sigh. After that she opens the door and walks slowly down her walk, and he notices there is something off about her stride, it's too slow and uncertain. He feels crappy about leaving her, but he has to go back to police headquarters. "I'll call you," he cries out, but she doesn't respond.

Paz saw the envelope sitting on his desk as soon as he entered the squad bay, a plain eight-and-a-half-by-eleven manila with no markings on it. He opened it and slid the contents out onto his desk.

"Anybody see who left this here?" he called in a loud voice. The other four detectives looked up but none of them responded. "Nobody saw who left this here?" Apparently not. "Jesus Christ!" Paz exclaimed. "This is a restricted area. You only get in here with a fucking card. Somebody with access must have brought this in."

More blank looks. A detective named O'Connell said, "What is it, Jimmy? Kiddie porn?" Paz stared at his colleagues and got hostile stares back, or nasty smirks.

He grabbed the envelope and its contents and stalked out of the bay, heading for Major Oliphant's office. There he blew past a protesting secretary and entered the major's office without knocking, earning a glare from the man, who happened to be on the telephone. He said, "Thanks, Arturo, but I got something here—let me get right back to you." He hung up and continued glaring. Paz slapped the two eight-by-ten color glossies down on Oliphant's desk. The major examined them, instinctively handling them by their edges. "Who's the woman?" he asked.

"Lorna Wise, the psychologist working with Emmylou Dideroff. Someone came in here and dropped this on my desk, which means either someone has a pass card who shouldn't or one of our guys is bent. This isn't supposed to happen."

"No, it's not," said Oliphant dully. He studied the two photographs. One was a shot of Lorna Wise and the other was of Paz, lying on his back asleep. Someone had carefully drawn, with a fine marker, a crosshair sight centered on each head. "Telephoto lens," he said. "Probably from a boat, the angle here. You took her to the beach?"

"Yeah, I did. We have a relationship." Oliphant was silent, staring down at the photos. Paz said, "What are we going to do about this, sir?" No answer.

"Sir?"

"Well, Jimmy," said Oliphant in a tired voice, "I don't know. Whoever's behind all this is cranking up the volume. I've had a couple of calls in the last hour, from friends. It looks like I'm going to be indicted."

"Indicted! For what?"

"Malfeasance. Misappropriation of government funds. I ran a kiddie-porn sting operation at the Bureau about four years back—I think I may have mentioned it—and it involved major buys. We were posing as a big operation, trying to suck in producers all over the world, working with Interpol and foreign police . . . anyway there was a lot of money flowing through my office, all cash, of course. Well, you know, in an operation like that, if they want to get you, they can. The boys with the green eyeshades get busy and they find you're a thousand short here, a couple of thousand short there. They get some scumbag to say, hey, I only got five grand, and they say you vouchered for eight. Like that. Then this call I was on when you came in, an old pal informs me the word is around DOJ that this all might go away if this thing with Emmylou falls right, meaning we act like good little locals, consider the case closed like we were supposed to, and move on. Also, I hear they're moving to pick her up on an old warrant, something with a drug operation in Virginia, some officers got killed raiding it. You know anything about that?"

"Yeah, I do, but the only way anyone else would know that our Emmylou and that Emily Garigeau are the same person is if they read it in the notebook that an armed robber took off Dr. Wise this afternoon. I haven't read it yet, but Lorna did, and the connection is apparently there in detail."

"Mm, like I said, they're cranking up the volume. It also means that there's a direct link between the Bureau and Justice and whoever is doing all these crimes down here." Oliphant raised his big brown hands to shoulder level, palms up, and then lets them drop. "Ah fuck it all, Jimmy . . . I don't know what the hell to do now. I'm open to suggestions."

"Hey, we got beat, boss. We had the Red Sox and they brought in the Yankees. Let's head for the showers."

"You're serious?"

"Absolutely. You should immediately dictate a direct written order to me and Morales, telling us not to waste any more valuable department time on a closed case. You could send your pal in Washington a copy of it."

"That would get me off the hook," said Oliphant. "And what about you?"

"Oh, well you already noticed that I'm exhausted, you've actually mentioned it to me. That's probably why I wasted so much time on this case. Probably my judgment is so impaired that you might think about directing me to take annual leave, four weeks or so. Write a letter and put it in my file. I have the hours."

"I could do that. What would you do on your vacation?"

"Rest and relaxation, sir. I would take my girlfriend, Lorna, on a trip, maybe to the islands."

"Sounds great. But I hope you won't take advantage of the free time to sneak in some work on this case."

"No, sir, that would be wrong. And if you found out about it, you could write a severe reprimand. You could break me back to patrol if you wanted, or suspend me."

"Yes, I could." Oliphant was grinning now, but Paz kept his face quite straight. "Well, I think we're done here, Jimmy. I'll get those papers moving. Thank you for your input."

Paz hung around the homicide bay until Oliphant's secretary brought him the letters, after which he filled out a leave ticket for twenty-eight days and showed it to Lieutenant Posada, together with the letter from Oliphant directing him to take it. Posada seemed delighted to sign the ticket and get rid of Jimmy Paz for a month. As he was heading to his car, Morales rang him on the cell to say that the parking garage attendant at Jackson had seen a white Explorer SUV with tinted glass tearing out of the place at about the time Lorna had been mugged.

"Plates?" Paz asked.

"Not any numbers. He thought maybe they were out of state." A pause. "You saw a car like that when we were going to see that guy Zubrom."

"Yeah, and here it is again, and we'll probably never find out who was driving it," said Paz, and then told him about what he'd discussed with the major, that they had to lay off the case now, that he was being put on leave, that they would probably get back on the chart when he returned, and in the meantime, the unit would find Morales some detective work to do.

"That sucks," said Morales.

"Win some, lose some," said Paz lightly. Just then all he could feel was delight that the white Explorer actually existed outside his own mind.

Lorna is wondering what to wear to the voodoo and finds that she can still laugh at herself. She thinks this is a good sign. More than the dissolution of her flesh she dreads the breaking of her spirit, sinking into the universe of Sick. At some level, she knows she is being a little nuts, she should be planning her cure campaign in consultation with Dr. Greenspan and a squad of oncologists, she should be discussing treatment options, she should be telling her near and dear, so that they could start treating her in that smarmy half-horrified way that people treat the cancerous, she should be getting biopsied and staged and starting chemo. But she doesn't make the calls. Instead, she looks the monster in the eye; embracing it; she says, You can have me, but first I'm going to live without fear. Then she finds herself thinking about Emmylou, about miracles, about living without fear. She wonders whether this is one of the famous stages of death, denial or whatever, but she doesn't feel mortal just now as she goes through her closet. She feels like she has laid down a load.

Paz arrives. He seems tense to her and she offers him a drink. They sit on her patio and drink vodka and lime. She feels his eyes on her and says, "This outfit is all right, isn't it? I never dressed for a what d'you call it before."

"A *bembé*," he says. "It's a ceremony where they call the spirits down to ride people. You just picked that out?" She is wearing a white wraparound cotton skirt and over it a yellow boatneck short-sleeved jersey with fine pale green vertical stripes, and yellow sandals.

"Yes, too dressy? Not dressy enough?"

"No, they're not big on dress codes in Santería. But you picked Ifa's colors."

"Ifa being . . . ?"

"The *orisha* of prophecy. You'll get your fortune told for sure." He drained his drink. "Let's go."

It is just a regular house, on a classless street in what they called Souesera, which is a corruption of the English "South-west area," the name for a substantial region of modest residences stretching south and west of Little Havana. The former lawn is being used as a parking lot, and both sides of the street are solid with cars. Paz parks at a hydrant, with a police card stuck on the dash.

They hear drumming as they walk past the parked cars. Inside, the living room is crammed with people, mostly women, and lit by many, many candles. It smells of incense, and the sweet holy sprays they sell at *botanicás,* and the perfumes of the people, and something else, earthier, almost rank. The drumming comes from a trio of black men set up in a corner, drums of three different sizes. They tap quick riffs and turn the tuning pegs.

Mrs. Paz drifts toward them through the crowd. She is in a

white dress trimmed with blue at the hem and wears a blue turban, and around her neck a pendant fan shell. Somewhat to
Lorna's surprise (not to mention Paz's) she greets both of them
warmly, with embraces and kisses. Her eyes are huge and liquid
in the candlelight, and Lorna wonders if she has taken some
drug. She is starting to feel a little nauseated now, from the
smells and the heat and the closeness. Mrs. Paz holds her arm
and guides her around the room, greeting people, introducing
her son and his friend to others, and exchanging a few words in
a language Lorna doesn't know. Mrs. Paz explains that it is Lu-
cumi, the language of the religion, from Africa.

The other people have the worn faces of the hardworking
nonrich Cubans of Miami, the moppers of floors, the caretakers
of the old, the sandwich makers. Many of these people are
dressed in odd colors, and Mrs. Paz explains that these indicate
the particular *santos,* the *orishas,* to whom they are bound:
white for Obatala the Calmer; red and white for Shango, spirit
of force; yellow for Oshun, the Venus of Africa; green and
black for Ogun, the Warrior; blue and white for Yemaya, the
Mother, the Sea.

"That's you," says Lorna.

"Yes, I'm made to Yemaya for many years now. Now, look,
you see we have palm leaves all over the walls and the ceiling,
because in Africa we danced under the sky in groves of trees."

"What are all those yams?" Lorna has located the source of
the earthy odor. There are perhaps two hundred large yams
piled around a pedestal draped in elaborately beaded yellow
and green silk brocade. Similar brocade hangs as a canopy from
the ceiling. Dozens of candles flickered around it, interspersed
with cut coconuts and opened bottles of beer, soda, and rum.

"Gifts to Ifa," said Mrs. Paz, "this is his *sopera,* that pot, you
see, it contains his *fundamentos*, his sacred stones, and all of
these, these little statues and medals, these are gifts from those
he has helped."

Mrs. Paz falls into conversation with a small man dressed all
in white, the *santero*, Pedro Ortiz, and Paz whispers into
Lorna's ear, "Are you having fun yet?"

"It's . . . fascinating," she whispers back, but when she looks
at his face she is astounded to observe that he is frightened. His
mother appears at his side with two stern-looking women, and

after a short conversation in rapid Spanish, the three of them whisk Paz out of sight.

Then without any particular signal or announcement, the drums start to beat. The throng reassembles itself before the drums, leaving a small sickle-shaped area of floor vacant. Lorna has never heard drumming like this; it is entirely different from the drumming of popular music, even Cuban popular music, enormously complex, like a language, dense with data, insistent; she feels her body taken over by it in a disturbing way. The people are swaying now, and chanting: *ago ago ago*. She sways with them despite herself.

Now people are entering the dancing area, they are barefoot, and although they are middle-aged women and men they appear to move with the grace of professionals. Lorna looks past them to the people standing on the other side of the dance floor and sees Jimmy Paz. He is dressed in a white robe and has a white cloth wrapped around his head. His face is blank, no, not blank exactly but presenting an expression she has never seen on it before, not at all an American face anymore, more like a carving in some tawny wood. She feels like an alien here, and fear starts to tug. The embarrassment monster cranks up in her head, What are you doing here this is crazy what are you doing with this idiotic relationship what will your friends say . . . ? The chants grow louder and louder, drowning out the monster's voice. Then, suddenly, the drums fall silent.

Something has changed in the room. Lorna is aware of it without knowing just what it is. The air seems cooler and drier, but at the same time harder to see through. The faces of the people glow oddly, and seem mysteriously beautiful. When she was in college Lorna took LSD several times and she recognizes this state as similar: something has happened to her brain. She knows she should be concerned but is not. She turns to the woman next to her and whispers in her primitive Spanish, "Why did they stop? What's happening?"

The woman says, "Eshu has opened the way for the *orishas*."

The drums start up again, a quite different rhythm than before. Now there is another dancer on the floor, and Lorna sees that it is Mrs. Paz. Her dance is a swooping undulating thing, all waves and spray, with a balanced force underlying the moves. The image of the sea pops into Lorna's mind and she seems to scent salt air and coolness. The people are chanting *Oké oké Yemaya l'odo, l'ari oké*. The drumming reaches a crescendo, the higher pitched drum utters a set of sharp reports, and Mrs. Paz falls to the ground as if shot. Women surround her, help her to her feet, and take her away. The drums are silent, people are chattering now as if at an intermission. Lorna asks the same woman what has happened. The woman smiles and in English says, "The *orisha* has arrived. Yemaya is here."

Mrs. Paz comes back to the room, and now Lorna for the first time feels a thrill of real fear, because this can't be happening. They have decked her in a cloak of blue and white that has thousands of small seashells worked into its surface and must weigh twenty pounds, but Mrs. Paz carries it like chiffon. She is at least ten inches taller than she was an instant ago and sixty pounds heavier, her breasts are like cannonballs and her belly is a whale's back. Her face is stern but ineffably kind and not the face of a human being at all. Her hair has been untied and falls down her back in dense stiff coils, as if carved from ebony. The drums start up again, and the drummers sing a song in some African language. Mrs. Paz-Yemaya circulates around the dance floor, inviting people to dance and whispering things in their ears. She approaches Lorna, pulls her out onto the floor. They whirl and stamp together.

Lorna looks into the eyes of the *orisha* of maternity and of the sea. Now she is not at the *bembé* anymore. She is lying with her mother on the glider on the porch of their beach house on the Jersey shore. She is four. They are alone in the house, the father and brother are off somewhere, and she has her mother all to herself. They are examining Lorna's shell collection, talking quietly, her mother reads from *The Golden Book of Seashells*. Lorna can smell the iodine breath of the sea and her mother's scent, sweet sweat and suntan oil. She is perfectly secure in love.

This just for an instant but so real!

Now Yemaya is stroking Lorna's body, her hands strong and soft, it feels as if they are penetrating her flesh, stroking her insides. She is talking in a deep voice, not Mrs. Paz's voice at all, but Lorna cannot make out the African words. Lorna feels her knees give way, but the women standing on either side of her hold her up. She feels tears breaking through, the knife-at-the-back-of-the-throat feeling, and she now recalls that from the moment the drums started the heaviness of her impending death has been absent. But now it returns.

The drums change their song. Now they are wilder, nervose, irritating. She sees Paz has returned to the circle. He's looking right at her but makes no acknowledgment that he's seen her. Mrs. Paz embraces him, she seems to tower over him, she seems to pick him up as if he were a child, which Lorna knows is impossible, but she seems to observe it. People are in the way now, she can't see them, but in any case this has become a sideshow. All eyes are fixed on a woman of about thirty with a round face, she is whirling and dancing with abandon, thrusting her hips, flailing her arms. The congregation is chanting Oya Oya, and after an impossible leap, the woman faints away. The older women help her up, they drop a tunic of maroon silk over her head and a necklace of skulls. In her hands they place a long black wooden lance, carved with figures.

Lorna asks the woman next to her what's happening. "Oya," says the woman, with awe in her voice. "Ruler of the dead." Oya is a popular fellow at the *bembé,* it appears. People gather around him for news of the dead, and press offerings of currency to his sweat-slick skin. After a good deal of this, Oya dances with some people, a wild bacchanalian fling, and then, before she can think to resist, Lorna feels her arm grabbed with an irresistible force and she finds herself dancing with Death. Sweat is in her eyes, stinging, and that must be why she sees not a round-faced young woman but a gaunt man with eyes that seem to fill their whole sockets with black, glistening oil and she recalls with horror what she saw when Emmylou showed her the demon. The *orisha* says to her be prepared this life of yours is almost over, perhaps in words, perhaps in her head. She feels light-footed, graceful, terrified, full of sexual abandon. But with the terror she feels a sense of deep comfort, for just behind her left shoulder is the loom of her mother's being, her scent. She knows if she turns now the ghost will be there and she will lose her mind, go screaming off into the night.

Nausea rises in her throat. With a heave she breaks from her partner, pushes through the crowd, and out the front door. It is a cool night and the air outside feels like air-conditioning's chill against her dripping face. She staggers to the curb, kneels, and pukes.

Lorna walks unsteadily away from the *bembé*. She finds Paz's car, climbs in, and within minutes sinks into grateful, exhausted sleep.

When she awakens, Paz is beside her and the car is moving at speed, heading south on Ludlum.

"You all right?" he asks, when she stirs.

"I guess. Somewhat wiped out, really. What happened to you?"

"Oh, they . . . I participated in what they call a *limpieza*. I got washed and anointed in the bathroom. Now I'm pure."

"What did they do to you?"

"It's hard to describe," said Paz carefully.

"Try."

Paz ignored this. "I heard Oya took you for a whirl around the floor."

"Yes."

"Any comments?"

"No. Why won't you tell me?"

"You first. Oya doesn't appear very often, and when he does it's a big deal. Did he say anything to you?"

"I couldn't understand any of it." Despite herself a groan escapes her lips. She says, "But . . . but anyway, it was a *lovely* evening, Jimmy, and I want to do it again *real* soon."

Hysterical laughter that they find difficult to stop. In Lorna's house, they are still sputtering in bursts as they rip each other's clothes off and fall together on the floor of her hallway.

# Nineteen

## The
## CONFESSIONS
## of
## Emmylou Dideroff

### Book IV

*My religion, such as it is, was a pure gift, a complicated
densely layered device that I can barely understand. I have
had the glory, yes, treats for beginners as St. Teresa says,
the sweetness, as St. John calls it, of God's embrace, but
probably I would have walked away from even that God
forgive me had I not loved Nora Mulvaney, of which more
later, although it was not what you probably think.*

*The Rome headquarters of the SBC is a vast seventeenth-
C. pile called the Palazzo Treschi, on Via Giulia between
the Palazzo Ricci and the Criminological Museum. You go
through an iron gate in a wall made of those purply brown
stones they like for palaces in Rome and then you're in a
paved courtyard with a fountain and the original bronze
statue of Marie-Ange and the dying lad. On its marble
plinth are carved the names of the sisters who have died in
service, and although the names are quite small two sides of
the plinth are already full and a third has been started.*

*They have the language school and the residence and the administration there, one in each of the three wings. Nora took me there just after we got to Rome and I found we were both in a heap of trouble. We were called in to see Constance Mucha, the prioress general, the woman in charge of the daily operations of the Society, second in command to the Mother General herself. She was a sharp little woman with the face and small round glasses of a Gestapo inspector in a bad movie, who for twenty minutes reamed us both out about my escape. Then I was sent out while she and Nora argued about my fate. The memory business was the key. Nora convinced her that I could learn languages real fast, and that I'd be a boon to her work in Africa, and so all through that damp Roman winter and for a year afterward I worked on learning Arabic and Dinka. My Arabic teacher was Mr. Sulieman. He said I had a terrible accent, but he was amazed by my progress in reading. Before the year was out I had read and memorized swaths of the Quran and the Thousand Nights and a Night, not particularly useful, we thought, but it gave him delight to see me do it.*

*Nora and I lived in a little apartment in Monti near Trajan's Market. Not much time for sightseeing, not interested much, Rome a little overwhelming for a hick white girl from Caluga County, the most distinguished architecture I had ever been in were the Caluga County Courthouse (1911) and Miami hotels. Out for daily mass at Chiesa Nuova, a tradition. In the old days we used to march out two by two from our palazzo to the church, but now we just show up. I didn't mind this at all, the one part of going to church that always pierced me through and through, the Eucharist as poor Robert Lowell said, perfectly real like getting your hand wet, well he was crazy too. Once to St. Peter's, horrified, clearly the Hall of the Demon King, full of Japanese tourists viewing the ruins of my dying civilization.*

*(Do you need to know about this? I am determined to finish this miserable story in the present notebook, the four*

books according to Emmylou, do I dare take more than the Gospels, no, and besides I am aware that I am a danger to you and others. Being crazy officially has been a nice rest, but this must end soon.)

Evenings, we hung out in an Irish saloon on the Via Leonina, drinking Guinness while she laid out for me the complex politics of the Society of Nursing Sisters of the Blood of Christ. Power corrupts she said, as our good old Lord Acton used to say and you know he was talking about the church and the pope. And money is power and it's corrupted us, I mean the Society. You have no idea how much money we have darlin', we're living on the interest of the interest of it, and now we have some of us saying, well why are we always sending our poor girls out to foreign shores to be shot and raped by ignorant heathens, why not change things so that the ignorant heathens get some lumps too, a bribe here and there, a little private army, so that we can do God's work and help more people? And you know the prioress bloody general Mucha-do-about-nothing, that's her goal in this life. Why, she says, the Templars and the Hospitallers took up arms to save the sick and the poor pilgrims in the Holy Land, forgetting that they also helped destroy the Holy Land and made the name of Christ a stink in the nostrils of those people unto the present day, and the Templars all got burned at the stake for their greed. But a lot of the sisters don't see that, especially the ones from the third world, they've got a different attitude, and the kind of war they've seen is different from the kind the Society used to know. Now it's just gangs of thugs wandering around looting and killing, not proper armies with front lines and command structures, and they're thinking, oh, if we just had us a troop of boys with rifles, maybe poor sister Angela wouldn't have got the chop, what's wrong with that? Now, see, the mother general's got a head on her shoulders, but she doesn't want to split the Society, so she temporizes and she's got me to toss in Sr. Con Mucha's face, so as to stay above the fray in a manner of speaking, between them who want us to hire *private armies and me and me friends, who think it's a rotten idea. And the whole issue would've never come up if it weren't for the Trust, our golden calf, because even though the Trust keeps us independent, and allows the pope to wink at some of the stunts we pull from time to time, it also lets us contemplate hiring soldiers, so it's still a gilded cage, d'you see.*

*I did not. Oh, darlin', she said, didn't you read the little book? Where do you think the Trust gets its money, and of course I remembered and I said, oil, and she grinned and said right you are, and oil means politics, and it puts us in with some of the world's worst, because what did oil ever do except make despots rich and ruin the people so unfortunate as to have oil under their feet, and I don't even mention burning up the world. By God, if it was me in her chair I'd sell up and give the money to the poor and beg on the streets for the little we need. Dying for Christ is the cheapest game in the world, you know, it hardly costs a thing.*

We didn't have a sexual relationship I should say here. Nora was a strangely asexual sort of person, but with terrific erotic energy channeled into charismatic rather than genital lovemaking. There are people like that, although rare. Her brother was another. I came back from my Arabic lesson one evening and there he was in our kitchen, pouring drinks, Nora in drag, and twice her size. Peter was on leave from the army, thinking about getting out, and when I asked him what he did he said quartermaster, counting the sheets, and Nora laughed and said, he's coddin' ya, he's in the specials, killed hundreds with his bare mitts, and he actually blushed red. I'd never met a man so sexy and at the same time without a hint of lust. Married with three kiddies and devout as Nora, it turned out. We went out and got drunk and he had to carry the pair of us home.

The next week we went to Nettuno, south of Rome, to the parachute center there, and I learned to jump out of airplanes. It took two weeks, one of ground school and leaping off towers, and then three actual jumps from a *light plane, wheeling above the Tyrrhenian Sea, flying through pure blue and landing on a broad beach, and then once at night. The Society runs its own planes and pilots and has the largest air force of any religious order, the reason being ubi vademus ibi manemur, the Society is often unpopular among nations, but that makes no difference so we sometimes have to stay off the roads and away from borders and then we move people and goods by air drop. Also parachute training tends to strip out the easily frightened and those with an excessive fear of extinction. I found I didn't mind it at all, no, going out the door after Nora seemed the most natural thing in the world, flying nuns, although it was considered tacky to so express it.*

*Last night in Rome, the fourteenth of March, me having been nearly two years in the city, and being able to make myself understood in Italian, Arabic, and Dinka, we wandered through the old city, giving away all our lira to beggars, something she did all the time anyway even though it was clear to me that nearly all of them were scam artists. But she saw them as suffering people doing us a favor, allowing us the grace of charity.*

*And off we go to Africa, a couple of plane rides, Cairo, Nairobi, and now a Land Cruiser over red dirt roads, to the border between Kenya and Sudan. I found I was right at home, because Africa is like one huge bad trailer park in north Florida, very hot, bug ridden, rich in biting flies, sweaty, smelling of sewage and vegetable decay and cheap cooking, full of poor poor people wearing T-shirts with sports logos. There are fewer shoes and no wrecked cars in the front yards, however. We went to Lokichoko, in Kenya, which is the main base for the vast empire of Help. Nora despises Loki and all it stands for, the rich working out their guilt in relatively comfortable surroundings, eating three squares a day among the starved, trying out their improving schemes upon the wretched of the earth, oops that didn't work, let's try this!, and when the bullets fly, it's oh my, so long poor folks, we can't stay, because we're white and our bodies are simply worth more than yours are.*

The Society had its Sudan operation headquartered at Mokilo about ten kilometers closer to Sudan so as not to be contaminated by the Helpers. There was an airfield, tents to sleep in, an office tent, a field of storage containers surrounded by barbed wire, and a wooden control tower. On the field was an antique Convair 580 being worked on by a couple of greasy sisters in cut-down bleus, and a little bit after we got there a newer Fokker 27 landed in a cloud of red dust.

In the Society the head of a regional operation is called a prefect, and the prefect here was Sr. Isobel Alecran, a barrel-shaped Filipina with a hard flat face that converted itself into a broad gold-toothed grin when my Nora walked into the office tent. She greeted me more formally and announced that since they had no need for my language skills at Mokilo, she was going to put me in logistics. It turned out that logistics was yet another thing, like religion and languages, that I was not much interested in but I was a dab hand at, I am a walking demonstration of God's mysterious ways.

Medical logistics starts with the patient-day (and the treatment unit for outpatient work) and from each of these there flows a physical stream of necessities from drugs to rubber gloves to pillowcases. These are embodied in packagings of a zillion different weights and dimensions and these in turn must be entombed in standard airdroppable palletized crates of particular volumes and weights, so given that say a F-27 can haul 6.3 metric tonnes in a usable volume of 62 cubic meters, figure out how to get the maximum number of packages per flight while ensuring that there is no day when your recipient has all catheters and no morphine. Needless to say the Society has been doing this for a long time and they have it down, but still it is useful to have a person who has all the logistics charts in her head, especially when the computers crash, as they so often do in African conditions.

So I worked in the ops center writing out pack tables for the Sudan sites, Wau and Juba and Bor and the outlying places, Wibok and Pibor Post, where we were going. Our flights were made at night because they are all into the no-fly zone that the Government of Sudan has declared in the regions controlled by the Sudan People's Liberation Army, with whom it has been fighting a war since 1955 except for a short break in the 1970s. GOS and SPLA, as we call them, have between them caused the death of around two million people and made another five million into refugees. There have been many efforts to stop the war but all have failed because all the valuable resources are in the southern part of the country, especially the oil in the Bahr al-Ghazal basin, and the political control is in the northern part, and the northerners think they are Arabs and thus superior to the southern people, who are Nilotics, although I believe every single person in that country would be considered a nigger in Caluga County, Florida. The northerners are Muslims and would like the whole country to be ruled by Muslim shari'a law, but the southerners are mainly Christians or traditionalists, what we used to call pagans I suppose, and they don't want this at all.

The real reason is racial and cultural, according to Nora. The Islamized Sudanese used to raid slaves in the south, that was the only real business in the country before the Brits took it over, and they still call any southerner _abd_, which means slave, and they still have slavery, that's how they drive the southerners away from the oil regions, they give Islamized tribes weapons and set them loose to raid and rape. And all that about Islam is a crock anyway because they attack the Nuer, who _are_ Muslims, but that doesn't count because they are also _abd_. And so the SPLA are the good guys? Well, no, not really because they're always breaking off little tribal or clan or warlord groups, sometimes siding with the GOS or some local confederation of thugs. Honestly I never got the politics and now it's so boring that I can't talk about it anymore and it would be just crap except it killed all those people.

But Nora loved the Dinka. Not what they call themselves, the first literate person who met a Dinka asked him

what people he sprang from and the Dinka said we are of
Deng kak, giving the name of their clan ancestor, and so
Dinka they became, but they call themselves Monyjang,
which means the husbands of men, meaning they are so
manly that other men are women compared to them,
which gives you some idea of their haughty views. But
they also call themselves the slaves of cattle. They loved
their cows, and not in the 4-H way they did in Caluga
County, cattle are wealth, pride, honor. They write love
poetry to their cows, one of their major art forms. Every
boy has what they call a personality ox to which he devotes
the kind of attention Americans devote to their girlfriends
if the girls are lucky. Women are valued by how many
cows they bring as bride-wealth and if they produce sons.
So women get the shaft as usual I said, but Nora said, not
really, it's hard to explain, the women are as proud as the
men, they're all aristocrats, even if they have nothing they
own except spears, cows, pots, and poetry. There's also a
great tradition of women warriors among the Dinka, the
thing they respect more than anything is spiritual power.
The Dinka we were going to stay with—the Peng Dinka—
traced their origin to a woman named Atiam 150 years
ago, who led them across the Nile to a promised land, just
like Moses.

Nora was a tribal kind of person like all the Irish are, she
thought Africa was like Europe was in the Dark Ages, desperate, murderous, but laden with hope, she thought it
could be converted, not missionary-converted, but really, by
the Holy Spirit and saints, like the European barbarians
were. She thought the Dinka were just like the Irish before
St. Patrick—warriors, poets, kings of little plots of land,
lovers of cattle, she saw in their tall black forms Cuchulainn
and Finn, Queen Maeve and King Ailil and the Cattle
Raid of Cooley. I believed her because she had a degree in
history from University College Dublin and besides I would
have believed the Dinka were Choctaws or the Ten Lost
Tribes on her say-so, not only because I was entranced with
her but also because she could talk the hinges off a door.

*What we did at Mokilo after the long days, we would lie in the hot tent under our netting and she would talk and drink whiskey from a tin cup, a drop to carry her off as she said. We're of a dying race me girl she would say, alas Babylon, with all our gold and power we can't make our women bear children or keep our children from killing themselves or keep off the hatred of all the world and don't you think one day it'll all come crashing down? Oh not next year or in our lifetimes even, but the mark of death is on us sure, and the church is dying and so is the Society, oh I don't mean it'll vanish, but there'll be a change of form into something new with its own new glory, by God even Rome didn't vanish after the sack, and the church is not after all a mortal thing.*

*T'ing. A morrtal t'ing, I can still hear her voice, the accent got thicker with the drink. I guess she was a drunk when all's told, but I never saw her take a sip between sunrise and sunset there was that much iron in her, but she needed her drop when it got dark in Africa. As who the fuck doesn't?*

*We were waiting for a full moon and for our complement of people going to Pibor, a town more or less besieged by GOS forces where we had a refugee hospital. Then a final planeload came in and we were ready, a couple of sister-doctors, some nurses, a sanitarian, some technicians, and among them I found my original Blood sister, Trinidad Salcedo from Miami. She was not surprised to see me or what I'd become, but I was surprised to find her an ordinary person, pleasant, efficient, nothing special, not the strange mystic figure I had made her out to be in Miami, and when I said all this to Nora she said, it's you who've changed darlin', Trini didn't shrink down, you grew and of course it turned out that Trini was some kind of special disciple of Nora, and had lived with her once upon a time, which made me jealous, no it was just the ghost of jealousy and I told Nora about it and we had a laugh.*

*We went in at night on the first of April, many jokes*

about the date, eight of us in blue coveralls and hockey helmets in the Fokker, flown by a couple of sister-pilots and a sister-jumpmaster and four men, Africans, for cargo kickers. We took off at sundown, a tin tube full of nerves and noise. I looked over at Nora her face strange in the red glow and she smiled a rack of pink teeth at me. Then the plane veered and dropped to altitude and the cargo kickers got up and harnessed themselves and the clam shell yawned open aft and the gritty African wind poured in and the kickers ran the pallets out. We came around for another run, leveled, the red light turned ghastly green, sister-jumpmaster gave the commands, we hooked up our static lines, and then in just a little more time than it takes to tell it, we trotted down the aisle and into the moonlight.

It was a good drop. None of the containers burst, the trucks from Pibor were where they should be, no one got a pallet on the bean, no brokens among the sisters. We sang as we rode back, a Salve Regina from the eleventh century in four parts and then "Finnegan's Wake," Nora's addition, she knew all the verses and the rest joining in the chorus, lots of fun at Finnegan's wake. Nora broke out one of her precious bottles of Jameson and we all had a taste and then Nora hung around my neck a chain with a little brass angel on it and everyone clapped and kissed me. That's what they were for. And thinking of where I was and who I was when I first saw one of the things, I cried shamefully.

Life at Pibor. Pibor is in the gók, a Dinka landscape term meaning a woody area with sandy fertile soil above the flood zone. This particular gók was well outside the usual Dinka tribal regions, which lie to the north and east, and people had fled to the area to escape the GOS depredations. There were Dinka cattle camps all around, with huge round cone-roofed thatched cattle byres and smaller sleep huts of the same design. The zone was considered relatively quiet, and the SPLA sent their wounded there for treatment and recovery along with the larger number of civilians who'd been hurt by the GOS bombings of villages. Our operation was protected by a SPLA militia, a not very effective-looking bunch of teens with Kalashnikovs and grenade launchers and a fleet of battered pickup trucks. The Society bribed the local warlord to keep up the protection and also bribed the local GOS commander to lay off. Nora said much can be done with a little money in a place where everyone is dirt poor and loyalties are local. She didn't think much of the SPLAs either. If there is a real soldier in the whole of the Sudan, I'd like to see him, was her opinion, she said one disciplined brigade could go through the whole blessed country like a dose of salts. But there wasn't one on either side, and so the war continued without hope of an end.

But something was up and Nora was worried. There had been two bombings in the last month, which meant that the orders had come from higher up, maybe from Khartoum, maybe they thought we were getting too comfortable in our little corner. So there was a lot of digging now, and filling of sandbags. They had an air raid shelter built under one of the tents and another under construction for the post-op ward, the sound of scraping went on all day and night. Wheelbarrows and shovels had filled one of my crates.

We had air raid drills. You could hear the slow Antonov 32s that they used from a long way off, so there was plenty of time and besides they were just cargo planes not real bombers, they just rolled the bombs, welded oil drums packed with Semtex, out the rear cargo door, just barely accurate enough for terror.

I saw Nora working as a nurse for the first time, and also for the first time I saw the white aprons of the Society actually soaked in blood. There was always a slow trickle of casualties, occasionally a flood when a village or another hospital got bombed. Also diseases, malnutrition, although we had plenty of food, if you consider sorghum porridge a food, and dysentery. When necessary I cleaned up diarrhea, working alongside Nora and the others, her always cheerful, ah the romance of the Cat'lic religion! she would call out, wiping filth.

*I made myself useful, inoculating and distributing stuff, keeping inventory, and since I was Dinka-speaking, I also helped Father Manes, our priest, another American. Manes was a classic whiskey priest, a big shambling man with a mess of long gray curls, wore a dusty cassock and a straw fedora, God knows where he got the booze. He was always half in the bag, never more, never less. Rumors of a voluntary exile because of a taste for altar boys. The sisters treated him friendly enough, like a large dirty hound, and besides his religious duties he ran the school.*

*That's where I met Dol Biong, at the school. I was teaching a class of boys. They loved me, not because I was anything of a teacher but because I had given each of them a notebook and a pencil. Giving an African kid a pencil is like giving an American kid a sports car. I had to insist that they use the pencil to write with, they were so much more useful as cult and status objects. Also, none of them had ever been to school before, so I had to invent the concept for them, me the high school dropout, and I was just describing the wonders of the alphabet, when I saw him, standing one-legged in the Dinka way just outside the circle of the class. I called to him, but he didn't budge. One of the boys said oh Dol Biong will never come to class he is too <u>adheng</u> for us. He says he is a chief's son but we don't know of what tribe, and they all laughed. So I went on. He never joined the class, but never missed one either, standing there, his eyes burning with something, hate or desire, black as tar, skin and bones, naked except for a ragged T-shirt and shorts. I asked Father Manes about him and it turned out he was an escaped slave, Baggara tribesmen had raided his village and stolen his whole clan. He was from north of here around Wibok. Manes intended to take him back there the next time he could join a SPLA convoy.*

*He ate alone too. On the other hand I seemed to run into him more than simple chance required. Once or twice he helped me carry the heavy ice chests we used for vaccines, just appearing at my side. Never said a word except*

with those eyes. The last week in May, the SPLA sent half
a dozen trucks with soldiers and supplies and some of our
sisters up to Wibok. Wibok was full of orphaned kids who
had fled the slave raiding in the north, around Nasir.
Manes went with them in the hope that he could get the
SPLA commander up there to let him start a school instead of recruiting them all into the rebel army. Trini went
to take charge of the aid station there. I thought that Dol
Biong would have gone with them, but I spotted him later
that day, lurking. I asked him in my best Dinka why he
hadn't gone, and got no answer but that stare.

In all a happy time and the days flew. In the evenings,
Nora and I would sit in our tent, she on a cot sipping
whiskey and pontificating about the events of the day or
the fate of man, me crouched usually at her feet leaning
against her thigh like a dog while she idly stroked my hair.
I liked being her dog. There is a lot to be said for mindless
devotion after a life such as I had lived. Looking back I
suppose she had the same relationship with Christ, she
was His dog as I was hers, although at the time that was
quite beyond my imagination. I would from time to time
recite poems from the 500 Best, she liked Yeats Auden
Donne Carlos Williams Southey Marvell Herbert. Ah,
you're a wonder, Emily, I niver could remember a blessed
thing I had to cheat like a gypsy to pass me exams.

Speaking of gypsy, I got dark again. When I was a tiny
kid I used to get very brown in the summers, my Cajun
blood, Daddy used to say, but after he died Momma
would make me cover up, them Garigeaus had a nigger in
the woodpile sure as shit she used to say, but now Africa
turned me brown as an Arab.

I am avoiding again I see and I mustn't there is hardly
space to tell the rest, how clever of me it means I will have
to stint on some of my crimes. June 13, a Sunday and we
are all gathered in the church of the old Italian mission,
even the atheists, for Father Manes has left for Wibok and
there is no one to say mass, except Nora is doing it anyway, yes our dirty secret we do it all the time in the Bloods

when there are no priests, as there very often are not where we work. Perhaps that's why the atheist Euro docs are in attendance, solidarity with feminism, or one in the eye for the patriarchy, although I know all that's far from Nora's mind. Technically the host is already consecrated by the priest on such occasions, but Nora is doing it proper, proclaiming the Gospel, giving the homily, singing the words of the mass in her clear voice, lift up your hearts and so on, and we lifted them up. I didn't actually see her do it because I was the youngest sister and by our tradition I had my back to the altar, looking out the door for the enemy.

Out the door I could see Dol Biong standing motionless in the shade of a water tank looking like a child's stick figure drawn in charcoal against its bright corrugated steel. Behind me they were singing the Agnus Dei. In a few minutes one of the sisters would bring me the bread and wine, another little tradition. Then I felt something brush by me and I saw that a little kid, maybe four years old, had dashed out of the church laughing and I called out to her mother I'll get her! and I ran out. I caught the little girl and tickled her and called her rac (naughty) and started back, at which moment I first heard the engines.

In the Spanish Civil War the fascist bombers used to cut their engines off over the sea and glide inland soundlessly, cranking up only as they approached the target, which worked pretty well before they had radar and it shows you that a good idea is ever green, because the pilot of the Antonov had done it too. I screamed out a warning and started to run back to the church, but they were all singing dona nobis pacem and besides it was too late. The Antonov coasted over at about twelve hundred feet and dropped four large bombs, I could see the long black cylinders tumbling out of the rear cargo bay door. The first bomb hit the motor pool and our fuel dump, the second a group of tents. I had not been bombed before but I knew something about explosives and these blasts were enormous, five-hundred-pounders, a mind-numbing bowel-loosening noise. The third crashed through the tin roof of *the church and exploded inside. I didn't see where the fourth one landed because I was standing there flat-footed with the kid on my hip when the shock wave and the rushing cloud of atomized bricks pews statues hymnals bread wine chalices and people knocked me flat.*

*I was blown out of your world, really, now that I think about it, and this makes the next part difficult to tell. Out of prose into poetry. Out of the secular into the mythos. Out of <u>chronos</u> into <u>kairos</u>, God's time.*

*No, but not at first. I came to myself and found I was blind and someone was pulling at my arm. Gelling blood lay thick in my eye sockets from a gash on my scalp. I wiped it away. I saw smoke and hanging dust and crumbled ruin with shards of tin roof sticking up, so small, these ruins couldn't have held so many souls. I screamed her name and began to claw at the rubble like a dog, but I was pulled back by the boy, Dol Biong. Emily, Emily, they are all dead, they are all dead, he said and I struck at him tears washing away the sticky blood, but he held me. Come with me he said there is nothing here, and after the bombings the Baggara always come. I cried no no and ran away from him to the dorm tent, I suppose I was thinking that somehow she was still there God had brought her away from the church at the last moment but no, and I saw that the refugees were already looting the possessions of the dead helpers. And why not? But still I screamed and beat at their dull black skins and forced my way to where Nora and I had slept and took the old rucksack she kept her things in and swept into it her crumpled clothes her little carved crucifix her rosary and some of her books, things that smelled of her alive I wanted to cover the stink of death that came from the ruins scorched hair and bone and the barbecue smell that's the most hideous thing about burning people your belly says mm good meat! Despite what you know.*

*Come come he was tugging at me and we pushed through the mob and out into the compound. The SPLA who had gone to church had neatly stacked their rifles out-*

side with their bandoliers and I saw Dol grab an AK and some ammunition. I saw he had a bag too. As we left I saw also the child who had saved me by running out, a bit of debris had ripped her from my arms and taken off half her head I envied her I wanted the flies to be eating me too. But I followed him, and again why not? Nora was gone and God was finally silent in my head, no medieval saints to guide me today only a Dinka boy.

We walked east. This was the _sudd_ itself, meandering rivers cutting across clay plains, and papyrus marshes that in the wet season make huge rafts of matting that sometimes blockade the rivers. _Sudd_ means blockage and gives the nation its name. It was the end of the dry season and so travel was easier than it would have been at another time. There was just enough water still on the land, and he had brought food, bean cake, mashed groundnut, dried fish, cooked rice. We barely talked. I sat where I was placed, I moved when tugged, when food lumps were placed in my hand I carried them to my mouth.

Several times we hid from Baggara raiders. The Baggara are Arabized tribesmen who traditionally prey on the _abd_, mainly the Dinka but also the Nuer. We hid in the grass, he with his rifle ready, I silent but uncaring. It's hard to recall emptiness, there is nothing there to respond to the world. I know we crossed rivers and there were crocodiles and hippos in the deep places. He was a fearless boy, but he was wary of hippos, ridiculous beasts that kill more Africans than crocodiles do, yet another example of God's deceptive ways. Once we waded across a wider river than usual and he said that is the Pibor and this is my land. Now we stayed at night in villages, in the round houses of the Dinka. Dinka manners require eating with the mouth open, but what did I care? It was a sad country then, the GOS was expelling Dinka from the oil lands, pushing them east, stealing their herds, making them paupers, arming the Baggara and the murahileen, the Muslim tribal militias, who took the girls and boys for slaves. No one paid me any mind. I crouched against the

*wall invisible. But him they treated well. Every Dinka is
an aristocrat, but some lineages are especially honored,
and he was the last of his line, the last male descendant
of Peng Biong and Atiam, the holy woman. There I first
heard the song*

> *In the days of Peng Biong and Atiam
> No one could count our cattle
> The holy people took us across the river
> To rich pastures
> But now the land is full of sin
> And our wealth is no more
> No one has the power of spirit
> Unless Atiam and Peng Biong return
> From their graves*

*How long we traveled I don't know. It was Ker by their
reckoning, the first division of the rainy season, and all
that the people talked about was the rains being late. The
sky was a thin stretched hot membrane the clouds hung on
the horizon and never seemed to come nearer they seemed
painted on blue china. The more we traveled the emptier I
became as all the days resolved into the same day, endless.
He was refining me in His holy fire to make me a fit instrument of His will. Now I know it but not then.*

*So we arrived one night at a reed-thatched hut such as
the boys make when they go on the summer herding, the
toc, and abandon to decay when they leave. There was a
dead thorn tree nearby and the boy built a little fire of
thorn sticks. We ate, we slept.*

*I awoke in the dark, and the hut was full of smoke, so
thick I thought I must choke, but there was no rasp in my
throat, and in the center of the smoke a flame glowed but
not from a little fire of sticks, it was bright as a welder's
torch. And the hut was full of beings, too, huge, inhuman,
full as a crowded elevator, I could feel them pressing
around me, not with my senses but with my soul and this
host cried holy holy holy is the Lord of Hosts the whole earth is*

*full of His Glory. Now imagine the worst embarrassment you have ever felt in your life the greatest shame that you know will stay with you all your days and I say that is nothing to what I felt then, I fell on my face and ground it into the soil, pissing my pants in terror, earth gritty in my mouth, clawing with my hands until my nails cracked digging with my knees to get away from It, light too hard to stand, away from Him. No no I said aloud I'm too filthy filthy but they held me and pulled me back and I howled in pain. And I saw one of them take a coal from that fire and it placed the flaming coal on my mouth (and it burned with the most terrible pain, but my flesh was not consumed) and it said lo your sin is purged.*

*Then I heard His small clear voice in the center of my head saying*

*Whom shall I send and who will go for Us?*

*And I heard my own voice saying aloud: Here I am. Send me.*

*And the Lord said, go and save this people who are despised and afflicted and make them understand My words with their hearts and convert and be healed. And lead them in the ways of righteousness for My name's sake, for they will be a great people.*

*Yes, what they call a topos, a set-piece chunk of religious experience, but who knows but that it's always like that when God chooses you, like chocolate ice cream it is always what it is or a hand in cool water, real. Maybe Isaiah also had to change his shorts, Scripture is silent here.*

*The remainder of the night was interesting too. Nora was there and St. Catherine of Siena and the Devil as well. I was so happy to see Nora again, covering her hands and face with kisses and she said don't be stupid girl don't you know when you love someone they live forever and surely you didn't think that the communion of saints was just a figure of speech? I was surprised to see my old shiny man there it now being holy ground, but when you think of it he has to be there to twist every good thing to evil if he can it is the way we play here on earth and he said con-*

*gratulations we're both working for the same outfit now and I told him to be quiet and sucked him into me again.*

*Then the morning and I was a different person, so different that Dol looked at me strangely. I ate with good appetite, more than I had for days, I was empty and needed my strength to do God's work, but I wanted more than a handful of bean paste I said I needed meat and he said there is no meat Emily the bush meat is all gone because of the war and all the hungry people. But when we came out of the hut we heard a thrashing in the reeds and out stepped a little reedbuck kid and stood there and I took our rifle and killed it with one shot and butchered it and we built a big fire and ate our fill of meat. Then we packed and I picked up a staff of thorn wood and set off. I set the pace now, no longer having to be tugged along, amazing the boy.*

*I saw his dismay and said I am not a witch nor have I been witched in the night, but the Lord (<u>Nhialic</u> as the Dinka call Him) has enlarged my spirit and told me to save the Monyjang Peng from the wars and the slavers and make them great in cattle again as in the time of Atiam. At this his eyes grew wide and he said but you are a pink foreigner. I said I am not very pink at all anymore and also, who saved me when the church was bombed and who sent the meat to us and who made you follow me around like a calf after a cow in Pibor? You knew it in your heart already. I saw in his eyes that he believed and that made me believe the more and so we set out again for Wibok.*

*We crossed the Kongkong the next day and there was Wibok close by the river. Nora had told me that it was once a place of considerable importance. Located on the confluence of the Kongkong and the north and south forks of the Sobat, it was the seat of a <u>beylik</u> in the Turkish days. Muhammed Ali, the khedive of Egypt, had built a fort there nearly two centuries ago to overawe the Abyssinians and also as a barracoon to confine the slaves he took in huge numbers from the lands between the Nile and the* other rivers. The Brits had taken it over in their day and built a little town, the seat of a district commissioner and his colonial troops. After independence the Sudanese had allowed it to fall into disrepair, and when the SPLA moved against Wibok in this recent war the GOS troops had not put up much of a fight. There was nothing to fight for in Wibok or its hinterland, the principal product of the area being a little arms smuggling from Ethiopia and a rich crop of starving refugees.

These lay in vast dying fields surrounding Wibok town, a valley of bones as in Ezekiel, and the hand of the Lord had truly set me down in the midst of them so they might again have life. They were women mainly and old people and young children, the military-aged men and boys having been swept up in the wars. We walked through these fields Dol and I unsurprised, for he had seen it all his life and I like everyone in the rich world had seen this on television but it's not the same without the smell: dust, and shit, and the abrading odor of thousands of dead and dying bodies. Stick-figure babies lying in the sun covered by flies and ants, being eaten alive actually, swell-bellied and red haired from the kwashiorkor. The first fifty maybe clawed at your heart and then it was like beer cans on an American street. The babies were starving, the women and the old people were starving, but sleek and fat were the men with guns.

I found Trini Salcedo in the Society hospital tent and she dropped a pan when she saw me walk in. Of course she had heard over the Society radio about the catastrophe at Pibor and she thought I was dead with the others. Are you okay, she asked looking closely at my face. I said I was fine and she said, good we need someone to organize this place. She told me that there were three different medical establishments, plus maybe twenty charities, operating, all with their own logistics, generators, distribution systems, priorities, whatever. The only thing they all had in common is that they gave the SPLA guys whatever they want, off the top, or else they get kicked out of town. The

*fort was stacked with food and medicine that the com-
mandant used for barter with the Ethiopian smugglers for
fuel, generators, booze, weapons. I said I would like to
help and I walked out of the tent.*

*With Dol by my side we went to the fort. First a crum-
bling wall with an arched Turkish gate and a square tower
out of Beau Geste on either side. There was a SPLA guard
at the gate with an AK. He was seated on a backless office
chair and drinking from a can of Orangina, both symbols
of unapproachable status in this part of the world. He
waved us through, my Euro-ness substituting for ID, as it
often does in Africa. In the center of the courtyard was a
two-story brick building with Turkish arches for doors and
windows, painted faded green with a square tower battle-
mented in the Moorish style on the two facing corners. It
had a wide tin awning running around it at the upper
edge of the first floor so that in the rains supplicants to the
bey or the Brits could wait dry. A flagpole rose before the
main door, but no flag flew. At ground level a row of small
windows grilled with iron had been blocked with concrete,
evidence of the old barracoon. There were tons of supplies
stacked in the courtyard, guarded by raggedy-assed
SPLAs.*

*I ignored them and went into the church. The church it-
self was built by the Verona Fathers in the 1920s and was
called St. Philip Neri, a substantial mudbrick structure,
nicely stuccoed in white, with a high tin roof set up on
posts and beams above the walls leaving a wide gap for
air, much like the blown-up church in Pibor. There was a
simple altar and a large crucifix in the Italian fashion and
a wheezy pump organ. Father Manes was there rehearsing
his choir. The Dinka are maybe the greatest singers in east
Africa, all they have ever had really besides their cows are
their songs. They sang an Ave Maria and a Dinka hymn
about Christ bringing the rain. Father Manes was also
surprised to see me and even more so when, later in the
tiny back room he used as his rectory, I told him what had
happened to me in the smoky hut and also what I in-*

tended to do. I could see he thought I was crazy and also I could see the fear that I might not be. White people go nuts in Africa all the time, and sometimes, especially among missionaries, it shows as religious mania. So he was smarmy-kind and solicitous through the whiskey fumes until I said he had to stop buying booze from the SPLA with the money he got from America for keeping the church. He stared at me gaping.

I guess he had some words later with Trini because she came to see me the next day. I was staying with Dol Biong in a mud-walled grass-roofed sleeping hut belonging to his mother's family. This was one of the traditional Peng Dinka villages that ringed Wibok, full of people trying to maintain the tribal discipline and customs and keep a small herd of cattle, although this was nearly impossible, given the thousands of starving refugees that surrounded them. We spoke outside, in the shade of a large fever tree. I could see by her expression that she was surprised to find me not obviously raving. Like many devout people raised in the faith, she had never had a religious experience. I have found that such people have a mixed attitude toward those who have, it is wistful longing mixed with resentment and just a taste of envy like the good son in the parable: I've worked in the vineyards all my life oh Lord and no fatted calf for me? I told her what had happened to me and what God had told me to do, but I don't think she really heard me.

I went back to Wibok fort then and confronted the SPLA commander, a chubby fellow named Nyoung. Feed the people, I said, in the name of the Lord, and the Lord then put into my mind all his iniquities and I spoke them out and he gave a cry of rage and called me a witch, and pointed a pistol at me and pulled the trigger. But the Lord protected me and the weapon did not fire. I walked very close to him and said, you know I am no witch, Nyoung, but a prophet of Nhialic Himself. Aren't you Monyjang? Did you learn from your fathers to steal food from the hungry? Is this <u>cieng</u>? Is this noble, to live like foreigners?

When did the Monyjang learn to stuff their mouths so? Your fathers are ashamed. Their spirits are calling on Nhialic to judge you. If you don't repent, will he not cut you off, you and your whole line?

I could see the terror grow in his eyes. The whole court-yard was silent except for the thump of the generators. Even the wind seemed to have stopped blowing. I said, in a voice only he could hear, Nyoung listen: God has sent me to cure the spoiling of the Monyjang and give them new life. For every measure of food you give, ten measures, a hundred measures will be given you. There will be cattle again and peace and the foreigners will trouble you no more. Only believe and follow me!

So then he believed and gave orders to distribute the food they had stored. I said that his soldiers must see that the food went to the women and that the women must feed their children first. After that, the men could eat. They were astounded at this, as it went against custom, it was not _cieng_. But I said that God had ordered a new _cieng_ for the Dinka and was watching and would strike down any man who took food meant for the children, and I went out then and said the same to the multitude. So it went over the next days, and two men who opposed this were found dead on the edges of the camp, their mouths stuffed with cooked rice and after that there was no more opposition.

I had Nyoung lend me one of his trucks and went with Dol around the neighboring cattle camps and villages, speaking to the people and the elders about my mission, or rather I had Dol speak for me and say what had happened at Wibok and how what the Dinka call the spoiling-of-the-world could be made good again. The young men were excited at this and wished to take up their spears, but I said not yet, not yet, because the government and the mili-tias were well armed and it would be a waste of life. I told them God would provide them with sufficient weapons when the time came and give them the victory. Dol was wonderful at this; he had _dheeng_ in great measure, the combination of grace, beauty, manners, comportment, *fine speech, that is the quality most prized among Dinka men. He looked like a chief, and I heard the people speaking of him and his lineage, and recalling the old song about Peng Biong returning. It is an interesting thing about being a prophet of God that you never have to think about what to say. Sometimes the words just come into your head and you say them out loud and for the rest it is a matter of relaxing into faith. God would act or not; meanwhile it was up to us to follow and be patient.*

*Some weeks passed while Dol and I preached the new <u>cieng</u>. The whole tenor of the settlement began to change. With a little more food, the people could begin to work. They could dig latrines and build sleeping huts. There were tools enough in Wibok for this. The women could begin to plant beans, groundnut, and sorghum against the coming of the rains. People began to sing again. I went to mass every day and sang with the choir. Around now I began to hear people calling me Atiamabi, or Atiam-again, I was sliding into the mythos as was foretold. They asked me, Atiamabi, when will the rains come? And I answered soon, soon, until the day when God spoke through me and I answered, tomorrow.*

*The next morning dawned red and off to the west we saw that the cloud that had lingered so long on the distant rim of the world had grown and become black and purple and full of lightning and there was a little wind. That was also the day we woke to find the town occupied by Baggara murahileen. They had captured or killed our few soldiers, finding them sleeping in the dawn, and had chased off the rest, and taken the town. Now they were spreading through the settlements and the huts, grabbing children and women and beating or shooting the men that resisted. They were hard-faced black men in turbans and robes and the scraps of uniforms, but they were well armed with assault rifles. Amid the screams and shots and crying we could hear the sound of thunder coming closer. As I ran into the courtyard of Wibok fort the first heavy drops began to fall and the sky lowered and became black.*

*There were a couple of dozen of them there, all of them had Kalashnikovs. Several SPLA soldiers lay dead. One was crawling away slowly like a crushed beetle, nobody paying him any attention. The Baggaras were assembling their catch, girls and young boys and tying their hands with commo wire or rope. I saw the whole girls' choir bound and weeping. There was a battered Toyota pickup parked by the corner of the fort, with a Russian 12.7 machine gun mounted in the bed of the truck, and behind the gunner stood the man in charge, a big confident-looking man in a camo uniform, shouting orders.*

*The rain had started in earnest now and the commander told his driver to move the truck under the tin eaves out of the downpour. I climbed up on an oil drum and cried over the sound of the rain and thunder Arabic words I had memorized in Rome: In the Name of God, the Merciful, the Compassionate. O believers! Dispute not with the People of the Book save in the fairer manner, except for those of them that do wrong; and say, 'We believe in what has been sent down to us, and what has been sent down to you; our God and your God is One, and to Him we have surrendered.'"*

*I spoke the holy words of the sura in the slow chant of <u>tartil</u> so my words would carry better. I saw wet black faces under turbans turn to me, amazed. They were not used to hearing Quran from people who looked like me, and never from a woman. I continued: hasn't the Prophet, peace be unto him, said, God is gentle and loves gentleness in all things. O believers, is this gentle? Stealing children? Is this what men do? No! Cowards and idolators do this, and assaulting the People of the Book is forbidden. Hear me now, who speaks in God's name. From this day all the land on this side of the rivers is proscribed you. Go to your own lands in peace and raise your cattle and your sons. Those who do not will meet death and their souls will be ladled with boiling water in Gehenna.*

*But the commander called me a whore of an unbeliever and they beat me to the ground with their rifle butts and kicked me into the mud. The rain was now coming in sheets and the thunder was an unremitting roar. I rose to my feet and cried out again, Let fire from God consume you and blacken your bones! Today, this very hour, demons shall eat your flesh in Hell. The curse of God be upon you and upon seven generations of your sons!*

*I saw the commander speak to his gunner and the muzzle of the 12.7 swiveled around to point at me and then the lightning struck the fort.*

*A great thick white bolt of fire, deafening all who heard it, traveled down from the tin roof through the drainpipe to the tin eaves and struck the roof of the pickup. The driver, the gunner, and the commander were instantly turned into smoking corpses, and all the ammunition in the belt and cartridge box went up at once, tracer rounds flying through the air. The murahileen were yelling and running around and a number were knocked down by the big bullets.*

*Nor did the lightning cease. North Florida has plenty of lightning and I'd seen some doozies in my time there, but I never set eyes on the match of this. The whole fort glowed blue from the strikes. Balls of white fire ran along the ground, and the sky was so black and the rain so heavy that everything seemed to be in stop motion like at a rock concert when they do the strobes the air so thick with ozone it hurt to breathe. I kept on yelling out the most bloodthirsty parts I could recall from both the Quran and the Psalms about the wrath of God and the punishment awaiting evildoers although it's hard to believe anyone heard me. I can't swear I saw a militiaman point his rifle at me and then explode into a pillar of flame, but it could've happened. Nearly everyone who was there saw wonders, one of which at least was real: aside from the SPLA shot in the initial attack, not one of our people was harmed. At last there was a God-almighty crack as a bolt struck the right-hand tower and the gas tank of the pickup went off in a smoky fireball at the same time and the whole tower came crashing down like Jericho.*

*The militia fled on horse and foot, leaving their dead and wounded. When they were gone and we were picking ourselves up, tending our own wounded and unbinding our captives, the rain lifted and out came the sun sending beams like church-painted heavens down on us, raising steam. It was like the creation of the world. Then I saw that the fall of the tower had ripped a hole in the building's side clear down to grade, and there was a triangle of black emptiness showing at the corner of the building.*

*Now everyone in Wibok believed that the Brits had filled the old dungeon with rubble and poured concrete in to seal it off, but I saw that this was not the case. They had poured concrete yes, but over a steel mesh, making a false floor. Beneath this was a void. I grabbed a boy and sent him to ask at the hospital for a flashlight and when he returned I sent him through the hole to see what was there. He came back out, covered in dust and cobwebs, and when I asked him what was there he said, boxes and things wrapped in cloth and there were guns too.*

*I said out loud, although there was no one to understand me, a Depot of the Damned, and I knew that God had sent this to us in our need. After what had just happened, of course, everyone was anxious to do my bidding. I directed men with pick and shovel to widen the gap and then went down into it myself. It was clear to me what this was. All over East Africa in the British days there were army units and army units have quartermaster sergeants and these had matériel in excess of regulation or broken under embarrassing circumstances that could neither be thrown away (for what if an officer should find it in some native souk with the broad arrow of British army bold upon it) nor returned to whence it came, and these quartermaster sergeants had said to their corporals I never want to see that bloody —————— again and off it had gone to an obscure place. No place more obscure than Wibok, and when the order came in 1956 to pull out and give the country back to the niggers, and at the same time orders to seal up the old barracoon so the niggers couldn't use it to enslave other niggers, why there was a gift from God. The crap was shoveled down into the cellars, landing mesh was dumped on top of it and concrete poured in afterward, all done at night surely, without any nosy natives looking. And off they went to Blighty singing a merry tune.*

*This is what we found:*

121 tools, entrenching, w/pick
200 shirts, undress, cotton, khaki, other ranks
650 sandbags, burlap, in bales
18,000 rounds .303 ball ammunition, in cans of 500, stamped "expired/for disposal"
12 Lee-Enfield Mk III rifles, in crates, in Cosmoline, crates stamped 1918 Aldershot
8 Lee-Enfield Mk V rifles, marked "unserviceable" in yellow paint
2 Mk III Bren guns, ditto
31 Bren gun magazines, empty
4 five-hundred-yard spools of concertina barbed wire
6 binoculars, Mk II, stamped 1943, all with at least one lens broken
2 Very pistols in boxes
6 Very flare sets in sealed boxes
3 immersion heaters, gasoline burning
12 whistles, chromed, NCO, for the use of
16 Wilkinson blade bayonets, 17 inch, w/sheath
122 helmets, steel, Mk II, 1916 pattern
10 machetes w/sheath, marked Sam'l. Kitchin & Co., Sheffield, 1917
214 cloths, ground, rubberized, 6' by 4'
plus boxes of metallic junk, webbing gear, bandoliers, rotting rubber products, unit shoulder flashes, chains, ropes, camouflage netting, tin cans bulging with bacteria, radios dropped off the back of trucks, puttees, various optical equipment of unknown function, holed buckets, left boots, etc.

*We brought it all out of its cave and spread it on the ground cloths and the people gathered around and stared at it amid the rising vapors and the acrid stench from the burnt truck. In the next days I showed the people how to clean off the Cosmoline with gas and how to grease and oil the weapons with the cleaning kits that came with each new one. I loaded and test fired each weapon. One of the Mk V's really didn't work, and one of the Brens was missing its bipod, but both of them fired. Not much, but my memory spat out that in 1945 the Viet Cong had owned three rifles and a pistol. I had the matériel taken into the fort with Nyoung and his remaining men to guard it. Then I went to the Dinka to prepare them for war.*

*The Dinka are great warriors, which means that they know nothing of war, although they are brave as saints in battle. Through yet another miracle, Dol Biong got it, my mélange of Clausewitz and The Combat Leader's Field Guide, eleventh edition, me pumping the germs of both volumes into his head as we sat together night after night after the militia raid. Then we went to the Peng elders, and he spoke and I sat and radiated spiritual energy, which is the only authority the Dinka recognize. The typical Dinka war starts with an affront; the tribe gathers, organized in age-set platoons. They beat drums and dance and make up <u>dor</u>, their war songs insulting the enemy and praising themselves. Then they run singing at the enemy tribesmen, with the women alongside them carrying food and extra weapons and they fight hand to hand. Wounded enemy are always killed. It is considered shameful to ambush and fight from cover. If they prevail they carry off the enemy's cattle. It is very plains-of-Troy, magnifique mais ce n'est pas la guerre against troops armed with Kalashnikovs.*

*The elders conversed and argued and at last they said we could have an age-set, the one called the Lion-men, aged seventeen, to train in the new way. Dol told them this would not compromise their <u>dheeng</u>, that ever-present con-*

sideration among Dinka men, this too a part of the new dispensation. Then I said I wanted a girl age-set too. More arguing, but I was after all now the voice of Nhialic, and they agreed and said the Tawny Lion Cubs could join our war. Dol picked the twenty most likely of each sex and we went into basic training.

They were good kids and easy to train, in perfect physical shape to begin with, agile and tireless, and they took to marksmanship with delight and impressive skill. They were naturals with the machete and the bayonet. The hardest thing to teach them was silence and patience. Dinkas love to sing and make noise; they were not born ambushers. But the most remarkable thing about them was their ability to run. Any of them could've wiped the floor with a top-ranked AAU college track team, and that with a full combat load. I gave them two months. When they could maneuver and dig in and establish a perimeter and fire twelve shots into a number ten can at three hundred yards in less than a minute, and I had picked out the best of them as squad leaders, we took up our pathetic arms and went after the _murahileen_.

It is very demoralizing even for trained soldiers to be sniped at long-distance by an enemy you can't see, and the tribal militias were mere bandits. They fired lots of bullets at random from their AKs and some of them charged us and we cut them down with the Brens. In a month we had cleared the whole country to the east of the rivers and took over two thousand head of cattle, as the Lord had promised, me riding ahead of the great herds on a black Baggara stallion, spoils of war, to the cheers and singing of all the tribe. And I divided the cattle among the fighters without regard to sex or clan and the people were angry because women had never owned wealth before, but I told them this is the new _cieng_ given you by God who gave you the victory, and they listened, for my word was law.

Yes my word was law among the Peng and my word was dig dig with our Brit shovels, air raid shelters at Wibok and at every village, because I knew the militia would tell the GOS that there was a powerful SPLA force in the *area, because how else could the mighty <u>murahileen</u> be defeated? Not by slaves.*

*One morning I awoke to the sound of gunfire and saw that some of my kids were shooting at a plane, which fortunately they didn't hit because it was the Society Fokker from Pibor and things were falling out of it on chutes, including a man, who turned out to be Peter Mulvaney.*

*He had come to collect Nora's ashes, and when he heard what I was doing here he insisted on coming. He said let the dead bury their dead, which was something Nora would have said if the situation was reversed and he asked what can I do for you and I said, I have warriors but I need infantry I need a battalion of infantry for I wish to hold this country. And he looked around at my people for a day or two and said it can be done, warriors can be turned into soldiers, it worked with the Irish and the Scots after all. So I taught him enough Dinka to give orders and insults and compliments, it was nearly like having Nora again, I was so happy, but then I asked Peter how come they let him use their plane to deliver supplies to us and he said you have friends in high places, by which I knew that the prioress general had heard about what I was doing and approved, and I thought another betrayal, Nora would have hated all this, I think, and I prayed for her forgiveness.*

*He was much better than I was, being a pro and all and he dressed the best of them in shirts from the Depot of the Damned and found packages of shoulder flashes and made half of them the Somerset Light Infantry and half the Royal Inniskilling Fusileers, which were the badges we had, divided them without regard to sex, age-set, or clan and he made them mock fight one another and compete in various ways, you have to break down any identity they have except the regimental he said and it was true, but painful all the same for them, church and regiment were the loyalties we wanted and also of course to Dol Biong, who understood the need for it, God bless him. And of course there were more recruits than we could handle now, and our original forty became the officers of them.*

A month went by and then they came just after dawn rumbling up to Wibok: a truck full of infantry with a 12.7 mounted on the cab, then the command car, a Humber Pig 4×4, then the gun and the other three-tonners. They stopped about five hundred yards from the fort and began blasting away, and for the first time I heard the terrible sound of what was to be my gun shooting at me for the first and last time. Well this is no fun, Peter said, that's an L70, it'll take down this fort in about ten minutes and I said let's get it, then. He took a squad of our best shots and I took the rest of our army and went out the back of the town and we made wide circles in both directions and of course they had no perimeter security at all. Peter's group sniped all the gunners off the gun before they knew what was happening and then shot down all the officers. Most third world armies are specialized for shooting helpless civilians and this one was no exception. Leaderless, they ran around and fired in all directions, showing that automatic firepower is of no use if you aren't hitting anything. It was over in forty minutes. The bearers came up, hacked the wounded to death with their machetes and stripped the corpses of boots, ammo, and weapons. We had two dead and ten wounded. In exchange we had the equipment of an infantry company and my gun. God forgive me I thought it was a good deal at the time.

Shortly after this, late in the day, we heard what sounded like artillery fire away to the east. Ride to the sounds of the guns is good doctrine, so we got into our new trucks and headed in that direction. There, about forty-five miles from the Akobo River and the Ethiopian border, we found an oil exploration team. The explosions we'd heard had been from seismic probes. The team had hired guards, but these all ran away when they saw who we were. The head of the team, Dr. Terry Richardson, a Canadian, invited me into the big RV he used as an office. It was air-conditioned, although it was the rainy season and cool for Sudan. He said they had not found anything significant as yet, and we talked a little about the exploration busi-

*ness, a civilized conversation until I told him that he was a prisoner of war and that I was confiscating all his gear. He said I couldn't do that, as he had permits from the government of Sudan, and I had to tell him that he was no longer in Sudan. I believe that was the first time I declared the independence of my people.*

By the spring of 1937, Mother General Roland, now aged eighty-five, understood that she was gravely ill and might not survive the year. She consequently did two things: first she went to Rome and met with Cardinal Ratti to seek his advice. At that period, most politically aware people understood that another European war was drawing near. Roland feared that, unlike the last one, it would be largely unsympathetic to nuns roaming the battlefields and caring for civilians, while it was likely, on the evidence of the Spanish Civil War then in progress, that there would be far more civilian casualties than ever before. The cardinal promised to consult his brother Pope Pius XI on the diplomatic aspects of this problem. Privately, he began to make available to the Society's leadership relevant pieces of intelligence gathered from the excellent Vatican diplomatic service.

Her second action was to call a convocation of all the Sisterhood. On May 17, 1938, over seven hundred sisters—all who could be spared from the work—gathered at the Mother House in Nemours outside of Paris. Most of them were young women to whom Marie-Ange de Berville was a legend, and the ancient woman, their general, who now addressed them, was hardly less so. The speech she gave was never published, but so impressive was her delivery and so prescient were her remarks that many there would be able to reconstruct it later on. The present writer had the privilege of attending and recalls it well, although in the interests of perfect honesty, it must be said that a speech that purports to foretell the future is subject to modification in accordance with how events actually turn out. She predicted the European war, and the war came. She predicted that the women there assembled would find themselves belonging to nations at war with one another, and so it turned out. She predicted that civilians would bear the brunt of the fighting at a level not seen in Europe since the Thirty Years War, and this happened, too, although to an extent not even the pessimistic Mother General could have imagined. She spoke of the propensity of modern states to make war on civilians as a matter of policy, nor did she blanch at naming the culprits. She said that the Spanish and Italian and German Sisters might have to defy their governments in order to fulfill their vows of protection, and might have to discard their habits and work in secret. She closed the speech with an admission that she was dying and that it fell to them to elect her successor.

The following day they did, choosing Elisabeth Maria Sapenfeld as the third Mother General of the Society. Three days later, Otilie Roland departed this life after a stay on earth as remarkable as a fairy tale. Born in a Parisian cellar, a thief and prostitute by the age of twelve, a communard and atheist at sixteen, she remains a testament to the possibility of regeneration through love, and a testament also of the charisma and perspicacity of the Foundress, who saw in her what no one else ever had and through her example and the grace of God saved her for a life of glory and service. When some churchmen complained of Otilie's unsavory antecedents, and the zeal with which the Society recruited from girls of the streets, the Foundress replied, with typical acerbity, "I can teach piety, I can teach skills, but courage is of God; we must have courage, and the *grisettes* have it."

—FROM *FAITHFUL UNTO DEATH:*
*THE STORY OF THE NURSING SISTERS*
*OF THE BLOOD OF CHRIST,*
BY SR. BENEDICTA COOLEY, SBC,
ROSARIAN PRESS, BOSTON, 1947.

# Twenty

They were both naked in Lorna's bed, but neither of them could recall getting there. Lorna threw a thigh over him. She wanted more. She regretted waking up, she wanted that blotting out, she was counting each fuck as her last, who knew when the disease would render her disgusting or incapable?

He said, "Look, we have a problem."

"You don't vant me anymore?"

"No I vant you a lot. But we have to spring Emmylou. They're going to come for her and she'll disappear."

"They can't do that."

"They can. They can call her a terrorist because of that drugs and guns thing she was in. Plus, she had some kind of connection with that Sudanese, and Sudan is a terrorist center, and they can make up any story they want. This is the new USA, and fuck habeas corpus. So we have to get her out."

"Jimmy, that's crazy."

"Is it? Wait here."

He slid out of bed and left the room. In a few minutes, he was back, dressed in his trousers and a T-shirt, barefoot. He had a manila envelope in his hand.

"Oh, God!" she cried when she saw them.

"Yeah. This is not good. This is a message that they can whack us anytime, and what I can't figure—"

"I saw the man who took those. At the beach. You were sleeping and I saw a man with a telephoto lens on a boat."

"Would you recognize him if you saw him again?"

"Maybe . . . probably . . . he had red hair. Oh, God, Jimmy! What are we going to do?"

"We're going to find these guys, find out what this whole deal is about, why they killed the Arab and Wilson, and why they want the confessions of Emmylou Dideroff so bad. And if possible, pull them in. You're going to come with me."

"Come with you? Where?"

"Grand Cayman for starters. We need to find out what happened in that hotel room when the Arab went out the window. I guess we should check out her native land, too, Caluga County."

"They won't have anything to add that's germane, and besides who cares? The key to what makes Emmylou tick is her religious life and she got that in St. Catherine's." To his inquiring look, she added, "It's a priory in the Virginia panhandle. Where she converted. Or so she told me."

"Okay, we'll tour the Blue Ridge, too. But first we have to get her out. Is there any way she can get off the locked ward? Special treatments or whatever?"

"She's scheduled for an MRI. It's in another building. I could go over there and say it was today."

"Perfect," said Paz, and together they worked out a plan, after which Lorna said, "You know, if someone had told me a month ago that I would be conspiring to kidnap a ward of the court from medical custody, I would have told them they were crazy."

"They would have been. You've changed."

"Yes. Your bad influence." She looked him in the eye. "How did you sleep?"

"Like a baby."

"The power of the voodoo mama."

"No," he said. "The voodoo mama says it's mainly you."

Lorna finds she is a natural conspirator and she knows why. She has been thinking about her mother a lot since the events of the previous evening and she understands that much of her upbringing has involved training herself to keep some personal space free from the didactic intrusions of her father and the demands of her big brother. Silences, false agreement, blandishments, and naked lies had been the essence of their family life.

She thinks more kindly of Emmylou—sisters beneath the skin actually. Thus she has no trouble faking an appointment at the MRI center, or obtaining a set of pink scrubs, a pair of Nikes, a clipboard, cheap steel-frame reading glasses and a blond wig. She also contributes an expired Jackson ID card to wear on a chain. Emmylou is instantly with the plan. She asks where she will be staying, and Lorna has to tell her she doesn't know. Paz has not contributed that part yet.

Darryla accompanies the two women for the short van ride across the Jackson campus to Building 403, where the magnetic resonance imager lives. They arrive at the suite. Darryla argues with the receptionist that yes they do have an appointment. Emmylou asks to visit the bathroom and Lorna volunteers to accompany her and stand outside the door. She passes her large handbag to Emmylou as she goes in. A few minutes later this obvious hospital employee, a blond woman with glasses and pink scrubs, walks out of the ladies' room, moving swiftly as such people do, consulting the papers on her clipboard. Darryla doesn't give her a second glance. She is on the phone with the scheduler for ten minutes, then slams the phone down, curses mildly under her breath, and goes into the ladies', where she finds Emmylou's hospital clothes in a heap. The alarm is given but Emmylou Dideroff has left the building.

Paz was behind the wheel of the rented white Taurus, driving fast and north up the center of the state. Lorna for some reason had climbed into the backseat, leaving the shotgun seat for Emmylou, who was wearing sunglasses, a Marlins ball cap, T-shirt, and shorts. Paz occasionally glanced her way and thought she looked like she had dropped ten years. She had one of her notebooks on her lap and occasionally scratched in it, otherwise she stared out the window with a contented smile on her face. Paz felt a certain discomfort. He liked a well-ordered life and, like many young men reared hardscrabble, was ordinarily a friend of discipline. He was conscious of going off the map now, not to mention all that wacko business at the *bembé*. He was doing his usual thing, replaying the memory tape in his mind and reinterpreting all the things he had seen and felt in terms more suitable to what he imagined was real life. He also occasionally glanced in the rearview at Lorna, another problem child. Paz was no enemy of hot sex in quantities, but he thought Lorna was a little strange in that department too. Something not right there, a fear there, she was using sex to drown something. He wondered when, if ever, she would tell him what it was. In fact, he now thought, really who gave a shit? He hardly knew the woman, and here he was dragging her over half the country to try to find out why this maniac next to him was a maniac. Was that what he was trying to do? He tried to recall why he had just torpedoed his entire career and set himself up for a stiff prison term . . . what was he *thinking*?

The road stretched out a dark two-lane ribbing through utterly flat greenness, tedious to get through, like his life, he thought, stupid and tedious, like this car ride to nowhere with a Jesus fruitcake in front and a fat, neurotic nympho in the back. A little roadside shrine whipped by, a white cross and some plastic flowers, and he thought there was someone with the right idea, he wished he had something to drink, rum or even vodka, but really he didn't need it, all it would take was a little flick of the wheel and why not, what was the fucking point anyway? A big semi appeared out of the heat shimmer, rushing closer, all it would take was a little twitch to the left, was a little . . .

An air horn, loud, and Emmylou's scream in his ear and then she had the wheel and they were rattling and jumping over the right-hand shoulder.

Paz brought the car to a stop, shaking and sweat-faced. "Holy shit, I must've gone to sleep. Christ . . ."

"No, you didn't," said Emmylou. "You were wide awake and in control. I was watching you. You steered us right at that truck."

"Oh, for crying out loud! I did not! Why the hell would I do a thing like that?"

"What were you just thinking about?" she asked.

"Nothing," he said, "just, you know, driving, the time, scenery . . ." Her eyes stopped the easy fabrication well before he could convince himself that he hadn't really tried to crash the car.

"You're not crazy," she said. "It's him doing it, and I don't know why. You had this kind of thing before, yes? Dreams, seeing things that weren't there, thoughts coming that weren't really you?"

Paz hesitated, then nodded and said, "That first time, in the interview room . . . your face changed. I mean I *saw* it."

"Yes, that's what's strange," said Emmylou, nodding. "Somebody said that the devil's greatest trick was convincing everybody he don't exist, and here he is popping up like a jackrabbit. She seen it, too"—looking back to where Lorna sat pale and twitching—"but she'll never say." Paz turned and searched Lorna's face, but she wouldn't meet his eye. He said, "So, Emmylou, we got any angels in there, any heavy hitters, or are we on our own?"

"Yes, everyone thinks it's a battle between good and evil, but the fact is there never *was* a battle. That's what omnipotence *means*. The devil is an employee."

"So what's going on, Emmylou?"

"I don't have an idea in the world," she replied blithely. "We're being used to some purpose and afflicted for some purpose, but we can't know what it is. It's like where the crust of the earth is weak and volcanoes shoot out? For some divine reason the stuff of nature is being penetrated by spirit around the three of us and God knows where it will lead. The main thing we're told is not to worry and have faith."

"Uh-huh. And that means we're going to be okay, right?" Paz was talking slowly and carefully, as to a child or someone with a lot of hostages and a big bomb.

"Oh, heavens, yes! All will be well and all manner of thing will be well."

Paz started the car. "You're sure about that? The three of us, we're cool as far as, you know, this crazy stuff, demonic, whatever . . ."

"Us? Oh, I didn't mean us as individuals. I meant the human race. The three of us are *doomed* for all I know." And she gave him one of those face-lighting smiles.

Nobody said much during the remainder of the ride. Twice Lorna asked him to pull off so she could be sick. Carsick, she said, although he had not noticed that as a problem the last time they had been this way. His cell phone sang several times, and twice he made calls. There were a number of arrangements to be made, and by the time he pulled into Cletis Barlow's driveway all of these had been handled. That was something at least.

He turned Emmylou over to Edna Barlow, declined an offer of lunch, and got back on the road, driving west across the state and then north on 75. By late afternoon Paz and Lorna were at Tampa International. They turned in the car, checked into the airport Ramada. He paid for the room with a credit card belonging to Cesar Somoza, the chef at the restaurant. Meal in the room and several drinks beforehand. He heard her crying in the bathroom. When she came out, dressed in the hotel's robe, he asked her what was wrong. She said, Nothing, just thinking about my mom. Really? No, she said, those were tears of sexual frustration. It's been hours. And dropped the robe.

The next morning they were on the early US Airways flight from Tampa to Georgetown, Grand Cayman, arriving just past noon on the vacation and corruption paradise. A huge black man in a safari suit met them and drove them to a substantial peach-painted villa, with grounds protected by high walls topped with glass shards sparkling in the bright sun. Their driver took them through a cool and shuttered house to the rear patio. There, seated in a wicker chair under an umbrella, was a bulky man in his midsixties, with a face a scant shade lighter than Paz's, a large fleshy nose shaped like an immature papaya, and curly pepper-and-salt hair combed straight back. The man stood. He was wearing a gleaming white guayabera shirt, fawn slacks, and woven leather sandals. He appeared to be a typical Cuban businessman, Paz thought, until you looked into his eyes. These were yellowish, bloodshot, pouched, and gave you a pretty good idea about what untypical kind of business he was in.

But Paz and Lorna were greeted cordially, seated, offered drinks and Cuban hors d'oeuvres. They admired the view. Ignacio Hoffmann kept his eyes on Paz; Lorna might not have existed.

"So, little Jimmy Paz. I remember you when you were busing tables at your mother's place, not the new one, the old joint, the hole in the wall on Flagler. Your head, you could barely see your head above the table, you know?"

"Long time, Ignacio."

"Yeah, and now you're a cop."

"Miami PD."

"Yeah. You know your mother and I go back a long way. We floated in about the same time."

"So I heard."

"I owe her my life. Did you hear that?"

"That I didn't hear."

"No. And you won't hear about it from me. Has to do with the *brujería*." Here Hoffmann made an odd gesture with his hand and a toss of his head. "Anyway, that's why I agreed to see you. Not that I don't always want to see an old friend, except, you know, I'm trying to keep a low profile here."

"Well, I appreciate that, Ignacio, and I'll try not to take up too much of your time. I'm interested in Jack Wilson and Dodo Cortez and why they whacked a Sudanese guy named Jabir Akran al-Muwalid."

"Hey, you get right to the point," said Hoffmann with a big gold-flecked smile. "Okay, first of all, this was Jack Wilson's deal, not mine. Totally. He came over here, what was it, maybe three months ago, and says he's got a business opportunity. He wants me to lend him some of my boys. I'm retired, you know? But I still got people want to do me favors. What's this for, I say, and why should I be interested? He says this is the feds, they want to do a black bag job, and if I go with it, I might get the heat off me a little, maybe even get this bullshit indictment they got on me lifted. So I'm interested, but I'm not going to make a move on the say-so of Jack Wilson. I mean, a nice guy, but he fixes boats. He'd *like* to be a player, but basically he's a mechanic. So I say, I'll talk to somebody and if I like the deal, we could make something happen."

"What did he want you to do?"

"Following. Looking in bags, drawers. Maybe distracting bodyguards in the process. He didn't say nothing about no killing, though."

"This was on al-Muwalid?"

"There were no names mentioned at the time. So I call my lawyer and he calls back and says he talked to the feds, and the word is I need to talk to a guy name of Floyd Mitchell, and whatever he needs I should give him, because he's connected up to the top. This is terrorism bullshit, or something, he wasn't all that clear on it, you know? Okay, so a couple days after that, Wilson calls and says a Mr. Mitchell and him will call on me. And they do."

"What did Mitchell look like?"

Hoffmann shrugged. "A white-bread American. Chunky build. Blue eyes." Hoffmann touched the top of his head. "That kind of short haircut, like the astronauts. But not a hard guy, you know what I'm saying? I'm a hard guy, and you're a hard guy, but this guy was a papers guy, a phone call guy. Anyway, we sat down. He told me this Arab was going to be in Miami, and he was going to be raising money for terrorist activity over there in the Middle East and they wanted to watch him, maybe break into his room, go through his stuff. I say, what's the matter you don't have people who do that working for the *federales* anymore, and he says yeah, but they don't want to go for a warrant because they think there's leaks somewhere, they don't want to spook this guy, they want to see where the money goes and so on and so forth. Bullshit, I'm thinking, but I listen and after he's done I say, well, no problem, Mr. Mitchell, but what's in it for me, does Uncle Sam have a present for Ignacio? He says there's money available, but I say I got plenty of money, what I need is some help with my legal problems and there he says, I'm not sure we have the pull to get that fixed. And then Jack jumps in and he says, 'Come on, you're saying Serpu can't get an indictment dropped?' And Mitchell gives him a look, I swear you could've fried a steak in it and Wilson goes all pale, and at this point I'm kind of amused by this pair of *pendejos* and I say, well why don't we call Mr. Serpu and find out, and Mitchell gets real calm and says, well, thanks for your time, we'll get back to you. And that was it."

"That was *it*?"

"Yeah. I never heard from them again. But before they left, while the big *guapo* was taking a leak, I said to Jack, listen what the fuck is the matter with you? You don't want anything to do with this *cagada*. But it turns out he didn't take my good advice."

"You're saying he was freelancing with Dodo Cortez?"

"That's exactly what I'm saying. They fucked with the bull and got the horns."

"Uh-huh. You know they whacked the Arab."

"I heard. Popped on the head and out the window. A little show-off, if you ask me. You got the whole Glades and the ocean you want to get rid of someone."

"Who'd you hear that from?"

"What? He got whacked? It was in the *Herald*."

"Not the part about him getting clubbed over the head. We kept that close. Dodo called you, didn't he?"

Hoffmann's genial mien evaporated. "What is this, Jimmy, you're *interrogating* me? In my own home, where you're a guest?"

"Ignacio, this's got nothing to do with you. You tell me Dodo paid you a piece of what he got, I'm cool. You tell me you whacked Hoffa, I'm still cool. But I have to know what went down in that hotel room and why, and you're the only one standing who knows."

"Jimmy, it's been nice. Give my very kind regards to your mother."

Paz took out his cell phone. "You can do that yourself. She said to me, 'Ignacio will help you, and if he gives you any trouble, you'll call me, we'll straighten it out.'" Paz punched buttons, waited. "Hello, Donna? Jimmy. My mom around? Uh-huh, well put her on . . ."

Hoffmann was waving his hand, as if to distract a charging bull. He said, "Come on, Jimmy, don't bother the lady with this crap." Paz said, "Hey, Donna? Forget it. Just tell her I'll call her when we get back." He put the cell away and turned expectantly to Hoffmann, who cleared his throat and said, "I'm only doing this because your mother, she's like family to me. I don't want you to think you can take advantage, you know?"

Paz agreed that he would never.

"Okay, then. Dodo calls me up, a couple of days before it went down. They had a meeting: him, Wilson, and another guy, who was running the whole thing."

"This was Mitchell?"

"No, another guy. Harding, Hardy, something like that. Tell the truth I didn't pay that much attention. Anyway, it was fifty K straight up, but they had to do it a certain way. This guy had it all figured. They had this woman they were going to pin it on, she worked for Wilson at his shop."

"Why? Why her?"

"Hey, how the fuck should I know? Is it my operation? So Wilson sends the woman to a parts place for an engine part, long and heavy, like a club, and then they call this Arab and tell him to wait by a phone booth right near the parts place. They want the woman to see him and follow him back to the hotel. They call him at the phone booth—go back to the hotel and we'll meet you there. It turns out the guy wants information about this woman. So that goes down, and Dodo and Wilson are at the hotel. Wilson calls 911 and says there's a disturbance at the hotel. Dodo has this monkey jacket like a hotel waiter. He waits for her to leave her truck, he opens the truck and gets the fuckin' rod or whatever and goes to the guy's room. He's a waiter, says he's got a basket of fruit, the guy lets him in. Bang over the head, and out the window, he leaves the part out there, and he splits. The whole thing took half a minute. He leaves the door open and hangs around until he sees the woman go in. A couple of days after it went down, my lawyer calls me with good news. Justice is making nice in ways they never did before. That's it, the whole thing, all right?"

Again high over the spangled sea, Lorna said to Paz, "You can't say I haven't been patient."

"You're right, I can't say that. But I didn't want to get into it until we were off the island. Call me paranoid, but . . ."

"I would never."

Paz explained what he'd learned in his Spanish conversation with Hoffmann.

Lorna said, "So this Mitchell guy is Mr. Big?"

"His name's David Packer. Or who the fuck knows what his real name is? And who's Harding or Hardy? Packer rented Emmylou her houseboat. I was ordered not to go near him."

"What about this Mr. Serpu?"

"There is no Mr. Serpu. 'Serpu' is how you say the acronym for Strategic Resources Protection Unit. Packer works for them. He's the last actual government employee before you get to the criminals. He ordered the murder of al-Muwalid and concocted this whole scheme to get Emmylou working for Wilson and framed for the crime, so that . . . so that . . ." Paz stumbled. It was hard to keep the mind on all the facets. Perhaps this too, this oily, murky confusion, was part of the plot.

"She would reveal this great secret," said Lorna in a tired voice. "Which Muwalid was also after and which has to have something to do with oil."

"You forgot the dope lord's hidden gold."

"Oh, right, that too. And there's the mysterious jade idol and the Nazi diamonds and the missing Rembrandt." Lorna lay her head back against the seat and looked down at the distant ocean. "It's so boring. How can people spend their lives this way, plotting and killing and stealing? What's the win for them? After everything works out perfectly and all the people who need to be dead are dead and the treasure is in the safe, what happens? Nice vacations? Wristwatches? A slightly larger office? A promotion to GS fucking fifteen? What?"

"It's the oil," said Paz. "This whole things smells of out-of-control bureaucrats. They're protecting strategic resources. It's a dangerous world. The bad guys play rough, and so the good guys have to play rough too. That's the theory." Paz thought back to his conversation with Oliphant, and about how easily Oliphant's passion and outrage had been derailed by the threat of a lost job and pension. He wondered briefly what would derail him from this strange wild-goose chase he was on. Not the job and pension anyway. "It's just a guy thing, I think. There're people like that on the cops too. They like to get away with stuff, and they want a small group of players to know it too. Shooting drug dealers and taking their cash, inventing evidence, lying to make a case. They like the wink, they like thinking they're inside something and everyone else is on the outside looking in. Hell, you're the psychologist, you explain it. But it has fuck all to do with national security. All that kind of shit is personal."

Lorna heard what he was saying, and it made sense, but she lacked the energy to follow on with the discussion. What did it matter after all? She squeezed his hand and settled more deeply into her seat. Her head felt hot and she rested against the cool of the glass. She never slept on planes, she was a white-knuckle flier usually, but now she could not keep her eyes open. Yet another upside of dying, she thought as she dropped off.

From Tampa they fly to Atlanta and then to Roanoke, arriving that night and checking into the airport Holiday Inn. She sits on the bed, staring at the floor while he goes out to get some ice, and when he comes back she is in the same position.

"What's wrong?" he asks, and she gives her usual answer, "Nothing."

He feels her forehead. "It's not nothing. You're hot and you're always tired and you've thrown up about ten times since we left Miami."

"It's just a flu," she says. How tedious, she thinks, to be fussed over. She wishes he was a brute, an animal, who saw her merely as a set of warm, slick orifices.

"Do you want to cancel out on the trip? You could crash here while I go."

"No. I'll be fine. It's just some bug." She hates lying to him. Worse, she now feels too miserable to contemplate sex. Galloping lymphoma. Is there such a thing? She recalls that lymphoma is one of the slower cancers and relatively easy to treat, but she also recalls that there is a wide range of types within both Hodgkin's and non-Hodgkin's. She will have contracted the worst type, or maybe it's a new type, violently metastasizing, they'll be amazed at the autopsy, faces will grow pale, oncologists will scurry to their terminals to get the news out, her cells will be preserved for research, she will live forever in tiny tubes all over the world. Someday, maybe, when science advances far enough she will be cloned and wake up on a table in a white laboratory. Of course, she will have superpowers then. . . .

"What's so funny?" he asks in response to the sound she now makes.

"Oh, just thinking about the peculiar life I seem to be leading." He mixes drinks, vodka tonics, they click glasses, she looks him in the eye and says, "You're really nice to me, Jimmy Paz. Is that 'cause you like me, or are you this way with everyone?"

"I think I'm marginally nicer to you than I am to most people."

"You don't seem to have many faults. Is that the case, or are you just good at concealing them?"

"The latter. It's just because we've been working together plus socializing that it hasn't come up, but when I'm on a case, I mean forget it, I get totally lost. That might be something you should think about. I mean missed dates, no calls for days. Often you might have to take little Jason or Jennifer to soccer when I promised I would. Like that."

"It's something to consider," she says, looking away. "I appreciate being told in advance." She gulps the rest of her drink. "Excuse me," she says and goes into the bathroom. She turns the water in the sink on full force and by wrapping her head in the bath towels and lying on the floor with her face jammed into the corner near the tub, she is able to weep hysterical tears for a good long time without Paz the detective detecting anything.

In the early morning they drove south out of Roanoke on 81 with the mountains ghostly on their right hand. He was worried about her. The ravening desire mixed with an obvious debilitation, something he had not experienced before in a partner, but he did not pry. Margarita Paz's little boy, although a professional detective, had a horror of personal prying.

"This is nice country," he said after an hour or so of silence. "The Blue Ridge is actually blue. It's nice to know you can trust something nowadays."

She looked out the window. "They probably spray it so the tourists don't complain," she said, and then gave him a weak smile. Her eyes were red, and he almost confronted her, he almost said, Oh fuck this, Lorna, the next time I see a hospital sign we're going to the emergency room, but he didn't. The moment passed and he started playing with the radio.

He had called ahead and explained briefly what they were about, and made an appointment with the prioress at St. Catherine's. They drove through an ornate iron gate and up a graveled road and parked in a corner of a pleasant quadrangle made by solid bluestone buildings. A group of sisters dressed in blue overalls were playing a vigorous game of volleyball on the lawn behind a large statue. A tiny brown-skinned sister in full habit greeted them solemnly and ushered them up to the office of the prioress, Sr. Marian Dolan.

They were offered seats and coffee. Small talk before the coffee arrived, the pretty country, something about the history and operations of the priory. Sr. Marian talked a little about the background of the Society and then asked, "So, how can we help? You say you're from the Miami police?"

"I am, Sister. Dr. Wise here is a therapist attending Emily at Jackson Memorial Hospital."

"She's mentally ill, is she?"

Lorna said, "Officially she's remanded by the court to Jackson until she's fit to answer the indictment against her."

"This murder of this Sudanese Mr. Paz mentioned on the phone."

"Yes." Lorna found she could not bring herself to use the title.

"Is she in fact mad?"

"We're still determining that."

"She was prone to visions. Is she still?"

"To an extent," said Lorna. And drives out demons, she thought, except for the one living in her. She shuddered involuntarily.

A silent young sister brought in a tray and left it. The coffee was in a filter pot, and excellent, as were the madeleines. Paz and Lorna shared a glance over these, which made him feel better than he had in some time.

Sr. Marian said, "I was subprioress at the time, and I had some contact with this person. What exactly did you want to know about her?"

Paz explained: subject originally a suspect in a murder, now not so sure, a conspiracy about some information held by Emily Garigeau, now Emmylou Dideroff; the necessity of tracking down all leads, tracing back along the course of subject's life.

Sr. Marian's eyeglasses glinted, reflecting the light from the window so that it was hard to gauge her expression. Paz imagined that the desk and chairs had been set up with just this in mind. He certainly would have done so.

"Well, you seem to know the woman better than we do. She wasn't here very long and I'm afraid she didn't make much of an impression. I guess you know this is a training facility, and I guess you know that the Society has a somewhat unusual means of seeking women with vocations. A good number of the women who pass through here are damaged or marginal in some way. Most of them decide the religious life is not for them and they leave here, certainly with no hard feelings on our part. On the other hand we do receive some really remarkable women, very tough, self-reliant, seasoned, the kind other religious foundations would never see. So it evens out, or it has in the past. She came in as a patient. A gunshot wound according to her records, and exposure. We patched her up and she was here for a little over a year, doing routine maintenance. Then she left."

"Did you know there was a felony warrant out on her?" asked Paz. "I mean you knew she was involved with that drug operation over on Bailey's Knob, right?"

"Detective, this Society is something like the French Foreign Legion. In fact, our foundress was a keen admirer of that organization. People come here looking for peace and a chance to serve the helpless victims of conflict and we don't ask questions about their former lives. Obviously, as good citizens we cooperate with the authorities. But certainly no official agency ever served such a warrant on Emily while she was here."

"Um . . . Emmylou tells a story about being sent to Sudan," said Lorna, "of fighting in the civil war there, on behalf of the Dinka tribe. She had the use of some kind of cannon . . ."

"Well as to that, I'm afraid Emily's unfortunate background gave her the sort of personality that plays a little fast and loose with the truth. I would be astounded if anything like that actually happened, and, in fact, we have no record of anyone named Emily Garigeau or Emmylou Dideroff serving the Society in Sudan, or anywhere else for that matter. I'm sorry, Detective, and Dr. Wise. I'm afraid you've come all this way for very little."

"I'm sorry for taking your time, Sister," said Paz, in his best parochial school manner.

They walked out of the building to their car.

Paz said, "You get the impression we're getting the bum's rush here?"

"Maybe they know we're unworthy."

"No, then they'd be bending over double to be nice. It's something else. What did you think of the boss lady?"

"Very smart. She managed to seem cooperative and yet convey no real information, while at the same time avoiding actual lies."

"Yeah. She would be really astounded. I bet she was, but that doesn't mean it didn't happen the way Emmylou said it did."

"No, but she also could've made the whole thing up."

"Uh-uh," said Paz. "We got what we came here for. I was worried that Emmylou had manufactured her past totally in her head, but now we know she really was shot on Bailey's Knob and was here. That woman we just saw was shining us on, and that suggests to me that Emmylou is telling the truth. What is it?"

Lorna had staggered and caught the side of the car for support. She opened the door and sat down.

"You're sweating," said Paz.

"It's hot."

"It's not hot, it's cool. It's September in the mountains. Why aren't you telling me what's wrong with you?"

Lorna was silent. Somewhat to her surprise, she found herself incapable any longer of the lie direct.

He said, "If you tell, I'll tell you what happened to me at the *bembé*."

A long pause. They heard shouts from the volleyball game and the soughing of the wind through the old trees planted on the grounds, horse chestnuts, pin oaks, and pines.

"All right," she said. "You first."

"They washed my head," he said. "Like at a haircut place when you get a shampoo, they sat me in a chair and leaned my head and neck back above the sink. They washed my whole head, though, not just the hair, with something that smelled like coconut. And they were burning something that smoked, incense I guess, the place was filled with smoke, I could barely see what was going on with the smoke and the water in my eyes. And Yemaya and the other two women, Marta and Isabel, were chanting—"

"Yemaya . . . you mean your mother?"

"I mean Yemaya. The thing was seven feet tall with a voice like a two-hundred-watt woofer. It picked me up like I was a little kid. Anyway, that went on for a while and then they smeared some kind of oil on my head, and the chanting got louder, and then . . . I realized there were more than the four of us in the room."

He stopped and had to swallow. She could see sweat beading on his forehead, although the afternoon was growing cool. "What do you mean, more?"

"They came through the smoke. I couldn't see their faces too good, but I knew who they were. Dodo Cortez and the other one, Moore. The Voodoo Killer. So, the theory is when you kill someone your spirit is tied to theirs and you kind of take on the evil they did in life and carry it. I mean spiritually. And before you can get free you have to experience it, what it means to kill someone, and after you do that they can wash it away. So I did and they did. Oh, the cherry on top was that there's a demon after me, but it's got nothing to do with Santería. Not their department, sorry, and I should be careful. Thank you very much, Emmylou Dideroff. End of story. Now, what's the matter with you?"

She pretended she hadn't heard this last. "I don't understand. You already experienced killing when you shot them."

"It's the wrong word, then. I *killed* two human beings. It doesn't matter that they were a couple of warped sons of bitches, or that they deserved it, or it was self-defense, or any of that legalistic bullshit. The theory is each person is a piece of Olodumare, the creator, and when you kill you disturb the order of heaven and you have to be cleansed. You have to experience the sadness of God. I was crying like a baby and I puked my guts out."

"But people kill hundreds, thousands even, and it doesn't seem to bother them. Why did you have to go through all that? It doesn't seem fair."

"Santería isn't about fair. It's about balance and walking with the saints. Christ, Lorna! Do you think I *comprehend* what the fuck is going on here? What my mother is up to with me? I just keep my head down and do what I'm told. And it works. I felt clean and I still feel clean. Except for the occasional demonic attack, there's less buzzing shit in my head. Things look brighter, I mean things in the world, like those flowers." He pointed to a bush of hydrangeas. "And your eyes." He stared into these. "Now, what's wrong with you?"

"I'm dying of cancer."

His face contorted into that ridiculous monkey expression we all wear, with the semismile, when we have heard impossibly bad news. "What do you mean you're dying of cancer? When were you diagnosed?"

"I haven't been yet. But I have all the classic symptoms of lymphoma."

"Oh, please! What is this, the do-it-yourself school of cancer research? Lorna, they have machines now, microscopes, chemicals, whatever. . . ."

"But I know. I *know*, Jimmy. My grandmother died of cancer, my mother died of cancer, and now it's my turn. I have enlarged lymph nodes, sweats, weakness, weight loss, skin itching. I feel nauseated all the time, which means it's really locked in there, it's spread to my internal organs, maybe even the pancreas."

Paz cursed in Spanish under his breath and hung his head like a boxer who's taken one hit too many. Time slowed down a little in the car; even the wind seemed to die. He asked, "How long has this been going on?"

"I don't know. Months maybe, but I've been in denial about it. It got so obvious recently that I couldn't do that anymore."

Paz started the car and tore down the priory drive in a spray of gravel. He was surprised at himself. He was usually a really focused guy, he prided himself on it, in fact, and the other parts of his life he kept in neat pockets—life as a fishing vest, a tackle box. He was on a case now, certainly the most difficult case of his career, with no backup, with no support above him, confronting forces of unknown dimension, not all of them in the material world, but certainly malign, and nothing else should have mattered very much. But now he found that this did matter, Lorna being sick, and it occurred to him as he barreled along the mountain roads that this was a real difference. He told himself he hardly knew the woman, sad sure if she was dying, but people die, and anyway the whole thing was a rebound from Willa, he needed something and she was it. Sorry, so sorry and good-bye. No! He caught that line of thought and strangled it in its cradle. And then he broke the speed limit more than he usually did driving to Roanoke, and bullied her into going to the emergency room, and he completely abandoned the tempo of his investigation to sit in waiting rooms in hospitals in Roanoke and then Washington while they looked at her and he pretended to be her husband and got in the faces of doctors and nurses to ensure that they treated her like a human person and not a diseased lump of meat.

Lorna wonders why he's doing this. She wonders why she has relaxed so entirely into the hands of a man she hardly knows, why her will, which she had thought was of steel, has proved in these last weeks to be taffy. She allows him to move her around like a mannequin, she submits to the probing and questionings and procedures, although previously she would never have allowed a doc to touch her without the most elaborate investigation of her background and record. It is very strange, and in a peculiar way, it contents her. She has never allowed strangeness to enter her life, and now she is with this strange man, who lights up her (unfortunately dying) body as it has not ever been lit up before, who defies her lifelong understanding of what a suitable mate ought to be, who participates in voodoo, sorry, Santería, and kills people. From time to time she finds a foolish grin arriving on her face, startling the oncology nurses. The tests take a good long time, days and days. She is in the hospital, the hypochondriac's wet dream, but she finds she has become passive about the practice of medicine on her body. Paz will take care of everything. He is in and out, seeing people in Washington offices. He tells her things he's learned, things he suspects. There really is an outfit called SRPU, it's part of the Department of Homeland Security, and they never heard of Floyd Mitchell or David Packer and they really can't tell him anything else, he doesn't have the clearances.

Now she is looking at a doc, whose name (Waring? Watson?) has slipped her mind, although she is certain Jimmy knows and has checked him out like a murder suspect. He is kindly and has a full head of gray hair, like the men on TV who sell drugstore remedies, and he tells her from a long distance away that she has non-Hodgkin's lymphoma, stage four, based on the biopsy and her symptoms, and that it may have metastasized to other organs, and that they would like to check her into George Washington University Hospital for more tests. She feels, oddly enough, not the horrified sense of denial that is usual in such interviews but a rush of something like satisfaction. She wants to tell the world, *See! Not a crock.* She looks over at Paz, the pseudo-husband, and sees his face, his eyes. No, she tells Waring or Watson, I think I'd like to go back home to Miami.

But first they fly to Orlando, and rent another Taurus, because there is still Emmylou to consider. This is Lorna's idea, Paz wants to go immediately back to Miami and get her started on therapy, but now she digs in her front paws and hunches her back and will not budge. She is not much interested in the criminal case per se anymore, but she desperately wants to talk to Emmylou Dideroff again.

**P**az knew he was driving like a maniac, weaving in and out of the interstate traffic, drawing outraged honks and hoots from the 18-wheelers he challenged. He told himself that it was because he wanted to resolve this whole thing so he could get Lorna into treatment, but at some level he knew it was not the real reason. Dangerous driving occupied his mind as ordinary freeway cruising did not; it blanked thought. Had it not been shut out he knew it would turn toxic. He would start asking the why questions, the gut rippers. He would have to think about his life and about his connection with the woman sitting quietly beside him. He would have to admit he'd lost control of his life, that he was scared to death, frightened that she'd die, frightened that she wouldn't and that he'd have to admit to love, the kind his mother was talking about when she'd yelled at him about Willa, crazy love. And what if she said get lost, bub, no high school grad need apply?

He exited onto the state road and drove toward Clewiston. At the little county two-lane he had to pull over for an ambulance and a state trooper, screaming by with lights and sirens. When they got to the Barlows' yard and he saw the cars from the state police and the county sheriff, his heart froze.

Sometime later they found Cletis Barlow in a waiting room at Community Hospital in Clewiston, sitting calmly and reading a Bible.

"How is she?" asked Paz.

"Oh, she's hurt, but she's a tough old lady," said Barlow in a tired voice. "You don't last long around a cattle ranch if you're any kind of fragile. She came to in the ambulance, and the first thing she asked was if Emmylou was all right. She didn't see their faces. Three of them, masked with cartoon masks, Porky Pig, Casper the Friendly Ghost, and Bugs Bunny. They pistol-whipped her for no reason when they took Emmylou. She's getting x-rayed and some other tests now."

"My God, I'm sorry, Cletis. If I had any idea something like this was going to happen . . ."

"It ain't your fault, Jimmy. We can't be constrained in doing good because evil might take advantage of it. The devil'd be the winner then for sure. What did you learn on your trip?"

Paz told him. Barlow was silent for a while, and Paz had the strange feeling that time had run in reverse, that he was still the junior partner on the detection team. Surprisingly, he felt relief rather than resentment. One of his virtues was that he knew when he needed help. Barlow was staring at a poster on the wall, the usual cheery art show thing.

Then he turned his tin-colored gaze onto Paz, with an expression that Paz had rarely seen in it, more Old than New Testament, and Paz felt the hair bristle on his neck.

"Vengeance is mine, saith the Lord, I will repay," said Barlow. "But I'll have their blood for this."

"What're you talking about, man?"

"Where you're going with it now. I figure you got one more card to play and I want to be in on the deal."

"Packer."

"Him. I'm coming with you. You'll wait while we make sure Edna's all right and then we'll go together."

"I don't know, Cletis . . ."

"Yeah, you do. We'll go after him together, only this time y'all're going to be the good cop."

# Twenty-one

## The
## CONFESSIONS
### of
### Emmylou Dideroff

### Book IV

*I see I am waxing prosy now though I said I would not, I can't help it because the memories come that way and besides I am a prosy person, a rude mechanical as Shakespeare says I was never meant to be the person He made me in Dinkaland. Now I have relapsed into my generations, coming as I do from a people used to fixing clutches on old cars and scraping knuckles on rusted iron. So I loved my gun. Peter Mulvaney being SAS knew much about all the nearly infinite varieties of the machinery of death and together we Read the Fucking Manual and we learned how to use the dreadful thing. I assembled a gun crew, the Dinka Nation Automatic Cannon Gurls and Alto Choir, four of them all named Mary and I called them Marys Tok, Rou, Dyak, and Nguan, counting in Dinka, and very regulation for shouting orders. The gun was built in Sweden about twelve years before I was born and was a Bofors Type A L-70 with the generator over the axles. You swiveled it with a little joystick, like in a video game. It had the standard NIFE SRS 5 close-range reflex sight with the integral predictor unit. The five-ton prime mover Bedford contained over a thousand rounds of HCHE multipurpose ammunition plus spare parts and tools and a box of twenty-four TPT practice rounds, and we shot them at long range against the wrecked pickup and at big kites we made, towed by running boys and then by our truck oh Christ Jesus running on running on so I don't have to*

S ister Prefect Alecran came for a visit prepared to declare anathemas, but she could see that something strange was going on in Wibok. She looked at me differently than she had in Kenya. It helped that I was not about to lead a crusade on Khartoum. I don't know whether she ever really got it, that it wasn't just an unruly sister with a knack for small unit tactics, but really the Holy Spirit once again entering history as of old. She left to repair the ruins of Pibor Post, saying she would get back to me. Most of the helpers left too. Some were made nervous by real religion, God walking in the cool of the day, which I guess they had not seen before and others were made to feel unwelcome, like the nice folks who bought slaves back from the Baggara, so that they would be encouraged to take even more slaves and not have the trouble of marketing them. The only solution to slavery, as I had just demonstrated, was to kill lots of the slavers and terrify the rest into taking up some other business.

In fact we didn't need much help anymore. The lands were fertile under the rains, and the durra grew lushly green in the flat acres, and the cattle were fat and bred generously. Trini and her people stayed of course, although she never gave me the time of day anymore. The Jamesons stayed too, a missionary couple who had come to start a mission but had turned instead to useful work, for the people were more interested in hanging out in church with Atiamabi than in points of Christian doctrine. Good sports, the Jamesons. He was a big florid guy who really liked fixing cars and machinery; she was a blond birdie with a steel core who kind of liked how I was reforming gender relations among the Dinka. She ran our primary school and I made an arrangement with her to teach my officers and Dol, my boy-king, how to read. They used the OT as a text. It was like reading the daily paper for us. Nice people.

Two weeks after we took the gun, the Antonov coasted silently down from the northwest. Warned by our watchers, we had just enough time to set up a mile or so north of Wibok, the four Marys and me in the commander's seat. It was a dot when we first saw it, no sound of engines, trying that old trick again. It switched on at two thousand feet and came in for its run. I engaged at about four thousand yards, throwing a stream of hopeful red dots into the sky and kept on shooting as the plane came directly overhead. The tracers intersected with the plane and it moved past seemingly unhurt except for a thin stream of black smoke. As it passed overhead I saw that the cargo doors were open and then black tubes rolled out of the bay, one fell and exploded another fell almost on top of us and didn't and then the Antonov seemed to roll to one side as if tired of flying and we saw thicker smoke with a heart of orange flame and then it went down, boom, and a black cloud somewhere to the west of Wibok.

We howled, we cheered, we waited to see if another plane would come, but nothing did, the GOS has few planes and its pilots are not used to taking flak. We walked over to where the dud had fallen. It seemed that the crew had tried to get rid of the bombs when their plane caught fire and had not armed this one. It lay broken and half-buried in clay and it meant that I now had nearly five hundred pounds of high explosives to play with. Later, looking at the smoking wreckage I felt no satisfaction in having killed, probably, the people who had killed Nora, although I was full of joy in an impersonal way, vic-

*tory is a thrill better than sex, why men leave their wives
and go to war.*

The shoe had dropped, the GOS had made its response,
and so I had a little leisure to deal with my oil men, for the
GOS runs on a slow tempo. Speed is of the devil, as the
Arabs say, and a good thing for our side. Terry Richardson, the oil team's leader, naturally demanded that I release him and his associates with all their equipment and
I said I considered him a hireling of the government, with
whom we were at war, and so all his goods were forfeit as
spoils of battle. It was a civilized discussion, although he
got a little pissed when I had all of them strip-searched
and found he had a CD taped to his lower back, which I
doubted was Joni Mitchell's *Greatest Hits*. I gave them
their clothes, food, water, their Toyota pickup truck, and
safe passage out of our lands. They left a lot of nice swag:
besides the customized RV, we now had a radio net with
four mobile sets, a couple of ruggedized laptops, a nice
HP Inkjet printer, all kinds of geological equipment, and
the prize, a satellite phone hooked to a laptop all set up to
squirt encrypted e-mails via satlink. I pulled out the old
wrinkled, red-dusted card from *The Gun Nut* that Skeeter
Sonnenborg had included with his fudge gift a hundred
years ago and one night I tapped the number out on the
keyboard.

Oil company encryption is very good, and Skeeter was
much relieved when I told him via satlink e-mail what I
was using, because the feds were still tapping his commu-
nications. Via e-mail I ordered four thousand rounds of
40 mm proximity-fused high-explosive antiaircraft rounds,
in case they ever sent serious jet combat airplanes after us,
and the same number of armor-piercing fin-stabilized dis-
carding sabot rounds for use against tanks, also ammunition for all our rifles and machine guns plus more AK-47s,
82 mm mortars and rounds, a couple hundred RPG-7 an-
titank rockets, grenades, mines, other warlike stores and a
thousand pairs of Malaysian tire-soled sandals, extra
large. To pay for it all, I sent him the location of some of

Orne Foy's golden hoards, with more to come on delivery. He said he would assemble all the stuff at Sharjah, in the Emirates, and fly it in, with a stop at Gore in Ethiopia. It came to a pretty penny including bribes, air freight, and commissions, very nearly all the money Orne had accumulated that I knew about, and so Nietzsche was funding a holy war by the slaves, yet another evidence if any was still needed that the Holy Spirit has a sense of humor.

By then it was _anyoic_ the end of the season of Ruel, when the rains cease and the second harvest is brought in. No one, not the oldest of Dinka, could recall such a harvest for abundance. We built round mud-wall silos to store the durra and other grains. Now began Rut, the start of the dry days, when the young men are available for labor. I had them build a landing strip and I had them dig bunkers and revetments and shelters under the earth, for people and cattle, sandbagged against flooding. I knew that when the GOS understood what was happening in our country they would send the full force of their military against us, for quite aside from the strategic position we occupied, it would be intolerable for them that the despised _abd_ could defeat them, and under the banner of the church at that. I thought we had perhaps half a year, for they would want the land to be perfectly dry and for our supplies (as they would imagine) to be at their lowest.

About a month after I placed my arms order, an ancient Hercules landed on our strip and I was not entirely knocked off my chair to find Skeeter himself at the controls. He hopped out of the cockpit carrying a flat box, crowing, anybody order a pepperoni pizza? I let him kiss me. He said, why pay for a pilot and besides I wanted to see Emmylou of Sudan for myself. Peter despised him from instant one and the same back and I pissed away a lot of energy I couldn't really spare just keeping them from killing each other. One night I caught Skeeter in the oil company RV going through drawers. He grinned at me, with that charming psychopath grin he had, and held up *an empty CD case. Lots of cases no data disks, sweetie, why is that? I said I'd given out all the CDs as gifts, the people liked to cut them into spirals and use them to orna-ment the horns of the cattle, and what was it to him? In-formation is money, he said, lotsa folks would like to know what Richardson found out there. You know he's dead. I didn't I said, and he told me that the burnt-out shell of their pickup had been found just north of Pibor, w/charred skeletons. Looked like they hit a mine, but they weren't in any mine field, you wouldn't know anything about that would you, sweetie?*

*At that moment I knew of a certainty, I can't explain how, that Skeeter had been the one who ratted Orne out to the feds, all kinds of stuff clicked in, like how come he was still in business when half a dozen survivors would've been glad to testify that he'd supplied most of the heavy weaponry on Bailey's Knob, and also the look on his face when I blurted it out. He laughed then and grabbed me, his hands crawling up onto my neck and I think he might've killed me right then if Peter hadn't barged in. Skeeter left the next day, good riddance to bad rubbish said Peter what a fucking plague those people are, and added that he thought he might take up a sideline assassi-nating arms merchants.*

*Now we came into the season called Mai, late winter to early spring on the planet, a bad time for the Dinka, when the rivers go dry and the heat is greatest and the cattle must be driven to outlying camps because the grass around the settlements is all gone. But we had so much fodder that we could keep the herds closer in, which was a good thing, because then the Sudanese attacked and we first heard the name of Jabir Akran al-Muwalid.*

*I guess there are people like him in every country, or in any case it doesn't seem that leaders interested in doing genocidal atrocities ever have a staffing problem. The at-tack came from the north at a place called Ring Baai, a village of about fifty families near the Sobat River. We had no warning at all. Later we found that they'd come at* night, which was very unusual for the GOS forces. They had tanks and armored personnel carriers, which we could tell from the tracks and also because they had bound nearly the entire population hand and foot, 658 men women children and lined them up and run a tank down the line crushing all of them and that was the worst thing I saw in Africa. They'd also knocked over the signal tower and crucified the clan elders on the supporting logs. The cattle they'd burned alive in their byres. Two days later they struck at Malual Baai, near the Pibor, way to the south of Ring Baai, the same destruction, only this time some boys had escaped with their cattle, having been in a distant camp with them. They spoke of many tanks, many soldiers, a whole army. In fact, we discovered that it was an armored battalion, obviously, this being Sudan, not a _real_ armored battalion, but bad enough: two dozen tanks, about half of them American M-60s and the rest Type 62 Chinese lites, plus a dozen or so M-113 APCs, self-propelled mortars, and an assortment of trucks and service vehicles. Troop strength was estimated at about 500. This was an unusually formidable force for that crappy little war, and I suppose we should have been proud that they had thrown it against us rather than the SPLA. I did feel pride God forgive me.

We set up a night watch and distributed pyrotechnics to the villages, and Peter organized a commando out of our Somersets and took them across the Pibor, where they lay in wait for the fuel convoy that had to be supplying the armor and blew it up with charges we'd made from our unexploded bomb. A very satisfying operation, which meant that the enemy no longer had enough mobility to go picking off settlements and I see I have about eight pages left in this notebook. All small wars are more or less the same and it's about as interesting to read the details as to read the report of a soccer game. We kept contact with them and sniped. Wibok got bombed, but all our people took shelter in the deep tunnels and my gun knocked a

Sukhoi bomber out of the sky with the new proximity ammo. I led the Somerset Light Infantry off to attack their squadron of light tanks, which were tearing up villages some forty miles distant. They sniped enough to keep the commanders' heads down, nothing blinder and dumber than a buttoned-up tank, and then they ran away at the usual Dinka fifteen mph lope, pursued by twelve tanks in a row and led them onto my gun, which was nicely camouflaged in a thicket. We blew the first two tanks and the last tank with concealed charges and then it was a matter of flinging out a lot of APFSDS until they were all burning. The Afrika Korps used to do this a lot with their 88s, and it took the Brits a remarkably long time to figure it out. Our forces were now divided and al-Muwalid chose this moment to launch his attack on Wibok. I raced back to the town in the command car and arrived just before he surrounded it.

There was no hope of defending the town of course, they blasted the place to rubble and blew up our vehicles and chased us into our tunnels. And their armor entered our ruins and their infantry followed us into the earth. Then came the close and hideous work in the dark, lit only by the flashes of rifles and the glare of grenades. They pushed us back of course they were so many more than we, until only the headquarters and the hospital bunkers remained together with short stubs of tunnel and a few strong points still ours.

I saw my brave boys and girls casting fearful glances at me waiting for the miracle, but there was no miracle, something had gone wrong with my plan I thought and so I crawled through a collapsed tunnel and arrived at the surface where I hid and waited and prayed until I heard the sound of my gun again, I saw a tank go up in flames as the tungsten darts tore into its stern and then the Somerset Light Infantry came trotting through the smoke having run forty miles with full gear in a little over ten hours.

Jammed among the ruins they had made, the GOS armor could not maneuver so our people destroyed it all with

RPGs and satchel charges, and then our people poured into the tunnels catching the enemy between us inside and safety and we hunted them through the dark, with bayonets and machetes and shovels at the very end, when we had all run out of ammunition.

So that was my little Stalingrad, my miniature ketelschlacht. My last battle. We had ninety-one killed, and two hundred wounded, and counted 488 of them killed, although Colonel al-Muwalid and his guards escaped.

The tunnels had drains down the center of their floors and these ran overflowing with blood I waded in their blood above my ankles it flowed over the tops of my French ammunition boots. As soon as I knew we were safe, I went to the hospital to see the wounded, me covered in blood, squelching it in my boots, and there Trini attacked me with vehement language, calling me monster traitor murderer maniac, and what hurt most, that Nora would have despised me for what I'd done and I said I knew but I hoped to explain it to her in heaven and she laughed hysterically saying look at you, you look like Attila the Hun. Heaven, don't make me laugh! Now get out of my hospital!

I don't know who betrayed me. Someone did, though, someone who knew that in the balmy days of peace I used to ride north out of Wibok along the Kongkong in the early morning and that I started doing it again after the battle. I suppose even after all the victory I had enemies among the people, what prophet doesn't? I imagine they will weave the traitor into their songs and so he will live forever like Judas Iscariot. It happened in high Mai, just past dawn, the sky with that fragile glassy look it gets in the dry season, hardly any green showing at all and the river shrunk to a stream you could practically leap across. Dol always wanted to send some people with me, but the whole point was to be alone for a precious hour or so.

They shot my horse from the cover of a burnt forest. I twisted my ankle when we fell, and the fall knocked the wind out of me, so I was just waiting for them when they came out, guns pointing, cautious, as if I were a bomb.

*I was quite harmless now, although they didn't know that. A moment earlier I had been what I had been since the night in the smoky room, a prophet full of God's presence, and when I hit the ground I was just Emmylou Dideroff again. He tossed me out without a word of warning like you tumble a sleeping kitten out of a sewing basket. I wonder if that happened to the real prophets after they'd done their mission maybe Jonah sold insurance in Nineveh for the rest of his life Jeremiah went into camel saddles and*

*Shit so little space left and here I am going on*

**W**ell of course they did the usual, bag over the head, beatings, abuse, gang rape and who really gives a shit it's going on right now in a thousand places, right now as you read this and you might say oh how awful if it was brought to your attention in some compelling and artistic way and then you'd maybe write a check if you are a particularly conscientious person before going back to the usual bourgeois oblivion of the rich world. I'm sorry, being tortured gives you a bad attitude sometimes. Whoever was tortured stays tortured, Jean Amery, French resistant, died in prison, my eternal quotations. Colonel al-Muwalid did the actual torture himself, not the physical part but the interrogations. It was mainly bastinado, shredding the soles of the feet with split cables and also the very common and convenient form that I don't know the name of where they bind your hands behind your back and hoist you off the floor and then drop you a distance, catching you just before your toes hit. It dislocates the shoulders and then they leave you there naked with your feet just touching the floor in my case since they'd flayed them to the bone thus unbearable pain either way. I say unbearable but clearly I bore it, praying continuously although to nothing I could feel. God had forsaken me as He so often does in our hours of need, playing His deep game. When I passed out from the pain I had visions, usually little replays of my stupid life but sometimes Nora was there which was nice

*but she wouldn't tell me what heaven was like or how soon
I would join her I figured maybe 150,000 years in Purga-
tory would do it. Pretty thin stuff considering. Pathetic. I
didn't even cry why have You forsaken me, not having expected even as much as I got of grace. Well, of course He
forsook me.*

*After some days of this they got bored I suppose or they
were afraid I was going into shock and they took me to
what I guessed was a military hospital, and I awakened in
a clean bed with my veins full of painkillers, my shoulders
reset and my wounds dressed. Dr. Izadi announced himself as my doc, a small, neat guy with a pepper-and-salt
mustache and glinting aviator glasses, so obviously a
mukhabarati that he might as well have been wearing a
T-shirt with* SECRET POLICE *on it. He was very concerned
about my health and informed me with much clucking
concern that if they got hold of me again my body
wouldn't bear it. You will die, my dear, and that will be the
end of you, you really should tell them what they want to
know, or you could tell me . . .*

*And so on. It would have worked too, that's the beauty
of the technique, having been tortured once and then
made comfortable and filled with dozy drugs, the thought
of being violated again appears insufferably awful, the
anticipation being even worse than the pain itself. But
what they wanted to know I did not have to give. The colonel was convinced that Richardson had discovered a bo-
nanza of petroleum in the Upper Sobat basin, he read me
what he said were transcripts of radio messages that the
oil team had sent out, predicting billions upon billions of
gallons, fifty, sixty billions, dwarfing the Bahr al-Ghazal
fields, and so he kept asking what did you do with the
data, who are you working for, you're not some nun, do
you expect us to believe that a nun could organize and
lead an army made out of slaves, who is helping you, the
Americans, the Russians, the Chinese, the Israelis? Where
is the oil data? Who did you give it to?*

*But there was no oil, Richardson was perfectly clear*

*about that and I can't figure out why he would lie to me. I'm no expert, but I did claw through Seely's Principles of Petroleum Geology while I was hosting the oil prospectors, enough to follow Richardson's argument and read his seismic data and he was telling the truth, at least to me. If he was playing another game with his employers I don't know, maybe lying to them, but al-Muwalid wouldn't buy it. I knew he was going to kill me, by torture if I didn't support his fantasy, and with a head shot in any case, and I made up my mind to make a break, on my hands and knees if necessary, in order to provoke a fatal encounter, foolish really, the idea of me escaping in the shape I was in, but in the event it proved unnecessary.*

*I awoke one night with a hand over my mouth whose owner pressed a finger to his lips drew back the covers and lifted me out of bed like a baby. He carried me from the room, down a hallway and out into the night. There were other men standing around, watching, holding short automatic weapons. I saw one body in a wide pool of blood before they had me strapped down on a litter in the back of a military ambulance. I heard a brief rattle of fire and a dull explosion and then we were off down a road. A man with a short beard was examining me with a tiny flashlight, checking my heart and pulse taking my temperature as we roared bumping along. I heard voices speaking German over the roar of the engine. Who are you? Friends, he replied. It's better that you sleep now. He had a slight accent, but before I could ask him anything else I felt a coolness on my thigh and a pinprick and I went out.*

*When I next opened my eyes I started crying because I wasn't in heaven with Nora, and the first face I saw was Peter Mulvaney's and for a second I thought it was her. Where am I the usual question and he said Malta, we're on Malta, in Valletta. He told me that he'd arranged the snatch, a bunch of special ops pals he'd organized on short notice, mostly Germans, came in and took over the military hospital where I was being held. For me? I said, calculating the cost. The Society footed the bill, he said.*

*Why? He looked a little embarrassed. We occasionally work together, he said. Mucha do about nothing, I said, and he nodded. Nora would have raised holy hell, he said, but we had a mutual interest. I brought your bag, he said, your things from Wibok, there's not much but I thought you'd want them. Am I going back to Wibok? Do you want to?*

*I thought about that for a while, looking around the room, a typical hospital room with a window through which came the smell of gasoline and cooking-scented air and the rumble of a city, which I had not heard since we left Rome. No, I said, I'm finished there. Where then? Florida, I said. I want to go home.*

*So when I was strong enough they flew me to London on a passport made out to Emmylou Dideroff and then to Miami, where I bumped into David Packer at the airport and it turned out that he knew the Jamesons and on that basis got me my houseboat and the job at Wilson's and I lived like a mouse, a church mouse, until the day I saw Jabir al-Muwalid on SW First Street and the river and you know the rest. I didn't kill him.*

*Here it ends and don't ask me to explain it because I can't. It's what I remember but who knows the sources of memory? Or fate? Only God. Or as the saint says at the end of his confessions, What man can enable the human mind to understand this? Which angel can interpret it to an angel? What angel can help a human being to grasp it? Only You can be asked, only You can be begged, only on Your door can we knock. Yes, indeed, that is how it is received, how it is found, how the door is opened.*

Emmylou Dideroff
Emily Garigeau
(late of the Society of Nursing Sisters of the Blood of Christ)

It is not possible in a small book such as this to recount in detail the sufferings and martyrdoms of the sisters of the Blood of Christ during the Second World War, and even now the fate of many remains obscure. Of the Polish Province, only three sisters survived, out of seventy-three in 1939. (The prioress general, Sr. Dr. Ludmilla Poniowski, died during the bombing of Warsaw. She had been making a visit of inspection when war broke out and she immediately made her way to the Society's hospital, where she treated casualties until her operating room was destroyed by a direct hit.) Many records were lost when the Mother House at Nemours was confiscated by the German occupation authorities for use as a convalescent home for the army, and most of the European leadership was murdered by various regimes. Mother General Sapenfeld was arrested in June of 1941, soon after the Gestapo obtained a secret memorandum directing her sisters to use their best efforts to rescue Jews and other innocent victims of the Nazis, since, she wrote, "The German Reich has declared war on a whole people and, since they are not combatants, they must be considered to be innocent victims and the subjects of our sacred vow of service." She died in the Ravensbrück concentration camp in the winter of 1943. In February 1944, the Society was outlawed in all German-occupied territories, its priories and assets were seized, and many sisters were arrested. A total of eighty-seven sisters perished in the camps.

—FROM *FAITHFUL UNTO DEATH:
THE STORY OF THE NURSING SISTERS
OF THE BLOOD OF CHRIST,*
BY SR. BENEDICTA COOLEY, SBC,
ROSARIAN PRESS, BOSTON, 1947.

# Twenty-two

It was nearly midnight when they arrived at the scruffy banks of the Miami River. Everything at the hospital had taken longer than expected, and Paz had not the heart to rush things. He had wanted to take Lorna home first, but she refused, and Barlow backed her up on it. He pointed out that they had no idea what they would encounter at Packer's houseboat, and they could not arrange for police backup without implicating themselves in the escape of a dangerous felon, besides which the point of that had only been to keep Emmylou out of the hands of the feds until they had the whole thing figured out. It was entirely possible that were they to retrieve Emmylou with the help of the police, she would be delivered from their custody by warrant to the very people who had snatched her from the Barlows, or their close cousins. So Lorna sat in the rental car a block away from the water with a cell phone in her hands and strict orders to get away and raise the alarm should the two men not return within the hour, or should something untoward take place.

"Untoward?" she asked. "I'm sorry, my standards for *toward* are a little bent. What would *un* be at this point?"

Paz regretted his use of the word. "Multiple gunshots, automatic fire, huge fireballs, cars full of gangsters tearing down to the water. Like that. On the assumption that we'll be in major trouble or dead."

"Okay, got it, gunshots, fireballs, cars." They stared at each other. "Don't get killed, Jimmy." The *L*-word floated in her glottis and strained to push itself out, but he beat her to it, the first time she had heard it from an unrelated male of her species.

"Me too," she said. "I'd like to spend the rest of my life with you, however short. Would that be cool?"

"Don't talk that kind of shit, Lorna. We'll be back before you know it."

They walk off into the dark. Lorna sits in the driver's seat, trying not to think about the passage of time, time on this terrifying operation, and the Time Remaining. She feels ashamed that she is so ill prepared for the ultimate things, her long career in hypochondria has not been helpful here. Oya told her that her life was over, perfectly correct, and she notices that she has started to think that it really was the Lord of Death and not a moon-faced nurse's aide there at the *bembé*. Perhaps a mercy, that, to accept the reality of an unseen world, maybe cowardice, but what was the point of stoic bravery, after all, whom were we trying to impress? She realizes too that whatever the second opinion says (and she is still Lorna enough to resolve to seek one), her life as it was is indeed over. She recalls now a story told to her by Betsy Newhouse. One of Betsy's friends had developed breast cancer, and Betsy had dropped her cold. I can't be friends with her anymore, Betsy said, she did all the right things, diet exercise, the best doctors, or so she said, but she must have done something wrong, *something*. . . .

Lorna feels a wave of self-disgust, how could she have spent so much time with a woman like that? Her precious moments listening to comments on this one's body and that one's sex life. She badly wants to talk to Sheryl Waits. Guilt here too, she hasn't called her in a week, maybe more. It is late, but Sheryl is famously available twenty-four/seven. She punches the keys.

"I'm sorry, we don't accept telephone solicitations from strangers," says Sheryl when Lorna speaks.

"Come on, Sheryl."

"Come on yo'self. You know how many messages I left on your voice mail? Where have you *been*, girl?"

"With Jimmy."

"Of *course* with Jimmy. Tell me how right I was."

"You were right."

"Of course I was. So? Give!"

"We went to Grand Cayman," says Lorna and converts the trip and its sequelae into a romantic idyll, provoking squeals of delight from her friend. She doesn't say she has had a bad biopsy, that she's dying, because she knows that Sheryl would want to come right over and hug her and hold her hand and she doesn't want to get into the B-movie aspects of her present situation, standing lookout for a desperate venture.

"So," says Sheryl, "this is now officially serious. Do we have the *L*-word yet? Do we have the *M*-word?"

"The former, but not the latter."

"But it's in the air, yes?"

"It might be. Time will tell."

"Hey, hon, is something wrong? Your voice sounds all funny."

There is a loud *boom* from the direction of the boat that echoes against the walls of the sheds and workshops that line the river here.

"No, I'm fine," Lorna says with a shaking voice. "Look, I got to go now. I just wanted to say that I love you."

A pause. "Well thank you, Lorna, I love you too. Are you sure nothing's wrong?"

"Nothing," she says and hangs up. She listens, straining her ears, and there is another boom, and then only silence and the normal night sounds of the district. Her phone buzzes. Sheryl again, but she doesn't answer.

They crawled low on the deck of Emmylou's old houseboat and looked across the yards of dark water at Packer's big box-on-a-barge. The windows were illuminated cheerily by a color television screen, and they could see the shadow of a man moving about against that light.

"What's that he got in there, a motorcycle?"

"Yeah, a big Harley. I guess he keeps it inside at night."

"Smart fella. A lot of crime down by the river," said Barlow.

"He's got a pistol," said Paz.

"Well, we'll just have to take it away from him then." Barlow reached into his pocket and brought out a pair of number one shells and slipped them into the old 16-gauge double-barrel Ithaca shotgun he was carrying. He also had a big revolver stuck in his belt. The clack of the breech closing seemed unnaturally loud to Paz. He worked the slide of his Glock.

"Now, let's do this," said Barlow, and in the dim sky glow Paz could see he was wearing his lynch-mob-leader face. Barlow jumped off the houseboat and started to run. Two steps on the deck of Packer's barge and he was at the jalousied glass door, which he shattered to pieces with his boot and the stock of his weapon. He had just dodged around the Harley when he saw Packer moving, a flash of white shirt in the dim light of the TV screen. He was heading toward the bow, toward his bedroom.

Packer was just reaching under the mattress of his bed when the butt of Barlow's shotgun cracked him hard over the ear. Then there was a knee in his back and the twin circles of steel pressing like a cookie cutter into the back of his neck. He went limp.

Barlow turned the man over and jammed the muzzle under his chin. Packer was paper pale and his eyes were rolling.

"What do you want? Money?" His voice squeaked.

"Shut up!" said Barlow. He pulled the pistol out of its hiding place, with his little finger in the muzzle and tossed it into a corner. He backed away, still pointing the shotgun, and said, "Get up!"

Packer rose and walked unsteadily to the living room of the craft. A trickle of blood flowed from the wound above his ear. The TV was still on, playing a car commercial. Barlow lifted the shotgun, pointed it at Packer's head, and pulled a trigger, twitching the muzzle at the last half second so that the charge fired past Packer's ear at the television, and scored a direct hit on a cruising Honda. Packer's face contorted and he lost control of his bladder. A pool formed at his feet. Barlow grabbed a chair from the dining area and threw it at the man.

"Sit down, you goddamn piss-baby!"

Packer sat. Without taking his eyes off him, Barlow drew a six-inch hunting knife from a sheath on his belt. He put the shotgun on the dining table and took a roll of duct tape from his trouser pocket. When Packer was fully trussed, arms, hands, and feet to the chair, Barlow stood in front of him and began to sharpen the hunting knife with a small stone that he took from a pocket in its sheath. He spit on the stone and drew the knife across it again and again. Packer watched the motion as if hypnotized. He cleared his throat. "Who. Who are you?"

"Well, I am the husband of the woman that your boys broke

into her home and pistol-whipped this afternoon up by Clewiston. And kidnapped a woman we had as a guest." *Snick, snick,* went the knife on the stone.

"I had nothing to do with that," said Packer. "Clewiston? I don't know what you're—"

The knife flashed out, quick as a snake strike. Packer felt a bite on his forehead and yelped. Blood flowed into his eye and he blinked it away.

"I swear to God . . . ," Packer began, but stopped when Barlow held the tip of the knife an inch away from his eye.

"None of that," said Barlow, "we don't hold with taking the Lord's name in vain."

*Snick snick snick.*

"What are you going to do?" asked Packer after several minutes had passed.

"Well, what do you think? What do you think is the right thing to do to a man who would hire hoods to beat a woman who never did an unkind act in her whole life? You got any ideas?"

"Look, I have money, a lot of money . . . I'll make it right. I didn't know . . . I never told them to hurt anyone. . . ."

"I don't want your money, you terrible chunk of dog shit," said Barlow in a slow calm voice. "Blood's been shed and has to be repaid in blood. I been thinking what to do driving down here and I guess I come up with something about right."

*Snick snick.*

Barlow replaced the stone in its little pocket. He licked the back of his wrist and shaved off a swath of hair. He held this in front of Packer's goggling eyes.

"Pretty sharp, huh?"

No comment from Packer. Barlow said, "What I come up with is I'm going to skin your head. That seem fair to you? My wife's poor face, you ought to have seen it. It just broke my heart to look at her. They cracked her cheekbone, you know."

"Oh, Jesus, oh God . . ."

"You hear what I said about taking the Lord's name in vain? You don't listen too good, Mr. Packer, that might be one of your main problems in life. My own main problem is anybody hurts my family I just go pure crazy out of control. Now I done this a bunch of times on deer, mostly when I was a kid, but I guess it'll work the same with you. First, I'm going to cut a circle around your scalp like this. . . ." Barlow drew the point of the knife lightly around Packer's head, too lightly to draw blood.

"Then I can get my point under there and work your scalp off. I ought to have a skinner, but I guess this old Randall's going to do the job good enough. It ain't as if I'm going to mount it. Anyway, after that, I'll cut in front of your ears, behind your jaw and on up. If I'm careful and slow about it and if you don't buck too much, I guess I can pull the whole thing off in one piece. The eyelids are the hard part, them being so delicate. I'm going to tape up your mouth now, since you're a goddamned coward who sends other men to beat up ladies in their own kitchens, which means you'll probably bawl like a little girl, and I don't want to wake up the whole town."

Barlow applied the tape and then walked behind Packer and placed his arm under the wildly squirming man's chin, pressing the back of his head against his own belt buckle. He placed the knife against Packer's forehead and began to move it slowly across.

The boat rocked and Paz burst into the room, his pistol pointing. "Goddammit, Cletis! What the *fuck* are you doing?"

"Stay out of this, Jimmy!"

"Put down that knife! What're you, nuts?"

Barlow put his knife on the dining table but picked up his shotgun and pointed it toward Paz, who pointed his pistol right back.

"Put it down, Cletis! I mean it."

Barlow fired the shotgun. The charge of shot hit the tank of the Harley, puncturing it in half a dozen places. The room filled with the toxic-sweet scent of gasoline.

Paz said, "Okay, Cletis, you made your point but now you got an empty shotgun there. I don't want to have to shoot you, but I will if you don't put the damn gun down and get the fuck off of this boat. Go out and cool off! I'll get with you later. Go!"

After a long moment of hesitation, Barlow placed the shotgun against a bulkhead and stalked out of the room. He climbed the stairway to the overhead deck and they could hear him pacing back and forth, reciting, "Thou shalt make them as a fiery oven in the time of thine anger; the Lord shall swallow them up in his wrath, and the fire shall devour them."

Paz pulled the tape off Packer's mouth. "Christ, what a mess! Are you okay?"

"What the fuck does it look like? Untie me! I'm going to put that fucking redneck maniac in jail for the rest of his life."

"Oh, you don't want to talk like that, Dave. You don't want Cletis in the same jail as you. No way."

"What the fuck are you talking about?"

"Murder, Dave," said Paz, strolling around behind the other man and into the bedroom. A little searching found an attaché case, locked. He brought it back into the salon and set it on the table next to Barlow's blade.

"You had a Sudanese named al-Muwalid killed by a man named Dodo Cortez, supervised by your pal Jack Wilson, and then you had Wilson killed too, to clear the decks. You're a thorough fellow, Dave. You couldn't have guessed that I had a way into Ignacio Hoffmann, but I did, and he was very forthcoming, for a gangster. He said that a Floyd Mitchell had visited him along with poor old Jack. Ignacio told me how and why Dodo killed the Sudanese and described you pretty well. Floyd Mitchell is you, Dave."

"You can't prove any of that."

"You're right, I can't. But, you know, I don't think I'm going to have to, because you're going to tell me the whole story, all about SRPU and the Sudan and Emmylou Dideroff and oil, every fucking detail. Or . . ."

"Or what?" said Packer. "You realize I'm going to have your badge for this?"

"That's good, that's a good movie line. Unfortunately, you're going to have to dig my badge out of the toilet. I'm now violating a direct written order from my superior officer, Major Oliphant, to lay off this case and specifically to stay away from you. My plan is to pursue a career in food services."

Silence, except for the thump and muttering above.

"Yeah, you're heavily protected, Dave, in high places. Unfortunately, right now, I'm your only low-place protection. From that."

Paz raised his eyes to the overhead.

". . . the righteous shall rejoice when he seeth the vengeance; he shall wash his feet in the blood of the wicked."

"He means it too. He's a fundamentalist. He will *literally* wash his feet in your blood. So start talking. I'm tired, I've been driving all day and I want a drink and bed."

Packer said nothing.

"Okay, your choice. You know, you messed with the wrong guy there. He was kicked off the force for trying to murder the chief of police. He's a religious maniac and you're the devil. In fact, after he finishes with you, he'll probably just toss a match into that gas puddle and walk away clean." Paz picked up Barlow's knife and worked it under the hasps of the attaché case locks. The lid popped up, revealing that the case was full of wrapped hundreds. He whistled. "Well we don't want *this* to get burned up, do we? What else have we got?" Paz riffled through the file folders in the portfolio built into the case's lid.

"Passports? Here's our old pal Floyd Mitchell, and gosh he does look just like you! Amazing. And here's a much-used one for Wayne Semple. A traveling man is Wayne. Spent a lot of time in the Middle East, Sudan too. And here's an ID card from the Strategic Resources Protection Unit, also in the name of Wayne Semple. I guess that's your real name, although I think I'll keep calling you Dave. You seem like a Dave to me. But it's a good thing I've got these, because I doubt they'd be able to identify the corpse after the fire."

"You can have the money," said Packer. "Just call . . . just call a number."

"This is incredible. You *still* don't get it. Dave, I *have* the money and you're all tied up with about twenty minutes to live after I walk out of here with it. I'll mail the passports back to SRPU. We don't want your family to suffer."

Paz picked up the case and walked toward the door. He was just stepping through when Packer shouted for him to stop. Paz walked back. He went to the refrigerator and took out a bottle of beer, opened it, and took a long drink. He saw Packer watch him and lick his lips. "You must be pretty dry, Dave. Fear'll do that. Want one?"

A pause. Then Packer nodded. Paz got another, cracked the cap and held it up to Packer's mouth. Paz sat down on a chair with his face about a yard from Packer's.

"So. Wayne Semple is your real name, yes?"

"Yes."

"And you're an employee of the federal government? In this SRPU outfit?"

"Yes."

"And what do you do there?"

"I'm a contract manager."

Paz laughed heartily. "In a manner of speaking. What do you do officially?"

"I told you. I'm a GS-13 contract manager. I'm not some kind of criminal mastermind. I never wanted anyone to get hurt. I just wanted some information, I wanted to know how much al-Muwalid knew. I didn't know those morons would throw him out the window."

"Uh-uh, Dave. We *need* a criminal mastermind here, and remember I got the whole story of how the murder went down from Ignacio. Someone traced Emmylou Dideroff to Miami. Someone got that little houseboat all available to rent to a poor lady on the run and someone got you this one where you could keep an eye on her. You got her the job with Wilson, we know that, and we know that Wilson set up the original murder and the frame and the attempted theft of Emmylou's confessions. Someone found Emmylou at the Barlows and kidnapped her. If that wasn't you, who was it?"

"The contractor. He arranged everything. I'm just managing the contract, paying out money, keeping records. . . ."

"What contractor?"

"GSE, it's called. Global Supply Enterprises. The local honcho is named John Hardy. He's the one who set it all up."

"What's his real name?"

"That's the only one I know. Why would he use a fake name?"

Paz stared at the man. He really didn't know. "John Hardy was the name of a famous outlaw. A desperate little man. So you didn't check this guy out in any way?"

"Check him out? You mean with the Better Business Bureau? Don't be stupid! The guy showed up in Khartoum and he could do the job. We hired him."

"How much of my hard-earned tax dollars did you give him?"

"About a million two so far. A lot of it was pass-through to the Sudanese."

"To a guy with a phony name? A million two?"

"That's chump change. God, you have no idea how much money is washing around in this antiterrorism business. I have a thirty-two-*million*-dollar budget I have to spend all by myself, me, a GS fucking 13. That's what they do when they don't know what to do, they throw money around. And you have to spend it before the end of the fiscal year or you get dinged."

"That's bad, getting dinged," said Paz. "And where's Mr. Hardy now?"

"I don't know."

"Uh-huh. Well, so long, Dave." Paz rose from his chair and picked up the case.

"*I don't!*" Packer cried. "Please, the whole point of using GSE is that it's all deniable. We pay in cash. I don't *want* to know what they do. Hardy handles everything. For Christ's sake, man, look at me? You think I'm a killer? I peed my pants when that gun went off. I'm a fucking bureaucrat. I live in Rockville and carpool to work. . . ."

"But you went to see Hoffmann."

"Hardy didn't want to go. He said Hoffmann knew him from another deal. He said Hoffmann wouldn't play if he knew he was involved."

"Okay, Dave. Let's start from the beginning. When was the first time you heard of Emmylou Dideroff."

"In the Sudan, but we didn't know that was her name. It's complicated . . . you don't know the background."

"You'll explain it, then. We have all night."

Packer asked for another drink of beer, and then, after a deep breath, began.

"The mission of SRPU is to keep the oil flowing. Oil is a big terrorist target, or it could be, so we have people in the oil-producing nations to make sure nothing happens. Sudan is a small oil producer but it's also a terrorist center, or was at one time, so we had people there. Mainly it was to make sure that the government had enough resources to keep the rebels out of the oil fields and away from the pipelines. No biggie, really. It was a shitty little post, just me and the guy I worked for, Vernon McKay, and a bunch of locals. But I needed foreign duty to get my ticket punched, a six-month posting. Okay, I'm there a couple of weeks, we started to hear rumors that an Almax survey team had made a major find in the southeastern part of the country, east of the Pibor River . . ."

"Who's Almax?"

"A survey outfit, working for a Chinese-French consortium. Anyway, we were monitoring their transmissions and we picked up the team leader, Terry Richardson, saying they'd found what looked like a major reservoir. It looked big, really big, maybe another Libya. A diagenetic trap."

"A what?"

"It's a rare formation and hard to find, which is why it'd been overlooked. Basically it's a fossil coral reef capping an oil reservoir. The Sirte basin in Libya is a trap like that, and it's around thirty billion barrels. Anyway, Richardson said that he'd send the data the next day. That was the last anyone heard from him or from anyone in the Almax team. They disappeared off the map. The government sent people into the area, troops, at first only a few and they disappeared, and then they sent planes, and stronger parties, and they disappeared too. The government was going nuts because there wasn't supposed to be anyone on the other side of the Pibor except bunches of starving refugees and a few SPLA militia. And then we started to hear about Atiamabi."

"Who's he?"

"She. A white woman. That's what the natives called her. She showed up in this little shit-hole east of the Pibor called Wibok, and all of a sudden these raggedy-ass locals are knocking off the Sudanese like clay pigeons. The whole area is closed off. We got onto our SPLA contacts and they say she's not one of theirs. They're pissed at her too, and when they sent people in there, they never came back either. Or they did, but with all kinds of insane stories. She was a nun, they said, she could do miracles, call lightning from the sky, all kinds of shit. So McKay told me to check it out, because he didn't believe that a nun was playing fucking Erwin Rommel down there. It had to be some kind of pro and he had to be interested in the oil. I mean there's nothing else there. We figured the nun was some kind of figurehead. So I hired people to go across the river, locals, and nothing, zilch. And then Hardy showed up. He knew who she was, an American named Emmylou Dideroff. A maniac like bin Laden, he said, but Catholic and she really was a nun. Hated Muslims, wanted to stake out a little oil kingdom of her own, use the resources to set up some kind of Christian theocracy. That's all we needed, right? Every fucking raghead in the world is going to say, See, we told you so, the crusaders are back and they're after our oil. It'd be worse than Israel. A catastrophe! But politically we couldn't do anything out in the open. I mean can you imagine the fucking right-winger fundies in this government if they learned we were helping the Sudanese Muslims knock out someone like that? Not to mention the pope getting on the horn with the president. So it had to be completely covert. Could I have another drink?"

Paz provided it. The man drank, belched, resumed his story.

"This is where al-Muwalid comes in. He was our liaison with the GOS—"

"The . . . ?"

"The GOS, the government of Sudan. He was doing what we were doing, keeping the oil flowing. He had a military unit, planes, a couple of tanks and armored personnel carriers . . ."

"To keep oil flowing? Tanks?"

"Yeah, he was chasing people out of Bahr al-Ghazal, where the fields are. Mainly he used Arab militias, but he had the heavy stuff too, if the SPLA gave him any trouble."

"I thought they called that ethnic cleansing," said Paz.

"It's part of the price at the pump. Those people were in the way and he moved them. Anyway, we funded Hardy and he was able to upgrade their equipment, I mean al-Muwalid's outfit, and he crossed the river and won this smashing victory, according to him. Well, fuck, we gave him pretty near an armored battalion, that's no surprise. And he captured the bitch. Which was good, but he didn't capture anyone else. No prisoners, no oil survey team, and no fucking data. I mean let's face it, the characters you're dealing with, in those places, you know . . ." Packer's face flushed around the cheeks.

"Niggers, you mean," said Paz helpfully. "Dumb-ass jungle bunnies. Go on, please."

Packer cleared his throat heavily and did so. "Okay, so it was critical to find out whether they really had a big strike or not. McKay got Washington involved here. It was a big policy deal. I mean all the way up to the top."

"Why?"

"Well, *if* it was all that big, like another Libya, say, then they had to decide what to do about Sudan. A country that's got reserves of point six billion is a whole nother thing from a country that's got sixty or more. Plus the country's run by a bunch of Islamist crazies make the Saudis look like Methodists. So do we try for a coup, get the crazies out of there? Or throw support to the SPLA, let them take over the region, push them to declare independence? Maybe it'd be a good thing to have a nominally Christian nation with a shitload of petroleum down there. It'd piss off the Muslims, though, which is all we need right now. The point was, the big fish couldn't come to a policy decision until we *knew* what the Almax team had discovered. We put the screws to al-Muwalid. He had the woman then. Could we see her? No. Did you find the data? No comment. You won this big victory, you got control of the region, let's get another survey going. The situation is too delicate at present, he says. And bullshit like that. No one'll give you a straight answer in the whole fucking country. Then we heard three things practically at the same time. One, the Almax team was dead, burned in their truck without a scrap of data, two, al-Muwalid had actually gotten his ass creamed by the n . . . by the locals across the Pibor, so there wasn't a hope of getting another team in there, and three, this Dideroff character had escaped."

"Who told you that?"

"Hardy. Some guys came in and snatched her out of the jail where al-Muwalid was holding her. A professional lift, not her people. We figured the Israelis, but our sources there said it wasn't them. Washington is going nuts by this time. Meanwhile, she's smoke for over a year. We looked for her hard, I can tell you that. The only Emmylou Dideroff on record skipped on a minor dope charge ten years ago and vanished. No record of employment, no criminal record, no credit, no passport. . . ."

"Just like you," said Paz. "And then . . . ?"

"Hardy found her, I don't know how. She was in some convent in Malta, but by the time we got our ducks in a row, she'd skipped. By this time she was important enough to have a federal presence on site, and they picked me. Hardy said she'd go to Miami, maybe he had people tracking her, I don't know, but she showed on the manifest of a London–Miami flight, no attempt at an alias, on a passport under her own name, for crying out loud, and I met her at the airport. I got into a conversation with her, fed her some names of people she trusted, and the next part you know, the houseboat, the job with Wilson. We watched her like fucking hawks and she didn't do shit. No long-distance calling, no contacts, no friends. She went to work and church and volunteered at a shelter, period. Then al-Muwalid showed up in town. Obviously, we were alerted. Hardy came up with the idea."

"What idea?"

"Get the two of them together, bug the place, see what they talked about."

"Dave, that's lame, even for you. The plan was to kill the Arab and frame Emmylou for it, period. You knew she was a religious nut and would go for mental evaluation, and you figured you could extract from the shrink's notes what you couldn't get in your torture session. That's why you've been trying to lift those confession notebooks."

No comment.

"Dave?" Paz pointed upward. Thump-thump of pacing feet and "He shall bring upon them their own iniquity, and shall cut them off in their own wickedness, yea, the Lord our God shall cut them off."

Paz picked up the knife. "Maybe I should make a start," he said. "How hard could it be? I bet it'll hurt a lot worse than getting *dinged.*"

Packer's face seemed to sag, and his shoulders. A tear trickled down from one eye. "Ah, shit," he said, "I can't do this kind of shit. Just let me go, okay?"

"When I have the story."

"Okay, yeah, that was the plan. And we had someone in the nuthouse too, an orderly, watching the doctor."

"Right, and who took the photographs of us at the beach?"

"Hardy. I told him it was dumb, but he doesn't listen."

"He's the redhead."

"Yeah."

"What about Porky, Casper, and Bugs?"

"He's one of them. He only has two men with him." He saw Paz's look. "Oh, God. I *swear.* I don't want to lie anymore. I want to go home." He drizzled for a while and Paz let him while he dumped out the files from the portfolio and looked at them.

"What are all these?"

"Just receipts. There's a checking account, besides all the cash. It's a front we use, to pay for things like rental trucks and equipment."

"This says you rented a storage locker yesterday. Tamiami Storage, Inc."

"If that's what it says. I sign a lot of vouchers."

"They have her there, don't they?" Packer's face gave the answer. He nodded.

Paz picked up the attaché case, grabbed the mini–tape recorder he had placed covertly on the shelf behind Packer's head, and walked across the salon, stepping around the pool of gasoline.

"Where are you going?" Packer shouted. "Don't leave! I swear I told you everything! Please!"

Out on deck, Paz motioned to Barlow, who stopped his declaiming and climbed down to the lower deck.

"Did he talk?" Barlow asked. They could hear Packer blubbering and screaming for Paz to come back.

"Yeah. They've got her in a storage place on West Flagler. Where're you going?"

Barlow stepped through the shattered door. "My shotgun. And my knife. It's a Randall."

Packer gave an unearthly shriek and fell silent. Barlow emerged, wiping his blade.

"For God's sake, Cletis . . ."

"I didn't touch him," said Barlow, replacing the blade. "Fella don't have the nerves for this kind of work. He fainted away like my old grannie soon as he saw me. I sliced the tape on his wrists a little so's he can get free and don't have to mess his pants." They started to walk back to the car and Paz asked, "Did you make up all that stuff you were spouting about killing and devouring fire?"

"Those're Psalms, Jimmy," said Barlow in an offended tone. "The word of the Lord."

"I'm glad I didn't know you when you were wild," said Paz in an amused tone, and then checked when, by the light of a street lamp, he saw the expression on Barlow's face. The lynch-mob guy had gone, replaced by a tired old man.

"You okay, Cletis?"

"Oh, I'll survive. But you can't do like I just done without letting the devil into you a little, and I still got the stench of him in my mouth."

**I** know this place," Lorna said as they pulled to the curb in front of a modest commercial strip. "This is the world's greatest Cuban sandwich joint. We stopped here when we went to the beach."

"That's right and there's Tamiami Storage right next to it." Paz swiveled to face the backseat. "How do you want to play this, Cletis?"

"You're the cop," said Barlow. "But I'd just go in that office and show the square-badge in there your tin and say you think you got a kidnap victim in such and such a locker. I'll just set here with Lorna and watch the street."

They watched Paz walk into the alley between the two four-story blank-faced cubes of Tamiami Storage, toward the lit sign that announced the office. Cletis loaded his shotgun.

"Do you think you'll have to use that?" she asked.

"I sure hope not," said Barlow. "But if someone shows with bad intent and they're armed and they don't throw down, I'm going to be thinking that they're the fellas who beat up Edna, and woe to them."

**T**he square-badge was a dozy fat man who looked wide-eyed at Paz's detective ID and made an effort to hide the porn magazine he had been studying. Paz showed him the rental receipt and demanded to be shown to the locker indicated. The man looked through a card file and led Paz down gray, ill-lit corridors to a door closed with a large padlock. Paz demanded a bolt cutter, snipped the thing off, and went in.

A long canvas package lay on the floor, wrapped with cords. He used his pocketknife to slice through the binding and peeled the tarpaulin back like a banana. At first he thought she was dead, but then he saw her eyelids flutter and heard her breathe. She sighed and opened her eyes.

"Edna . . . ?"

"She's okay," Paz said. "Banged up, but fine. How are you?"

"Conked on the head one more time," she said, and there was

that smile again. He stripped away the rest of the wrapping and helped her stand.

"Did you recognize any of them?" he asked.

"No, they had cartoon masks on. Bugs was the one giving orders. I thought I recognized the voice, but I couldn't tell for sure. He didn't say much. They wanted the notebook. That's why they beat Edna, may God forgive me."

"Does the name John Hardy mean anything to you?"

She nodded and recited, " 'John Hardy was a desperate little man, he carried a six-gun every day. He kilt him a man on the West Virginia line, you ought to see John Hardy gettin' away, good Lord, see John Hardy get away.' It was Orne Foy's favorite song. Why?"

"Packer said that was the name of the guy who ran the operation. Any idea what his real name is?"

She shrugged. "I couldn't say."

Liar, thought Paz, but said nothing, and led her out of the room, past the stunned guard, through the dim halls.

Outside, Cletis Barlow stood by the Taurus, cradling his shotgun. It was past two, and misty, the traffic light, the sidewalks deserted except for the occasional man or woman pushing a shopping cart. It was a great neighborhood for the homeless.

The sound of an engine roaring, and it came fast around the corner out of Nineteenth Avenue, a white Ford Explorer with dark-tinted windows. The driver pulled it to a sharp stop across the street from Tamiami Storage and jumped out, as did the man in the front passenger seat. They were big men, wearing black jeans and dark hooded sweatshirts. Their faces were covered with plastic masks, Porky Pig and Casper the Ghost. As they crossed the centerline of the roadway, Barlow stood in their path, pointing his old Ithaca at them.

The men stopped. They saw a skinny old guy with an old two-barrel shotgun and were not impressed. Barlow could see their thoughts spinning that way by the set of their bodies. Each cast a quick glance at his companion and both bolted, one going east, one west. Four steps and they spun around, pulling out heavy-caliber pistols. It was a good trick but not against a man who had been hunting dove for forty years. Barlow emptied both of his barrels, filling the air with sixteen .30-caliber pellets from each, one right, one left.

Lorna had never seen a shotgun fired before in real life. It was much, much louder than it was in the movies, and the targeted men did not fly through the air backward for twenty feet. They collapsed in place like punctured balloons and lay in two dark heaps.

Paz came running out, pistol in hand, with Emmylou walking slowly some paces behind him. He inspected the bodies on the street and saw that they were beyond help. Together, he and Barlow dragged them from the road, leaving long, wide trails of blood, black as oil in the anticrime light's yellow glare.

"Well, you got to see their blood all right, Cletis."

Barlow said, " 'I have pursued mine enemies, and overtaken them: neither did I turn again until they were consumed.' Psalm 18:37. I hope you don't think I take any satisfaction in this, Jimmy. They come at me tricky and I had no choice. Thirty-two years in the PD and this's the first time I ever shot a man to death. . . ."

Barlow sat down on the curb and put his head in his hands. Emmylou sat beside him and embraced him. Lorna came out of the car and sat on the curb on Barlow's other side, taking his hand. Paz observed the tableau stone-faced; he thought it looked like an allegorical sculpture: Faith and Reason Consoling Justice. He couldn't look at Barlow's face, because he knew that had he been the one with the shotgun he'd be dead, not because of his reflexes but because the power to deal out death had been taken away from him.

Then he heard the sound of a car door opening behind him, turned, and saw a man jump out of the back of the white Ford SUV. He was small and slight, so that for an instant Paz thought he was a boy. He didn't have a boy's face, though. His hair was short and red, and he was dressed in the same dark jeans and sweatshirt as the two dead men. He held some kind of submachine gun, an Uzi or an MP5, Paz couldn't tell.

"Bugs," said Paz. "Or John Hardy."

"What's up, doc?" said the man with a broad grin. "Paz, why don't you carefully draw your weapon by the butt and place it on the ground, and then go and sit down with your pals."

Paz did so.

"Hello, Skeeter," said Emmylou Dideroff.

"Emmy," said the man with the gun, "it's nice to see you again after all these years."

"Don't hurt these people, Skeeter. Take me, and let them go. I'll tell you anything you want to know."

"Oh, you can put *that* in the bank! But I need all these folks, honey bunch. Torture don't work so good on you, as our late Sudanese friend found out, but when I put it to your buddies here, maybe it'll work better. I actually haven't done a lot of torture, but maybe I'll have beginner's luck."

Paz couldn't take his eyes off the man's face. He was happy, delighted, like a kid at a carnival. Paz had always thought that happy was the whole point of life, but no longer, not if this guy existed.

"This is about the oil," Paz said.

"Right you are, boy. The oil. Emmy knows it's there and she wants it safe for her little jungle bunnies, so she keeps telling these lies. I thought she would come clean in her notebooks, or to Dr. Wise over there, but no. All lies. Oh, I forgot you guys didn't see the last one. She had it hidden away, but I worked over that old lady and she came up with it pretty fast."

From Barlow came a low growl and he stirred, but the two women grabbed his arms.

Skeeter chuckled. "Yeah, Gramps, you don't want to get your head blown off." He looked again at Emmylou. "Shit, girl, what the fuck're you doing with these people? A nigger, a yid, and a dumbass hillbilly, what a combo! You were a lot better off as a nihilist whore, if you want my opinion."

"Skeeter, please . . . ," she said.

"You'll excuse me, I have to make a call. I'm a little guy and it's going to be hard to handle this crowd without some help." He pulled out a cell phone and switched it on. He asked Lorna, "You think that's why I have a bad attitude, Doc? Because I'm a half-pint?"

Lorna said, "No, I think you'd have been the same piece of shit you are if you were a gorilla."

Skeeter laughed. "Not very therapeutic, Doc. You need to take a cue from Emmy, sympathy, empathy, all that good shit. And just for that, I think I'll start on you when we get to where we're going."

His weapon didn't waver as he pressed the buttons. The beeps seemed unnaturally loud in the quiet street.

From the alley between the storage building and the commercial strip Rigoberto Munoz has been observing the goings-on for some time with a mixture of satisfaction and fear. He has drunk most of his bottle of white port and he has wrapped his head in tinfoil, but the voices still come through. What he is witnessing clearly confirms all of his extraterrestrial messages. That nice doctor and the woman with the wonderful smile have been captured by the aliens, which means the aliens are real, and all those stupid people at the Jackson mental health are wrong. This makes him glad. Now he sees one of the space aliens take out a controller and press its buttons. Rigoberto feels a terrible wrenching in his groin, but he fights against it. He takes out his old-fashioned Cuban fisherman's knife and scuttles out of the alley, keeping to the shadows between the street lamps, working his way around the cars, to attack from behind. He knows what a submachine gun is from his time in the Cuban army, in Angola. Rigoberto is crazy, but not stupid.

"I thought you only had those two guys," said Paz.

"Oh, you've been talking to Dave," said Sonnenborg. "Yeah, you know it never pays to lay out all your cards, especially to dumb fucks like him. No, I got people watching your place and the doc's. . . ." Into the cell phone he said, "Yo, Benny. Yeah, get over to the storage. Yeah, like now, asshole." He broke the connection and dialed another number. "Yeah, it's me. I need you at the storage right away. . . ."

Paz saw Emmylou come to a decision, her mouth went thin and she nodded her head, and then she started to walk toward where Paz had dropped his pistol.

Skeeter pointed his weapon at her. "Stop right there, you stupid bitch!" he cried and shot a short burst into her path. The bullets went screaming down the street and a car alarm started wailing. She knelt above the pistol. Skeeter extended his arm and pointed his weapon at Lorna. "You touch that fucking gun and I'll blow her head off," he yelled.

Emmylou picked up the Glock and at the same instant Rigoberto Munoz came fast around the end of the white van and shoved his knife into the small of Skeeter's back. Skeeter dropped the cell phone. He spun around and saw a bum shouting at him in Spanish, a filthy, nearly toothless man with a cap of shiny foil on his head. The man danced away and ran behind a car. Skeeter sent half a magazine after him, shattering glass, puncturing steel, but there was no indication as to whether he'd hit him. He reached around to where his back ached unbearably and felt the rough wooden handle. "What the fuck is this . . . ?" he said to no one in particular, and collapsed.

Paz began to move as soon as Skeeter's head hit the ground. He kicked the man's weapon under the van, then checked his pulse. Finding none, he took his own pistol from Emmylou and entered the white vehicle. There he found, as he had expected, the fourth and final notebook.

"Is he dead?" asked Emmylou when he emerged. She was standing over the body.

"Yeah," said Paz. "You knew he was involved in this, didn't you?"

"No. I'm not a criminal mastermind, Detective."

"Oh, yes, you are," said Paz, "in your own sweet way. And you were going to let him shoot Lorna too, weren't you?"

She said, "He wouldn't have shot Lorna with me pointing a gun at him, he would have shot me. But the Lord sent an angel."

"That was a schizophrenic Cuban, Emmylou."

"Yes, an angel of the Lord. Not all of them are pretty blondes with feathery wings."

Paz wanted to shoot her himself just then but instead spoke to Barlow. "Cletis, if you would, get the ladies into our car and take them to Lorna's place. I'll be there as soon as I can. You all need to get out. By now that guard in there has called the cops."

"You *are* the cops," said Lorna.

"Maybe not for long," Paz said and looked sadly at Cletis Barlow.

Then he called Tito Morales.

It is unfortunate that the title of this work seems so technical; not everyone after all is interested in the formation of nursing sisters. Were it not so, then perhaps St. Marie-Ange de Berville's great work would have taken its place beside *The Spiritual Exercises* of St. Ignatius Loyola or St. Teresa of Avila's *The Interior Castle* as monumental guides on how to live the life of a vowed religious focused on a particular aspect of God's work. Marie-Ange begins her introduction with the famous lines "What is this life that we should love it so, even though we are assured by God Himself that bliss lies beyond the sleep of death?" She thus confronts head-on the great paradox of the Christian religion: if there is another, better world ahead of us, what is the value of the only one we know? This is the core of her training method, which is different from the training methods of her two great predecessors, in that it is anascetic; she focuses instead on the appreciation of the gift of life in all its forms, and is relatively unconcerned with a narrow propriety with respect to the sins of the flesh. "Our Lord loved sinners for a good reason," she writes in her introduction, "and in any case, blood is the best washing."

—FROM *THE FORMATION OF NURSING SISTERS*,
BY MARIE-ANGE DE BERVILLE, 8TH ED.
FOREWORD BY SR. MARGARET CLARE MCMAHAN, SBC,
NEW YORK, 1975.

# Twenty-three

Paz arrived at Lorna's in a car driven by his partner, Tito Morales, who had been told just enough about recent events to give him cover. The young cop seemed glum and irritated, and as Paz was getting out of the car he said, "What was that line about telling your partner everything?"

"That's only for honest cops," Paz said. "Take care of yourself, Morales. Stay away from crazy people."

He rang the bell and Barlow answered it, holding his S&W Model 10 revolver by his side.

"Any problems?"

"No. The ladies are sleeping. Emmylou went down in a jiffy. Lorna stayed up reading that notebook."

"You read it too?"

"I did. 'And after these things I heard a great voice of much people in heaven, saying, Alleluia; Salvation, and glory and honor, and power, unto the Lord our God.' Revelation 19:1."

"As good as that, huh? Well, I guess I better read it myself."

"Go ahead. It'll do you a world of good, I believe. And now, if there's nothing else, I reckon I'll be going. I'd like to be with Edna. I'll take your rental, if I may. If they want me, y'all know where I'm at." Barlow handed over his big pistol without being asked and walked out.

Paz went into the living room and found the notebook on the coffee table and read it through, and as soon as he finished he went into the bedroom, dropped his clothes in a pile on the floor, a thing he rarely did, and slid into bed beside Lorna. He lay flat on his back, exhausted but so jangled by what had hap-

pened and what he had just read that sleep remained a distant
rumor. He thought of Emmylou's confession—the maniac had
actually signed it!—and of what any prosecutor would say if he
presented it in evidence, and it made him laugh out loud, an unpleasant and high-pitched sound on the near edge of hysteria.
The sound made Lorna stir and moan, and slide closer to him,
and he slid his hand under the curve of her butt, and brought his
face close to her shoulder, breathing deeply of the sleep-scent
that rose from her skin, like vanilla he thought, or was that
synesthesia, she was so creamy.

At which point Paz let the reptile brain take command. She
responded in her sleep and then awoke quite in midfuck, and
made pleased and pleasing sounds, somewhat louder than was
her usual wont he thought, a gasp 'n' groaner rather than a
screamer or talker, which was actually his favorite type of the
three. He thought the increased volume might have had something to do with the woman sleeping (or not) in the guest room
on the other side of the headboard. Some women liked to ad-
vertise they were getting it, he had found, or maybe it was the
special circumstances here.

In any case, it blew most of the static out of his brain, and afterward she rolled around and he saw her face in the rosy glow
from her digital clock and was pleased that it seemed once
again drained of the pinching tension it had worn, suffused with
pleasure, looking years younger. He said, " 'A woman touched
by a man pretends, sometimes, to sleep, for the pleasure of letting him think that she awakens. After, her thighs sleep differently from before.' "

"Did you just make that up?"

"No, it's from one of Willa's poems. 'Sleep,' it's called."

Lorna stiffened and then let out a long, deep sigh, like an un-
raveling of something tangled in a dank internal place. "I don't
mind. You can go back to her after I'm dead."

"Oh, would you just shut the fuck up," he said gently and
kissed her face innumerable times until she drifted off again.
Moments afterward he joined her in sleep.

She was still out when he rose in the morning. He took a
quick shower and dressed in fresh clothes from his suitcase,
then peeked into the guest room and was pleased to see the
cropped dark head of the Former Suspect from Hell on the pil-

low. By the bed was the bag he'd used to bring her possessions from the houseboat.

Lorna was stirring when he went back to her room. He leaned over and kissed her, which turned into more than a simple farewell smack.

"Get those clothes off!" she ordered.

"I can't. I have to see Oliphant first thing. He's out on a long limb on this and I owe him an explanation."

"Are you going to tell him the . . . what the hell's that?"

"It's a .38 revolver. I'm leaving it with you, and your cell phone's right next to it. We might've got all the bad guys last night, but who the fuck knows? Don't let anyone take her without, one, seeing a warrant, and two, calling me. Okay?"

"Yes, captain," she said sourly, touching the brim of a notional hat. "If I go to sleep again, will all of this not have happened when I wake up?"

He laughed, kissed her again, and left to call a cab.

This morning Paz had his police coffee in a mug that said NA- TIONAL TAX FRAUD CONFERENCE, SALT LAKE CITY, 1999, which did nothing to improve the flavor of the brew. Oliphant looked tired, as if he had not been able to return to sleep after Paz's call had roused him in the middle of the night.

Oliphant tapped the stack of papers on his desk, the report Paz had knocked together in the small hours. "It says here you were pursuing a lead in connection with the Wilson killing, which is not our case, and which I specifically ordered you to stay off of. You were alone, also against orders, and armed with a shotgun. Two men drove up in an SUV, pointed weapons at you, and you killed them both with the shotgun. Then, while you were examining the bodies, a third man jumped out of the SUV and disarmed you, threatening you with a submachine gun. Next, this person, while making a cell call, was stabbed in the back by a homeless man, who fled. You called for backup and later arrested two other men, who had been summoned by Mr. Submachine gun, who turned out to be behind both the Wilson killing and the al-Muwalid killing, a Siegfried W. Sonnenborg, aka Skeeter Sonnenborg, aka John Hardy, an arms merchant and international security consultant, also our long-sought criminal mastermind. Approximately how much of this is true?"

"Say half?"

"Let's hear it."

"You're sure? You lose deniability."

"Oh, fuck that! I'm so fucking tired of deniability I could puke."

"Okay, boss. First of all, we have Emmylou. They snatched her from a place I stashed her upstate after breaking her out of the hospital. They had her locked in a storage locker. She's now at a secure, undisclosed location."

"Along with the vice president. I'm sure they'll have lots to talk about."

"Right. Second, I didn't shoot those guys. Cletis Barlow did. He was backing me and they drove up and jumped him. Both of them had federal fugitive warrants out. They were skinhead gunrunners and meth dealers, and probably won't be missed."

"No. And what about Sonnenborg being stabbed by a street person? You make that up too?"

"No, that's true. Sonnenborg had the drop on us, I mean me, Emmylou, Barlow, and Dr. Lorna Wise . . ."

"Wise too? What, you didn't bring the Hurricane Marching Band?"

"No, they had a game. Anyway, this guy came out of nowhere and put a big fish knife through his liver and ran away. Rigoberto's real, a Marielista fruitcake. We'll pick him up and put him away for good. He needs to be inside."

"I guess. Still, pretty strange coincidence, him showing up like that, just when you needed him. Forty years of law enforcement work have taught me to be suspicious of coincidences like that."

"What can I say, Major? That's how it went down. But the fact is that weird coincidences pop out like mushrooms after the rain when Emmylou Dideroff is in play. It seems to be part of her M.O."

"Mm. I guess there's not much doubt that this Sonnenborg guy is the mastermind?"

"Oh, yeah, he's our guy on al-Muwalid and Wilson and on the assault and kidnap upstate, him and his gang, also confirmed by the pair of mutts we grabbed later. Same kind of lowlifes, and they're anxious to talk. On the mastermind thing, well, Sonnenborg officially worked for a fed named Wayne Semple, aka Floyd Mitchell, aka David Packer."

"Who we don't have."

"No, but do we want him? My sense is that all the nasty stuff came directly from Sonnenborg, who was apparently quite a piece of work. Packer wrote the checks, but he's not a player down here anymore. When me and Morales went by there at four-thirty this morning, there was no houseboat at all. Packer must've called his cleaners. He's probably back in the 'burbs outside Washington and the boat is somewhere out at sea, heading for a watery grave."

Oliphant said nothing. He pursed his lips and stared up at the ceiling. Paz had the strange feeling that he could see the man's thoughts, like the news feed that runs along the bottom of the screen on CNN. Paz took a microrecorder cassette out of his pocket and laid it on Oliphant's desk. "This is for you."

"What is it?"

"A full confession from Packer, naming names. This whole thing is about Sudanese oil and the attempt by agents of the U.S. government to influence Sudanese oil policy and get information about a huge oil find. They committed God knows how many illegal acts both here and over there in furtherance of that goal, including ethnic cleansing, attempted genocide, and torture, plus the two murders here in Florida. My thought was that if you had that in a safe place, and let people up in D.C. know about it, you'd be off the hook as far as any pressure from that end was concerned. I mean it'd be a Mexican standoff. Or am I missing some subtlety?"

Oliphant stared at the little rectangle for a good while and then slipped it into his shirt pocket. "No, I'd guess you were right. They won't indict me. They might kill me, but they definitely won't go the other route. I'd thank you . . . no, I do thank you, but by Christ, I hate all of it like poison!"

"You're welcome," said Paz. "Only two other items. One is the dangerous nutcase fugitive Emmylou Dideroff me and Dr. Wise illegally sprang from state custody. I vote for letting her disappear just like Mr. Packer."

"Second the motion. You have a plan, I presume."

"Sort of. Last night I put in a call to Rome a little after three-thirty A.M. our time. I spoke to a very nice woman at the Society of Nursing Sisters of the Blood of Christ. I told her who I was and I said that her prioress general might be interested to know the current situation of one of their ladies. They call her Emily Garigeau. Rome seemed pretty interested."

"What are they going to do?"

"I haven't got a clue. But they're a resourceful outfit. I'm sure they'll think of something."

"Yes. What's the other item?"

Paz took out his Glock and his shield wallet and placed them on Oliphant's desk.

"I'm handing it in, Major. I suggest you put it out that you forced me to resign. It'll cover you better if any of this stuff starts to work loose. Irresponsible cowboy resigns under pressure of squeaky clean new administration. I'll take the pension in a lump sum."

"Christ, Jimmy, you don't have to do this." Oliphant's face showed real concern, but at a somewhat more veiled level, Paz observed, it showed relief as well.

"I do. I killed two guys already on the job, and I just realized last night I can't do it again, and if I stay on the street, one day I'm going to choke and get someone killed." He stood up and held out his hand. "Been a pleasure, Major," he said. "Come by the restaurant sometime. I'll buy you a dinner."

Lorna abandons sleep with some reluctance and toddles naked into her bathroom. There is a wall-spanning mirror there, placed by the former owners, and she pauses to check herself out. Still a long way to go before she looks wasted, but it's starting. There will be a brief phase, she thinks, when I will be fashionably thin, before collapsing into yellowing skeletal wreckage. On the other hand, I'm getting the best sex I ever had from the nicest man I ever went out with: what is this, a terrific dessert at the end of a crappy meal? *What?* She realizes she is addressing the Deity and recalls the last notebook, where Emmylou refers to the putative sense of humor of the putative Holy Spirit. What would it be like, she wonders, to believe in all that? She reaches briefly inside her mind and finds no handle for it; instead there's something like a damper that muffles any exploration in that direction and sets up, like an interior PowerPoint slide show, a materialist explanation for everything that has recently befallen her.

Now she palps her glands, finding them swollen but unchanged. She is feverish and has, she now determines, an actual fever of 100.2 F. Still slightly nauseated, but not enough to chuck up. She feels like death, but not that soon. She showers, and as she swabs love's ichors out of her, she wonders yet again how long it will last, how long before she becomes too sick or too unattractive to have it anymore, and thinks by then I'll have pills enough to slip away. It hasn't really kicked in yet, she thinks as she dresses, I should be more depressed and I'm not, I feel like I'm floating over it, like it's happening to someone else. The famous Denial stage? Probably.

As she emerges, she notices the guest room door is open and she hears movement in her kitchen. The refrigerator door swishes closed. There is Emmylou, all dressed in her shorts and T-shirt, with a container of yogurt in her hand.

"Oh, you're up!" she says and wiggles the yogurt. "I hope you don't mind . . . I can't remember the last time I ate."

"No, don't be silly. I could make you bacon and eggs if you want."

"No, this'll be fine."

Lorna makes coffee, and they take it and the rest of their breakfast out to the back patio. It is cool now, and the neighboring air conditioners have entered their fall silence, and they can hear the mockingbirds singing in the overarching foliage. Lorna sips coffee, nibbles a corner of toast. She is never hungry anymore. But Emmylou sits cross-legged in a basket chair and consumes her yogurt and eats four slices of toast and jam with total concentration and enjoyment.

She looks about fourteen now, and Lorna can hardly believe that this person has experienced the life she has presented in her confessions, murdering, whoring, leading armies, wading in blood. . . . Where does she keep it all? Lorna can see one of the woman's feet poking out and registers the scars, the thick keratinized tissue, like rubber cement spilled and dried out. Where is the shattering, the crushing of the spirit, the post-traumatic stress? She recalls her battery of tests, administered with such confidence not long ago, by a Lorna that hardly seems to exist anymore. The damned woman is an affront to the science of psychology. Lorna catches herself thinking along these lines and feels absurd.

Emmylou becomes aware of Lorna staring and grins sheepishly. "I'm sorry. I'm such a pig now. The Dinka would be mortified."

"Don't they eat?"

"Yes, sure, but modestly. It's against *dheeng* to show hunger or gluttony. Of course their cooking is pretty bland. It's mostly sorghum porridge studded with dead flies. Insects ingested with food or eaten purposely are a big source of protein in Africa."

Lorna feels her stomach heave.

"You get used to it, everything crawling with flies, and it's interesting," says Emmylou, picking up the yogurt container. "The Dinka have tons of milk but they don't have yogurt or cheese. I made some of both while I was there, but it wasn't a hit. They have butter, though. Also, they don't care about the actual yield from their cows, only how many cows, like thinking twenty nickels is more valuable than ten quarters."

Lorna listens without comment, recognizing nervous chatter when she hears it. A précis of Dinka husbandry and custom flows forth, including items that Lorna could have lived without knowing—such as Dinka men pressing their lips to the anus of a cow and blowing air into its gut, to fool it into thinking it was still pregnant—and then the phone rings. Lorna goes into the house and comes back a moment later with a surprised look on her face and the cordless in her hand.

"It's for you," she says.

Emmylou takes the instrument as if it were a live grenade. She listens more than she speaks, and that mainly monosyllables. When she closes the connection she says, "That was the Society. They want me back. Unless our friend is going to arrest me again."

Lorna barely wonders how the Society knew what number to call. "I very much doubt that. What will you do, go back to Sudan?"

Emmylou looks up at the mango tree. "No, I don't think so. As you probably picked up from my writing, there's a debate going on about arming our missions, and I'm a prime example of the success of that side of the debate. That's why they paid to have me rescued and that's why they're sending someone to take me away."

"So you'll be a military consultant to the nuns?"

She laughs. "Sisters. Yeah, right, a master of war, just like Skeeter. Sister-Colonel Garigeau. No, Nora was right and the prioress general is wrong. I'll be happy to fold sheets or do anything they want, but all that's over with for me."

"But you won your war. You proved her point—I mean the prioress general."

"God won the war. Saying it was me is like saying a bat and ball won the World Series. No, He formed me from the beginning, the memory thing, making me sneaky, sending the devil into me, my family, Orne and his war library and his weapons, meeting Nora and getting civilized, the bombing of Pibor, all those things made me into an instrument of His will and He used me and gave the Peng Dinka what he wanted them to have. He chose another people for His covenant, and that will go on. They don't need me anymore, just like the Israelites didn't need Moses once they got to the Promised Land."

Lorna now experiences a flash of irritation. She has been keeping a good deal of her real feelings about Emmylou Dideroff bottled up, but now that the woman is no longer a patient, she feels them froth into new life. The infernal arrogance! The shameless manipulation! The lack of caution and respect for the lives of others! Every string of her liberal heart twanged ire and she says, "What about the oil, Emmylou?"

"There is no oil. Didn't you read the notebook?"

"Yes I did and I saw what you were trying to do. You were totally frank throughout the whole thing, letting out all the awful things that were done to you and that you did, creating an impression of guileless honesty, all to conceal one big lie. They found oil, a lot of it, or Richardson wouldn't have radioed out, and the Sudanese wouldn't have launched a huge attack on you, and especially Richardson wouldn't've tried to smuggle out a CD when you searched him. What was it, a *blank* CD pasted to his skin? You slipped up a little there, it was a detail we didn't need to know. Sonnenborg must've spotted it too."

"There was no oil. The CD had financial records on it. He was a consultant and he was interested in getting paid."

"I bet."

"Lorna, if there was an oil find, don't you think I would've confessed it? He tortured me for days. . . ."

"You're a religious fanatic. Torture doesn't work on religious fanatics. As a matter of fact, you're the kind of paranoid fanatic who regards torture as a vindication. You would have let him shoot me."

"No, I explained to Detective Paz. He would have only shot me, and in any case there was the angel—"

"Oh, please! And what if Sonnenborg had been able to pull us off the street to some secret basement? You would have watched the bunch of us being tortured to death and you still wouldn't have said a word."

The other woman looks away. "God allows people to be tortured to death all the time."

"*You're not God!*" This comes out in a yell, and Lorna is gratified to see Emmylou jump a little.

"No, of course I'm not God, but I believe he used me for a time. For a while we made one little tribe secure. We did something against the toxic, vicious misogyny of Africa, we turned them away from being stupid proud victims, and taught them that God had a special use for them, that He cared about them being righteous. There'll be a seed, like the one He planted in Israel. When the rich world collapses—"

"Oh, thank you! I should have figured there'd be apocalyptic stuff in there too. Do you have a date figured yet?"

Emmylou looked startled for a moment. "Oh, gosh, no, I'm not talking about *judgment* day. I'm talking about the fact that it's unreasonable to assume that ten percent of humanity is going to control ninety-eight percent of the world's wealth forever. I'm talking long time scales here. A thousand years ago Paris and London looked like raggedy-ass trailer parks and Baghdad was the intellectual capital of the world. There were more books and literate people in Timbuktu than there were in England. New York was an Indian village. For all we know the world will be ruled from Wibok a thousand years from now, or someplace we never heard of. It's no crazier than telling some sheik in Basra in the year one thousand that his descendants would be kicked around by Englishmen. And look around you, Lorna, look at what's happening to your country, the stupid apathy, the addiction, the violence, the mercenary army, the corrupt political system, the rich and the poor becoming practically different species again, the collapse of religion . . ."

"I thought this was the most religious country in the world."

"I'm talking about actual religion, not these rich pharisees with their rules and their delicate purity, rotting inside painted tombs, hypocrites, and the pagans praying for washing machines; they are all utterly corrupt and God has cast them out. Can't you see it? 'And the kings of the earth who have committed fornication and lived deliciously with her, shall bewail her and lament for her when they shall see the smoke of her burning, standing far off for the fear of her torment, saying alas, alas that great city Babylon, that mighty city! For in one hour is thy destruction come.' " Her voices rises, becomes a different voice as she recites this, not unlike what happened with the Oya lady at the *bembé*.

A little breeze rattles the croton leaves and Lorna shivers and tries to think of some logical argument against the fall of the West, and then she thinks What am I doing here, trying to make sense to a maniac? But the maniac has something else to say.

"And have you ever thought that He may be using you too? That this between us, our passing and touching, is part of a larger thing, vast and twisted? He's brought you through all these dangers for some purpose, some great thing, even if you never learn what it is. You or your seed, a child who might be the one who saves the world. We never do know."

Now Emmylou swings her head around slowly and faces Lorna and fixes Lorna with her eyes. In these she sees bottomless sorrow, unlimited compassion. Lorna feels all the anger running out of her, although she wishes to cling to it, it is like water through her fingers.

"I'm not going to have any children," Lorna cries. "I'm going to die and there is no God."

And collapses utterly. She shrieks loud enough to frighten the birds away and pounds on the table and throws a cup shattering against a tree trunk. I'm going to die and there is no God, this is her wail, interspersed with wordless blubbering, shameful, beyond all control, God was going to torture her to death even he doesn't exist, unfair, unfair! Emmylou jumped from her chair and held her in a wiry grip, stroking her hair and cooing meaningless comforting noises.

"I'm sorry," she says when she can speak sensibly again. "I have cancer. Would God cure me if I prayed?" Lorna was appalled listening to her mouth say this, and in a little squeaking voice too.

"I don't think it works that way," says Emmylou, "but it never hurts to pray. If you want, I'll pray for you."

"Oh, what's the point!" Lorna snaps as her self-disgust rises to overcome the terror. "Every plane that goes down must be screaming with prayers, but the plane still crashes."

"That's true, but if any of them are praying sincerely, they're praying for God's mercy in their final moments. That's really the only thing we *can* pray for, you know, thy will be done, and let me align myself with it."

"This is all about heaven, right? The so-called afterlife?"

"That you don't believe in," said Emmylou.

"Of course not!"

"Then what are you afraid of? Extinction? You have extinction every single night of your life. What can it possibly mean if the lights go out permanently? You'd never know it, by definition."

Lorna blows her nose into a paper napkin. "Oh, thanks! Why am I not comforted by that? I suppose for you it's going to be choirs of angels and eternal hymns."

"You know, I have no idea. We're advised not to speculate: eye has not seen nor ear heard nor has it entered into the heart of man what the Lord has prepared for those who love him. I'm assured of a welcome into eternity and the resurrection of my body, but we really haven't the faintest idea what that's going be like, having an exalted body like the risen Christ had. It's outside time, you see, and my brain just can't bend around that, the idea of existence without duration, just like I guess the caterpillar doesn't understand the butterfly, though it's the future him."

Lorna is staring at her, preparing some cynical remark, when a butterfly flies in from the yard and lights on Emmylou's shoulder. It is small and bright blue, with orange eyespots in its wings. Then another comes and another, dozens of them, on Emmylou, the table, the chairs, on Lorna herself. Time slows and seems to halt, the breeze dies, the leaves fall silent, and for some incalculable period they share existence without duration.

Then, in a blue flash the creatures take off all at once and disperse into the sky.

"And gone," says Emmylou, smiling with delight.

Lorna felt something wrong in her mouth, a peculiar dryness, and realizes that her jaw has been hanging open for the whole time. Emmylou goes on as if nothing unusual has taken place. "I'm remembering something Teresa of Lisieux said. She was real sick, she died when she was twenty-five or so, and she said something like, It really doesn't matter to me if I'm alive or dead, because I feel like I'm in heaven now, so what could death change? That's pretty much how I feel, I guess. Of course, most people are in hell."

Lorna misunderstands. "You think I'm going to hell?" she cried.

"Of course not. You have a much better chance of getting into heaven than I do. You've probably never done a consciously evil thing in your life. You work with the sick and try to cure them, and accept less money than you could earn in other ways. And you do it from pure goodness, since you don't fear hell or seek heaven. I'm commanded to goodness and charity by my Lord, but you generate it like a pure fountain from your soul. You're a far better person than I'll ever be, and the devil has no grasp on you at all."

Now Lorna jumps to her feet. These last remarks, with the butterflies, Eskimos, schizophrenic angels, the Little Flower: all too much for her. "I have to go," she blurts out, "I have to go to the hospital now." Racing toward materialism, escaping from all this . . . *hope,* whatever, but she can't help herself.

She doesn't even wash her face, just grabs her keys and her wallet and the medical records from GWU Hospital and gets in her car, and while she drives she dials Dr. Mona Greenspan and gives her secretary such a good impression of a patient just falling over the edge of psychosis (not much of a stretch now) that the frightened woman tells her to come right in.

Lorna in her paper smock, hours have passed, she has been probed and rayed and she has been waiting a long, long time, and now the door opens and Dr. Mona Greenspan, a small woman with a cap of silvery hair and an intelligent open face, enters holding a thick sheaf of folders. She sits on her little stool. "Well, the good news first," she says. "You don't have lymphoma."

"What do you mean? I have all the symptoms of stage-four lymphoma and I had a positive biopsy and CAT scan in Washington."

"What can I say? GWU is a good outfit, but people make mistakes. There are abnormal lymph cells there, but they're not malignant. You have an infection. That's why your nodes are blown up and why you've got a fever and why you're losing weight."

"An *infection*? What kind of infection?"

"Brucellosis, strange to say."

"What? I thought that was a cattle disease."

"It is, but people get it too, and it's no joke. Have you been around any livestock lately?"

"Some cows. But the symptoms started before then."

"Then what about unpasteurized or imported milk products, cheeses, like that?"

Lorna thinks back to before the weirdness started. The gym. Betsy. "Oh, God. I had some Albanian goat cheese in a health food restaurant. It was zero fat. Oh, Jesus, what a moron!" She slapped her head.

"I'm not done. I assume you don't know you're pregnant." There was the usual stunned, gaping pause here.

"I can't be pregnant. I'm on the pill."

"I know you're on the pill, dear, I'm your doctor. But you seem to be the lucky one in a hundred for which it fails. In any case, there it is, about five weeks. Didn't you realize you'd missed a period?"

"I thought it was the cancer," Lorna wails. "Oh, God, and that's why I was puking up all the time."

"Right. And the itching is an allergic reaction to sand flies, very common down here in South Florida. In any case . . . when I was an intern we called it Von Veilinghausen's syndrome—a group of unrelated symptoms interpreted as a novel or more complex disease. But back to the brucellosis. There's a real danger of spontaneous abortion here, not so much in human females as in cattle, but real enough. So what did you want to do about the condition? I'm assuming it's an accident, in which case—"

"No! I want to keep it," says Lorna, without any conscious thought at all.

Dr. Greenspan gives her a swift, sharp look and then smiles. "In that case, mazel tov. We'll start you on rifampin right away."

No one answered the doorbell, and Paz felt a little tickle of fear. Lorna's car was gone from the carport, but that could mean anything. He used his key and paused in the short hallway, placing the grocery bag on the floor and listening. Nothing, the sound of an empty house, and then something else, a murmuring drone. Oh, right, he knew what *that* was. He took the bag into the kitchen and unloaded it onto the counter. Taking his cell phone, he punched the key for Lorna's, and got the service. He left a call-me message, and the thing was no sooner back in his pocket than it played its tune.

"Where are you?" he asked and learned where and then heard the news. "Well," he said, "that's great." More listening. "I thought brucellosis was something you got from guys named Bruce, sort of a gay community thing. No, you're right, it does go to show I don't know everything." Now an even longer pause. Paz felt queasy now and had to pull up a kitchen chair. "Is she sure?" he asked. "Well, well, lucky us. I guess I'll have to marry you and give up my dreams of a career on the concert stage. No, I'm not kidding. No, listen to me. It's not a question of *pressuring*. Pressure doesn't even begin to describe it. Ever since that asshole got tossed out the window, my whole life has been on a railroad track with somebody else driving. All I've been doing is looking out the window at the scenery going by. Don't you feel that way?" She did and told him about Emmylou's phone call before they said good-bye.

Paz cracked a beer and went into the living room, where he found Emmylou Dideroff on her knees before the little African crucifix standing in front of her on the coffee table. He cleared his throat. She let out a little cry and sprang to her feet, her face flushing.

"Oh," she said, "I didn't hear you come in."

"You looked like you wouldn't have heard a bomb." He instantly regretted that figure of speech.

"No, I would have heard a bomb." With that unearthly smile. "Lorna isn't here. She went to the doctor."

"Yeah, she called. So, how's things with God?"

"Fine, as always. Is Lorna . . . okay?"

"Yeah, it wasn't cancer. She has some rare disease, which they can apparently fix with antibiotics. She's also pregnant. How about that?"

"Yes," said the woman, as if confirming something she already knew. "God be thanked. What will you do?"

"Oh, the usual. Marriage, house in the 'burbs, driving to soccer games."

"Not that usual anymore. Well, congratulations and God bless you."

"You should stick around for the wedding. My mom will be in her glory—every witch doctor in Miami will be there. You could be a bridesmaid. I bet you'd fit right in."

"Thank you, but I think my ride will be here soon. I have to get ready. Do you know if Lorna has an iron and board?"

Paz directed her to the laundry alcove on one side of the Florida room and then walked through the glass doors to the back patio. He lay down in a padded lounge chair and sipped his beer. He felt very peculiar, and for a while he couldn't figure out what it was, and then he realized that for the first time in his memory he had absolutely nothing to *do*, no people to see, no cases to keep track of, no naggings from Mom to avoid, no girlfriends to juggle. He was between lives, and he felt like a sage of the East. Something Willa used to quote popped into his mind, Thomas Merton:

> *Who can free himself from achievement*
> *And from fame,*
> *Descend and be lost*
> *Amid the masses of men?*
> *He will flow like the Tao, unseen.*
> *Such is the perfect man: His boat is empty.*

Paz spent what seemed like a week lying there, watching clouds sweep across the sky and observing the lives of the birds and the larger insects, until Emmylou Dideroff came out and stood in his field of vision. She wore a dark gray calf-length cotton dress, with a freshly starched and ironed white apron over it, black leather boots on her feet and a white headcloth over her hair, marked with a thin bloodred stripe. She smelled pleasantly of spray starch and shone with an austere beauty.

"My boat is empty," said Paz.

"Yes," she said. "Good for you." She held up a grocery bag. "Well, I'm all packed. My earthly goods."

"You kept the habit."

"Yes. I couldn't bear to throw it away, and here I am. Will Lorna be back soon? I'd like to say good-bye to her."

"Half an hour, maybe," said Paz. He rose from the lounger. "So, off you go to further adventures."

"I certainly hope not," she said with a smile.

"Uh-huh. Little Emmylou rides off into the sunset, her work done. Although no one is really sure what that work was, are they? It's like all the big boys sit down at the poker table, the U.S. government, the city, the state, the oil companies, the Church, the Sudanese rebels, the Sudan government, and Mr. Sonnenborg—can't forget *him*—and somehow, by dawn's early light, when the game is all over, who do you think is holding all the chips? Why, good gracious, it's little Emmylou Dideroff! Let's see if we can count 'em up."

Paz plucked at his fingers as he spoke: "First, we have the fortunate death of the oil explorers. They could've hit a mine, but they also could've been purposely blown up by someone who didn't want them talking to anyone. Next we have the fortunate rescue of our heroine, who gets tortured just long enough to convince any normal person that she's telling the truth. No Joan of Arc last act for Emmylou. Rescued by a mysterious military gang who seem to be financed by our heroine's own Society, which just happens to get all its income from—hello?—oil company stocks. Next, somehow, one of the two people who really believes there's a lot of oil there, and also happens to be the very guy who tortured our heroine, arrives in Miami looking for her. Now how did he know to come?"

"Skeeter must've told him."

"Skeeter was working for the feds, for Parker. Who was watching you. Why in hell would he have done that?"

"He was a strange man. He always wanted to be the one controlling the play. That was his only pleasure, to make fools out of the whole world. He had no interest at all in how the game came out. He thought every outcome was equally meaningless. That's why he blew the whistle on Orne Foy."

"Did he? I kind of figured you for that one."

"You're very cynical, Detective."

"True, but you have to admit you got a history of getting even. As a matter of fact, all the people, every single one of them, who ever crossed or messed with Emmylou Dideroff are dead. Except old Packer, and I'll lay odds that something'll happen to him, if it hasn't already. Add to that, the one other guy who knew you were blowing smoke on the oil business is dead too, of course, although I'll give you that Skeeter getting knifed was a coincidence pure and simple and—"

"Just another damned Eskimo."

"What?"

"You want to believe that there are giant wheels turning, deep games being played, and there are, but not by men. God has preserved me in wonderful ways and done his will through me, using what means were at hand, including the plots of evil people. You know, God really wants to talk to us. He tried Scripture, he tries the still small voice, but we're all unbelievers now, so he mainly speaks to us through a conspiracy of accidents."

"That's a way of putting it. Come on, Emmylou, just between the two of us, what's the true story on the oil?"

She stared at him for what seemed a long time and part of him was terrified that her face would start to change and he'd be having this conversation with the Prince of Darkness. He went on. "I had an idea you might like. If you tell me the real story I'll get your confessions to SRPU in Washington. That should convince them there's no oil in your part of Sudan. I mean they don't really know you."

Some moments passed until he saw her give a little nod of decision, as if getting a message from somewhere.

She said, "Now I put lives in your hands. Are you ready for that?"

"Yes. I'm used to it."

"I know, and I'm telling you this not only because of what you propose, which would be an act of mercy in itself, but because you love the truth more than anything, and I don't want you to dig into this ever again." She took a deep breath and said, "Richardson found a huge diagenetic trap on the upper Sobat basin, sixty billion barrels or more. I destroyed all their data and I sent them out by a road I knew had been freshly mined by the enemy."

"Because God told you to?"

"No, it was my own idea."

"Playing God?"

"Yes. And don't judge me. It's not good for your soul, and I'm being judged in a much harder court."

"But why? The oil would make them rich. Your people. Don't you want them rolling in it?"

"No. They're happy. They have their cows and their God and a peace they can defend. Oil would destroy their world. Money and arms would come pouring into Sudan from every oil-addicted country on earth, and there would be mercenaries and the GOS would exterminate them to the last baby and the world would go tut-tut and fill their gas tanks. Now they have a chance. When the world collapses they'll have a little secure place maybe. Maybe Dol Biong's heirs will be prince-bishops of a little state, and maybe something good will come of it. I don't know. But I would and will do anything to give them the chance. *Anything*."

Paz saw the mad saint start to come back into her face and then the doorbell rang.

"And I guess we'll have to leave it at that," said Paz, moving toward the door. He opened it and there stood a towering, thin young woman in an SBC habit. She had cheekbones like wings, huge slanted eyes, and skin as shiny and black as a pocket comb.

"You're a Dinka," Paz said, with his neck hair wriggling at the reality of her presence, and *The Confessions of Emmylou Dideroff* burst into vivid life.

"Yes, I am," said the woman, but then Emmylou was there and with a cry she threw herself at the Dinka girl and they embraced and chattered away in that ringing tongue. Introductions were made: this was apparently Mary Dyak, Mary number three, from the famous gun, now all grown up and a novice. Then more Dinka. Paz waited a decent interval and said, "Well, so long, Emmylou."

She said, "Give my best to Lorna and please don't think bad of me."

"I don't," he said. "You played the cards you got dealt. But I'm a cop, or was, and people lying to me gets on my nerves."

He held out his hand for a conventional shake, but she grabbed it in both of hers and fixed him with her blue eyes, gas flames now, and she said, "Remember, lives in your hands."

"You going to have me whacked if I tell?" he asked lightly.

"No, but you may sleep uneasy. *You know what I mean*."

He did and he felt sweat on his brow.

Then the two sisters trotted down the walk, and at that moment Paz saw the way their dark dresses swung with their walking and realized that one wore a dress of cotton, one of wool. He had to lean against the doorpost, so rubbery were his knees, as they got into a black car and drove off.

"Well, we won't see her like again," said Lorna later on, after their glorious reunion, having been to bed and become hungry and giggled around the kitchen with no clothes on, Paz making omelettes in a silly position so as not to spatter his groin with spitting butter, and afterward eating a hilarious naked lunch, or supper, outside on the patio to the scandal of the birds.

"I sure hope not," agreed Paz. "She was a pisser all right. Saint or devil—you choose."

"I don't think you do choose. She once told me something to that effect. Not even saints ever get rid of the demons, maybe especially not saints. One other thing, though, and don't laugh, but I knew at the bottom of my bones that I had stage-four lymphoma when I walked out of here, and she said she'd pray for me, and when I got to the doctor's office I didn't have it anymore. And I don't believe in any of that stuff."

"A miracle, you think?"

"Or a medical error—you choose. In a funny way I think I'm going to miss her."

"You'll get over it," said Paz. "And whatever it was, it couldn't've happened to a nicer person, is what I say, and I'm sure little Jennifer or Jason will agree."

"Little Amy," said Lorna. "My mother. Is that cool?"

"Absolutely. Amelia, to give it that Cuban tang. And if a boy, how about Jésus?"

"That will guarantee my dad will never speak to me again, although marrying someone without a graduate degree will start the disownment process."

"You can tell him I'm a full professor at the University of Girl."

"Which has closed its doors and is no longer accepting applications."

"Boy, that's harsh. You'll have to take total responsibility for improving my mind. Can you do that?"

"I can but try," said Lorna. "But back to Jennifer and Jason, what's your position on sonograms? I mean do you want to know the sex beforehand?"

Paz looked at her with a kindly look, but one tinged with some sadness too. The poor woman really had no idea. He said, "Dear, in this family we don't need sonograms. My mom will tell you what sex the child is if you ask her, and probably even if you don't. In fact, she'll probably call us right now and let us know."

"Plate o' shrimp," said Lorna with a laugh. "The old voodoo man's trying to scare me," but she stopped laughing when the phone rang. They both stared at the cordless on the table. It rang and rang, but neither of them was in any hurry to pick it up.

# Acknowledgments

The poems attributed to the fictional poet Willa Shaftel in this novel are real poems written by a real poet named Jane Hirshfield, who has never had anything to do with a policeman in Miami. They are printed in her book *Given Sugar, Given Salt,* and are used in this way with her permission.

The Dinka of the Sudan are real people, and their words and customs are as described here, following closely the report by their own Dr. Francis Mading Deng in his book *The Dinka of the Sudan.* The sufferings of the Dinka under the Sudanese government are also real and were for decades unrelieved by God or anyone else. There is indeed oil in the Sudan, although I hope none where I said there was, and it has been a prime cause of the monstrous thirty years war in that land.

*The me I remembered no longer existed. Except for Mark. And now I was terrified of Mark. Mark was God now, he could erase me with a word. So I passed the time until he chose to reappear. I played solitare. I cleaned my nails with my Swiss army knife. While I had the knife out I carved my monogram into the side of his desk drawer. In case this was a complete hallucination and I was really someplace else, I could come back and check. If I remembered.*

From THE FORGERY OF VENUS

Chaz Wilmot has inherited all the talent—and more—of his famous artist father, but his paintings, steeped in craft and tradition, don't sell nearly as well as the contemporary products of his peers. Their unrecognizable abstract constructions sell for millions while Chaz earns a meager living painting *pastiches* to illustrate vapid magazine pieces about the celebrity *du jour*. Chaz can paint Cate Blanchett like Gainsborough, Jennifer Lopez like Goya, and Madonna like Leonardo, but he can't paint like *himself*. Tortured by this abnegation of his talent, he takes on a commission to restore a fresco for an Italian millionaire, a job set up by his friend and gallery owner, Mark Slade. Once there, Chaz finds there's little left to restore—it's more a "re-creation" than restoration—but he does the job brilliantly; so well that it leads to other opportunities that he finds impossible to resist. But during all this, Chaz has become subject to hallucinations and begins to question his own existence: Is he who he thinks he is? Or is there another Chaz, a man he himself wouldn't recognize? Is he crazy? Or is someone trying to drive him crazy for their own purposes? Michael Gruber has created an intricately layered, absorbing novel of psychological suspense, a fascinating world of secrets, genius, and conspiracies. Intelligent and fast paced, *The Forgery of Venus* cements his reputation as one of the most imaginative and gifted writers of our time.

> "I'll lay a bet," said Sancho, "that before long there won't be a tavern, roadside inn, hostelry, or barber's shop where the story of our doings won't be painted up; but I'd like it painted by the hand of a better painter than painted these."
>
> "Thou art right, Sancho," said Don Quixote, "for this painter is like Orbaneja, a painter there was at Ubeda, who when they asked him what he was painting, used to say, 'Whatever it may turn out'; and if he chanced to paint a cock he would write under it, 'This is a cock,' for fear they might think it was a fox."
>
> —Miguel de Cervantes, *Don Quixote*

Wilmot showed me that one, back in college; he'd written it out in his casually elegant calligraphy and had it up on the wall of his room. He said it was the best commentary he knew about the kind of art they were showing in New York in the eighties, and he used to drag me to galleries back then and wander through the bright chattering crowds muttering in a loud voice, "This is a cock." A bitter fellow, Wilmot, even back then, and it should not have surprised me that he came to a bad end. Whether the story he tells is merely remarkable or literally fantastic I still cannot quite decide. I would have said that Wilmot was the least fantastic of men: sober, solid, grounded in the real. Painters have a rep, of course—we think of van Gogh and Modigliani flaming out in madness—but there's also stodgy old Matisse and, of course, Velázquez himself, the government employee and social climber, and

Wilmot was always, even back in college, on that zone of the spectrum.

Did this all begin in college, I wonder? Were the lines of relationship, envy, ambition, and betrayal set that early? Yes, I believe so, or even earlier. Someone once said life is just high school, on and on, and it does seem that the great of the world are only familiar schoolyard figures—the obnoxious little shit we recall from ninth grade becomes the obnoxious little shit in the White House, or wherever. There were four of us then, thrown together by chance and by our mutual dislike of dorm life at Columbia. Columbia is technically an Ivy League school, but it is also neither Harvard, Yale, nor Princeton, and has the additional misfortune of being located in New York City. This tends to make its undergraduates even more cynical than undergraduates tend elsewhere to be: they're paying all this money and yet they might as well be attending a suburban community college. And so we were cynical, and affected also a paint-thin coat of sophistication, for were we not New Yorkers too, at the center of the universe?

We lived on the fifth floor of a building on 113th Street off Amsterdam Avenue, across the street from the great futile mass of the unfinished Cathedral of St. John the Divine. I roomed with a fellow named Mark Slotsky, and in the other apartment on the floor were Wilmot and his roommate, a reclusive, pasty pre-med whose name I had forgotten until reminded of it somewhat later in this tale. Aside from the pre-med, the three of us became pals in the manner of students, deeply, but provisionally: we all understood that school was not real life. This was perhaps unusual at the time, the waning days of the great patriarchy, and there was still floating around in the air the notion that this experience would mark one forever, that one would always be "a Columbia man." This none of us bought, which is what pulled us together as a group, because it would have been hard to find three young louts with less in common.

Slotsky's parents only appeared at graduation, and I sensed that he might have excluded them then had he been able. They were actual refugees from Hitler, with dense accents, almost parodically overdressed, noisy and vulgar. Mr. S. had made a modest pile as a soft-drink distributor and loudly wondered what items of the college's property his money had paid for. They seemed, to my eye, oblivious to their beloved college boy's desire to stay as far away from them as possible, indeed to be mistaken, by reason of dress, speech, and comportment, for another scion of Charles P. Wilmot, Senior.

The name of C. P. Wilmot (as he always signed himself in a thick black scrawl) is not as famous now as it was then, but he was at one time considered the natural heir to the throne occupied by Norman Rockwell. He'd made a rep as a combat artist during the war and had flourished as a delineator of American life in the mass-circulation magazines of the fifties, and at the time of our graduation it was not at all obvious that his profession and livelihood would utterly vanish in the succeeding decades. He was rich, and famous, and happy with his lot.

I should add that upon this graduation day I was an orphan, parents killed on the road when I was eight, only child, raised by a responsible but distant aunt and uncle, and so forth, and therefore I always had my eye out for appropriate father figures. During the various graduation ceremonials I found myself staring at the elder Wilmot with filial lust. He wore on that occasion a soft cream-colored double-breasted suit, with a foulard bowtie and a Panama hat, and I wished I could stick him in a shopping bag and take him home. I recall that the dean came by and shook his hand, and Wilmot told an amusing anecdote about painting the portrait of both the president of the university and the president of the United States. He was much in demand as a fellow who could paint into the faces of world leaders a nobility of spirit not always apparent in their words and deeds.

After the graduation was over, the great man took us three friends and our families to Tavern on the Green, a place I had never been to before and which I then regarded as the pinnacle of elegance rather than what it is, a sort of higher Denny's with a terrific location. Wilmot sat at the head of the table, flanked by his son, and I was down by the foot, with the Slotskys.

During lunch I therefore learned a good deal about the distribution of carbonated beverages and what little Mark had liked to eat as a child, but what I chiefly recall about the afternoon (and it's amazing I can recall anything, so generously flowed the champagne) was the senior Wilmot's voice, rising witty and mellow above the restaurantish murmur and clink; the laughter of the company; and once, the sight of Chaz's face, illumined by a chance bar of sunlight from the park outside, and its expression as he regarded his father, a look that combined worship and loathing in equal measure.

Or perhaps I am interpolating this based on what I later learned, as we so often do. Or I do. But there can be no doubt about what I am now to relate, and this bears more directly on the veracity of Chaz Wilmot's remarkable, horrible tale. He was one of those sons who, looking upon their father's profession and finding it good, set out to match or surpass the old guy's achievement. He was therefore an artist, and a surpassingly good one.

I first met him in our sophomore year as I was moving in. He happened to be going out while I was struggling up the filthy marble stairs with an enormous suitcase and an over-full grocery carton, and with hardly a word, he pitched right in and helped me with my things and afterward invited me into his place for a drink, which was not beer, as I had expected, but a Gibson, made in a chrome shaker and served in a chilled stemmed glass. My first ever, and it went to my head, as did the appearance somewhat later that afternoon of a lovely girl who removed all her clothes so that Chaz could paint her. I was reasonably experienced in that area for an undergraduate, but this was for me a new and expansive level of the louche—Gibsons and naked girls in the broad light of day.

After she was gone, Chaz showed me his work. His room had the street-side windows and for a few hours a day the light was fairly good and to obtain this light he had agreed to occupy the smaller of the two bedrooms, even though he was the lessee. There was an immense professional easel in it, a ratty pine table smeared with paint, a junky student desk, a brick-and-board bookcase, a plywood wardrobe, and a beautifully made antique brass bed, this last brought from home. One wall was covered with pegboard, from the hooks of which depended an astounding variety of objects: a stuffed pheasant, a German lancer's helmet, a variety of necklaces, bracelets, tiaras, a stuffed beaver, an articulated human skeleton, swords, daggers, odd bits of armor, a large flintlock pistol, and an array of costumes representing the last half-millennium of European dress, with a few tastes of the Orient thrown in. This collection, I soon gathered, was a mere overflow from his dad's, who had a virtual museum of paintable objects installed in his studio at Oyster Bay.

The place stank of paint, gin, and cigarettes; Chaz was a heavy smoker—always Craven A's in the red cardboard box—and you could see the yellow nicotine stains on his long fingers even through the omnipresent blots of paint. I still have a little self-portrait he did that year. I watched him do it, in fact, entranced: a few minutes staring at himself in a dusty mirror of a Broadway saloon and there he was—the pall of coarse black hair falling heavily over the broad forehead, the elegant straight nose, the long jaw, those remarkable large pale eyes. When I expressed appreciation he ripped it out of his sketchbook and handed it to me.

On that first afternoon, however, I woozily stood in front of his easel and caught my first sight of his work, which was a smallish painting of that naked girl done against an ochre ground. Without thinking I gasped and said it was terrific.

"It's shit," he replied. "Oh, it's alive and all that, but overworked. Anyone can do a figure in oils. If you screw up, you just paint over it, and who cares if the paint is half an inch thick. The thing is to catch the life without trying, without any obvious working. Sprezzatura."

He said the word lovingly, with a roll; I nodded sagely, since we were both being formed into little Rennaissance manikins by the Columbia great books program and had both read Castiglione's Courtier, with its admonition to achieve excellent results without showing obvious effort. One was languid, therefore, one whipped out brilliant papers at the last minute, one despised the sweaty grinds in the pre-med program. I should mention here that Chaz rather set the tone of our little community, which was as aesthetic as all get-out. The three of us were in the arts: Chaz painted, of course, and I was acting seriously at the time—I had some off-Broadway credits, in fact—and Mark had a Super 8 camera and was making short films of intense existential dreariness. In memory it was a lovely era: bad wine, worse marijuana, Monk on the record player and an endless stream of lanky girls in black tights and heavy eye makeup with straight hair down to their butts.

Strangely enough it was something Chaz did that knocked me out of acting for good. This was at the start of junior year, and they had brought in a visiting professor, a real Broadway director who was mad for Beckett. We did a series of his plays and I was Krapp in *Krapp's Last Tape*. Chaz went to all three performances, not, I think, to support me, for we sold out the Minor Latham Playhouse straight through, but because he was genuinely fascinated with the idea of taping one's whole life—of which more later. At the cast party I got into a drunken argument with some frat boy gate-crashers and there was a modest spasm of violence. The police were called, but Chaz hustled me out through the restaurant kitchen and back to our building.

We sat in his room and we drank some more, vodka out of the bottle, I recall, and I talked and talked until I noticed that he was looking at me peculiarly and I asked him what was wrong. He asked me whether I realized I was still in character, that I was using the querulous, middle-aged voice I had devised for Krapp. I tried to laugh it off, but the realization generated a deadly chill that penetrated through the booze. In fact, this happened to me a lot. I would get into a character and not be able to get out, and now someone else knew about it too. I changed the subject, however, and drank even more sincerely until I passed out in Chaz's armchair.

And awoke to dawn and the sharp stink of turps. Chaz had set up a large canvas, maybe five feet by three, on his easel. He said, "Sit up, I want to paint you." I did so; he adjusted the pose and began to paint. He was at it all day, until the light was gone, pausing only for the necessary toilet breaks and a Chinese meal delivered to the door.

I should say that although I had scrubbed the theatrical makeup off my face, I was still wearing powder in my hair and my Krapp costume of collarless white shirt, baggy, dark trousers and waistcoat with watch chain; and I'd grown a three-days beard to add to the seedy effect. I believe I said, "Holy shit!" when at last he allowed me to see what he'd done. I'd taken the obligatory history of art survey course, and the apposite name popped into my head.

"Jesus, Chaz, you're painting like Velázquez," I exclaimed, with a peculiar combination of feelings: astonishment and admiration at the feat of art, and an absolute horror of the image itself. There was Krapp, with the impotent lust and malice playing on his face and the little lights of incipient madness around the eyes; and beneath this mask there was me with all the stuff I thought I had successfully hidden from the world staring out, naked. It was like the picture of Dorian Gray in reverse; I had to make myself look, and smile.

Chaz regarded it over my shoulder and said, "Yeah, it's not bad. A little sprezzatura working in there, finally. And you're right; I can paint like Velázquez. I can paint like anybody except me." With that he snatched up a brush and signed it with the black colophon he would use throughout his career, the "CW" with a downward pothook drooping from the "W," to indicate that it was Wilmot *Junior* who'd done it. I have the thing still, rolled up in a carboard tube on the top shelf of a storage closet in our house, never shown to anyone. A couple of days after he made the painting I went to my advisor, dumped all my theater courses, and switched to pre-law.

I should say a here a little something more about myself, if only to frame, as it were, the story of Chaz Wilmot. My firm is one of those anonymous outfits denoted by three capital letters, and we specialize in insuring the entertainment industry, broadly speaking, everything from rock concerts to film locations, theme parks, and so on. Still in showbiz after all, I like to say. We have offices in L.A. and London, and for about twenty years I was based out of town in those places. Currently, my domestic arrangements are ordinary in the extreme and related to my business life, in a way, for I married my travel agent. Someone in my position necessarily spends a good deal of time on the phone with the person who arranges flights and hotels and so forth, and I developed an attachment to the voice on the phone, so helpful and accommodating at all hours, so unflappable in the many emergencies, blizzards and so forth, that afflict the traveling man. And I liked her voice: Diana is a Canadian, and I grew accustomed to those long vowels and the perky little "eh?" she appended to her sentences; I found myself calling her number late at night with pretended routing changes, and then we dropped the pretence. We have been, I suppose, happily married, although we see little of one another, except on vacations. We have the canonical two children, both now in college, and a comfortable house in Stamford. I am not rich, as wealth is calculated in these imperial times, but my company is both rich and generous.

Chaz and I were fairly close up until our senior year, and then I went off to law school in Boston and we lost touch. I saw him for about twenty minutes at our fifteenth college reunion, when he walked off with my date. She was an arty type with a wonderful name—Charlotte Roth-schild—and I seem to recall that they eventually got married, or lived together or something. As I say, we lost touch.

Mark kept in touch, being a keep-in-touch kind of guy, active in alumni affairs, always a call for the annual contribution. He tried his hand as a screenwriter in Hollywood for a season, got nowhere, then got his parents to set him up in a downtown gallery when SoHo was just taking off, and he flourished at it, but not before changing Slotsky to Slade. I got invitations to all the Mark Slade gallery openings and we occasionally went to them.

We didn't discuss Chaz much on those occasions, and I gathered that he was working as an artist with some success. Mark mainly likes to talk about himself, somewhat tediously, if you want to know the truth, and in any case I am not terribly interested in the art scene. I own only one original work of any distinction, curiously a painting by none other than C. P. Wilmot, Senior. It's one of his wartime paintings—the crew of a gun tub on a carrier at Okinawa, the antiaircraft cannons blazing away, and hanging in the air in front of them like a hideous insect is a kamikaze on fire, so close you can make out the pilot and the white band wrapped around his head, and there's nothing they can do about it, they're all going to die in the next few seconds, but the interesting thing about the picture is that one of the crew, a boy really, has turned away from the oncoming doom and is facing the viewer, hands outstretched and empty, with an expression on his face that is right out of Goya, or so I recall from my liberal education.

In fact, the whole painting is Goyesque, a modern take on his famous *The Shootings of May Third 1808*, with the kamikaze standing in for those faceless Napoleonic dragoons. The navy did not approve, nor did the magazines of the time, and the painting remained unsold. Thereafter, it seems, Wilmot was more careful to please. Chaz had it on the wall of his bedroom all through college, and when we were packing up just before we graduated he gave it to me, casually, as if it were an old Led Zeppelin poster.

As it happened I had just flown into town the weekend Mark threw a party at the Carlyle hotel to celebrate his coup in acquiring the painting that has become known as the *Alba Venus*. I'd followed the saga of the painting's discovery with more than my usual interest in things artistic, mainly because of Mark's involvement, but also because of the value of the object. They were quoting crazy figures for what it was expected to bring at auction, a couple of units at least, a "unit" being a movie mogul term I like to toss around for fun—it's a hundred million dollars. I find that sort of money very interesting, whatever its source, so I decided to stay at my firm's suite at the Omni for the evening and attend.

Mark had rented one of the mezzanine ballrooms for the party. I spotted Chaz as soon as I walked through the door, and he seemed to spot me at the same time—more than spot, he seemed to be looking for me. He stepped closer and held out a hand.

"I'm glad you could come," he said. "Mark said he'd invited you, but your office told me you were out of town, and then I called later and they said you'd be here."

"Yeah, Mark really knows how to throw a party," I said, and thought it was strange that he'd taken all that trouble to establish my whereabouts. It's not like we were best buddies anymore.

I looked him over. Pale, with what seemed to be the remains of a tan, and waxy looking, with his bright eyes circled with grayish, puffy skin. He kept glancing away, over my shoulder, as if looking for someone else, another guest, perhaps one not so welcome as I. It was the first time I'd ever seen him in anything like what he was wearing then, a beautiful gray suit of that subtle shade that only the top Italian designers ever use.

"Nice suit," I said.

He glanced down at his lapels. "Yes, I got it in Venice."

"Really?" I said. "You must be doing okay."

"Yeah, I'm doing fine," he said in a tone that discouraged inquiry, and he also changed the subject by adding, "Have you seen the masterpiece yet?" He indicated the posters of the painting that hung at intervals on the ballroom walls: the woman lying supine, a secret, satisfied smile on her face, her hand covering her crotch, not palm-down in the traditional gesture of modesty, but palm up, as if offering it to the man revealed smokily in the mirror at the foot of the couch, the artist, Diego Velázquez.

I said I had not, that I'd been out of town during the brief period it had been on public display.

"It's a fake," he said, loud enough to draw stares. Of course, I'd seen Chaz drunk often enough in college, but this was different, a dangerous kind of drunk, I realized, although Chaz was the mildest of men. The taut skin under his left eye was twitching.

"What do you mean it's a fake?" I asked.

"I mean it's not a Velázquez. I painted it."

I believe I laughed. I thought he was joking, until I looked at his face.

"You painted it," I said, just to be saying something, and then I recalled some of the articles I'd read about the extraordinary scientific vetting of the painting and added, "Well, then you certainly fooled all the experts. As I understand it, they found that the pigments were correct for the era, the digital analysis of the brushstrokes was exactly like the analyses from undoubted works by Velázquez, and there was something about isotopes . . ."

He shrugged impatiently. "Oh, Christ, anything can be faked. Anything. But as a matter of fact I painted it in 1650, in Rome. It has genuine seventeenth-century Roman grime in the craqueleur. The woman's name is Leonora Fortunati." He turned away from the posters and looked at me. "You think I'm crazy."

"Frankly, yes. You even look crazy. But maybe you're just drunk."

"I'm not that drunk. You think I'm crazy because I said I painted that thing in 1650, and that's impossible. Tell me, what is time?"

I looked at my watch and said, "It's five to ten," and he laughed in a peculiar way and said, "Yes, later than you think. But, you know, what if it's the case that our existence—sorry, our consciousness of our existence at any particular now—is quite arbitrary? I don't mean memory, that faded flower. I mean consciousness, the actual sense of being there, can travel, can be made to travel, and not just through time. Maybe there's a big consciousness mall in the sky, where they all kind of float around, there for the taking, so that we can experience the consciousnesses of other people."

He must have observed my expression, because he laughed and said, "Mad as a hatter. Maybe. Look, we need to talk. You're staying in town?"

"Yes, just for the night, at the Omni."

"I'll come by in the morning, before you check out. It won't take long. Meanwhile, you can listen to this."

He took a CD jewel box out of his inside pocket and handed it to me.

"What's this?"

"My life. That painting. You remember Krapp?"

I said I did.

"Krapp was crazy, right? Or am I wrong?"

"It's left ambiguous, I think. What does Krapp have to do with your problem?"

"Ambiguous." At this he barked a harsh sound that might have been a laugh in another circumstance and ran his hands back through his hair, still an abundant head of it even in middle age. I recalled that his father had such a crop, although I couldn't imagine Mr. Wilmot wrenching his tresses in the way Chaz was now doing, as if he wanted to yank them out. I had thought it merely a figure of speech, but apparently not.

"Great, but if you don't mind me asking, why are you handing this to me?"

I can't describe the look in his eyes. You hear about lost souls.

He said, "I made it for you. I couldn't think of anyone else. You're my oldest friend."

"Chaz, what about Mark? Shouldn't you share this with—"

"No, not Mark," he said with as bleak an expression as I'd ever seen on a human face. I thought he was going to cry.

"Then I don't understand what you're talking about," I said. But I sort of did, as a queasy feeling cranked up in my gut. I have little experience with insanity. My family has been blessed with mental health, my kids went through adolescence with barely a blip, and the raving mad, if you except the people who make movies, are not often found in the fields where I have chosen to work. Thus I found myself tongue-tied in the presence of what I now saw was a paranoid breakdown of some kind.

Perhaps he sensed my feelings, because he patted my arm and smiled, a ghost of the old Chaz showing there.

"No, I may be crazy, but I'm not crazy in that way. There really are people after me. Look, I have to go someplace now. Listen to that and we'll talk in the morning." He held out his hand like a normal person, we shook, and he vanished into the crowd.

I went back to the Omni, then, poured myself a scotch from the mini-bar, and slipped Chaz's CD into the slot in my laptop, thinking, Okay, at worst it's eighty minutes, and if it's just raving, I don't have to listen, but it wasn't just a recording. It was a dozen or so compressed sound files, representing hours and hours of recorded speech. Well, what to do? I was tired, I wanted my bed, but I also wanted to find out if Chaz Wilmot was really around the bend.

And another thing. I have sketched my life here, a singularly bland existence strung around the cusp of the century, and I suppose I wanted a taste of, I don't know, extravaganza, which is what the life of an art-ist, which I had declined in terror long ago, had always represented to me. Perhaps that's why the Americans worship celebrities, although I deplore this and refuse to participate, or only to a slight degree. But here I had my own private peep show, and it was irresistible. I selected the first file and clicked the appropriate buttons a few times, whereupon the voice of Chaz Wilmot, Jr., came floating from the speakers.

# BOOKS BY MICHAEL GRUBER

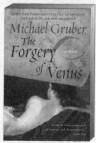

## THE FORGERY OF VENUS
### A Novel
ISBN 978-0-06-087449-0 (pb) • ISBN 978-0-06-145304-5 (cd)

"A tour-de-force combination of suspense and characterization, as well as a primer on the world of art and art forgery." —*Seattle Times*

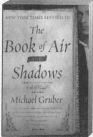

## THE BOOK OF AIR AND SHADOWS
### A Novel
ISBN 978-0-06-145657-2 (pb)

A *NEW YORK TIMES* BESTSELLER

"Breathlessly engaging . . . brilliant . . . unpredictable." —*USA Today*

# • THE JIMMY PAZ SERIES •

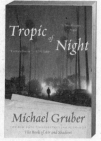

## TROPIC OF NIGHT
### A Novel
ISBN 978-0-06-165073-4 (pb)

"A blockbuster. As unsettling as it is exciting." —*People*

## VALLEY OF BONES
### A Novel
ISBN 978-0-06-165074-1 (pb) • ISBN 978-0-06-075930-8 (cd)

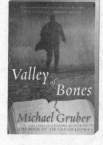

"Dazzling, literate, and downright scary." —*Cleveland Plain Dealer*

## NIGHT OF THE JAGUAR
### A Novel

ISBN 978-0-06-057769-8 (mm)

"An astonishing piece of fiction." —*Washington Post*